PRIME NUMBER

17 Stories from
Illinois Short Fiction

Edited by
Ann Lowry Weir

With an introduction by
George Core

University of Illinois Press
Urbana and Chicago

This book is printed on acid-free paper.

Library of Congress Cataloging-in-Publication Data

Prime number : 17 stories from Illinois short fiction / edited by
   Ann Lowry Weir ; with an introduction by George Core.
      p.   cm.
      ISBN 0-252-01572-X (alk. paper).   ISBN 0-252-06032-6
   (pbk. : alk. paper)
      1. Short stories, American. I. Weir, Ann Lowry, 1946- .
   PS648.S5P7 1988
   813'.01'089773—dc19   88-10076

Contents

Ann Lowry Weir

Preface

In the days of Top 40 records, or the sportswriters' list of Top 20 college basketball teams, a collection of 17 stories may seem to fall outside the realm of symmetry and order. Perhaps, however, this number—a prime number—is a fitting departure from the norm, a first, for an anthology of work from a series that has been extraordinarily symmetrical from the outset.

The first four volumes in the Illinois Short Fiction series appeared simultaneously in 1975. The program was initiated by the current director of the Press, Richard L. Wentworth, who was expanding on the kind of program that he had instituted while he was director of the Louisiana State University Press in the 1960s. (The LSU editor at that time was Charles East, who now directs the Flannery O'Connor Award selection process for the University of Georgia Press.) In the l960s and early '70s the University of Iowa Press was the only university press to have a structured fiction program in that it annually published a book by the winner of the Iowa School of Letters Award for Short Fiction. In the early '70s, before the inception of the Illinois Short Fiction series, Illinois tested the waters with three collections by local writers. Two authors in that experiment, Dan Curley and Paul Friedman, have since joined the series with the publication of second books bearing the Illinois imprint; the third, Mark Costello, received widespread attention for *The Murphy Stories,* which served as the prototype for the Illinois Short Fiction series volumes and has so far remained the Press's best-selling fiction collection.

As the volumes continued to appear, four by four, and as the years continued to roll by, the Illinois Short Fiction program began to receive recognition as "a familiar and welcome addition to American publishing" (to quote Joyce Carol Oates, in the *New York Times Book Review*). The time for an anthology, an idea often discussed but just as often deferred, finally seemed right. Now that the work of fifty authors has appeared in the series, only through such an anthology is it possible to introduce the fictional riches of the Illinois Short Fiction program to individuals (and libraries) of limited means and limited shelf space.

The evaluation process that led to *Prime Number* closely resembles that for the scores of individual fiction manuscripts received each year. Each collection chosen for the Illinois Short Fiction series normally has an in-house evaluation followed by at least two favorable outside readers' reports. The anthology manuscript originally contained one story nominated for consideration by each Illinois Short Fiction author. A panel of judges consisting of journal editors, creative writing teachers, and fiction writers made the selections that have resulted in *Prime Number*. It was impossible to include some outstanding fictions, owing to length constraints on the volume as a whole and the judges' very positive responses to the long pieces and novella that do appear here; indeed, each judge found that at least one of his or her favorite stories ended up on the cutting room floor, as it were, after all of the votes were tallied. On the other hand, there was remarkable agreement on the high quality of the stories that appear here.

While the stories are here arranged in alphabetical order by author's last name, George Core alludes to some other possible configurations in his introduction. We are pleased to have him as a participant in *Prime Number*, for, in addition to serving as the editor of the *Sewanee Review* and as a reviewer for other periodicals, he has served as an active recruiter of Illinois Short Fiction talent. His comments have led us to approach writers whose collections have added immeasurably to the quality of the series—Susan Engberg, William Hoffman, Rebecca Kavaler, Kermit Moyer, Helen Norris, and Barry Targan among them.

The final pages of this volume contain a list of all books published in the series to date, grouped as "annual quartets" starting with 1975, for those who wish to read more by the seventeen writers showcased here, or to sample the collections by more than thirty other series authors.

Prime Number contains seventeen stories that appeared in fourteen journals over a thirty-one-year period, reprinted here with the hope that readers will respond to the talent and ambition that each displays. As the editor who has been most involved with the series for the past decade, I was delighted to read Alan Cheuse's comment, in the *Los Angeles Times*, that "the editors of the series can feel proud of their part in preserving the strength of the genre." The University of Illinois Press *is* proud of the volumes in the Illinois Short Fiction series. We salute all of their authors, and we hope that *Prime Number* will lead readers to seek out and explore the riches that can be found in the hundreds of other stories contained in the individual Illinois Short Fiction volumes.

George Core

Introduction

For generations—at least from the time of Poe and Hawthorne—the short story in America has been treated as a stepchild, often even as a bastard arriving uninvited at the family reunion. That reunion, it hardly needs saying, is held by publishers occupying grand addresses in New York and Boston.

In sharp contrast, the short story is welcome in nearly every kind of periodical—little magazines, quarterlies major and minor, slick magazines of large circulation, even newspapers on occasion. Indeed, the short story has been a staple of everything from *Godey's Ladies Book* in the 1800s to the *Saturday Evening Post* in its heyday to the *New Yorker* throughout its history.

When it comes to collecting stories—particularly by a given author, not in an anthology by divers hands—many publishers get cold feet. They often become the victims of their own shibboleths and propaganda: they start subscribing to the old canard that the short story in book form, especially if written by the relatively young or obscure author, will not sell. When they do agree to take a collection of stories, they usually torpedo the effort by not properly advertising and distributing the resulting book. This is being hoist on one's own petard. When the work fails in the marketplace, the prophecy of doom comes true; the canard seems unimpeachable.

Lately, more collections of stories do seem to be making their way when published under the imprimaturs of trade houses. Meanwhile, for more than a decade university presses and small presses have been regularly issuing collections of short fiction. The quality of these books has rivaled, and in some cases exceeded, the quality of the collections being published by the best trade houses. This development parallels the same phenomenon in the periodical press: many of the best stories regularly appear in little magazines and in quarterlies, only to be ignored by the people who edit the annual anthologies of "the best short fiction" published in the United States.

At the same time, what is going on with the short story in America is often happening with other modes of writing as well, and I would be remiss in not remarking that often the bad drives out (or at the very least overwhelms, or perhaps only obscures) the good. We are living in a madly overproductive society, and this overproduction applies especially to writing of all kinds. Over 40,000 books are published annually in the United States; the sheer bulk of new books, not to mention periodicals, means that good work is overlooked—or, if not overlooked, is scanted by its publishers.

Writers themselves constitute a large part of the general problem in that they write far too much and read far too little. If every person who seriously calls himself or herself a poet or a story writer would actually *buy* eight or ten or a dozen books of poetry or short fiction annually, the market for these forms would improve remarkably, and publishers could afford to issue many more collections as a result.

While trade houses have been less and less innovative and have been lured into competing wildly for bestsellers, university presses have been moving into territory formerly held only by trade houses. That is especially true of fiction and poetry, but it by no means applies to only these modes, for university presses have lately published everything from garden books to cookbooks to the memoirs of spy masters.

The University of Illinois Press has published four collections of short fiction annually since 1975. The success of the Illinois Short Fiction series can be measured in several ways—by the quality and number of reviews, by sales, by the number of collections still in print, by how well the authors involved have done before and since. That such authors as Susan Engberg and David Long, whose first collections appeared in the Illinois series, have since had volumes published in New York by large and small trade houses is but one sign of the prescience and perspicacity of those who are involved with evaluating and publishing the press's short fiction.

The seventeen writers whose work appears here spring from a great diversity of backgrounds, colleges and universities, and locales; only one is associated with the University of Illinois. A good number of them, including Janet Shaw, John William Corrington, Susan Engberg, Lester Goldberg, and Anthony Stockanes, are professional writers without ongoing academic affiliations.

These stories cover more than three decades of publishing history, with Abraham Rothberg's "The Red Dress" having first appeared in *Epoch* in 1954. The latest story to have been published serially is Merrill Joan Gerber's "At the Fence," which won the Andrew Lytle Prize for the best story published in the *Sewanee Review* in 1985. The seventeen stories reprinted here appeared in fourteen different periodicals—from the *Atlantic* (Janet Shaw's "A New Life") to such relatively obscure magazines as *Matrix* (Russell Banks's "Indisposed") and *Sun Dog* (Helen Norris's "The Christmas Wife"). But the quality of a story in no way depends upon its appearing in a well-known or even fairly visible publication. "The Christmas Wife" is perhaps the most dazzling story in this anthology. Of the fourteen periodicals involved, twelve are still in business, a high ratio in a time when little magazines—and larger ones, too—are constantly dying. The longest story here, "Surviving Adverse Seasons," also one of the best, could not have appeared in most periodicals owing to its length.

A vast amount of talent is represented in the pages of this anthology and elsewhere in the Illinois Short Fiction series. Let us now look more closely at the seventeen individual stories that have been chosen to appear here. I shall group and measure them, principally by considering common themes (and, to a lesser extent, common situations, characters, and techniques). This should not lead the reader to assume that these fictions were chosen for inclusion because they involve a general commonality of purpose. On the contrary, these seventeen fictions have been chosen for one reason only: excellence.

John J. Clayton's "Bodies of the Rich" (1982) and Gordon Weaver's "The Two Sides of Things" (1973) are fictions involving the archetypal theme of coming of age. Each is a variation on the usual situations and characters that we associate with initiation into the adult world and into manhood. (Jean Thompson handles the female counterpart of this theme in "Birds in Air" [1974].)

"Bodies of the Rich" is narrated by a fourteen-year-old boy. We do not know how the action affects Richard Stein after the story ends or what happens to him later, although we can speculate that the story he relates about Arlene Koffman not only oddly reflects the difficulties of his parents' marriage, especially his mother's frustrations, but also may wind and reverberate through his own adulthood. In contrast, the story that Weaver's narrator and protagonist tells us is a paradigm of his own life as well as his uncle's. Uncle Adolphe dreamed of walking with kings but did not; so, too, will be the case of his nephew, who is really his adoptive son. Weaver expertly presents this relation and its implications in a single sentence: "In shaping my deportment he was treating his own sense of failure in life." We realize when "The Two Sides of Things" draws to a close that the narrator has not lived up to his own dreams. "There are the moments when we suddenly feel we have failed ourselves, have betrayed or frittered away what was once best in us . . . when only sour memories come to us when we call on the past for help." Uncle Adolphe's farfetched stories suggest the failures of uncle and nephew, as does the central action of "Bodies of the Rich," which is amplified against the thoroughly detailed background of the contrasting lives of the rich in the hotel and the lower-middleclass lodgers in the boardinghouse. In both stories generational conflict and love are neatly balanced against the way the younger generation seems doomed to repeat the lives of its elders.

Lester Goldberg's "One More River" (1976) is another story drama-tizing generational conflict. The time in which the action unfolds is essential—the worst part of the Great Depression. Goldberg's protagonist grows up the hard way: after being mistreated by his father, he hits the road, riding the rails. One of the ironies involved in his journey is that he actually becomes, willy-nilly, the delegate that his cultural club had wanted to send to the Scottsboro trial; but then he finds himself fleeing Alabama, treated like one of the Scottsboro boys. He is on the run from the law but headed toward home.

In "Home Fires" (1980) David Long also explores the magnetic pull of home—but from an entirely different perspective. Pack, a trucker, has spent the last "ten years . . . living in the dark." When he falls asleep and has an almost fatal accident, he awakes to realize that he has the chance to create a new identity—and a new life—for himself. By chance he runs into two women who firmly believe that "the only good road leads away from home." When Pack's wife hears that he is missing, she suddenly realizes that "she had not seen Pack as he actually was in a long time," even though she long since had recognized that he knew his loneliness better than he knew her. The story turns on his realization, and hers.

The theme of "A New Life" (1980) is announced in the title of Janet Beeler Shaw's subtle story of the ways that death and frustrated love affect two women who are friends and who are hungrily seeking more from their own mundane existences. But Ronna and Kristin may accomplish very little in searching for new lives before they will be overtaken by middle age. When the story ends, Ronna has lost her lover, a policeman who feels trapped by marriage (or does he?); and Kristin has lost his child, who has become the child she hoped for before her husband died. Kristin is attempting to avoid taking Ronna's place in the policeman's life; we are unsure that she will be successful. Home and family are what she and Ronna lack—and what Gene has but isn't entirely comfortable with. Yet his very domesticity (as a father who takes good care of his son and who can cook) is what particularly appeals to these fretful young women.

A different kind of fretfulness invades the life of Anna in Abraham Rothberg's "The Red Dress" (1954), although she in some ways envies her friend Jessica, whom we learn has "quit social work and become a housewife." Anna is living her life secondhand by experiencing the lives of the sixty people whose "cases" she must deal with in her job as a social worker. Gradually we learn that buying the red dress seems to Anna to be the only solution for her repressed and difficult life. She is living on the margin, barely making ends meet, and, in desperately trying to buy the red dress at a discount, she finally exposes herself not only to the financial difficulty that she tries initially to avoid but even, perhaps, to actual harm. What Rothberg achieves is an almost Kafkaesque sense of impending danger, and we fear that Anna will meet it when she returns to the seedy discount shop run by the sinister Mae Rumage and her daft sister.

The world of "At the Fence" (1985) is no less claustrophobic and frustrating for the protagonist of Merrill Joan Gerber's story. But here the mood is essentially comic and not marked by terror (albeit sometimes tinged by fearfulness), although both stories are invested with pathos.

The Anna of "At the Fence" is entrapped in suburban life. She feels paralyzed, unable to escape the narrow round of her family and neighborhood; out of her frustration she makes common cause with the dog next door, who is driving her mad with his constant frantic barking because he is confined for long hours. Anna herself is fenced in by the circumstances of her dreary life. Although we sympathize with her plight, we are amused by the ways in which she envisions it: "It will end as a headline in a tabloid newspaper. Her husband will kill the black Doberman with his bare hands and the young man will get out his gun and shoot her husband. Karen will marry Ben. Her other daughters will run off to a commune. The wind will blow away her invitations, and the ink will come out of her pen nib in blots."

In Susan Engberg's "Pastorale" (1976) the leading character feels even more restricted by her life's boundaries, but there is an added measure of pathos: Catherine has lost her daughter and is now alone in a masculine world. "Beneath this methodical impassive continuance of life," we are told, "she could feel her grief changing into something less bearable than the immediate anguish." "Pastorale" powerfully embodies the story of how Catherine comes to terms with that anguish and finds the strength to remake her life and carry on.

In "Early Morning, Lonely Ride" (1967) Nancy Huddleston Packer explores the life of a woman who feels as confined as the protagonist of "Pastorale." The locale is entirely different, of course, as is the general situation; and the marriage between Frances and Emery Benedict is not nearly so stable and rich as that between Catherine and her husband, John. Emery is very successful as an attorney and a provider, but he is a failure as a lover and husband, and he is helpless outside the worlds of boardroom and courtroom and drawingroom. His wife, who has no career, not even as a housewife or mother, is much more capable than he of confronting the messy situation that occurs when they have a flat tire. They are left to contemplate this fine irony.

Irony irradiates Barry Targan's "Surviving Adverse Seasons" (1975), the longest story here—in fact, a short novel. Targan gives us the lives of two people who seem, almost despite themselves, to be on the verge of finding new life in a winter romance; but as the action unfolds we find the expectations that the author has carefully developed suddenly being reversed. The promised new life is wrenched by fate, and we see Abel Harnack's fortunes repeating themselves. In this complicated action we learn about Latin language and its poetry, about mechanical inventions, and about the mysteries of nature; but most of all we learn about the vicissitudes of human life—its seasonal turns, its apparent triumphs, its certain defeats.

Defeat is the theme of one of the four long stories reprinted here— "Ladies Who Knit for a Living" (1980) by Anthony Stockanes. Dover, an anti-hero if there ever was one, is gradually and painfully coming to realize that life is slowly going stale on him and that he can do nothing to restore its freshness. We come to perceive that Dover is little more than the sum of—and the victim of—a lifetime of habits, many of them vulgar and embarrassing, wholly out of keeping with his deeply held convictions about his dignity. If "habits," as Dover thinks to himself, "are the gears of life," he is enmeshed in those gears and being ground to bits by them. Finally he is left only with a can of peaches to satisfy his lust for life—just like the peaches he had more than fifty years earlier, when he was a boy lusting for experience and the chance to savor life's juices. Between these two scenes in his life is a long stretch of fatuity, which Stockanes surely unfolds in a series of artfully detailed scenes.

If romance as a theme is stood on its head in both "Surviving Adverse Seasons" and "Ladies Who Knit for a Living," it is turned inside out in Helen Norris's "The Christmas Wife" (1982). Norris characteristically examines the fuzzy intersection of reality and fantasy, and seldom has she done it with such grace and authority as in this story. The lives of the Christmas wife and the man who is her Santa Claus and putative husband are changed forever.

Thwarted or soured romance is a common theme in three stories that are related also by the fact that they may be called history as fiction— Pamela Painter's "The Next Time I Meet Buddy Rich" (1979), Robert Henson's "Billie Loses Her Job" (1979), and Russell Banks's "Indisposed" (1978). In each a historical figure is convincingly depicted, and a fictional character is measured against that character. Without the social and historical dimension provided by the actual people—from William Hogarth to John Dillinger to Buddy Rich—the protagonists would not fully come to life. (The historical dimension—through the various allusions to Abraham Lincoln—plays a lesser but not negligible role in Jean Thompson's "Birds in Air," a story about generations that is set in the late 1940s or early '50s.)

Each of these authors brings his or her protagonist to life by giving us the background of that life history. Banks has the most difficult job, for the world of William Hogarth (1697-1764) is a long way from us—and a long way from what we might expect from a great painter and satirist. Hogarth, as Banks depicts him, might well have appeared in his own *Rake's Progress*. We sympathize with his indisposed wife, just as we sympathize with Billie Frechette, the displaced mistress of John Dillinger, a woman who finds herself, an Indian and ex-convict, with no place in his romanticized past and no share of the money involved. Painter depicts Tony, her narrator and protagonist, so skillfully that he comes to represent all drummers in his general situation. Tony is developed against the other drummers (especially Buddy Rich) who appear in action. When he finally genuinely succeeds as a drummer, he fails as a lover, for he will pursue his vocation to the detriment of his commitment to the woman he loves and is traveling with. The moral of this story— that the artist will give up everything in his pursuit of art—also has a place in "Billie Loses Her Job," if we think of Dillinger as an artist among bank robbers; but it applies only by indirection in Banks's "Indisposed," for Hogarth seems as intent on sating his sexual desires as on realizing his art.

"Last but not least" runs the handy cliché when one comes to the end of considering a long list, as I do now in looking at John William Corrington's "The Actes and Monuments" (1975). The well-worn phrase does not do justice to what, aside from "Surviving Adverse Seasons," is the most complicated fiction included here. Corrington, whose several vocations include law, has given us a richly complex action that includes the juxtaposed histories of several lives, especially that of the narrator, who at age thirty-eight leaves the high-powered world of Manhattan to practice law on a much reduced scale in Vicksburg, Mississippi. With such a narrator as Harry Cohen, Corrington enables the reader to see the South from the outside, while at once presenting a series of rich literary allusions and introducing a grotesque figure, Rand McNally, who could be the grandson of Faulkner's Popeye, had not Popeye been impotent. Indeed, W. C. Grierson, the highly cultivated and learned attorney who befriends Cohen, might well be Phil Stone, the well-educated and savvy friend who introduced Faulkner to modernity. Corrington is engaged in all these possibilities and much more. His story is a meditation on crime and punishment, on history and grace ("grace is history transcendent, made true at last"), on how life can be atoned for through death, on the conjunction of other matters physical and metaphysical. "The Actes and Monuments" can be read in many ways, with its luminosity reflected through several prisms and in a dozen mirrors.

I have necessarily scanted many of the virtues of these seventeen stories. To have commented on the precise dialogue of "Bodies of the Rich," "The Two Sides of Things," and "Early Morning, Lonely Ride"; to have remarked the use of indirect discourse in "One More River" and "The Actes and Monuments"; to have explored the use of detail in "The Red Dress" and "Ladies Who Knit for a Living"; to have pondered historicity in "Indisposed" and "Billie Loses Her Job"; to have scrutinized exposition as a dimension of action in "Surviving Adverse Seasons"; to have noticed some of the most dazzling beginnings ("At the Fence," "A New Life," "Indisposed"); to have reflected on the sinuous movement of the best plots ("Home Fires," "Billie Loses Her Job," "Surviving Adverse Seasons," "Pastorale"); to have lingered, even briefly, on the most effective conclusions ("Ladies Who Knit for a Living," "The Red Dress," "At the Fence," "The Next Time I Meet Buddy Rich")—all of this and a good deal more would have been possible and was tempting. But I was invited to write an introduction, not to provide an exhaustive treatment of each story.

What I particularly relish as a reader and editor of short fiction is the richness and diversity these stories offer. I would put them up against any recent anthology of contemporary short fiction in the expectation that this gathering would more than hold its own.

The stories presented here are traditional in the sense that they have beginnings, middles, and ends; they have definite narrative pulses; they embody plots with conflicts, rising actions, and resolutions. They are fictions, as fiction has been written for centuries, not minimalist exercises with feeble narratives and no plots, exercises that are drowning in mundane description and exposition.

The fictions here—a dozen short stories, four long stories, and a short novel—show the possibilities of short fiction at its best, which are possibilities that life itself, fully lived, offers to us all. Good fiction, needless to say, does not offer a prescription for living; but it shows us experience outside our own ambit (as well as within) and reveals new aspects and dimensions of life. In this sense, as Henry James said in a famous letter to H. G. Wells, "it is art that *makes* life, makes interest, makes importance," and there is "no substitute whatever for the force and beauty of its progress." I commend the force and beauty of these stories to you.

Notes on the Authors

Russell Banks is the author of five novels, including *Continental Drift* (Harper & Row, 1985) and *The Book of Jamaica* (Ballantine, 1986), as well as four collections of stories. He teaches in the Creative Writing Program at Princeton University and has been the recipient of grants from the Guggenheim Foundation, the National Endowment for the Arts, the Merrill Foundation, and the American Academy of Arts and Letters. "Indisposed" first appeared in *Matrix* (1978).

John J. Clayton is the author of a novel, *What Are Friends For?* (Little, Brown, 1979), and is a professor of English at the University of Massachusetts in Amherst. His stories have been reprinted in O. Henry and *Best American Short Story* anthologies. "Bodies of the Rich" first appeared in *Shenandoah* (1982).

John William Corrington resides in Hollywood and writes screenplays. His most recent books (written with his wife, Joyce H. Corrington) are *A Civil Death* and *A Project Named Desire* (both Viking, 1987). He lived for a number of years in Louisiana, where he was an attorney in New Orleans and, previously, a member of the English faculty at LSU. "The Actes and Monuments" first appeared in the *Sewanee Review* (1975).

Susan Engberg, a Milwaukee resident, received the Society of Midland Authors Award for *Pastorale*. Her second collection is entitled *A Stay by the River* (Viking, 1985), and she is currently at work on a novel. Her stories have been awarded O. Henry and Pushcart prizes and chosen for

The Ploughshares Reader: New Fiction for the Eighties (1985). "Pastorale" first appeared in the *Sewanee Review* (1976).

Merrill Joan Gerber's fiction has appeared in the *Atlantic, New Yorker, Mademoiselle, Harper's Bazaar, Virginia Quarterly Review,* and elsewhere, including several dozen stories in *Redbook.* The author of several novels, Gerber resides in southern California. "At the Fence" first appeared in the *Sewanee Review* (1985) and won that journal's annual Andrew Lytle Prize.

Lester Goldberg is the author, most recently, of a novel, *In Siberia It Is Very Cold* (Dembner Books, 1987). His stories have appeared in *Epoch, Iowa Review, National Jewish Monthly,* and elsewhere. A longtime resident of Cranford, New Jersey, he was for many years the manager of housing developments in New Jersey and New York. "One More River" first appeared in *Ascent* (1976).

Robert Henson, who lives in New York City, is retired but continues to write short stories. *Transports and Disgraces,* his Illinois Short Fiction volume, contains four other historical pieces; two (including "Lizzie Borden in the P.M.") were chosen for O. Henry anthologies. "Billie Loses Her Job" first appeared in the *Antioch Review* (1979).

David Long lives in the Flathead Valley of western Montana. *Home Fires* won the St. Lawrence Award for fiction. Of his second collection, *The Flood of '64* (Ecco Press, 1987), *Publishers Weekly* observed, "Long's prose can grip the reader with a sense of the vitality and treachery of the Western landscape." "Home Fires" first appeared in *Canto* (1980).

Helen Norris was nominated for the PEN-Faulkner Award, the only award given by writers to honor their peers, for *The Christmas Wife.* The title story (which appears here) has been made into a Home Box Office film starring Jason Robards and Julie Harris. Norris, who lives in Montgomery, Alabama, is also the author of three novels and of *Water into Wine* (1988), her second collection in the Illinois Short Fiction series. "The Christmas Wife" first appeared in *Sun Dog* (1982).

Nancy Huddleston Packer is a professor of English at Stanford University. In addition to *Small Moments* (from which "Early Morning, Lonely

Ride" is taken), she is the author of *In My Father's House: Tales of an Uncomfortable Man* (John Daniel) and *The Women Who Walk and Other Stories* (LSU Press), both published in 1988. "Early Morning, Lonely Rise" first appeared in the *Southwest Review* (1967).

Pamela Painter's Illinois Short Fiction collection, *Getting to Know the Weather*, won the Great Lakes College Association Award in 1986. Since then her stories have appeared in *Harper's, Mademoiselle, Ploughshares*, and other magazines. A resident of Boston, Painter teaches in the Vermont College MFA program and received a National Endowment for the Arts grant for 1988. "The Next Time I Meet Buddy Rich" first appeared in the *North American Review* (1979).

Abraham Rothberg is a native New Yorker who, after a variety of jobs in industry, government, publishing, journalism, and university teaching, now resides in Rochester, New York. The author of seven novels, three nonfiction books, and two children's books, as well as *The Four Corners of the House*, he has twice won the John H. McGinnis Memorial Award. "The Red Dress" first appeared in *Epoch* (1954).

Janet Shaw makes her home in Ridgeway, Wisconsin, with her husband, Bob. In addition to *Some of the Things I Did Not Do* (in which "A New Life" appeared), she is the author of two books of poetry, a novel entitled *Taking Leave* (Viking, 1987), and five novels for children, as well as numerous short stories and poems in magazines and journals. "A New Life" first appeared in the *Atlantic* (1983).

Anthony E. Stockanes, a Chicago native, lives in Urbana, Illinois, where he continues to write. His stories have appeared in *Chicago* magazine, *Sewanee Review, North American Review*, and elsewhere. "Ladies Who Knit for a Living" first appeared in the *John O'Hara Journal* (1980).

Barry Targan continues to write short fiction and informal essays while teaching creative writing at the State University of New York at Binghamton. His first collection, *Harry Belten and the Mendelssohn Violin Concerto*, won the Iowa Award for Short Fiction in 1975. Targan lives in New York near the Vermont border, where he gardens and builds boats. "Surviving Adverse Seasons" first appeared in *Salmagundi* (1975/76).

Jean Thompson, who teaches creative writing at the University of Illinois at Urbana-Champaign, is author of two novels, *My Wisdom* (1982) and *The Woman Driver* (1985), and of *Little Face and Other Stories* (1984; all Franklin-Watts). "Birds in Air" first appeared in *fiction international* (1974).

Gordon Weaver is the author of five collections of stories and of four novels, most recently *The Eight Corners of the World* (Chelsea Green, 1988). He is a professor of English at Oklahoma State University. "The Two Sides of Things" first appeared in the *North American Review* (1973).

PRIME
NUMBER

Russell Banks

Indisposed

Lie in bed. Just lie there. Don't move, stare at the ceiling and don't blink. Keep your fingers from twitching. Let your weight press into the mattress. Take shallow, slow breaths, so that the covers neither rise nor fall. Feel the heavy, inert length of your body. The whole of it, from your head to your feet, like the trunk of a fallen tree moldering and sinking slowly into the damp soft ground of the forest.

For that is how he likes you best—your husband William. You are Jane Hogarth, wife to the painter, keeper of his house and bed. He sees you as a great tall tree that he is too short to climb, except when you are prone, cut down by the ax of his temper, or drawn down by his words, his incessant words, the need that drives them.

It's now mid-morning. You are indisposed and have remained here in bed, as if it were a choice, a decision not to rise at dawn, empty the pots, wash and dress, brush out your hair, descend the stairs to the kitchen, build the fire and start preparing the day's food, send Ellen to the market, organize the wash, beat the carpets, sweep and wash the floors, the two of you—the big, slow-moving, careful woman and her helper, that skinny, nervous, rabbit-like girl Ellen.

You're a poor combination, you and that girl. Together you seem to break more crockery, waste more time, do more work than either of you would do alone. You follow each other around as if setting right what the other must have done wrong. You never should have agreed to take her in, but she is your cousin, a Thornhill, and her family could not hold her at home in the country any longer. It was the only way to keep the girl from becoming a harlot. William insisted on it. Absolutely insisted.

Of course he insisted, you reflect. They're just alike, he and that tiny quick girl. They probably have the same appetites. If he did not have this house and you to run it, to keep it clean and comfortable and filled with food and drink for him and his friends, he would have long ago died a rake's miserable death. And he knows it. He saw that girl and recognized the temperament and he knew the way she would go if you did not take her in. He sat there in his short-legged chair in the corner, the only chair in the house that lets his feet rest flatly on the floor, and his eyes and hands and mouth would not stop moving until you relented.

We can't set her onto the streets, and your uncle won't let her return home, and her mind seems set on the city life, and on and on he chattered, while his hands moved jerkily across the paper on his lapboard, and his eyes jumped like blue fleas, and the girl wrung her hands and spun around, dropping her bonnet, stooping to retrieve it, knocking over the water pitcher and basin on the table next to her, all the while apologizing and blathering as much family gossip into your face as she could think of, probably making most of it up, just to keep on reminding you that you too are a Thornhill and that she is the daughter of your famous father's country brother.

Maybe my father—, you tried to say, but he wouldn't let you finish. No, no, no, no, he said, his eyes still hopping over the girl, leaping from her clear face to her fresh young bosom to her slender hips and back again, as she spun and wrung and bumped into things. No, your father's house is already too crowded. All those apprentices, maids, all those children, patrons, hangers-on. And how many cousins already in from the country. Even he himself, your father, couldn't say. No, our house is quite large enough, she should stay here with us. After all, there's only the two of us . . . and you need a helper, he said, suddenly turning his gaze on you, as if you had just entered the room.

His eyes filled wetly with sympathy for you. You nodded your head slowly up and down, and his eyes went swiftly back to the girl, his hands back to the drawing on his lap. Then, the matter settled and the drawing finished, he stopped, folded the sheet of paper in half, stood up and went out the door to the street, calling over his shoulder as he rounded the corner that he wouldn't be back till later this evening.

Which you knew. No reason for him even to say that much anymore. He'll come home sometime after midnight, smelling of wine and beef fat and whores, humming downstairs in the kitchen as he rummages for a piece of cake or a slice of cold meat. Then he'll bump his way up the stairs, and he'll be on you, climbing up and over you with his nervous little body, already stiff and pressing against you with it, prodding, poking, groping, his hands yanking at your breasts, his wet mouth jammed against your dry throat, until finally, to stop him from jabbing himself against you, you spread your large thighs and let him enter you, and for a few moments, as if searching for your womb, he leaps around inside you.

Then, at last, he sighs and releases his grip on your breasts and slides out of you and off. You hear him standing in the darkness buttoning himself up. He wobbles unsteadily from the room and down the hallway to his own room. A few minutes pass in silence, and he begins to snore. And you lie in your bed and stare blankly into the sea of darkness that surrounds you.

Now, this morning, when Ellen comes to your door and asks what should she do today, you say that you are indisposed, meaning that you cannot come down today—as if it were a choice, a decision. You almost remind the rabbit-like girl that after three months in the house she should know what to do. You remember that you yourself knew after three months what was expected. And you had no patient, calm, competent older woman to teach you the intricacies of housekeeping. Ellen walks off with her chamber pot in hand, and you lie there in your bed, preferring to have the girl think you have decided to stay in bed today, like a lady of leisure, than that she know the truth.

For the truth is that you have made no decision at all. Not to rise, and not to stay abed. When you woke at dawn, it was as if you had not wakened at all. You had merely slipped from sleep into a world where neither sleep nor wakefulness existed, where you could neither act nor not act. And so you lie here, hoping that by imitating a corpse you will at least seem to be in the same world as the people around you. They will think you are present, even if only as a corpse.

But you are not present. You are absent, gone from this house, its clutter of beds, pots, chairs, tables, bottles, linens, carpets, dogs, and clothes, and gone from the people who live here, that taut young woman downstairs in the kitchen and the man who went out to his studio early this morning, as always, that man, that chattering, growling, barking, little man, his bristling red hair and bright little eyes, his jerky hands and his sudden switches of mood, words, movement, direction. You are absent from them both. Gone. Your body remains behind you, like your clothes and hairbrush. Your large, strong, smooth-moving body. Your barren body.

And so, helpless, you lie in bed. You can't move. You stare at the ceiling and you cannot blink your eyes, even as the shadows fade and the afternoon light scours the plaster to a white glare. You feel your weight press steadily into the mattress. You take shallow, slow breaths, and the covers neither rise nor fall. You feel the heavy, inert length of your long body, from the crown of your head to the soles of your feet, as if it were the trunk of a fallen tree moldering and sinking slowly into the damp soft ground of the forest.

Suddenly he is in the room, standing next to the bed. Your husband, William Hogarth, the famous painter and engraver. You stare at the ceiling but you know he is standing there beside you. You can hear his quick, gulping breaths, can smell his sweat and his mouth, the kidney pie and ale he had for lunch. He is asking questions, making demands for answers. His voice barks at you. Then, leaning over you, blocking your view of the ceiling, he stares into your eyes, and his expression changes from that of an annoyed man to that of a wondering man. But he is not happy when he is a wondering man, and his expression swiftly changes back to one of annoyance.

It occurs to you that he will beat you again, will double those hard small fists of his and throw them at you, as if you were in a pit and he were stoning you from above. You are not afraid. Not now. Not anymore. You are absent now, and though he may bury you in this

pit with his stony fists, he will bury only your barren body, as if he
were pummeling a pile of some poor woman's old clothes.

Then, as suddenly as he came, he is gone. You are alone again.
The shadows on the ceiling, long grey wedges, have returned. Falling—, you are falling and flying away at the same time, from this
thick body, from the bed, its four carved posts, from the room itself,
the clutter, the babble of furniture, crockery, clothes, and carpets,
even away from the house, and the crowd standing wide eyed on the
narrow street in front, gaping skyward as you fly and fall away from
them. It's what he would want. You are pleasing him at last. You
have left behind what he wants—your large, slow body, your silence,
and your acceptance of his blows, his words, his pushing, stiff little
body, his seed. You are pleasing him at last.

You watch him return to the house with the doctor in tow. They
are both out of breath and red faced as they come through the door
and enter the bedroom. It is dusk. The doctor asks for light, and in a
few seconds Ellen appears next to them with a lit candle. The doctor,
a short man, almost as short as your husband, but older, rounder,
dirtier, takes the candle from the girl and holds it near your face.
You watch them all—the somber, wheezing doctor with the stained
fingers, the fair-haired, pink-faced girl, her new breasts popping
above her bodice like fresh pears, and your husband, bobbing ner-
vously behind, talking, talking, making suggestions, asking quick
questions, recalling similar cases. From time to time he looks at the
girl's breasts and goes silent.

You watch them all, including the one they are examining, the
body on the bed. It is the largest body in the room, the strongest, the
only healthy body in the room. The doctor's lungs are bad, his face is
red and blotched with purple islands and broken veins, and his
hands are stunted and bent from arthritis. The girl, though young, is
nervous and cannot eat without suffering great stomach pain. Her
blonde hair has started to fall out in thatches when she brushes it in
the morning. And your husband, when he rises, coughs bits of blood,
suffers from excruciating headaches, and has had three attacks of
gout in this one year. Your body, though, lying there below you, is an
athlete's, unblemished, bulky, powerful, and smooth. That's what

they're trying to save, that's what they believe they can save—your big, healthy body. They need it, and it lies on its back, like a wagon without wheels. They are all annoyed. Why won't it work? they ask each other. What's wrong with this big, strong, in all observable ways healthy body?

The doctor asks the girl what were the exact words your body uttered this morning when she came to the room to check on it, to see why it was not performing its usual tasks.

Indisposed. It said it was indisposed, the girl tells the man. Nothing more. No complaints or anything. The girl's hands are in fists jammed against her hips.

The doctor takes a small vial from his case and with one crippled hook-like hand prods open the mouth of your body. With the other he empties the vial into it. Then he closes the mouth, massages the muscular throat, forcing the body to swallow. It swallows the thick, salty fluid, and the doctor releases the throat, content.

He wipes the mouth of the grey vial with his fingers and places it neatly into his case. I've given it a purgative, he says to your husband. By morning it should be back to normal again. You can do without it till then, can't you? the physician asks him, winking.

Your husband grins and looks at Ellen's breasts. Of course, he says, and invites the doctor downstairs for a drink and something to eat. The girl Ellen runs ahead to prepare the table for the men.

Now your body lies alone in the darkening chamber. You watch it from above, from a place touching the ceiling. The body hears the doctor laugh, a rumble of voices, chairs against the floor. Then the sound of the doctor's hearty departure. Laughter of your husband and Ellen. A door between rooms somewhere downstairs opens and clicks closed. Carriages pass in the streets, a pair of harlots argues with a vendor. Someone calls to a departing friend.

The body shudders slowly. A bubble grows inside the belly and then bursts. The body shudders again, this time more violently. It is the grey purgative working. Then the body erupts with rumbling noises from its several orifices, and its surface ripples with muscular contractions. It is wet with sweat yet goes on shivering as if chilled. The body continues barking and erupting with noise, sounds of air under pressure being suddenly released. The sheet is wet, at first with sweat, soaked, but with urine now as well. Then a watery stool trickles from between the buttocks and spreads, foul smelling, beneath the thighs.

The body hears the call of your husband downstairs as he opens the door to the street and informs the girl Ellen that he won't be home till later. Then the sounds of evening drift up the stairs and seep under the closed door of the bedroom—the creaking of the pump, dishes being washed, the sound of cupboard doors being opened and closed, and, after a while, the clicking steps of Ellen past your closed door and up the stairs beyond to her tiny room in the attic. Then silence, except for an occasional passing carriage, a cry from the street, a dog barking.

The body lies motionless in its waters and extrusions, quiet now, the heart beating slowly, regularly, peacefully, the bladder, kidneys, and intestines emptied and at rest, the lungs expanding and contracting with perfect symmetry and ease. For the first time that you can remember, you look down at your large, slow body, and you pity it. For the first time, you pity your body. Until this moment, you have felt either indifference or dislike, annoyance. For it has made you the plain daughter of a famous and demanding father, the one passed over in favor of your smaller, prettier sisters when the young artists and budding courtiers came to call at the home and studio of the grand and official court painter, the newly knighted Sir James Thornhill. It was the body presented at last to that persistent, abrasive one, the tiny man with the grandiose ambitions, almost as a joke, as a way of getting him to go away and cease his incessant talking. Hogarth wants a Thornhill, eh? Well, let him have Jane, let him have the body we call Jane, the cumbersome one, the one that's larger than most men. Let him wake every morning and be reminded of his smallness. Ho, ho, she may turn out to be barren. A good joke on a desperate man, and a solution to the problem posed by a daughter too large and too plain to marry off easily.

You did not pity it then, you were angry with it, annoyed that it should get caught so helplessly in other people's designs for themselves. But you pity it now, tonight, as it lies there below you like a great and dignified beast trapped in quicksand, resigned, yet all its systems functioning efficiently in the darkness, as close to a state of rest as a living organism can come without descending into death. Stasis. You pity it for its very presence in the world, its large and pathetic demands on space, the way it tries and constantly fails to avoid being seen. And the way it has at last given up that attempt, has at last agreed to be seen, to be wholly present. You pity it, and finally you understand it. You understand the body of Jane Hogarth.

From below comes the abrupt noise of your husband returning from the company he keeps, drunkenly bumping furniture and walls as he makes his way in darkness up the narrow stairs. He stops outside your room, where your body lies in its cold juices, pauses for a second, then moves down the hallway. At the attic stairs he stops again. Then slowly he ascends to the attic. His feet scuffle overhead, like rats in the gutter.

Your body slowly stirs, then rises and plucks itself gracefully from the sopped and stinking bed. At the sideboard there is a china pitcher of water and a basin. With a wet cloth and soap, your body slowly washes itself. Delicately, lovingly, the hands move over the shoulders, breasts, and belly, across and between the buttocks and thighs. Even the feet are washed and carefully dried. Then it slips a clean white linen gown on, and, relighting the candle left by Ellen on the sideboard, your body takes its leave of the room, as if the body were a queen leaving her private chambers for court. The body turns left at the door and stops at the bottom of the attic stairs, turns left and mounts the stairs to the attic.

There they are, the man atop the girl in her narrow bed in the corner. They are twined together in a tangle of limbs, blotches of hair, bedclothes in a snarl. You watch as your hands place the candle on a stool by the door and reach across to the man, who, suddenly aware of the presence of your body in the low room, filling it with bulk and swiftness, turns from the girl's shut face and faces yours, as your huge hands grab his shoulders as if they were chunks of mutton and yank him away from the girl's stickily clinging legs. The little man is hefted into the air, and the girl screams. He groans helplessly and is pitched across the room against the wall. Your left hand grabs his throat, lifts him to a standing position, and your right hand, balled into a fist, crashes into his face. Your hand releases his throat and lets his body collapse on the floor, a marionette with its strings cut, where he moans and spits in pain and fear. When your gaze turns back to the girl, the man scuttles like a crab for the door and clatters down the stairs to the hallway below, and, while the girl pleads for her life, he flees through the darkened house for the street, howling through his broken mouth like a dog kicked by a horse. Your right hand slaps the girl powerfully across the side of her small head, then in one continuous motion sweeps through the air to her wicker satchel next to the bed, draws it up and hurls it at her. Her wardrobe is wrenched open and its contents spilled onto the floor, then thrown at the sobbing girl on the bed.

Calmly, with dignity, your tall, broad, powerful body turns and leaves the room, descends the stairs and somberly returns to your bedroom. A new candle is lit, and the bedding is removed and swiftly replaced with clean linen. Then the body slides into the cool, broad bed, covers itself against the chill of the late summer night, and soon falls into an even sleep.

The morning will come, and though many things will still be the same, some things will be different. The girl Ellen will be gone, on the streets of the city or else returned to her father's home in the country. Your husband, his mouth tender for weeks, will be silent but brooding and filled with the resentment that feeds on fear. But he will go on behaving just as before, and in time he will forget this night's fury and your immense power, and his fear will abate, and drunkenly one night he will climb onto your prone body to take his pleasure from it. People will still smile when they see you in the company of your diminutive husband, and it will irritate him, as always, and he will hurriedly walk several paces in front of you. You will remain childless. But never again, for as long as you live, will you be indisposed. You will live in your body as if it were the perfect mate, the adoring father, the admiring handmaiden, the devoted child of your devotions. You will live in your body as if it were your own.

John J. Clayton

Bodies of the Rich

I was fourteen the last summer we spent at Feingold's Manor.

Feingold's Manor — past the lights of the boardwalk — and I still think of it as cast into darkness, old three-story beast. And why beast? — Its clumsiness, clunkiness, iron fire escape askew and gritty stairs that smelled of family cooking, of ocean tracked up every day by mothers and children.

We had, my mother assured me, too much class for Feingold's. Too much class — but hardly enough money to pay our way. In spring my mother haggled with Mrs. Feingold, sighing poverty and years of loyalty to the manor. Mrs. Feingold wouldn't answer; she cleaned her glasses on her sour-smelling skirt. Finally a curt snap of the shoulders: disgust but agreement. Feeling like a beggar, I smiled a lot at Mrs. Feingold and didn't overuse the toilet paper in the hall "facility."

Mornings I ran barefoot past the hot-dog stand, through the parking lot dangerous with broken glass to the sand, still cool from the night. Plunging like a horse into the waves, I broke through the whitecaps, a wrestling match, love match, my only sexual combat. Out to the calm water, where I floated, my baby fat not a problem, our lack of money irrelevant, king of the deep, rolling ocean.

One morning my mother joined me early. "So," she said as if in the middle of an ongoing conversation, "shall we go for a walk?"

I waited for her, and we finished the walk together. Half a mile, jetty to jetty, from the beach near Feingold's Manor to the beaches of the great hotels, red brick or white stucco hotels from the 1920s with their roped-off plots of sand raked every night by beachboys, wooden reclining chairs awaiting the bodies of the rich. Maybe not so rich, but to me then, prince of a family that couldn't afford Feingold's, rich enough. That she was willing to walk all that way to be surrounded by these rich bastards who kept us roped off their sand!

We sat halfway between the roped-off plot of the Ocean Royal and the ocean, far enough from the ropes so as not to seem envious. "The ocean," I told her, "they can't rope off."

"With money, my dear, you can rope off whatever you like."

I swam, then read—but only with one eye. With the other I watched the guests of the Ocean Royal come out in rhinestone-edged sunglasses, bellies distended from hotel breakfasts. Fat matrons in gold lamé one-piece bathing suits fell into reclining chairs. Kids my age formed a circle around a huge portable radio. For no reason, I hated them.

But loved the young women with yellow hair who lay like roasts, first on one side, then, for even tanning, on the other, wearing tiny eye-lid covers to avoid the untanned ovals left by sunglasses. Women I could touch with my eyes without fear of being touched by their eyes. I could watch their breasts rise and fall—such beauty to walk around with, those breasts. And, still reading, I waited, as I had all summer, for a girl. All summer inventing her. She didn't have to have breasts yet, please, dear God. Or small, new breasts would be okay...

Then, looking up from my book, I saw a girl nearly my own age. Hopping on one foot at the edge of the ocean, she did an Indian dance to shake water from her ear: lean-legged, slight, with long brown hair and animal eyes, troubled eyes.

And she had breasts.

Standing up and stretching, I put down my book and pretended to hunt shells along the edge of the incoming tide. I think I picked up a shell, any shell, and rehearsed: Did she know what kind of sea animal—but she was gone, up to the roped-in beach front. I saw her with towels and beachbag and mother, leaving. For the morning? The day? The rest of her life?

At once I resented her for being rich. I hated her mother, who would be cross, bored, middle-aged, face smeared with protective oils she would in turn have to protect by staying out of the water. The fancy hotel was a castle, the beachboys castle guards. I was the peasant at the gate.

I didn't tell my mother. Peasant turned spy, I trailed them. I slipped the rope and trotted up the sand. Waving casually to the beachboys who leaned against a post, I jogged along a planked walk, past a shut bar, down a damp corridor. I could hear their voices, the daughter's murmur, the mother's soothing, lyrical comforting voice I'd soon get to know so well. But turning the corner in panic, I found they'd escaped—I stood watching the indicator arrow above the elevator rise along its half-circle to 3.

I turned away, suddenly washed through with a floating, high-pitched craziness: What was I doing here? Suppose I'd met them. What could I have said?

I whistled my way back towards the beachboys. "Hi," I said, stretching and scratching and yawning. Then I ran, young athlete in training, to plunge into the ocean.

When the girl didn't return after lunch, I waited for my mother to take her nap, then slipped the rope again. "Some terrific waves," I said to reassure the single beachboy. He didn't care. Jesus, he said, he wished he could go for a swim. "Great waves," I said, passing on, towel over my shoulder, to the hotel basement, feeling callow, spoiled, that I could swim and search for a girl while he had to work. As if I were in *fact* the rich guest who belonged at the Ocean Royal.

I'd invented a friend, Arnold Zweig, in case the management asked what I was doing there. Still, it was hard to get up the courage to walk up to the lobby. So I wandered through the basement. I opened a door wide enough to see a huge laundry room, hot as a steam bath, where two black women were ironing sheets. I could hardly believe it: to be ironing in such heat? One of the women looked up and I smiled a cramped, false smile at her, as if to say, I'm not one of those who put you here; she didn't smile back. Closing them in again, I considered calling the Department of Health.

Then, from the end of the corridor, I heard echoing voices.

Forgetting the laundresses, I snooped on. Found a pile of old newspapers and took one. I think my fantasy was of finding a castle dungeon. But, turning the corner, I came upon an open doorway, daylight so suddenly bright I couldn't see. Stepping through I found myself at the hotel swimming pool.

I hadn't known about the pool—a small guest pool in the courtyard, not visible from beach or boardwalk. Surrounded by a low brick wall, tiled in aquamarine, it was, except for kids, empty. Easy work for the lifeguard, who sat by the little kids sunning himself. But the patio surrounding the pool was full of guests in loungers. A waiter in white uniform was serving drinks. At one table, women played bridge; mah-jongg at another.

I dropped my towel and dove in, dove deep, came up and sat at the edge of the water, delighted with myself for finding the pool. Then, as my eyes cleared, I saw the girl and her mother standing in the entranceway, looking around for a place to sit.

The girl pointed to a pair of lounge chairs; they carried bags and towels over and sat down. The girl walked in halting, rushing, delicate, embarrassed steps: I loved her. But the mother—she was the surprise.

She wore a white bathing suit that was almost a bikini. This was ten, fifteen years before bikinis came to the United States; maybe I'm remembering badly. Could I really have seen the bony points of her hips, the cleft of her full breasts, even her belly button? I saw the other women around the pool look up and stare. Resenting. But she smiled, self-consciously, blissfully, as if to say, My my, what a lovely day! She was the first mother I'd ever seen who was beautiful. Not beautiful, really: a sweet-faced, slightly fleshy woman. Beautiful isn't the point. *Sexual.* Mothers were never sexual. Mothers were mothers. Was she the girl's *sister,* then?

I went back to my towel and my newspaper, unable to finish a column of print without looking up. The girl stood, put down her sunglasses, and ran in quick little dance steps to the water, stopped cold, eased herself down the ladder and floated away.

I felt misery, felt my own fear like a cripple's gimp, imagining it visible, knowing she'd swim and I'd hunger but say nothing. Just haunt them both with my eyes, while I felt them watching me watching.

The girl swam so clumsily—sidestroke—it made me want to protect and teach, though I was no special swimmer. I stood up and jumped in. I swam the width of the pool in perfect form, as if a March of Time newsreel camera were looking down, then turned over to float gracefully near her serious sidestroking.

"Mother? Come on!" she called. Her voice wasn't nearly so elegant as I'd imagined: an ordinary New York whine, the kind of voice my mother loved to parody. But I erased the criticism. "Come *on,* Mother!"

So it was her mother! "You know I'm no swimmer," her mother laughed. But she put down her glasses and came over. The other women poolside stopped playing cards, sat up from sunning themselves, to stare as, in all her bare skin, she slipped into the water.

Three of us now. Easier for me to talk when there were three. I swam forth, I swam back, I yawned and called out, "Isn't it funny —nobody but us in the pool?"

"And the water is just right—so warm," the mother said, feeling it with her fingertips as if it were a pet animal.

"But I like the ocean," I said, playing Male. "You get used to it."

"Are you staying here in the hotel?"

Hot-faced, I shrugged—"No—a friend. At least I think he's supposed to be staying here—"

"What a lovely day," she sighed. "This is Sandra," she said. "I'm Arlene Koffman."

"Richard Stein," I said.

"Thank God," she said. "Company for Sandra."

"Mother!"

Arlene Koffman laughed. Sandra pouted and splashed off for a Coke. "I think I said the wrong thing? Oh, but Richard, Sandy knows nobody here—it's so boring for her. She's exactly the way I was at thirteen. A little shy. Always alone, reads too much, I feel sad for her. It's nice to find somebody she can talk to."

"Sure," I said. "Great." But I had been trained by life with my mother to know that it was Arlene who needed someone to talk to.

Of all the adults I knew, only my mother ever exposed pain to me. My mother thumped her chest and wept: her brother, flesh of her flesh, was gone—up in smoke or turned to soap, God knew where...And wept—equally—at her lot in life. A side-street apartment in Washington Heights. Feingold's in the summer. But what got to me most was her loneliness. "Your father is a decent man," she'd say. "But is he company for me? Tell me." He wasn't. I had to try to be.

"So are you staying here all summer, Mrs. Koffman?"

"Two weeks. They fatten you up here. More than two weeks, I'll be ready for the meat market." She laughed. We were out of the pool, drying off. I had to notice her tan torso, breasts exposed half-way to the nipples, and my breath bulged inside me. "But before the meat market gets me, I'll be bored to death."

Now a curious thing happened. I felt Arlene stiffen and stir in her chair and I followed her eyes. A distinguished, well-built man came out of the hotel. The man looked like an ambassador or—still more impressive to me then—a movie star—Cary Grant, say. Handsome, hair waved, with more than a touch of gray at the temples. James Mason, say. He stood by himself, towel toga-like across broad, tan shoulders, smiling at Arlene Koffman in a way that made me hold my breath. I'd never seen a look of such intimacy and tenderness between adults—except on the screen. Real adults seemed to have very little tenderness for one another. On weekends my mother and father would smile at each other—his smile expressing guilt and a desire to be approved, hers expressing affectionate, mocking irony. Those looks I turned away from, not comprehending the precise nature of her irony or his guilt. But the look of this handsome man I understood enough to bulge the front of my bathing suit and have to cover up with the *New York Post*.

Then Sandra was back, with three Cokes, and Arlene waved to her. Just behind Sandra, a mammoth woman in a one-piece suit like the cover of an overstuffed chair came out into the sun and stood behind the handsome man. She pointed, he took the beach-bag from her and led the way to a pair of recliners, while she, certainly his wife, followed like some proud bird, examining the other guests. I imagined it a look of challenge: You see me in this enormous cage—I dare you to laugh!

Three hundred pounds. Maybe more. Was her face calm or furious? Somehow, I remember both. Calm I suppose but I presumed a hidden fury—to walk across a patio dedicated to the glorification of women's bodies, to be appraised by these jeweled, creamed, bleached, tanned women-without-men and your husband is gorgeous and you look like an overstuffed chair—how could she be less than furious? I felt bad for her. I guessed—and I was right—that she held the pursestrings, and I imagined a Hitchcock plot of romance and murder.

Sandra handed me a Coke. Turning, I saw that Arlene had lowered her chair and was sleeping or pretending. I invented tears for her.

"You want to take a walk?" I asked Sandra.

"All right."

We walked the beach, kicking wisps of sand and staring at the arc the mind made of their fall. I was dying to ask about James Mason, but did Sandra know? Did *I* know—maybe I'd invented the whole encounter. We were halfway to the next jetty, done talking about where she lived (Central Park West, the expensive street facing the park) and where she went to school (Ruxton School for Girls). I yawned and asked, "Did you see that gigantic woman at the pool?"

"Her? Sure."

"That's Mrs. Cole. She's very rich. I think it's sad. She's not very nice. I think it's sad."

I stopped playing detective. I imagined taking Sandra's hand and looking at her with the look James Mason gave her mother. Instead I found a bronze stone for her. We examined it on my palm.

"Beautiful," she sighed, a breathy *beautiful* that I thought I could feel tickle my palm. I shivered. I placed it in her hand, the stone.

I led her to the jetty, rocks stretching out into the ocean. Here I had the courage, somehow, to hold out my hand. "Let's climb, okay?" As we touched, the first hand, first girl since I'd slipped over the line into guilty adolescence, I grew hot and hard and had to hide my body—but casually—from her eyes. We walked to where the waves crashed around us, then sat and took the spray. I told her about Hemingway and Steinbeck. She told me about her flute lessons. Next summer she'd be at music camp. She took art classes at the Metropolitan. She was reading *Lust for Life,* Irving Stone's novel about Van Gogh's life. Her mother had given it to her, but it was really good, really sad. I asked, did she know *Starry Night?* I didn't say, Can I see you tonight? I didn't say, We live in a roominghouse past the end of the boardwalk. I didn't tell her, I have baby fat around my waist so that all this time I've been sucking in my belly and throwing out my chest.

"And your father?" I asked, walking back.

"He's in business for himself. The dress business. He's only here on weekends."

"I think it's terrible the way husbands only come out on weekends."

"He doesn't even like his job," she said.

"I feel sorry for husbands," I said.

"But they love each other," Sandra said. "Whatever happens."

"Whatever happens?"

"I mean it's not like some parents. They'll never separate. They fight, but they love each other."

"I wish," I told her coolly, "my mother would leave my father. He'd be a lot happier. She would too." Actually, it was the last thing I wanted. The night my mother packed her suitcase and left for my aunt's, I begged her to come back. "It's terrible," I said, "how miserable people make each other." I liked sounding free; it let me take a broad view of her mother's romance with Mr. Cole. If there were a romance.

My mother was waving her handkerchief at us. "I'd like you to meet my mother," I said, not in the least liking it.

"Aren't you going to introduce me to the young lady?" my mother said from some yards away. Her cultured voice. British.

"Sandra Koffman, this is my mother, Mrs. Stein."

"You did that beautifully," my mother said.

"I have to go now," Sandra said. "Nice to meet you."

"I'd love to hear you play the flute," I said quickly.

"I'll be at the beach tomorrow." In a stumbling, jerky, delicate dance, she ran through the sand back to the hotel.

"Charming," my mother growled. "That's what they're like nowadays."

"Tomorrow" was a rainy day. I moped at Feingold's Manor while my mother tried to interest me in books or food. After lunch we played a few hands of gin rummy but before the game was over, I threw down my cards, got my raincoat, and ran along the slick, deserted boardwalk to the Ocean Royal. Leaving my raincoat folded up behind a potted plant, I ambled through the lobby, the card room, the solarium. Nowhere. At the front desk I said, "Arlene Koffman—that's 322, right?"

"305," a bored voice answered. The clerk never even looked up.

I took the elevator, heart in my ears. Down a plush-carpeted hallway, 309, 307, 305. Flute music in my ears. I knocked.

Arlene Koffman in a peignoir. I remember translucent white with raised flowers. Probably some other woman, at another time. And through the lace at the front, her breasts.

The flute kept playing. Then I noticed the record player, turntable turning. "Hello, Mrs. Koffman. Is Sandra in?"

"She's at the movies. The one downtown. Maybe you can catch her."

"Sure." But I had no money for movies. Arlene Koffman kept her hand on the knob. Suppose she asks me in? I just stood there. Finally—"Mrs. Koffman, I wonder, what was the name of that book she's reading? About Van Gogh?"

"*Lust for Life?* Would you like to borrow it, Richard? It's Richard, isn't that right? Wait there a minute."

"Yes, thank you." What was I thanking her for? Getting the book? Remembering my name? She opened the bedroom door and I heard a shuffling. And another voice, a man's voice. I found myself getting hard while my eyes looked at the record player and my face pretended I was just a kid and what did I know?

She came back, book in hand.

"If you're short of money for the movies—"

"No, nothing like that, Mrs. Koffman. I just want to read it so I can talk to Sandra — she was telling me — "

"Wonderful. Well, goodbye, Richard." I was cut off by the door. And did I really hear laughter from inside?

I protected the book under my raincoat and, back at Feingold's, read *Lust For Life* the rest of that dreary afternoon, read it as a gospel of spiritual adventure, a message from both daughter and mother.

Next day, thank God, was clear, dry, hot. Again we walked up the beach to the Ocean Royal; again my mother lay out our blanket halfway between the roped-off hotel beach and the ocean, reading Winchell, then turning to a book of Chekhov stories in translation. I followed Van Gogh to Arles.

It wasn't until after lunch that Sandra came down to the beach. I put down her book and yelled; she smiled hello. I ran up to her, but, approaching, I felt her mood and slowed my pace to hers. We swam for a while, touching as a form of play. Floating together, we agreed that Long Beach was *boring*. "Can you even imagine Vincent Van Gogh in Long Beach?" I said. "Oh, God," she said.

Later, I followed Sandra through the roped-off beach to the plank walk, along the basement corridor — I didn't mention the laundry women in the terrible heat — to the pool, where her mother sat writing letters. I invented loneliness and sorrow and an ugly husband for her, so I could accept her taking an elegant fop for a summer lover.

Her lover sat with his wife on the other side of the pool, a *Wall Street Journal* on his lap, a drink in one hand. Once in a while he looked up to smile — ahhh — at Arlene Koffman. On behalf of husbands cooking in the city, I resented him — but I sympathized with her. And Arlene sighed. Up to that moment I'd heard only my mother sigh so deeply — and that to indicate the depth of her daily suffering. But this sigh of impossible love! There they were — separated by that ocean of a pool — he a gallant flyer, she a wartime nurse, their love hopeless.

Or, perhaps, not all that hopeless. In the middle of the afternoon, I saw Mr. Cole get up, slip on his terrycloth robe, and, leaning over to say something to his wife, go back to the hotel. Five

minutes later, Arlene yawned and stuck her lettercase and cigarettes
into her beachbag. "Dearest, I'm going up for a nap. I'll see you
here later on. You don't mind?"

"We'll be at the beach, Mom."

We watched her go. "Mother and her naps," she laughed. Was
she covering up? Or didn't she know? Walking along the beach
again, we traded secrets like kisses. Hers: I don't really care about
the flute. Mine: my father wishes he had a football player instead
of me for a son. . . There was one secret I held on tight to, but I
couldn't stop visualizing a cool bedroom, shades drawn and sheets
scattered, ecstasy tumbling hot in the center of the world. Imagining the mother, I could scarcely concentrate on the daughter. But I
took her hand — and ached, trembled, at the contact, ashamed that
I wasn't the hero who had the right. The golden flyer.

We ended the afternoon reading together by my mother. I held
the book, Sandra turned the pages, until, looking up, I saw Arlene
Koffman: her nap done, there she was, waving at us. My breath
locked inside my throat.

"This is my mother," I said. "Myra Stein. And this is Mrs. Koffman — Arlene."

"How *nice,*" my mother drawled in her British charm voice. She
reached out a hand. "My son, it seems, is very taken with your
family."

"Richie is very sweet," Arlene said. I rolled my eyes to get a laugh
from Sandra. She wasn't a laughing girl. I stopped. I couldn't stop
looking and imagining. Mixed in with the sea wind must be the
perfume of Arlene's lovemaking. But they were talking about Long
Beach in the 1920s, "when it was really *something.* I remember
when the Ocean Royal was built," my mother said. "But what
hasn't come down in the world?" Arlene sighed — in agreement? I
thought I detected something else in that sigh.

My mother was maybe ten, fifteen years older than Arlene, who
must have been young, very young, when Sandra was born.
Although she came from Feingold's Manor, my mother played the
older *grande dame,* but it seemed to me that Arlene only half
listened. Was she sad because they could be together so brief a
time? How strange, how immense, that afternoon lovemaking

seemed. But my mother just chatted to Arlene about the brilliant, wealthy people she used to know before she married and, like Long Beach, came down in the world.

I noticed that Sandra had dug a little hole and was burying her foot. Instantly I grew panicky she'd felt me neglecting her for her mother. I added sand to the hill above her foot, then burrowed down, my fingers a strange animal, to touch the underside of her foot and force her to explode her hiding place. "Come on," I said. "One last swim?"

"We're invited to the pool tomorrow," my mother said on the way back to Feingold's. "A spoiled woman. Not an ounce of class. But very sweet. And *très jolie,* don't you think?"

I *did* think.

"Believe me, I was a lot prettier at her age. She's a child herself." She heard me not answering.

"You don't think so? You think your mother was always a frump? Aach! As God is my judge, I could have married a million-aire. Many millionaires."

"Well, you didn't."

"No, I had to marry for love. Love!" She lit a cigarette in the wind and exhaled all her aspirations. "Love is a luxury, my boy... Now, in all seriousness—will spaghetti do for you tonight? For tomorrow, when your father gets here, we have lamb chops. You're pleased?"

Friday morning. My mother took her sweet time at the mirror. She dolled up: creams and mascara. Didn't fix lunch. And instead of the old, patched beachbag, she carried a fancy Italian straw bag she'd bought in the city for just such a purpose. Down the sad stair-case at Feingold's.

We walked the boardwalk. I didn't like her eagerness. "It's just a tiny pool, Mom. No big deal."

"If they ask us for lunch, leave the answering to me."

We entered the Ocean Royal from the boardwalk and asked at the desk.

Arlene had left a message: *We're at the pool.* I started for the stairs—my mother tugged at my shirt. "The *elevator.*"

We walked along the basement corridor that led to the pool. "You see this door?" I said, stopping at the laundry room. "I want to show you something." I opened the door; the room was dark. "The other day — two black women were working in this terrible heat. Like a steam bath."

"People suffer," my mother explained. Dutifully, she sighed. "But you — you shouldn't go near laundry rooms. That's not your business."

She was, I knew even then, being contrary. If I had said I cared nothing at all about poor people, about suffering, she would have said, I can't bequeath you a heart, my boy. I knew she had a heart, but I preferred to let her take the role of social climber, leaving the good stuff for me.

We stood in the sunlit doorway to the pool. Sandra and Arlene Koffman waved from the far corner. My mother stood a moment, hand on hip, taking in the canasta players, the mah-jongg players, the sunbathers. I could feel her contempt.

We sat together, the four of us. My mother sighed with pleasure. "I've always loved a good pool."

Someone's husband arrived early from his week in the city. So pale he looked. Laughing and an embrace. Arlene was nodding without listening. She watched the doorway, seemed upset. I invented a lovers' quarrel. Had he stopped caring about her? Oh, that bastard!

My mother was telling Arlene about Paris. Oh, how she used to love Paris! The magnificence of the Louvre. And that "pretty little jewel of a chapel" — Sainte Chapelle. And the great synagogue... That darkened her mood, and she talked about her cousin, who'd lived in Paris. Who knows where she is now?

"Yes," Arlene said. "It must all be very different." But she wasn't really there. She looked past my mother toward the hotel.

Sandra and I swam in the pool. Stopping at the ladder, I laughed. "My mother doesn't always talk that much."

"It's nice for my mother," Sandra said. "The only other people she knows at the beach are the Coles. That fat woman and her husband."

"You're friends? You didn't tell me that."

"Oh, personally, I can't stand her. He's okay. Not exactly friends. They just eat at our house once in a while. Or my parents go to their parties. But that's not why we're here. Why we're here is my mother thinks *I* care about the beach."

"I'm glad you're here."

"Thanks." Sandra kicked into a sidestroke. I followed. Then, bored, we sat down by our mothers and let the sun dry us.

We were hardly dry when we saw Mrs. Cole. She filled the doorway, scowling. I imagined what she must look like without that sack of a bathing suit around her. And instantly I groaned inside for the pain I imagined in her. The laundresses in that hot room were in a palace compared to her prison of fat. I touched my own belly—belly I was too vain not to suck in—and imagined what agony it must be for her to walk past all those women.

She carried herself her lumbering way along the side of the pool. Sandra said, "Here comes Mrs. Cole, Mom. I guess she's got to snoop about our guest...Want to go to the beach, Richie?"

But Mrs. Cole was upon us.

"Please sit with us," Arlene said—and stood up to introduce her to my mother.

"Sit with *you?* I came to tell you what you are," she said, loud enough for all the women at the pool to hear. "You—a tramp is what *you* are. You're nothing but a tramp!" Very formal, her delivery. A public announcement.

Then, in slow motion she pressed forward, a tank, her arm pulled back for a slap, and Arlene tripped backwards over the leg of her lounging chair. Finally, Mrs. Cole slapped—but she was too stiff or too proud to swing with her whole arm. Thank God. The slap became a swing of the fingers, as if this giant beast were swatting a fly. The tips of her fingers grazed Arlene's face. A ritual slap. But Arlene screamed twice and cried behind her own fingers, leaving Mrs. Cole on stage.

"I'm very sorry to do that in front of you, Sandra. I thought it was all over a year ago. They kept on behind my back."

Sandra had been standing, stunned, gawking. Hearing her name, she came alive, shoved at Mrs. Cole but couldn't budge her. I took her enormous arm and pulled. She stood her ground. "A tramp!"

she said again. Then, satisfied or embarrassed, she turned and walked away.

The women around the pool stared. They stared and then they talked. I helped Arlene into her chair—she was still weeping. My mother said, "Garbage like that. Lice! Don't worry."

Arlene shook her head.

"I'd sue," my mother said, holding Arlene around the shoulders. "I knew a doctor once—" then she stopped talking and just held.

Sandra was brooding. Her eyes wet, she looked like a hurt little girl. I rubbed my hand along her arm. Downy hair. "It's okay."

She bent to her mother and kissed her and put her arms around her mother's neck and took a wet kiss in return.

"Oh, he's such a coward," Arlene sobbed.

"Oh, Mommy," Sandra said. Then she was crying. Then she was off—walking fast by the pool. I followed, caught up to her in the corridor to the beach. She leaned against a column, weeping. I held back, but finally I held her shoulders and loved her.

"You want to take a walk?"

"I've got to see Mommy."

"Sure—you want to go back and see your Mom?"

"Why did she do it?"

"To get back—revenge, I guess."

"I mean Mom."

"I guess she loves him. I'm sure she loves him."

"But she didn't tell me. Why didn't she tell me?"

We both knew why. I kissed her cheek. Somehow, that got me excited and I didn't feel I ought to be.

"Daddy's coming tonight," she said.

"So you want to go back?"

"No. Let's take a walk," she said. We went past the beachboy, past the ropes, to the water. Sadly, we walked down to the jetty. The tide was out, leaving small pools in the depressions between the rocks. Sandra lay belly down on the hard, wet sand and, head in hands, stared and stared until the big world had maybe disappeared for her. I lay next to her, self-conscious, awkward, until I was able to make the rock seem a giant cliff and the pool a lake and the hermit crabs and starfish giant sea creatures. A string of kelp became the jungle of some other planet. We hiked the landscape together. But it was impossible to live there. "Richie? Want to go back now?"

But we didn't have to. Turning, we saw that my mother and Sandra's mother had come down to the beach. They sat on towels spread out near the water. As she talked, Arlene was drawing with a stick, patterns in the sand. My mother listened. "Yes," I heard her say as we approached. A breathy "yes."

Like a trial lawyer, my mother extended an open palm toward Arlene and offered her to me. "Why does Mrs. Koffman have to put up with trash like that? So — we decided — this noon we'll eat lunch at *our* place. Decent, simple, home cooking. Tell me, Sandra, do you eat lamb chops?" My mother gave me a Look.

Back at Feingold's Manor, my mother broiled the lamb chops and reheated last night's vegetables. Not once — not climbing the Lysol stairs, not showing Arlene the hot-tar terrace nor opening the old, shaky, wooden icebox for food — not once did she criticize Feingold's. Queen reduced to this broken-down flat, she simply moved in the old kitchen with the grace of one used to better things.

"My dear, you want a cup of tea?"

"Oh, Mrs. Stein..." Arlene began to cry. "Mrs. Stein, I love him..."

"Life," my mother sighed. From the O'Neil apartment below came an infant's shrieking. Without undue haste my mother closed the door to the porch.

"Sometimes," Arlene said, "someone comes along in your life and you can't help loving them."

My mother provided a Kleenex.

Arlene and Sandra picked at their chops. I ate my own, then ate their leftovers. Arlene fumbled for a cigarette. "Mrs. Stein, what you must think of me..."

"Nothing of the sort. Call me *Myra,* my dear."

"Myra, this is the romance of my life." Arlene looked beautiful in tears. I felt a furtive pleasure at being in the presence of such high emotion. "Oh, we've been in love for years."

Sandra, slumped in her chair, poured salt from the shaker into a tiny mountain on her plate, then etched with the tines of her fork in the salt.

"Sandra," her mother said. "What are you *doing?*"

Sandra shrugged.

"Sandy? Please."

"So does Daddy know?"

"No, Daddy doesn't know. Sandy—I love your Daddy. I do. But Stan...is the romance of my life," she said again."We tried to stop seeing each other. We just couldn't, that's all."

Sandra shrugged. "Then *that's* why we had to come to Long Beach."

"Sandra," my mother said, "your mother is an angel. I know an angel when I see one."

"Isn't it, Mother?"

"Partly, yes."

Furious, Sandra turned back to the salt. Arlene cupped Sandra's face in her palm. "Please, Sandy?"

"Well, what's Daddy going to say?"

"Do you want me to tell him?"

"I don't know. No."

"I will if you want."

Sandra shook her head.

"Would anyone like some nice fruit?" my mother asked.

"He's my heart," Arlene said and was touched to tears by her own words.

"That isn't a woman," my mother said. "She's a Hitler. A Nazi tank. To make such a scene. Would a lady make such a scene?"

"Mommy? How did she know?"

"She was waiting in the corridor yesterday afternoon. We weren't thinking. It was such a beautiful hour together. That's all we have."

"I knew a Very Rich Man once," my mother said, slowly, so we'd know this was wisdom, "who was married to money. 'Myra,' he said to me, 'you want to know what hell is? Married to money is hell.' Finally, he divorced her. Of course, she didn't give him a penny."

"How can I go back there, Mrs. Stein?"

"With your head held high—that's how," my mother said triumphantly.

Watching the sway of Arlene's body on the way back along the beach, I felt cut off within my adolescence from a depth of sexual life she knew. And cut off from Sandra. As if to touch her now I would have to be a man. I felt unable even to imitate manhood.

When they went back to the hotel, Arlene's arm around Sandra's waist, I sat with my mother outside the ropes, looking out at the ocean. It seemed, the ocean, drab. Boring. I fell asleep. Woke to my mother's "Well, how *nice.*"

A tall, good-looking man with tan face and pale chest stood above me. Athletic. In his thirties. Arlene, in gold lamè swimsuit, hung on his arm. "Mrs. Stein, I wanted you to meet my husband. This is Harry. Mrs. Stein has been wonderful to us."

"Oh, my dear—"

"You have. Saved us from those boring people at the hotel. And we wanted to say goodbye."

"You're leaving?"

"We're checking out today. I can't stand it another day."

I was fully awake now. Sandra stood behind her parents. We looked at each other; she turned away. "Richie—you want to go for a swim?"

I ran after her. "Wait up. Sandra?"

She stopped. "Don't say anything in front of my father."

"Of course not."

"She has to go away from him. She loves him so much. And she loves my father too. She promises she'll stay away from Stan. It's so sad. He won't leave his wife. You know—money. I think it's disgusting. But this way it's better, really..." So much talk bursting out of her silence. I followed her into the water. We watched the waves heave and explode into white, then die around our ankles. "If I write you," I said, "will you write back? Will you see me in the city?"

"Of course. Come on, Richie—last swim for the whole summer."

We dove into the same wave and I imagined her tumbling lost inside the roller and me saving her and her father inviting me into their lives. But we both spluttered through to the other side and smiled. My smile was phony. "So goodbye," I said, wanting at least to sip the pleasure of tragedy from the moment. But she swam a couple of strokes and said, "So have a terrific rest-of-the-summer, Richie. We're going with Daddy for a week to the mountains. It was all arranged so fast."

"I never heard you play the flute."

"Well, I'm awful anyway. Richie? Don't think bad about Mommy."

I watched her skinny beauty almost catch a wave. She danced, stumbled, ran the rest of the way to shore. I floated till they were off the beach.

"Well," my mother sighed on the trudge back along the beach to Feingold's Manor, "so it goes. Now I have to get more lamb chops. Do you think your father would mind hamburgers? Maybe meatloaf? I'll make a nice gravy."

"Sure," I said, feeling, somehow, sorry for her.

"You know, my dear, I felt in my heart for what that poor woman is going through, but you know, a high-class woman doesn't follow her boyfriend to hotels. That's not high-class people."

But the further we got from the Ocean Royal, the emptier I felt. Whatever my mother said, high-class didn't mean meatloaf and fidelity; it meant money and romance.

As we passed the end of the boardwalk and crossed the final jetty, we saw my father waving. He'd just come out from the city, down to the beach, a few hours early. Still wearing city pants, carrying his shoes, his big belly and chest pale, he looked so out of place that I felt ashamed, then ashamed of myself — remembering that his labor kept my mother and me there at the beach, gave us our tans.

"Well, what a pleasant surprise," my mother called across ten yards of beach. "We didn't expect you till dinnertime."

"I worked late last night. Max let me out at one o'clock so I could beat the rush."

"Well, my dear, *aren't you taking a chance?*"

But not listening to her, he said to me, "Well, look how brown m'boy's getting. Another couple of years, you'll be knocking 'em dead. Like your old man."

"Aren't you taking a chance?" she said again. "I remember Bea Altman once saying, 'If you want to find a faithful wife at home, make sure first you telephone.' "

"Your mother's kidding," Dad said.

"Don't you think the boy knows *that?*" she snapped.

"So how's the water?" my father said.

"Seaweed," she said. "It's nicer down the beach." She pointed back at the great hotels.

"The seaweed's gone," I said, fatigued. "Let's just stay here." But *here*—the beach near Feingold's Manor—seemed drab, less in the sunlight than it once had.

"You look tired," she said to my father as we stood by the water. "It was a hard week?"

He admitted it.

"You'll rest this weekend. So. So tell me," she said, as they both looked out at the waves, "for tonight will meatloaf do your majesty?"

John William Corrington

The Actes and Monuments

After the coronary, I quit. I could have slowed down, let things go easier, taken some of the jobs where little more than appearance was required. But I didn't do that. I like to believe that I cared too much for the law. No, I *do* believe that. Because if I had cared nothing for the law, I would have played at being an attorney—or else simply stopped being involved with law at all. But I did neither.

Rather, I let go my partnership and began looking for some way to use all I knew, all I was coming to know. It wasn't that I couldn't stand pressure; I could. I could stand quite a bit of pressure. What I could not stand was the tension that never lets up, the sort of thing generated by corporation cases that might go four or five years without resolution. Brief peaks followed by relaxation: those, the doctor said, would be all right.

So I was thirty-eight, a good lawyer by any standard—including the money I had let collect in stocks. A bachelor, and a one-time loser on the coronary circuit. What do you do? Maybe you settle down in Manhattan and have fun? Maybe you don't. There is no room in Manhattan for fun—not in the crowd I knew, anyhow. You are either in it or out of it; that was the rule, and everybody understood and accepted. Poor Harry wasn't in it. So Harry had to walk out of it. Who needs to be pushed?

But Harry is no loser. Not since Harry climbed out of Brooklyn Heights and into Yale Law School. No, Harry has to find himself a blast he can live with. Out of New York. So where? London? Not really. We don't function well in other places. Rio, Athens, Caracas, Tokyo? Any one of them is easy with my contacts. But they are imitations of what I am having to leave.

So Harry comes on very strong. Much stronger than anyone can credit, believe. Who knows where I caught the idiot virus that took me down there? Maybe it was *Absalom, Absalom* which once I read, not understanding a word of it, but living in every crevice of time and space that the laureate of the Cracker World created.

It is no overstatement to say that my friends paled when they received postcards from Vicksburg. It was much too much. They were old postcards. Pictures in mezzotint of the Pennsylvania memorial, of the grass-covered earthworks outside the town. Postcards which must have been printed at the latest in the early 1920s, and which had been in the old flyblown rack waiting for my hand almost half a century. I cannot remember what I wrote on the cards, but it must have been wonderful. I can say it was wonderful, because except for one slightly drunken phone call from Manhattan late at night about a week after I arrived, I got no answers to those cards at all. Perhaps they never arrived. Perhaps they slipped back into the time warp from which I had plucked them at the little clapboard store outside town where there was a single gas pump with a glass container at the top, which the proprietor had to pump full before it would run down into the tank of my XKE.

Should I tell you about that man? Who sold me gas, counted out my change, made no move at my hood or windshield, and told me in guarded tones that he had seen a car like mine once long ago. A Mercer runabout, as he remembered. Never mind.

I rented a place—leased it. Almost bought it right off, but had not quite that kind of guts. It was old, enormous, with a yard of nearly an acre's expanse. I came that first day to recognize what an acre meant in actual extent. I stood in my yard near an arbor strung with veiny ropes of scuppernong, looked back at the house through the branches of pear trees, past the trunks of pecan and oak strung with heavy coils of that moss that makes every tree venerable which bears it. My house, on my property. Inside I had placed my books, my records, my liquor, what little furniture I had collected in the brownstone I had left behind.

My first conclusion was that the coronary had affected my mind. I could have committed myself to Bellevue with my doctor's blessing. Or, secondly, had I found in some deep of my psyche a degree of masochism unparalleled in the history of modern man? Is it true that Jewishness is simply a pathology, not a race or a religion? Perhaps I had, in the depths of my pain and the confusion attendant on my attack, weighed myself in the balance and found my life and its slender probings at purpose wanting utterly. Could it be that a man who, in the very embrace of probable death, can find no reason for his living except the sweating grab of life itself housed in a body, looks at all things and condemns himself to Mississippi?

Or finally, grossest of all, was there an insight in my delirium whereby I saw Mississippi not as exile, not as condemnation, but as a place of salvation? Must we somehow search out the very pits and crannies of our secret terrors in order to find what for us will be paradise? Consider as I did, in retrospect, that no man of normal responses raised in Manhattan is going to look for himself in the deep South. And yet how many of those men of normal responses are happy? How many die at the first thrust of coronary, dreaming as life ebbs of a handful of dusty dark-green grapes, a sprig of verbena, the soft weathered marble of an old Confederate monument within the shadow of which might have lain the meaning of their lives? I offer this possibility only because we are, most of us, so very miserable living out the lives that sense and opportunity provide. I wondered afterward, when I came to understand at least the meaning of my own choice, if we do not usually fail ourselves of happiness—of satisfaction, anyhow—by ignoring the possibilities of perversity. Not perversion. Those we invariably attempt in some form. No, perversity: how few of us walk into the darkness if that is what we fear. How few of us step into a situation which both terrifies and attracts us. If we fear water, we avoid it rather than forcing ourselves to swim. If we fear heights, we refuse to make that single skydive which might simultaneously free and captivate us. If we cannot bear cats, we push them away, settling for a world of dogs. You see how gross my insights had become.

In order to live, I thought, standing there, staring at the strange
alien house which was now my legal residence and the place where I
was determined to create, as in a crucible, the substance of my new
life, it may be essential to force, to invade, to overwhelm those
shadowed places we fear and, fearing, learn to ignore as real possibilities even when we know them to be real, to be standing erect
against a hot sky windless and blind to their own beauties, realizable
only to those of us who come from distant places.

A simpler explanation was offered me later by one of Vicksburg's
most elegant anti-Semites, a dealer in cotton futures who, loathing
my nation and my region, my presumed religion and my race,
became a close friend. He suggested that Jews, for their perfidy, are
condemned to have no place, to strike no roots.

—Don't you live always out of a moral and spiritual suitcase, he
asked slyly. —Isn't it notable that there has never been any great
architecture of the synagogue? How many of you speak the language
of your great-grandfathers? Isn't placelessness a curse?

—Yes, I told him in answer to his last question. —Indisputably
yes. But think of the hungers of a placeless man. Can you even begin
to conceive the mind of a man who has suffered a failure of the heart
once, who has fled all ordinary lives and come to Mississippi?

—No, he said, no longer joking or arch. —No, I can't conceive
that mind. But I expect there must be riches in it. You'll be using
your talents, he half-asked, half-stated. —You'll be going to help
niggers with the law, won't you?

—Yes, I told him. That certainly. Not that it will mean a great
deal. Only the reflex of the retired gunfighter who no longer hopes
either to purge the world of good or evil but whose hand moves,
claws at his side when pressed, out of a nervous reaction so vast and
profound that the very prohibition of God himself could not stop it.

—Good, he said.—Not about the niggers. Everybody in the
country wants a try at that sack of cats. But not your way. We've
never had a man who came loving, needing, down here to do that
kind of thing. I want a chance to see this. It has got to be rich.

—What, I asked. What will be so rich?

—Why, seeing a yankee Jew fighting in the South because he

needs her, because he loves her. Did you ever in your life hear the like of that?

How could I help loving? Where else could I come across such a man? But he was the least of it. There was, at the garage which saw to my car, an avowed member of the Klan who asked me why I had come so far to die. My answer satisfied him. —Because, if you have got to die, it is stupid to die just anywhere and by an accident of some valve in your heart. If it comes here, I will know why and maybe even when.

He looked at me and scratched his head. —My Christ, he said. I never heard nothing like that in all my life. You are a fucking nut.

—How do you like it, I asked him over the hood of my Jaguar, now dusty and hot with April sun.

—Why, pretty well, he said, grinning, putting out his hand without volition or even, I suspect, the knowledge he had extended it. I took it firmly, and he looked surprised. As if the last thing on earth he had ever expected to do was shake hands with some skulking yankee kike determined to stir up his coloreds.

By this time you have dismissed me as a lunatic or a liar or both. Very well. You only prove that the most profound impulses of your spirit can find their fulfillment in Fairlawn, New Jersey. Good luck.

But if your possibilities are . . . what? More exotic, then I want to tell you the proving of what I found here in Vicksburg, Mississippi. I want to tell you about Mr Grierson, and the cases we worked on together—cases which, whatever else, have found me for myself. So saying, I have to retreat to my first conclusion. The coronary affected my mind. This I'm sure of. Because, satisfied beyond any hope I brought from Manhattan with me, I am still enough of a rationalist to see that my satisfaction, my new life, and what Mr Grierson and I do—have done—is beyond even the most liberally construed limits of ordinary sanity. I am not a mystic, thus able to excuse any deviation in myself, blessing the lunacy as a certain portent. I am a sensible man who, so cast, must admit that he has found sense nonsense and empty, and that a tract of lunacy laid out before him has bloomed like the distant desert glimmering before Moses as he lay down at last, his final massive coronary denying him the power to cross over Jordan and dwell some last loving days or months or years amidst the plenty that his lip-chewing endurance had reared up out of the sands.

I was handling now and again the smallest of cases for certain black people who had heard that an eccentric yankee lawyer had come to town and would do a workmanlike job of defending chicken thieves, wife-beaters, small-time hustlers, whores, and even pigeon-droppers. This alone would have drawn me little enough custom, but it was said, further, and experience proved it true, that the yankee did his work for free, a very ancient mariner of yankee lawyers doomed to work out his penance for bird mangling or beast thumping by giving away his services to whatever Negro showed up with a likely story. It was said that if you had no likely story, he would help you make one up—not inciting to perjury, you realize. Only fooling with the facts in such a way as to produce a story diverting enough to keep the judge from adding a month or so to your sentence for the boredom you caused him in addition to the inconvenience of having to keep court for the likes of you. All that aside, I seduced by asking no fee. It was at first amazing to me how a Negro was willing often to take a chance of six months or a year in prison to avoid a fifty-dollar fee, even when he had it. For some reason I could not at first grasp, my own logic had no purchase with them. Think: suppose a man offered you free legal service. Wouldn't you, like me, presume that the service would be about worth the price? Yes, you would. But how do you suppose the blacks reasoned? One of my chicken—actually, a pig—thieves explained why he trusted me. You got a nice house, ain't you? Yes, I said. You out of jail yourself, ain't you? Yes. You look like you eats pretty good. I do, I eat very well. Except no pork. No saturated fats. Huh? Never mind. O, religion, huh? All right. Anyhow, if you got a good house, if you look like eating regular, and if the judge let you stand up there, you got as much going for you as any jakeleg courthouse chaser I seen.

It was that very pig-robber who carried me down to town one day in search of a law book. Something to do with statute of limitations on pig thievery. It seems that my man was charged with having stolen a pig in 1959, the loss or proof of it having come to light only in the last few days. I wanted to make absolutely sure that there was not some awful exception to ordinary prescription in Mississippi law when the subject was pigs. There are some oddities in Texas law having to do with horses. I had never had much practice connected with livestock in Manhattan. I thought I had better make sure.

So I was directed by a deputy, who was everlastingly amused by the nature and style of my practice, to the offices of Mr Grierson.

They were on a side street just beyond the business district. Among some run-down houses that must have been neat and even prime in the 1920s but which had lost paint and heft and hope in the 1950s at the latest, there was a huddle of small stores. A place that sold seed and fertilizer and cast-iron pots and glazed clay crocks that they used to make pickles in. Just past the pots and crocks, there was a flat-roofed place with whitewashed doors and one large window, heavy curtains behind it, across which was painted

FREE CHURCH OF THE OPEN BIBLE

There was a hasp on the door with a large combination lock hanging through it. I wondered what might be the combination to the Open Bible.

Just past the church, there was another storefront building standing a little to itself. There was a runway of tall weeds and grass between it and the church and it was set back a little from the sidewalk with a patch of tree-lawn in front. On either side of the door was a huge fig tree, green and leafy and beginning to bear. Through the heavy foliage, I could see that there were windows behind the trees. They seemed to have been painted over crudely, so that they looked like giant blinkered eyes which had no wish to see out into the street. Above the door itself was a sign made of natural wood hanging from a wrought-iron support. On it was graved in faded gold letters cut down into the wood

W. C. GRIERSON
Atty at Law

The door itself was recessed fairly deeply and I got the notion that it was not the original door, that it had nothing really to do with the building which was, like those nearby, simply a long frame affair—what they—we—call a shotgun building, although much wider and longer. I stood there in the early summer sun looking at that door as if it were the entrance to another place. Why? I rubbed my chin and thought, and then I found, back in the fine debris of my old life, back behind the sword-edge of my coronary, the recollection of another summer afternoon spent with a lovely woman at some gallery, some wealthy home—somewhere. We had gone to see paintings, and there had been one among all the others that I could not put out of mind. It had been by the Albrights, those strange brothers. Of a door massive and ancient, buffed and scarred, the very deepest symbol both of life and of the passage through which life itself must pass. On its weather-beaten panels hung a black wreath, each dark leaf pointed as a spike, shimmering in the mist of its own surreality. My God, I remembered thinking, is death like that? Is it finally a door with a wreath standing isolated from air and grass—even from the materials which are supposed to surround the fabric of a door? And then I thought, the lovely woman beside me talking still about a Fragonard she had spotted nearby, of Rilke's words: "Der grosse Tod. . . . —The great Death each has in himself, that is the fruit round which all revolves. . . . " But the title of the painting was *That Which I Should Have Done I Did Not Do*, and I could find neither sweetness nor rest in that.

Later, when I had done with the lovely woman, I remember somehow managing to go back and see the painting again. It was evening then, winter I think, and whether in a museum or a private home (I could remember such things with perfect clarity before my heart failed me) I was alone, standing before it with the light soft and nothing but loneliness stalking the roofless windowless doorless walll ess room there with me.

I had come back looking for some release from it, I think now. I had gone back not for appreciation—any more than one goes back to see Grünewald's Isenheim altarpiece for reasons of art. I wanted to find the key to that door—the flaw, the crack in its reality. To be free of the Albrights and their loathsome portal, I had to find, somewhere in the canvas, a false note, a tiny piece of sentimentality or stupidity. But there was nothing. The weather of the painting was unfathomable. It did not change. Even with the summer brightness purged from the room, it was the same—as if the door, the wreath,

the very canvas had the power to absorb or reject exterior light so as
to keep the painting always within that awful twilight which flowed
like sidereal influence out of the door's dead center—the wreath
which lay hanging against it like a demonic target or some emblem
of absolutism linked with the imperturbable power of death itself.

Yes, I am standing still in front of that frame building in my town
of Vicksburg, and yes, looking inward past the great fig trees at the
shadowed door which now after all looks only the least bit like that
other one, the weather, the light, the substantiality of all things
about being so much less dense. Reality spares us; we do not have to
know what else there is very frequently, do we? A colored boy, no
more than twelve, walked by in a polo shirt and worn corduroy
pants. He exchanged a quick glance with me and stepped on past, a
transistor radio hanging from his neck, a tiny tinny thing which
crooned:

> . . . *looks like the end, my friend,*
> *got to get in the wind, my friend,*
> *These are not my people, no, no,*
> *these are not my people . . .*

Surely he had his radio aimed at me. How could he tell? And was
the announcer a friend of his? He an agent of the station which had
discovered me, an alien, waxing in their midst. All of this I thought
in jest, putting sudden flash-cuts of the Isenheim crucifixion out of
mind, reaching for the doorknob, and stepping inside.

I do not know why I was not prepared. I should have been. No
reason for me to suppose that a lawyer's office here, in an old frame
building, would have the sort of Byzantine formality I remembered
from New York. Receptionist, secretary, inner office—with possibly
a young clerk interposed somewhere between. But the mind is
stamped inalterably with such impressions when we have done
business a certain way for a very long time.

So I was not prepared when Mr Grierson turned in his chair and
smiled at me and said

—Well, this is nice. Mighty nice. I don't know as I expected it.

—I beg . . . I began. Then I tried again. Best not beg. —I'm
sorry. Have we met? Is it better to be sorry than to beg, I thought instantly. Too late.

—You'd be the lawyer just come down. Got you a house and everything.

My God, I thought, even a B-movie would tell you that things travel like lightning here. He probably saw the deed, the note of transfer on the title. Knows what you paid for the lease, what you owe on the house if you pick up the option. Knows your last address, your last place of employ. Knows about your little chicken-thief cases, your car . . . I almost thought, about your coronary.

—Yes, I said, putting out my hand as he rose and offered his.

—I'm Harry Cohen.

He motioned me to a chair near his desk and I sat down, trying as I did to begin the task of seeing him, of seeing this place in which he worked. Trying at the same time to put out of mind the impressions I had created, had begun to suppose from the moment the deputy had told me where to come. If we could only stay free of our own guesses, what would ever make us wrong in advance?

He walked over to a large safe against the wall to the left of the door. It was taller than he was, and the door opened slowly as he turned the handle. He stood reaching into its dark recesses, his back to me. I wondered what he was looking for as his voice came to me, small talk like a magician's patter, over his shoulder.

—Yes, Mr Cohen. It's kind of you to pay a courtesy call. A custom languishing. Not dead, but in a bad way. A fine custom. Men who stand to the law shouldn't meet for the first time arguing a motion before Basil Plimsoll or one of the other boys on the circuit here . . .

I scanned the room as he spoke. I would deal with him later. It was a bright room—almost the opposite of what the door suggested. Or was it only the opposite of what the Albrights' door suggested?

On the wall over his flat desk, the shape and design of which had vanished long ago, I suspected, beneath a welter of papers and books, there were three old tintype portraits. Only they were not tintypes. They were fresh modern reproductions of tintypes. In the center, in a military uniform I almost recognized, was that stern beautiful face one recognizes without ever even having seen it. It was Lee. To his right, left profile toward me, hung that other one, that crafty rebel whose religion had almost severed the continent, Jackson. I did not know the third. He had a Tartar's face, long, bony, richly harsh—as if only in that uniform, only involved in that calling of arms, had his life meant anything to him at all. His eyes were straightforward and overpowering even at a hundred years' remove. And yet they were somehow at ease, their intensity more a matter of something evoked in the viewer than something essential to the eyes themselves. He had a high forehead, hair long, black, brushed back. His beard was a careless Vandyke, and the effect was that of seeing the man who had last closed the Albrights' door, nailed the wreath on it, and walked away, hands in uniform pockets. Whistling.

The rest of the room was austere and predictable. Near a long window there was a rocking chair done in some kind of chintz. Another table covered with papers. A third table in a corner with a coffeepot on it, a wine bottle or two, half a loaf of bread, and a plate upon which rested, glowing faintly, a large wedge of cheese. It looked like cheddar from where I sat. It was a room without quality—except for the portraits which were, I thought, a ritual observance no more meaningful to this man whose life had been lived in another country than washing his face in the morning, spitting at noon, closing his eyes at night.

Mr Grierson turned from the safe, hands filled with two tumblers and a dark brown bottle without a label. It had no cap. There seemed to be a cork stuck in it. He set all of it down on the edge of his desk and pulled the bottle's stopper with his teeth. The liquor was the lightest possible amber, a cataract of white gold as it twinkled into the glasses.

He smiled up at me. —You'll like it, he said. —Maybe not this time. But you let me send you a couple bottles. You'll come to like it.

—Corn, I said.

—Surely. Comes from upstate. Costs more than it used to. Bribes are just like the cost of living.

I sat back and sipped a little. It was peculiar, nothing like store whiskey, really. It was a shock in the mouth, vanished as you swallowed. Then it hit the pit of your stomach and paralyzed you for the briefest moment. Then great warmth, a happiness that spoke of cells receiving gifts, of veins moving to a new rhythm, muscles swaying like grain in a breeze-swept field. It was lovely. Nothing like whiskey. More like sipping the past, something intangible that could yet make you feel glad that it had been there.

Mr Grierson sat watching me now. As I took another swallow, deeper this time, I watched him back. A man of middle height, aged now but hale. Steel-rimmed glasses revealing large innocent blue eyes that seemed never to have encountered guile. He had that almost cherubic look that one associates with country doctors—or, in certain cases, with Southern politicians. He wore an old suede coat cut for hunting. I had never seen anything like it. It was a soft umber and fit as if it had been his own pelt originally.

—Your jacket, I couldn't help saying, feeling the whiskey lift me and waft me toward him, toward his smile. —Could I get one . . .

—At Lilywhite's, he said.

—Here?

—London, he said apologetically. —And even there back in 1949. I wouldn't reckon they make 'em like this anymore.

He wasn't putting me on, I could tell. But I could tell too that he enjoyed that level of conversation. It pleased him to please with pleasantries. One moves from one series of set exchanges to another. An infinite series. And when the last series is exhausted, it is either time to go, or you have lived out your life and death clears its throat, almost loath to interrupt, and says that it is time. I thought I would not want to go on like that.

Did I tell you that, on the far side of the coronary (O God, how that word has come to press me with its softness, its multiple implications. Corona. Carnal. Corot. Coronary. A place, a name, the vaguest warm exhalation glimmering from an eclipsed sun. Shivering golden and eternal around the glyph of a saint. Called then a Glory. I lay for weeks thinking Coronary, wondering when it would reach into my chest once more and squeeze ever so gently and bring out with its tenderness my soul, toss that gauzy essence upward like a freed dove to fly outward, past morning, past evening, past the blue sky into the glistening midnight blue of deep space, and past that even to the place where souls fly, shaking great flakes of its own hoarded meaning outward, downward on all suns and the worlds thereunder.) I had had a certain gift with exceptionally sharp teeth. Yes, I had been cruel. I had enjoyed finding certain lawyers in the opposition, men I had known who were blessed with a kind of unwillingness to go for blood. They worked within the confines of their dignity, their gentleness, their inadequacy. But I worked elsewhere and won invariably. But such work tightens the viscera. One cannot play bloodster without gradually coming to possess the metabolism of a jaguar, a predator. Was it imagination, or did I come to see better in the dark as I aged in my profession? Was I a little mad, or did I move more smoothly? Did my walk take on a certain ease, a bit of stealth? Did I smile with that humorless lynx-eyed expression that flows from the second sight of the killer? If it had not been for my success, I would have gone to a psychiatrist saying, Doctor, there is in me a germ and I fear it grows. Watch your throat, Doctor. What? Yes, I invent metaphors for killing. I am not psychopathic. Never that, not at all. No, I must kill without killing. I am a child of the century. Do you understand?

But Coronary came upon me, slackened the knotted nerves, the plaited muscles. I cannot say if I look younger or older now, but I am much different. I do not—no, will not—want to pursue and strike and rend. I am more peaceful. I want to do my part. And what is my portion will come to me. It is chess after professional football. But, even so, not Mr Grierson's gambit, not at his tempo. Though even as I looked at his pink uncreased face and considered the folds and inlets of the world behind him, I wondered if his pleasantries, his kindliness were not analogous to mine. What if one has, in passion or confusion, or as habit, taken men of another hue out and strung them to a near tree? What if that is how, for a small age, we have shaken from ourselves that rage that can tear a whole society to pieces? Suppose, from outside, something like Coronary should come? What might we do in the shadow of knowing that we cannot ever lynch again on pain of dying? Chess, after all, is a pleasantry profoundly complicated, Byzantine in its intricacies. Is there something in this?

—Another little drink, Mr Grierson suggested. —I believe you've already found something in it.

—I was thinking . . . of martinis.

—No comparison. Next step from corn would be . . . perhaps a pipe of opium.

I did not even wonder if he spoke from experience or from some book by Sax Rohmer. I wanted to go on.

—Mr Grierson, I wonder if you have the *Southwest Reporter* fro . . .

He poured each of us another glass. —I have it all, he said. —I think my . . . library will fill your . . .

I looked around. There was a single bookcase across the room, and only a handful of books in it. I must have looked doubtful. He gave me the oddest of small glances, and I took refuge in my whiskey.

—Maybe we should go on into the library, he said, rising and walking toward a door at the back of the room which I had not even noticed until now. It was painted the same dull color as the rest of the office. There was a hook nailed badly to the door with coats and jackets and what looked like an old fishing hat hanging from it.

I followed him and stepped ahead of him as he opened the door.

What shall I say? I have to tell you that Coronary fluttered not far away and I stepped in and turned in the new room slowly, slowly, taking it in, feeling, thinking in a simultaneity resembling that first moment of the attack.

So this is what lies behind them, Southerners. There is always that front room, the epitome of the ordinary, a haven for bumpkins. And behind, in one way, one sense or another, there is always this. No wonder even the most ignorant of them is more complex, more intricate than I have ever been. They stand upon this. This is behind them, within them. My God, what does that make . . . us?

Because it was, properly speaking, not a room. No, many rooms. It went on, back at least four more rooms and perhaps side rooms off each of the main rooms toward the back. And I knew without even entering the others that they were all more or less like this one I was standing in.

Filled from floor to roof with books. Thousands upon thousands of books. Books in leather and buckram, old, new, burnished bindings and drab old cloth. Behind and around the shelves the walls were paneled in deepest cherry wood. Before me was a beautiful nineteeth-century library table surrounded by chairs. It was like the rare book room of a great private library. I moved spellbound toward the nearest shelf. It was . . . religion. What was not there? Josephus. The Fathers in hundreds of volumes. The Paris edition of Aquinas. Was this a first of the Complutensian Polyglot? Scrolls in ivory cases. Swedenborg, Charles Fort. A dissolving Latin text from the early seventeenth century. The *Exercises* of Ignatius. Marcion, Tertullian. And I could see that the rest of the room was of a kind with those I was looking at.

—I had a house once, Mr Grierson was saying. —But even then it didn't seem fitting to have all this stuff out where my clients could see it. Folks here can abide a lot of peculiarity, but you ought not to flaunt it. You want to keep your appetites kind of to yourself.

This in a deprecating voice, as if possession of books, especially in great number, was somehow a vice—no, not a vice, distinctly not a vice, but an eccentricity that must disturb the chicken thief or the roughneck with a ruptured disk. Was it a kindness to spare them this?

—I think you'll find most anything you'll need here, Mr Grierson said softly. —Except for science. Not much science. Darwin, Huxley, Newton—all the giants. I kind of gave up when they went to the journals. They stopped doing books, you know.

—Yes, I said. Still thinking, this is where the Southerners have stored it all. You ask, how could Faulkner . . . how could Dickey . . . down here, in this . . . place . . . ? This is how.

I knew that this was madness. I did not question that. This time, had there been a psychiatrist close by, I would have gone to him at once without a doubt. Because, after all, this was not what I thought, but worse: what I felt. I *knew* it was not so, and still I *believed* it.

—This is where I do . . . my work, Mr Grierson was saying.

—Work, I repeated as we entered another room filled with literature. All of it. My hand fell on a shelf filled with French. Huysmans, Daudet, de Musset, Mérimée—and a large set of portfolios. They were labeled simply Proust. I took one out. It was bound in a gray cloth patterned in diamond-shaped wreaths, each filled with starlike

snowflakes, smaller wreaths, featherlike bursts gathered at the
bottom, nine sprays flaring at the top.

—It was the wallpaper, Mr Grierson was saying. —That pattern . . .

I opened the portfolio. In it were printed sheets covered with
scrawling script, almost every line of print scratched out or added to.

—Proofs. Of *Du côté de chez Swann.* I was in Paris . . . in 1922.
Gide . . . anyhow, I came across . . .

—Of course. You've studied them?

—O yes. The Pleiade text isn't . . . quite right.

We went on for a long time, shelf by shelf. But we did not finish.
We never finished. It could have taken weeks, months, so rich was
his treasure.

I left at dusk with Grierson seeing me to the door, inviting me
back soon, offering me the freedom of his library. I was back home
sitting under my arbor with whiskey and a carafe of water on a small
table beside me before I recalled that I had never gotten around to
checking in the Mississippi code as to its position on pigs and those
who made off with them.

The pig had prescribed, sure enough. But on the way out of court,
I found myself involved in another case dealing, if you will, with
similar matters.

They were bringing in a young man in blue jeans, wearing a peculiar shirt made of fragments, rags—like a patchwork quilt. He had
very long hair like Prince Valiant, except not so neat. He was cuffed
between two deputies. One, large with a face the color of a rare
steak, kept his club between the young man's wrists, twisting it from
time to time. There seemed somehow to be an understanding between them: the deputy would twist his club viciously; the young
man would shriek briefly. Neither changed his expression during
this operation.

—What did he do, I asked the other deputy who looked much like
a young Barry Fitzgerald.

—That sonofabitch *cussed* us, he told me with that crinkly simian smile I had seen in *Going My Way.* —We should of killed him.

—Local boy, I asked.

—You got to be shitting me, he answered, watching his partner doing the twist once more. —He's some goddamned yankee. Michigan or New York, I don't know. We should of killed him.

—Did you find anything in his car?

—Car your ass. He was hitching out on U.S. 80. We better not of found anything on him. I know I'd of killed him for sure. I can't stand it, nobody smoking dope.

—What's the charge?

—Reviling, he said, eyes almost vanishing in that attenuated annealed Mississippi version of an Irish grin. —Two counts.

—Two?

—We was both there. He was vile to Bobby Ralph and me both.

—What did he say?

—Wow, Barry Fitzgerald's nephew crinkled at me. —We should of killed him and dumped him in Crawfish Creek.

—What?

—Pigs.

—Sorry?

—You heard. Called us—Bobby Ralph and me—pigs. My God, how do you reckon we kept off of killing him?

I think it was a question of free association. Pigs. I had had luck with pigs so far. Maybe this yankee sonofabitch—pardon me—was sent for my special care. God knows the care he would get otherwise. Just then Barry's partner gave the young man a final supreme wrench. He came up off the floor of the courthouse hallway at least three feet. He squealed and looked at me with profound disgust.

—You old bastard, he drawled, hunching his shoulders, —would you let 'em book me so I can get these things off?

—I'm a lawyer, I said.

—You're fucking bad news, the young man said wearily.

—See, Barry said, as his partner shoved the young man down the hall toward the booking room. —Reckon we ought to take him back out and lose him?

—No, I said. —You don't want to do that.

—No, Barry said, walking after his partner and their day's bag.
—No, you lose him and the feds shake all the feathers out of your pallet looking for him. Christ, all you have to do to make him important is lose him. Or paint him black.

—You leave the ninety-nine lambs and seek the one that's lost, I said, striving for his idiom.

—Anyone does that is a goddamned fool, Barry said over his shoulder. —And he's going to be out of the sheep business before he knows it. Lost is lost.

Later—you guessed it—he sent for me. On the theory that I seemed to be the only one in the town able to speak English as he knew it, as opposed to lower Mississippian. We talked in a corner of his cell. There was a sad Mexican and a local drunk in the cell with him. The three had reached a kind of standoff between them. None could understand the others. Each seemed weird to the others. Since they had no weapons and were roughly the same size, an accommodation had been arranged. No one would begin a fight which could not be handicapped.

His name was Rand McNally. He might have been a nice-looking young man if he had wanted to be. But he was not. His eyes were circled, his skin dry and flaked. I could not tell precisely what color his hair was. He had a small transistor radio the size of a cigarette pack stuck in the pocket of his shirt. It was tuned to a local rock music station:

She's got everything she needs,
She's an artist,
She don't look back . . .

— the Spic stinks and the redneck keeps puking over there in the corner, Rand McNally told me. —But that's all right. I've got it coming. I deserve it. Jesus, I wish I'd kept my mouth shut.

—Or stayed out of Mississippi.

—It was an accident, Mississippi.

—Some say that, I told him.

—Oh shit. I mean being here. I was running away from a . . .

girl. It came up Mississippi.

—Where are you from?

He sat back and .fingered his essay at a beard. It was long and a kind of dark red. I supposed his hair was probably the same color if it was washed. The beard was sparse, oriental. Above it, he had large green eyes which somehow gave me a start each time I looked squarely into them. I am not used to being put off by a physical characteristic, but those eyes, deeply circled, seemed to demand a concentration and attention I had no wish to muster. They seemed, too, to require the truth. Not knowing the truth, I evaded such demands whenever possible. I wished I had let him pass on with Barry Fitzgerald's kinsman and his partner. No, I didn't.

—I don't know, Rand McNally said. —From one place after another. I just remember serial motels and rooming houses. The old man was an automobile mechanic. I never had the idea it started anywhere. I mean, it had to start somewhere. I got born, didn't I? But I remember it being one dump after another forever. Al's Garage, Bo-Peep Motel; Fixit Tire Company, Millard's Auto Court; Willie's Car Repair, Big Town Motor Hotel. Somewhere the old man had a woman and she had me—told him I was his—and then on to the next place. She dropped off somewhere. I think he whipped up on her. I seem to remember something. About money? Sure, probably. I don't remember her.

I saw his father, a great tall harried man with grease worked permanently into the skin of his knuckles, under his fingernails, with the soul of Alice's white rabbit, an ancient Elgin running fast in his pocket, and a notebook listing all the small towns, garages, and motels he was obliged to move through before it was done. One entry said: *Get Son.* Another said: *Son Grown. Leaves.* There were faded, smeared pencil checks beside each entry. Life lived between Marvin Gardens and Reading Railroad.

—How do you want to plead, I asked him.

He shrugged. —Make it easy on yourself. I've got a couple of months to do here. Price of pork.

I had not thought him intelligent enough to have a sense of humor. We smiled at each other then. The transistor was quacking another of its vast repertoire of current tunes:

> *These are not my people,*
> *No, no, these are not my people.*
> *Looks like the end, my friend,*
> *Got to get in the wind, my friend . . .*

—I'm going to plead you innocent. No malice.

He tossed his hair back and smiled up at me. His green eyes seemed to hang on mine for a long while. It surprised me that someone so worn, so ground off by the endless procession of new people in his life could reach across to the latest in that anonymous parade with even the appearance of interest.

—No malice, he said. —That's true.

It was late that evening when the phone rang. At the other end was Billy Phipps, one of the county attorney's assistants. His voice was lazy with an undertone of something like amusement or exultation. I did not like him. He was provincial as a Bronx delivery man and took pleasure in the webbing of paltry law as it snared those who had not the slightest idea of its working. His own ignorance made him delight in that of others.

—Well, what do you think of your boy Rand McNally, he asked.

—Not a lot, I said, wondering why he would bother with a call on such a matter. —It seems silly to put him on the county for a little mild name-calling. Hadn't you ought to leave room for rape-murderers?

At the other end of the line, I could hear Phipps draw in his breath.

I pause only to say that I neither believe nor disbelieve in magic, precognition, spiritualism, and so on. I am not prejudiced. But I come to feel that all we do in the four dimensions of our world is like the action of water beetles skating on the surface of a still lake, turning our tricks between water and air, resident truly, fully, in neither, committed vaguely to both. Are we material—or other? I receive hints from varied sources. If you have loitered at the gates of Coronary, you must wonder. Is a massive heart seizure only a statistically predictable failure of meat-mechanism? Could it be counted a spiritual experience? Who, what seizes the heart? Who, what attacks the heart? Could it be an entrance into the indices of those currents which play above and below the beetle, in the great eternal world where there are neither serials, sequences nor statistics. Where forever, possibly, dear God and his precious Adversary choose to disagree as to the purpose of their copulation. At my worst—or best?—moments, I seem to hear, like a radio signal from the most remote reaches of time and space, the voices of the Entities making their cases over and over, yet never the same, because each permutation is a case unto itself. Is it the voice of God one hears, arguing point by point, A to B to C, coolly, without rancor or regret —like Herman Kahn? Is it Satan who sobs and exults, demands, entreats, laughs, chides, tears a passion, and mutters sullenly? Or are those voices reversed? Maybe I am gulled believing in polarities. Why not? Could not God howl and sob the Natural Order of Normal Occasions, while Satan urges quietly the Stewing Urgencies of Madness? Why not? And why should we not in one way or another receive darts and splinters from those age-long and intricate arguments?

So much to explain my mind as I heard Phipps draw in his breath. *Jesus,* I thought, *a message.*

—What did he tell you, Phipps asked quietly, his normal sneering country manner gone altogether.

—Nothing, I said. —What do you mean?

—Counselor, we got a telegram from Shreveport. They want to talk to Pig-Boy. About a rape-murder.

—Ah, I said, and felt those faintest stirrings in my chest. Not even a warning, only the dimmest—can I say, sweetest—touch of recollection, of terrible nostalgia, from the distant geographies of Coronary. Like the negative of a photograph of a memory, saying: this twinge, this whisper, is what you felt without noticing before you came that day for the first time upon the passage to Coronary. Be warned and decide. Is it a landscape you wish to visit again? Is it, pulsing once more, a place where gain outmeasured loss? Stroke the contingencies and wonder your way to a decision. You have been

once across the bourn from which few travelers return? Do you have
it for another trip? And will that trip too be round?

—Ah, I said again to Phipps. —Let me get back to you, all right?

It was all right. Spatially, Rand McNally was fixed. This allowed
certain latitude with time. Tomorrow would be just fine. Since the
rape-murder, evocation of a nameless victim cooling after life's fitful
fever 350 miles away in North Louisiana, was fixed irrevocably in
time and there could be, for those to whom its being was announced,
no moving from it even as it receded backward and away now, one
more permutation in the patterns spoken of in that bower where
God and His Son ramble on to no probable conclusion.

Is it strange to say that, after the call from Phipps, I found myself
thinking less of the long-haired boy than before? Before, I had been
searching for a way to free him from, at most, a three-month term in
jail. Now, when he might stand within the shadow of death or a lifetime in prison, he seemed somehow less a point of urgency. Perhaps
because I believed not only that he had committed that rape-murder
in another place and time, but that he had, in passage from one
serial point called Shreveport to another called Vicksburg—both
noted as mandatory in a book like his father had been slave to—
placed upon that act, called rape-murder by authorities who have
the legal right to give comings-together names and sanctions, his
own ineradicable mark: a fingerprint, a lost cap, one unforgettable
smile caught by a barmaid in a cafe as he passed toward or from the
fusion with another—presumably female—in that timetable inheri-
ted from his father, and for all either I or he could say, from the very
Adam of his blood. However that might be, there was no hurry now.
Ninety days in the county jail, so implacable only a little while
before, no longer mattered. Which called to my mind, making me
laugh inordinately, that on the day of Coronary I had developed a
painful hangnail, had given it much thought. Until it vanished in the
wilderness of my new world. Had it healed in the hospital? One presumed. I could not recall it after I had stepped out of that world in
which one nags for the sake of a hangnail. It is a question of mag-
nitudes. When Coronary came, I was transformed into one who,
having disliked mosquito bites, now used the Washington Monu-

ment for a toothpick. Mosquitoes, landing, would fall to their deaths in the vastness of a single pore. And later, drinking off my bourbon and water and sugar, I slept without dreams. Or, as I am told, dreaming constantly, but remembering none when it came time to awaken.

—I hear you reached in for a kitty and caught yourself a puma, my telephone was saying.

It was Mr Grierson calling. He wanted to know if he could be of assistance.

—Seeing you hadn't figured on anything quite like this, he said blandly.

—Yes, I told him. Hell yes. Only small boys and large fools stand alone when they might have allies. Anyhow, I thought, McNally will barely have representation anyhow: a heart patient obsessed with the exotica of his complaint; an old man gone bibliophile from sheer loneliness. We would see.

We did. It was noon when we got in. Rand McNally stared out at the jailer in whose eyes he had obviously gained status. When he opened the cell, he loosened the strap on his ancient pistol. *This here bastard is a killer,* I could almost hear him thinking.

Mr Grierson hitched up his pants, passed his hand over his thin hair, and sat down on a chair the jailer had provided for him. I made do with the seat of the toilet. Mr Grierson studied the boy for a moment, then looked at me expectantly, as if protocol required that I begin. I nodded, returning the compliment to my elder. I had divined already how such things would move in Mississippi. Mr Grierson returned my nod and cleared his throat.

—Well, sir, it appears that clandestine hog-calling is the least of your problems.

Rand McNally stared at him in astonishment. Then he laughed, looked at me, saw me smile despite myself. He went on laughing while Mr Grierson sat quietly, an expression bemused and pleasant on his face.

—I'm glad you got such a fine spirit, son. You're gonna need it.

Rand McNally took the earplug of his transistor out and hung it through the spring of the empty bunk above his. The Mexican and

the farmer were gone now. Perhaps released to the terrors and punishment of sobriety; perhaps simply transferred to other cells in
honor of Rand McNally's new status.

—Huh, McNally said to Mr Grierson.

—If you did to that lady in Shreveport what they say you did,
you're gonna have a chance to stand pat whilst they strap you in the
electric chair. Shave your head, I believe, before you go.

Rand McNally shuddered. Whether it was the standing pat, the
chair, or the head shaving I could not tell.

—Well, Mr Grierson asked him. —What about it?

Yes. Well, he told us. He was glad it was over; was tired of running. ("Sonofabitch only did what he did three days ago," Mr
Grierson observed later. "What do you reckon? Think he's been
reading *Crime and Punishment?*") He had gone to work for an
elderly widow in Shreveport, had cut the yard for a meal, had hung a
shelf for a dollar, and came back the next day to whitewash a fence
for two dollars. Had whitewashed most of the day with her looking
on from her kitchen window past the blooming wisteria and lazy
bees. Near sundown, covered with sweat and whitewash, he had
gone inside to get a glass of ice water and his two dollars. As he
drank, the woman squinted out at the fence, saying, "It'll take
another coat." "Huh," Rand McNally said. "Another coat. Then
I'll pay you," she said softly, smirking at him, some last wilted,
pressed, and dried whisp of her ancient femininity peeking through.
At the very worst time.

She said something else that he could not remember and he
picked up a knife with which she had been dicing peaches and
pushed it into her throat. Then he pushed her over on the kitchen
table, pulled off her clothes and down his pants, made with that
agonized and astonished crone the beast with two backs, blood,
coughing, and great silence between them. In retrospect, he was
mildly surprised by it all. It was not, he told us, a planned happening. He was curious that, following the knife, he had discovered
himself erect. Why he pressed on with it, distasteful and grotesque
as it was, he could not say. But when he was done—he did get done,
by the way—he found that she was still very much alive, admonish-

ing him with one long bony liver-spotted finger.

So he got the remainder of the whitewash, dragged it back into the house in a huge wallpaper-paste bucket while he held up his pants with one hand. While she lay there mute, violated, bleeding, he whitewashed the kitchen: the walls, floor, cabinets, stove, icebox, calendar, and four-color lithograph of Jesus suffering the little children. Chairs, hangers, spice rack, coffee, tea, sugar and flour bins, breadbox, and cookie jar. All white. At last he rolled her off onto the floor, whitewashed the table, and put her back in the middle of it. After studying it all for a moment, he decided, and whitewashed her too. Which, so far as he could remember, was all he could remember.

—Ummm, Mr Grierson said. —So she was alive when you were done with your fooling?

—Alive and kicking, Rand McNally said without smiling. —You see I got to die, don't you?

—Well, Mr Grierson said, looking at me, —you ain't done much by way of making a case against that. Do you want to die?

—Everybody wants to die, Rand McNally said. He was picking his toes, disengaged now, considering certain vastnesses he had talked himself to the edge of.

—Right. At the proper place and time. How do you like the Chair?

—Ride the lightning? What a gas, Rand McNally almost smiled.—Anybody'd do that to an old lady has got to pay the price. You know that's so. The price is lightning in this state.

—Well, Mr Grierson said, getting up stiffly. —Let me study on it, son. I'll see you.

As we left, Rand McNally was screwing the transistor's plug into his ear. —Christ, he said, —a sonofabitch would do that has *got* to die.

Outside, we passed Billy Phipps talking to a couple of police we didn't know. Phipps nodded to us. I supposed they were from Shreveport.

—Do you smell Rand McNally . . .

— . . . sneaking up on an insanity plea, Mr Grierson finished my sentence. —Indeed I do.

—It looks good. From slimy start to filthy finish, doesn't it?

—Ummmm, Mr Grierson hummed, smiling. —All he's got to do is convince a jury he's Tom Sawyer . . .

— . . . and she was Becky Sharp . . . ?

He looked at me sorrowfully and shook his head as if only a yankee would have pressed it that awful extra inch. —Thatcher, he said. —But there is a question still . . .

— . . . ?

—If he *is* trying to get himself decked out with an insanity plea, the question is, why *did* he kill the old lady, and then do that to her? If he hadn't, he wouldn't need any kind of plea at all, would he?

That afternoon under the scuppernongs I felt as if I were waiting for some final word, some conclusive disposition of my own case. There was a dread in me, an anxiety without an object. I thought ceaselessly of Rand McNally and his insane erection in the midst of an act of violence. I thought of his surprise at it. I thought of my own prophecy over the phone to Phipps. What had brought him to this place, this conclusion? He had stepped from life into process: extradition, arraignment, indictment, trial, sentencing. I came to feel that he had ceased to exist, to be a human being owed and owing. He was no longer a proper object of feeling. Now one only *thought* about him. One took him into account along with Dr Crippen, Charles Starkweather, Bruno Hauptmann, Richard Speck, and the others of that terrible brotherhood whose reality is at once absolute and yet moldering day by month by year in antique police archives or grinning dustily in the tensionless shadows of wax museums.

It was just after supper when Mr Grierson appeared. He pulled into the drive in a 1941 Ford Super DeLuxe coupe. It was jet black and looked as if it had been minted—not built, minted—an hour or so before. He wore a white linen suit and a peculiar tie: simply two struts of black mohair which lay beneath and outlined the white points of his narrow shirt collar. It was not that his car and clothes were old-fashioned; it was that while they were dated, they were not quaint or superannuated or amusing. As if by some shift Mr Grierson had managed the trick of avoiding the lapse of time, of nullifying it so that what had been remained, continued unchanged. Could one pile up the past densely enough around himself so as to forbid its dwindling? And what would happen if the rest of us shared that fierce subterranean determination to drag down the velocity at which today became yesterday? It would fail, of course. You cannot disintegrate the fabric of physics. But what would happen?

We spoke of the weather, hot and dry, the bane of planters hereabouts. No sweet June rain. Only scorching sun, the river lying like a brown serpent between us and those like us in Louisiana. It was the mention of Louisiana that Mr Grierson chose as his pathway past the amenities.

—He's crossing the big river tomorrow. Waived extradition.

—Oh? Did you . . . ?

—Talk to him again? O yes. Surely.

He smiled at me, knowing what thoughts had crossed my mind and instantly been dropped as I asked my question.

—He was forcefully apprised of his rights. Not once, but several times. And he repudiated every one of them in obscene terms.

—What? I don't . . .

—He said it was a goddamned piss-poor legal system that gave all these rights to a . . . fucking pervert.

Mr Grierson looked embarrassed for the sake of the quotation.

—Jesus, I said, almost dropping the bottle of sour mash from which I was pouring our drinks. —Christ, he *is* crazy. He *must* have been reading Dostoevski.

—I don't know, Mr Grierson said. —He gave me this. Said it was your fee.

He handed me a greasy fragment of oiled paper—the kind they wrap hamburgers in. There was what looked like a quatrain scrawled on it in No. 1 pencil:

> *It's bitter knowledge one learns from travel,*
> *The world so small from day to day,*
> *The horror of our image will unravel,*
> *A pool of dread in deserts of dismay.*

—What's that, I asked Mr Grierson. He smiled and sipped his whiskey.

—You can come over to my place and look it up, he said. —The idea is interesting. Wine don't travel well.

— . . . the horror of our image . . .

—Seems what broke him up was that business after he stabbed the old lady. He didn't seem much concerned about the stabbing, you know. It was . . . the other.

—And the finale . . . ?

—The whitewashing? O no, he liked that fine. You can't make up for it, he told me. But you do the best you can. That boy is a caution . . .

We sat drinking for a while. I shook my head and said, not so much to Mr Grierson as to myself, —It's . . . as if Rand McNally was a . . . historical figure.

—Well, yes. That's so. But then, we all are.

—Yes . . .

—But history ain't like grace, is it? It has different rules. Which is to say, no rules at all.

I stared at him. Grace? What might that be? Luck? Fortune? I had heard the word. I simply attached no meaning to it. Now this old man set it before me as an alternative to history. I felt that dread again, some low order of clairvoyance wherein I imagined that Coronary might open once more: at first like the tiny entrance to Alice's garden—then like the colossal gates of ancient Babylon. It struck me at that instant with ghastly irrationality that grace was the emanation of vaginal purpose and womb's rest. Is grace death?

—Is grace death, I heard myself asking aloud.

—It could be, Mr Grierson answered. —I can imagine in a few years I might ask for that grace. But not altogether. History is the law. Grace is the prophets. History comes upon us. I reckon we have to find grace for ourselves. The law works wrath rather than grace, Luther said.

—That line . . . the horror of our image . . .

—Yes. Well, that's what brought grace to my mind. I think that boy has just broke into and out of history.

— . . . ?

—Something else I remember from Luther: certain it is that man must completely despair of himself in order to become fit to receive the grace of Christ . . .

—I didn't know you were a Lutheran.

—Hell, I'm not. Never could be. Most often, I quote Calvin. But you always go for water out of the sweetest well, don't you?

—You mean Rand McNally doesn't care anymore? He's done with the motels, the garages?

—No and yes. He cares all right. He wants to get on with it, don't you see? He's sick of problems. But no, there won't be any more motor courts and repair shops for old Rand McNally.

—Problems . . .

—What happened to him that evening in that old woman's kitchen? Do you know? How is it that killing moved to something like what they call an act of love? Neither fit the hour's need. What happened? That's the problem.

I felt very warm, my face flushed, my hands wet as if I had just climbed out of the river. Believe me, I was afraid. I thought it was another attack. They call the coming of Coronary an attack. Tryst might be better. Liaison, assignation.

—You feeling bad, Mr Grierson asked, pouring us both a little more whiskey.

—No, I lied. —I'm fine. Just thinking. Was it grace that came on Rand McNally? Is that what you want to say?

—Lord no, Mr Grierson smiled deprecatingly. —That'd be crazy. Grace to kill and rape an old woman? Naw, I never said that. I wasn't speaking *for* grace, you know.

—He's insane. They'll find him insane.

—Sure. So was Joan of Arc. So was Raymond of Toulouse . . .

—Raymond . . . ?

—A hobby of mine, he spread his hands. —I take on old cases sometimes. Not Joan. She's all right, taken care of. But Raymond . . .

Who was an Albigensian—or at least no less than their defender in his province. Tormented by orthodox authorities most of his life, he died outside that grace which Rome claimed to purvey exclusively, and lay unburied in the charterhouse of the Hospitalers for 400 years. Mr Grierson told me much more—told me that he had written a 300-page brief in Latin defending the acts and character of Raymond of Toulouse as those of a most Christian prince. But that was, he said, with a perfectly straight face, ancient history. He was working now on the defense of Anne Albright, a young girl burned during the Marian persecutions at Smithfield in 1556. It was to be a class action, aimed at overturning the convictions of all those Protestants burned under Mary Tudor.

—What about the Catholics, I asked sardonically, draining my whiskey.

—Fisher, Southwell, Campion? No need. The world's good opinion justifies them. As well waste time on More or Beckett. No, I go for those lost to history, done to death with no posthumous justification.

—That's a mad hobby, I told him. Somehow his pastime made me angry. At first I supposed my anger came from the waste of legal talent that so many people needed—like Rand McNally. But no, it was deeper than that. Could it be that I, a child of history, descendant of those whom history had dragged to America, resented Grierson's tampering with the past? How many of yesterday's innocents, perjured to their graves, can we bear to have thrust before us? Isn't the evil in our midst sufficient unto the day?

—The past is past, I said almost shortly.

Mr Grierson looked disgusted. —My Christ, he said. I had never heard him speak profanely before. —You sit under an arbor in Vicksburg, Mississippi, and say that? You better get hold of history before you go to probing grace.

We were quiet for a long while then, Grierson's breach of manners resting on us both. At last he left, walking slowly, stiffly out to that bright ancient automobile that came alive with the first press of the starter. I stood in the yard and watched him go, and found when I went into the house again that it was much later than I had thought.

I found myself gripped by a strange malaise the next day, and for weeks following I did no work. I walked amidst the grassy parkland of the old battlefields. I touched stone markers and tried to reach through the granite and marble to touch the flesh of that pain, to find what those thousands of deaths had said and meant. It was not the Northern soldiers I sought: history had trapped them in their statement. It had to do with the union, one and indivisible, with equality and an end to chattel slavery. That was what they had said, whether they said it or not. But the Southerners, those aliens, outsiders, dying for slavery, owning no slaves; dying for the rights of states that had no great care for their rights. In the name of Death, which had engulfed them all, why?

But I could find nothing there. It was history, certainly: the moments, acts frozen in monuments, but it told me nothing. I could find nothing in it at all. One evening as the last light faded, I sat on a slope near the Temple of Illinois and wept. What did I lack? What sacred capacity for imagining had been denied me? Could I ever come to understand the meaning of law, of life itself, if all history were closed to me?

Or was it not a lack but a possession which kept me from grasping the past as it presented itself, history as it laid down skein after skein of consuming time about us all? I imagined then that it was Coronary. That I had been drawn out of history, out of an intimacy with it by that assault. What was time or space to an anchorite who stared forever into forever? How could sequence matter to one who had touched All at Once? When I tried to concern myself with practical matters, I would remember Coronary and smile and withdraw into myself, forget to pay the net electric bill on time, suffering afterward the gross. Surely, I thought, I cannot care or be known within history because I am beyond it, a vestal of Coronary, graced with a large probable knowledge of how I will die. Knowing, too, that superflux of certain action can even hasten the day of that dying. I know too much, have been too deeply touched to succumb to history. I have no past, no particulars, no accidents. I am substance of flesh tenderly holding for an instant essence of spirit. I am escaping even as I think of it. Surely, I thought, a vision of one's dying must be grace. Yes, I am in grace, whatever that means.

Toward the end of some months of such odd consideration, I saw a small notice in a New Orleans paper that announced, purported to announce, the judgment of Louisiana on Rand McNally. He had been found incompetent to stand trial. Yes. The People had adjudged him insane. Not culpable. Simply a biological misstep within history. To be confined until the end of biology corrected the error of its beginning.

I found that I was sweating. As if in the presence of something immutable, and preternaturally awful. It had no name, and I could give it no shape. I began to reduce the feeling to an idea. Was I sorry? How is that possible? Capital punishment is a ghastly relic from past barbarism. To place a man in such a state that he knows almost to the moment the time of his death is . . .

Is what? The blessing of Coronary? My God, is it punishment or grace? I sat with my face in my hands, feeling my own doomed flesh between my fingers, trying to plumb this thing and yet trying not to let the juices of my body rise stormlike within, carrying me toward that dark port once more.

One evening a few weeks later, I drove downtown and bought two dozen tamales from a cart on a street corner. It was an indulgence, the smallest of sneers behind the back of Coronary. It was possible to go on with bland food and a rare glass of wine so long as the notion dangled there ahead that one day I would buy tamales and beer and risk all for a mouthful of pretended health.

I carried home my tamales, opened a beer, and began to eat with my fingers. The grease, the spices, the rough cornmeal, the harsh surface of the cheap beer. Before the attack, in New York, I would never have dreamed of eating such stuff, but to live in grace is to dare all things. Then I looked down at the faded stained palimpsest of the old newspaper. Above Captain Easy, next to the crossword puzzle, was a short article. It told of a suicide, that of a mad rapist-killer about to be sent to the State Hospital, how he had managed to fashion a noose of guitar strings and elevate himself by a steel support in the skylight.

It was Rand McNally, of course. No doubt enraged by a system so blind and feckless as to suffer his kind to live, a self-created lynch mob determined to do justice to himself. My hand trembled, spilling beer. A rapist-murderer will lead them, I think I thought. A little later that evening, my second cardiac arrest took place.

Dr Freud, with the most fulsome humility, I say you should have been in there. You would have forgotten physiology: it was not the smooth agonized tissue of my heart which sent tearful chemicals upward to trek the barren steppes of my brain. No, in there, within the futureless glow of Coronary, I was constructing my soul. What, precisely, transpired there? Why should I not smile like Lazarus and suggest that the price of such knowledge is the sedulous management and encouragement of your own coronary involvement? Because I need to tell it. That is why we do things always, isn't it? Because we must. Not because we should. Which is what Rand McNally came to know, isn't it? And why he came to want death, demand punishment for himself, because he was no longer able to count on himself: what he did was outside any notion of *should*, was wholly given to *must*. Isn't that the way it is with animals?

But never mind. I am not guessing. That is part of what I have to tell you. I saw Rand McNally in there, and Joan of Lorraine, Raymond of Toulouse, and Anne Albright. All in Coronary, yes, Dr Freud. Being a man dead, there is no reason one must honor time or space, chronology or sequence, in his hallucinations.

It was the Happy Isles, where I was, looking much like the country around Sausalito. There was worship and diversion, of course, and the smoky odor of terror. Two Mississippi deputies dragged Raymond before the Inquisition. Anne Albright was condemned once more for having denied the doctrine of Transubsegregation. They claimed that Joan had stolen something: Cauchon, pig? A Smithfield ham? Mary Tudor curtsied to Lester Maddox as they sat in high mahogany bleachers in Rouen's town square. Agnew preached against the foul heresies of all spiritual mediums while shrouded Klansmen tied Rand McNally to a stake, doused him with whitewash, and set him afire.

I think I saw Jesus, now only an elderly Jew, in a side street weeping, blowing his nose, shaking his head as the Grand Inquisitor passed in triumphant procession, giving us both a piercing stare, blowing us kisses. Behind him in chains marched Giordano Bruno and John Huss, Mac Parker and Emmett Till. Savonarola was handcuffed to Malcolm X and Michael Servetus walked painfully, side by side with

Bobby Hutton. The line went on forever, I thought, filled with faces I did not know: those who had blessed us with their pain, those suffering now, those yet to come. I wondered why I was not among them, but old Jesus, who was kind, and whom they ignored, said that there were those who must act and those who must see. It was given, God help me, that I should see.

There were other visions which I have forgotten or which I must not reveal. I saw, in the ecstasy of Coronary, the end of all things and was satisfied. It was only important that nothing be lost on my account. What does that mean?

—What does that mean, I asked Mr Grierson when he came to the hospital to visit me, as soon as they allowed anyone to come at all.

—Ah, he said, his pink scalp glistening in the weak light above my bed. —Economy. You got to note all transmutations. Correct all falsehoods. Don't you see that? Lies, falsehoods, perversions of reality—those are man's sovereign capabilities. Only man can rend the fabric of things as they are. Nothing else in the universe is confused, uncertain, able to lie, except man. And through those lies, those rifts in reality, is where all things are wasted. But . . .

—But what . . . ?

—Well, Mr Grierson smiled. —That's what my hobby is about.

—Your . . . cases . . . Anne Albright . . . ?

—Sure. No lie survives so long as the truth is stated. Those are the terms of the game.

—I don't see . . . what if people *believe* the lie . . . ?

—It doesn't matter. Tell the truth. Sooner or later that mere unprovable undefended assertion of the truth will prevail.

—How can you believe . . . ?

Mr Grierson shrugged. —How not? We got all the time in the world. When the profit goes out of a lie, nobody wants to bother defending it any longer. That's where grace joins history, you see?

I did. I *did* see. He was right. A lie *couldn't* stand forever. Because there is no history so old, so impervious to revision that the simple truth doesn't establish itself sooner or later. Like gravity, the consequences of truth can be avoided for a while. Sometimes a little while; sometimes a great while. But in the end, that which is false crumbles, falls away, and only the truth is left. So long as that truth has been once stated, no matter how feebly, under whatever pain.

—Yes, Mr Grierson said quietly, taking a sheaf of yellowed papers out of his briefcase. —What with all the time you've got on your hands just now, I reckoned you just as well get started . . .

—Started . . . ?

He handed me the file. —In southern Texas, summer of 1892, there was this Mexican woman . . . they gave her something like a trial, then they went ahead and lynched her which was what they had in mind all along. It was the late summer of 1892. There was a panic that year, a depression, some trouble in Pullman Town . . .

I lay back, eyes closed, veteran of trances. Why not tell you of one part of my final vision? Why not? Yes, I saw, larger than the sky, what they call the Sacred Heart, burning with love for all the universe. I saw its veins and arteries, how we every one moved through it and away again, the sludge of lies and torture and deceit choking its flow like cholesterol. I saw that heart shudder, pulse erratically. I saw the fibrillation of God's own motive center, and I cried out that I should share his pain, and rise to the dignity of sacrifice.

Yes, I came then to realize why Rand McNally had gone out of himself. In order to find himself. To tell the truth. Time matters only to liars, and they are, at last, worse than murderers, even rapists of old ladies. Because, caught in the grid of His truth, they yet try to evade, even as they see time vanishing before them. Grace is history transcendent, made true at last. And faith is the act of embracing all time, assured of renewing it, making the heart whole once more.

—It's an easy one, Mr Grierson told me.—They did Rosa Gonzales wrong. You won't have any trouble . . .

I smiled and reached for the file.

—I don't think I'll ever have any real trouble again, I told him.

Susan Engberg

Pastorale

There was a woman who for a time loved a younger man. Her name was Catherine, and she had lost a child. Her daughter had been in a coma one week, two weeks, and then one morning in October her expression had changed slightly and she had died. Hanna. She had had honey-colored hair and pale eyes with an outer rim of darker blue to the irises. Until the brain tumor she had been healthy enough and lively and competent. She had bought two goats with her own money, raised them up, rode with John to have them bred, and when they freshened, milked them herself, morning and night, and with part of the milk made yogurt for the family. Catherine took over the milking. The boys should be doing that, John said, but she wanted it for herself; the goats, at any rate, were almost dry.

She was forty; Hanna had been ten. Sometimes the rounded numbers rose up in her mind as a meaningless chant—ten, twenty, thirty, forty—and then she would look backward and forward and see nothing but inexpressive decades. Her own face, resting against the goat's fur above the stream of milk, felt used up, like a landscape of dry runnels. She cleaned the stall methodically, accepting everything—the smells of urine and dung, the impatience of the goats, the cold in her hands as she fetched the water—as she had begun to accept the death itself.

But beneath this methodical impassive continuance of life, she could feel her grief changing into something less bearable than the immediate anguish; it was a sense of absolute physical loss, of strange yearning: she wanted to touch the child again. There had been no chance to be alone with her, dead. At night Catherine would lie in the dark and think that she might be all right if only she could cradle the child's actual corpse one more time.

But of course that was impossible. Months were passing. The adolescent energy of their two boys continued on a course of its own, as if it had been a stream of water passing through the house and out again, seldom anything to hold on to, and she had the feeling that wherever they were going, they were already on their way. Childhood had never seemed to her so brief.

She and John were the maintainers. In the past they had occasionally joked to each other, companionably, about how they were merely the keepers of an establishment. A door would slam somewhere, there would be a thumping on the stairs, a call from the barnyard, and when they looked at each other, what was between them had to do with seventeen years of marriage and the pleasure they could still take in each other and the way these people who were their children had invaded their house, but only for a time. Now between them Catherine sensed a self-consciousness that it seemed discussing would only aggravate, and although they might be alone, she no longer felt the same privacy. She would lie in bed, watching him undress, and the sight of his bare back, twisting to pick up a shoe in the half-light, or of his hair and beard—how grizzled he had become!—made her want to cry out to break through this theatrical intimacy, but the sound remained voiceless. He seemed to have become gentler with her, sometimes distant. They talked, of course, and they had wept together and with Tom and Drew, and they both had their work, which was a blessing.

John had been having good success with his pottery; he would be showing at two large invitationals that early summer in addition to the usual regional exhibits, and he was working steadily now, seldom sleeping late in the morning, seldom coming in early from the shop to read or tinker with an odd repair. She herself was finishing up one commission from the nursing school, the illustrations for a handbook for expectant mothers, and on the strength of this had been given another by a biology professor, an essay on reproduction intended for high school and college students. The coincidence between these subjects and Hanna's death she endured, because of her desire for work; she was practical and energetic by nature, and she had always handled periods of unclarity or doubt simply by applying herself to what was at hand. Several times a month she drove in to the university with her sketches, had quiet conferences in one office or another, ate lunch in one of the cafeterias around the science and medical complex, shopped a bit perhaps, or saw a friend, and then drove home.

Once she had felt drawn up to the fourth floor of the hospital past the room where Hanna had died; another child lay in the bed, and another mother sat in the green vinyl chair by the window. A shout of laughter came down the hall from the nursing station; a metal cart was clattering along a hallway out of sight. She didn't go back again.

She looked at children on the street, blond children, and at mothers who didn't seem to understand the full value of what was theirs. Once, in the checkout line of a supermarket, she had rushed away in confusion, leaving behind the basket of groceries, because of her overwhelming desire to pick up the child in front of her and hold her close, perhaps even to run away with her and to keep running until she could find a quiet place to talk.

She tried to tell herself that it was natural her sorrow should be taking these different forms, and that she must simply wait and accept its evolving transformations.

One late afternoon as she drove into their lane, a thick wet February snow was beginning to fall, windless, very still, like a false oblivion, and two crows were screaming over the catalpa skeletons at the bottom of the pasture. Her body was worn down by the last stages of the flu. John too had been ill, and she found him in bed, muffled in a shawl, reading, smoking his pipe. His clay-splotched trousers hung from a chair.

"You look ravishing and curative," he said as he stretched and threw aside his book. His stiff hair was raked up and the creases beneath his eyes looked personal and contemplative.

"I'm frazzled and sick," she said. "You're just playing the lascivious old man again; none of it is genuine." But she went to him and sat down close, laying a hand on his chest.

"Spending an afternoon in bed has had certain effects," he said.

"You've improved your mind and the state of your health, I hope."

"My mind has been rotting away with carnal lust. For you, of course, my dear," he added.

"You sound venereal," she said as she rested her weight against him. The play of their bantering went on by itself, remote. Outside the window the snow continued, thicker now and bluish. "Where are the boys?" she asked.

"I told them to go out and do the goats for you."

"That was nice." It was all distant, even the sadness, even the dried mask that was pretending to be her face.

They were snowed in the next day, and on the following noon Louie came with the tractor to clear the lane. He brought in the mail, standing huge and good-natured in the mudroom in his layers of sweat shirts and coveralls, talking about the snow.

"That was some snow," he said.

Catherine watched him trudge out to the corncrib. Once in the army in Alaska Louie's legs had gotten frozen from the knees down. Watching him work made her think of life as being a matter of putting one stolid foot in front of another, endlessly.

"Well, he's coming," said John, holding out a letter, "Laurits Jorgensen—that fellow I told you about. He's taken the apprenticeship and has agreed to twenty hours of work per week in exchange. How does that sound?"

"For how long?" asked Catherine. She read hurriedly down the paragraphs.

"Six months or so—we'll see how it goes." He sat in his ragged down vest, nursing his pipe and coffee and slowly working himself up to go out to the shop. It was a familiar sight. He had been up until four that morning with a firing.

"This is going to be good for you, isn't it?" said Catherine. "You might actually get the new kiln finished."

"He does say he's good with tools. He's a find, I'd say."

"You'll take him sight unseen?"

"I trust Merton—he wouldn't send a slouch."

"He'll get a room in town, I suppose?" asked Catherine, returning to her dish of fruit and yogurt. She had been up at seven with the boys and for most of the morning, while John had slept with the covers over his head, had been at her drawing board in their sunny bedroom.

"He could do that," said John.

Later in the afternoon he came in for a sandwich and brought it up to the bedroom. He squeezed the back of her neck, kissed her ear, and then sat down in the old wing chair. She heard him biting through lettuce and sucking from his can of beer.

"I've been thinking," he said as he set aside his empty plate and leaned back with the beer can balancing on his chest, "that fellow Laurits could take Hanna's room, if you'd agree. It seems a waste of time for him to go back and forth to town every day when he could just as well stay right here."

Catherine turned her pencil around and around in the sharpener. She squinted at the network of mammary ducts on her paper.

"We'd have to do something about the curtains," she said at last.

"That's simple enough, isn't it? It just seems to me that it's time now to start using the room; I mean, love, we've got to do it some day."

She heard the school bus on the road and looked out to the lane where Tom and Drew were jumping down from its steps.

"All right," she said slowly, turning back to her husband. "I think we could manage that."

II

"You must be Catherine," says the voice in the barn door. She turns from the fresh straw she is forking down and sees his shape against the light. It is April.

She goes over and sees him better. He has blond hair that is parted in the middle, and it hangs straight on either side of his face. His eyebrows are black.

"Then you're Laurits."

"The master there sent me out to meet you." He tosses his head slightly toward the shop.

She smiles as he smiles. It is one of the first warm days.

"This is quite a place; it's really beautiful. What else do you have besides goats?"

"Nothing, except a hundred or so cats."

"You own it all?" He is leaning against the old timbers of the doorway and looking out towards the undulating Iowa fields.

"Just the house and the barn and the shop. Louie has the land. You'll meet Louie before long." The pregnant goats are outside the door drinking from a trough. She has filled a large pan with grain. Now she heaves up a basket of old straw and droppings.

"I'll take that," says Laurits. "Where to?"

"That dung heap over there."

"This is fantastic," he says as he jauntily brings back the basket. He tosses the hair from his eyes.

They walk together toward the shop where they find John sponging smooth the rim of a large tureen. The reddish clay glistens like a moistened lower lip. Catherine has seen John take a finished piece like this, to her eyes perfect, and slice it relentlessly apart to reveal a slight inconsistency in the thickness of the form. There are other days when he is unable to work at all; then he might lie hour after hour in the darkened bedroom, harshly humorous against himself and the world. She has understood for a long time that her strength is different from his.

"Well," he says to Catherine, screwing his face above the pipe smoke, "the slave has arrived. Have you shown him to his miserable quarters?"

"Not yet," says Catherine, "he's been helping."

"That's good, lad. I'm glad to hear you haven't wasted these precious minutes cavorting aimlessly in the barnyard. It's work we want around here. Work! do you hear?" He makes his eyes look fierce and insane.

"Yes, sir," drawls Laurits. He has propped an arm along a drying rack and seems as much absorbed in the tureen as in either of them. Catherine wonders where he has gotten his confidence.

John seems invigorated, boyish himself. He stops the wheel and draws a taut string under the base of the tureen. "That's it," he says; "let's go talk about the future."

They are very gay. Catherine sees that it is a good combination of personalities. When the boys come home, they hang on the railings beside the porch swing, fascinated. Laughter gushes out over the lawn and the beds of spring flowers and freshly tilled garden. They are talking about the new kiln for salt glazing, about the distances to the surrounding towns, about the farm girls in the neighborhood. John allows himself a leer. "They grow up fast around here," he says.

A meadowlark is singing from the walnut tree by the lane, a piercing, slurred call that seems to contain the entire moment. Clouds are rapidly riding out of the west, fanning out into an expanse of sky and disappearing over the house. Catherine feels herself breathless at the spaciousness these approaching masses make visible. She is sitting on the steps with her coat collar up, hugging her knees. Tonight she will make a large salad with fresh mushrooms and chopped cress. Her mind is planning. She looks at her sons, and it seems weeks since she has noticed them. They are growing quickly. Their heads of identical brown curly hair are like lively, irrepressible masses of energy.

Later, in the night, she wakes and feels the house full of sleepers. Catherine turns her face into her pillow and smells her own hair. Her body is radiating heat, her cheeks feel smooth. Sometime during the night the first of the goat kids is born.

Laurits makes competent pottery, mostly smaller pieces like bowls and mugs and casseroles. He does not seem apologetic about what he has to learn. He listens carefully, and he is keeping a chart of glazing mixtures. When he sits at the kitchen table for tea, he turns the mug thoughtfully, sometimes holding it by the handle and sometimes cupping both hands around its belly.

Today he has come back from town with the onion sets Catherine has ordered. When he has made the tea, he calls up the stairs to her. He seems to like the kitchen. He talks to Catherine about an idea he has for building some shelves over the stove; getting up, he shows her how they would span, from here to here, with hooks underneath for pans and open space above for pottery. He has started to grow a blond mustache, and now when Catherine looks at his face she notices even more the darkness of his brows. She has stopped being surprised at how comfortable Laurits seems talking about these everyday household matters. He makes himself useful, but he doesn't seem to need their praise.

When they finish their tea, they go down the side yard together to the garden. They take turns making trenches with the hoe and placing the onion sets. Catherine has already planted radishes, beets, and carrots. Laurits says that when the time comes he will make some circular supports for the tomatoes from some old fencing he saw in the corncrib loft. He follows along beside her, pushing dirt onto the onions with the flat of his hoe. Catherine can feel the heat of the sun through her jacket, and she thinks that there are only seven weeks until the summer solstice. She has stopped being surprised at how comfortable she is working with Laurits; it is almost as peaceful as working alone, and yet even the simplest of motions seems to be enhanced. She is crumbling compost into the bottom of a trench, and her hands seem to be understanding exactly the nature of its richness. When she was a girl Catherine used to sketch her own hands, with wonderment, and now, remembering that, she seems to be reminded of the richness of her own nature. She straightens up to see Laurits at the edge of the garden, aiming walnuts up into the tree at the last few nuts still clinging to the branches in their green casings.

Laurits is reading in the rocking chair by the dining-room window. After lunch he always takes this rest; Catherine has told him he reminds her of her grandfather, and he has told her that he reminds himself of his own grandfather. She has come up the lane with the mail, and she taps on his window as she passes on her way to the shop. In a few minutes she returns to the house.

"You have two letters today, Laurits," she says. "I think your lovely lady must be missing you." The postmarks are from California. Laurits has said that her name is Leah and that she is studying marine biology. She is twenty years old; Laurits is twenty-three.

Laurits puts down his magazine and takes the letters. A Swedish ivy plant is hanging in the window above the library table; Laurits begins to read his letters beneath this cascade of scalloped leaves. Outside the window green maple-blossom discs drift in the sun.

Catherine sees Louie in the south field beyond the garden making a sweeping turn at the end of a row with the corn planter lifted from the ground; he drives with one hand as he twists in the tractor seat to gauge the beginning of the new row. Her own hands feel empty.

She pours herself a cup of coffee in the kitchen and goes upstairs to her drawing board. The bed is unmade, and the air is warm and still, almost like a summer afternoon. She is working on a schematic frontal section of the female reproductive organs, using books and charts loaned by Maxine, the biology professor. The new women's center has inquired about the publication date of this booklet; it will be used as well by high-school family-life classes and will be among the free literature available to incoming college freshmen. Maxine is in her late fifties. One of her daughters ran away from home at the age of seventeen; it was very bad for awhile, Maxine has said, but then gradually things worked themselves out. Catherine looks at her drawing and understands that what she is seeing is a section through a moment in evolution.

It is June. The boxes are packed, the van is loaded for John's Chicago fair. Today Tom is fifteen. They are having his party at lunchtime, before Catherine and John must leave, and while Tom assembles his new fishing gear, Catherine cuts down through the cake. John is at the other end of the table, waiting for the coffee to be ready. His effort the last few weeks has been tremendous. Even he has called himself a maniac. The kiln has been fired twice a week. His final project has been a series of huge vases, almost human in their forms, with gentle bellies and flared rims and handles akimbo—his vestal vessels, he has said, giving one of them a pat.

He works at his pipe and squints at Tom; Catherine can see him searching for a humorous attack: no son of his is going to come off easily from a birthday.

"That's pretty sophisticated gear for a young whippersnapper like you," he says.

"Whippersnappers are good at things like this," says Tom as he carefully fits together the sections of the rod. He is barely suppressing his excitement with the gleaming tackle and newly fitted-out box, all chosen by his father, everyone knows. Laurits has promised to take the boys catfishing and camping overnight on the river. Drew watches everything from a calculated slouch.

"So, Laurits," says John, "do you think you can keep these lads in line? No ruckuses on the Mississippi?"

"We kids will not besmirch the family name," says Laurits. "Simply think of us as young gentlemen off on a naturalistic holiday."

"Mind you look to the goats before you leave," says John to the boys.

Catherine pours the coffee in silence. She is disorganized; her bag is scarcely packed. She is remembering the long labor of her first son's birth, her partial disbelief that it was actually happening . . .

"Now there's a well got-up woman," says John to her later in the bedroom. "The brow, the bosom, the lovely thighs—a figurehead for our ship, worthy, if you pardon the expression, of breasting the crest. Together, my dear, we will navigate the evil city and bring back lots and lots of money."

"John, will you please be quiet? You're exhausting me."

"I'm exhausting you?"

"How was I exhausting you?" he asks on the highway.

"Just talk straight now, all right? We're alone, there's no one listening."

"We are alone, aren't we?" he says that night in the hotel, smiling down at her. City sirens pulsate on an eerie stratum of air, disembodied. All night there are voices and shouts, neon-light waves. Catherine does not feel that she is sleeping, but then she wakes, terrified for the safety of her children; in a moment she remembers that one child is already dead. John sleeps curved and dark.

The bathroom is white, white everywhere, but she can only think of the thousands of people who have touched its slickness without leaving a mark. She sees that her period has begun: her skin, their toothbrushes, and the brownish blood are the only colors in the room.

She sleeps again, floating on sound and the sensations of her body. Hanna is calling her on the telephone, a child's voice, difficult to make out. Yes? she says to her. Yes? Speak up! Everything but her own voice is indistinguishable; the telephone cord is slowly disintegrating. She wakes into the morning.

"This hasn't been too bad for a rickety-dinky hotel," says John, pleased with himself.

He is opening the curtains. "Will you come with me to the village square, my love, to peddle our wares?"

She puts on a large straw hat and over her swollen breasts a white blouse, open at the neck.

The week before Laurits had worked bare-chested in the garden, and she had seen that he was smooth and compact, self-contained. He had knotted a red scarf around his brow, and his back had glistened.

"Come on, lass, let's get a move on," says John.

Movement: she must move in spite of herself; she can no longer be in last week's garden, bending over vegetables.

"Are you all right, love?" asks John in the coffee shop.

Outside in the street the light is too bright; there is too much light, everywhere; even beneath the mottled plane trees at the fair she finds only an overexposed confusion of dapple. She hides beneath her hat.

"You're quiet, love," says John after he has made another sale. Year after year many of the same people return to his booth. Catherine looks up to see the face of Dr. Avakian, inviting them to dinner that night. She feels herself nodding. Dr. Avakian has greyed remarkably in the past year. He and his wife live childless in a high apartment near the lake. Catherine knows all about the evening already; she can see the iced wine, the crepes filled with crab, the fresh strawberries, the strong coffee and pastry in the living room above the reflecting water. Each year Dr. Avakian buys two, perhaps three or four hundred dollar's worth of pottery. It is obvious that he considers himself a patron and that he must search for ways in which to spend the money of his middle age.

Catherine presses her knuckles into her eyes. The innards of her body are heavy and sinking toward the gravity of earth; within and without the world seems constructed of motion and loss. She tries to imagine her sons in a rented boat at the mouth of a Mississippi slough; what she sees is Laurits, selecting bait from a bucket.

As they speed home across Illinois the next afternoon, the landscape for many miles outside the urban fringes seems tentative and barren, as if it had already lost its vigor in the face of the impending lava-creep of the city. It is not really until the Mississippi itself that Catherine begins to relax. Looking down from the bridge, she sees the wide river flowing effortlessly between its banks and feels reassured, as if she herself had caught an easier current. Inland John turns onto back gravel roads and they approach the farm into the sun, beside newly cultivated corn rows that look like giant thin-man legs running with the car. Catherine opens her window and takes a full breath of earthy air; she feels the presence of her heart.

The weather turns very warm. At the end of the month Tom and Drew prepare to take a bus out to camp in Colorado where they will ride horses, backpack, and fish for trout.

"I hope those whippersnappers appreciate this," says John as he closes the van on their gear.

Catherine takes the pipe from his mouth to kiss him. "Take care of yourself in that big-town bus station."

"I plan on being alert," says John. "Not a hussy will pass my notice."

"You sure know how to talk big," she says, feeling his arm around her. The boys are in the shop saying good-bye to Laurits. The yard is still and empty except for scattered dozing cats, and yet Catherine thinks that perhaps she and her husband are being observed. He seems charming and inscrutable, and as she lets him shuffle her through a few dance steps and lower her into an embrace of mock passion, she finds herself looking up with alarm into his grinning face.

"John," she says suddenly. "Maybe I should come along for the afternoon. Do you want company?"

"I thought you wanted some precious solitude."

"I did. I do." She looks at her watch. "There really isn't time to get ready."

"Look," he says, taking her by the shoulders, "I'll take care of our sons, and I'll take care of myself, and you take some time for yourself the way you planned, all right?"

Catherine stands silent in front of him, and for a moment his mannerisms seem to fall away, and what slams against her is his suffering.

The boys come loping across the yard from the shop.

She wants to touch him. Her throat tightens into pain. Hanna! John!

Laurits follows slowly behind the boys, wearing a rubber apron, his forearms and hands reddish.

"The troops are assembled," says John, and the moment has passed.

Catherine kisses her sons, everyone is joking, and then the doors slam and the van pulls away.

"I hope they get some good trout," says Laurits; "there's nothing in the world like mountain trout."

Catherine nods. She goes inside the back door and presses her fist to her mouth. "O, my God," she hears herself whispering, "O, my God," and she feels that her hands are being flung, taut, above her head. And then she picks up a rainjacket from the floor and puts it back on a hook. In the kitchen she watches her hands finishing the dishes. When they are done and the plants hanging above the sink have been watered, she takes down a sketchpad from the top of the refrigerator and goes out to the side porch. She draws the walnut tree and in the foreground the trunk of the wounded maple. Then she goes down to the garden and sits close to a pepper plant, letting her pencil understand the way the white blossoms are giving way to tiny green buds of fruit. She is sitting on a mulch of straw. Not far away a yellow and black spider is zigzagging a reinforcement in his web between two tomato plants. It is almost too hot to stay where she is, but she continues, turning from the peppers to the fuzzy eggplant leaves, and then to the squash vines and nasturtiums. For a long time she feels as if only the motions of her hands are keeping back the tears; then gradually she begins to forget about everything but the nature of what she is observing. At last she takes off her shoes and lies back on the hot straw.

All around her are the rustlings of insects or of plants growing. A hawk circles several times overhead and then banks out of sight. She shields her eyes with a forearm smelling of tomato leaves and herbs.

She doesn't know if she has slept, but at an indeterminate moment the air has changed; a faint cool dampness has swept the garden. She sits up. From the south a mass of round white clouds is approaching rapidly; from the north a front of blackness is bearing down with amazing speed. It is fascinating, she thinks, and the heat, thank God, will lift; then an instant later she knows the danger.

"Laur-its, Laur-its," she yells scrambling into her shoes and running to the shop. She throws the sketchpad inside the screen door, shouting, "Laurits, a storm is coming," and without stopping further heads for the small goat-pasture behind the barn. "Here babes, here babes," she calls to the already frightened animals. She has to lift the kids over the stone sill of the barn. One door after another she runs to secure; the cloud masses converge as she is struggling with the huge double doors of the barn's central passageway. Laurits appears beside her. By the time they are running for the house, a whipping rain has begun. A trash can sails across the yard, then a tree branch.

They tend to doors and windows. The house is moaning, the windows rattling, the metal weather stripping whining above even the high-pitched fury of the storm. Outside the air is greenish through the almost horizontal slant of the rain. A bolt of lightning to the west appears to stab a nearby field; thunder shakes the house. Laurits thuds down the stairs with a blanket around his neck. He takes her by the arm—"Upstairs is all right, let's get down"—and they descend into the basement fruit cellar where the hundred-year-old lime foundation stones are damp and motionless. Laurits sinks down underneath a workbench and opens his blanketed arm like a wing for her to enter.

They are in one of Hanna's old forgotten playhouses, one of the many hideouts that she had fashioned for herself around the farm. This one consists of a few peach crates beneath the bench, set up as shelves, and on the floor a mildewed playpen pad. The child had tied some yarn around one of the crates as a sort of decoration, and inside Catherine finds a canning jar filled with rotting kernels of corn and one large spider, alive. She puts it down slowly. The mind of her child seems near enough to touch.

Catherine cannot stop the tears now; she feels that she has never been so close to her sorrow. Lowering her forehead to Laurits's knee, she lets herself become a rounded shape of grieving. "Hey," he says, "hey," as he begins to stroke her hair and back. Her body is wracked by an accumulation of feeling, as if the sobs are coming out of her bones. "Catherine," says Laurits, "here, here." He has taken her close to him in the cramped musty space; from upstairs comes the faint screaming of the wind. "Catherine, what is it, what is it? There, don't talk. Catherine." His hands over her ears are muffling all sound. Her brow is being stroked; he is kissing her eyes. They are underneath a storm, in a space made by a child. "You're having a bad time," says Laurits, holding her head against him. She is snuffling now and breathing more quietly; her brain feels as if a searing connection has been made between its two sides, leaving behind a warm fluidity. "That's better now," says Laurits. She feels herself being rocked slightly; with her eyes closed she has a slight sensation of weightlessness. Laurits is cupping her breast with a gentle hand of comfort.

"There now," says Laurits after a time. "Let's go upstairs and see what's been happening. Do you think it's safe?" He wraps the blanket around them both and pulls her in close against him as they start up the stairs. "Catherine," he says, stopping halfway up to kiss her hair. He lowers his forehead to hers, and she lets her hands rest upon his chest.

They go from room to room, window to window. The yard and lane are strewn with tree limbs, and one huge branch has crashed down through the electrical wires to the shop. "Laurits, that's a hot line then, we should call," but when they go to the telephone, those wires are silent. They test random lights and all are dead. In the wake of the lightning and thunder and furious wind is now a heavy turbulent rain, being blown in thick curtains across the fields. The light inside the house is a brownish chiaroscuro.

Laurits sits down in a chair against a kitchen wall. Catherine goes across the room and sits beneath the useless telephone. They are being careful now. "I'm going to guess that for you there has always been only John," Laurits says quietly.

"How do you know that? Do you find it strange?"

"I think I would have expected it."

"It's not that I haven't loved others, but well, yes, there's been only John. We moved from place to place; we went through a lot together. And then, too, I've been a mother for a long time." She draws an uneven breath. "You must understand that has something to do with it."

"You don't have to apologize."

"It's different for you?"

"Literally, yes, but I've told you, Catherine, I'm my own grandfather; I'm not sure where I belong."

"And Leah?"

"Leah? Leah is like water, you could say she follows her own natural laws. She's living with someone else this summer."

"I had no idea," says Catherine. "Is that all right with you?"

"I take large chances," says Laurits. "She's a brilliant girl; she's absolutely set in her scientific interests." In the half-light Catherine watches him shrug. "We'll see," he says.

"And meanwhile, back at the farm?" she asks gently.

"God, Catherine, don't mock me—are you mocking me?" He comes and stands in front of her. "Answer me." He is smiling.

"I'm not mocking you, Laurits. It's just us, here; I'm seeing it all."

He hunkers down in front of her and circles his arms around her hips. "Why were you crying? Can you tell me that?"

She tips back her head against the wall and feels how close the tears still are. Images are welling to the surface: the face of John that noon, the layers and layers of his reality; the countless vibrant expressions of her daughter, her lovely child; her own life, obscure essence, visible movement, change, desire.

Laurits has laid his head in her lap. "Come on," he says, "we can't talk here." He lifts her to her feet. "Come on, follow grandpa." He leads her up the stairs and into Hanna's room, his room, and to the same bed where the child had first wakened in the night with the pain—a headache no mother's hand could touch.

"Laurits—"

"We'll be good. Just talk to me." He covers them both with a light blanket. "Just tell me." He opens her blouse and lays his cheek against her breast; she can feel the steady waves of his warm breath across her nipple. She strokes his hair and begins to talk. She tells him about the hospital, the days and nights that became indistinguishable, the one resurgence of hope when the child's eyelids fluttered and her mouth seemed to be straining to speak; she tells him about the dreams, how she is certain that the child's spirit is present, that the other side of death exists even though it's untouchable; and then she is talking about John, about the days when he cannot work at all and his mockery turns inward and consumes his energy and her own as well, about the way the death has cut through their marriage to reveal a section-view of bewilderment barely concealed by stylized action—not that they aren't tender, not that there isn't pleasure in each other and in life: it's just—how shall she put it—it's perhaps that a reality has been given them that they haven't been able to incorporate yet; it doesn't fit into the old patterns. Does he understand, is she making sense at all? And then she realizes that it is herself she is talking about, grieving for: the inability of her hands to help her child, the weakness of her mind to understand what is now happening, the confusions of her heart. Her voice continues. She doesn't know what is coming next, she simply doesn't know, and she is asking herself, will she be able to live it?

When John returns at dark, they are in the kitchen making supper in candlelight. He is drenched from having run up through the rain from the end of the branch-choked lane. "The survivors!" he exclaims, coming to the stove and putting an arm around each of them. "Did you know, my children, that you have only narrowly escaped the fate of Louie's great-aunt?"

"We haven't had any radio, John," says Catherine. She has laid her own cheek against his wet one.

"The tornado touched down four miles north of here."

"That close!" whistles Laurits.

"Was anyone hurt, John?" asks Catherine.

"No one reported, but I saw damage to buildings, and lots of trees."

"What's this about Louie's great-aunt?" asks Laurits.

"You mean you haven't heard that story yet?" says John. "Catherine, love, I'll leave you to the telling while I go get dry and then may I suggest a bottle of wine for this murky night?" He shudders dramatically in his clothes.

She lays a hand on his arm. "And how were the boys? Did they seem to feel all right about leaving?"

"They couldn't wait to get away, and that's the honest truth. They said, bye, Dad—that's all, just bye old Dad." John waves his own hand in farewell and soft-shoes himself out of the kitchen.

Catherine begins to set the table.

Laurits is looking at her. "So? the story?"

"Well, once upon a time Louie had a great-aunt. I don't know her name but she lived in the days of high button shoes. Now this great-aunt was caught up in a tornado, picked up bodily; and she was finally found in a field two miles away, unhurt but covered with scratches and bruises, her hair was a mass of brambles, and—here's the crazy thing—the wind had left her absolutely stark naked except for one high button shoe."

"One high button shoe?" repeats Laurits.

"One high button shoe."

"She was lucky. But she must have been mortified."

"So to speak."

They are laughing, and it is a great relief. The thought of Louie's great-aunt being propelled naked through the air with one external item of dignity intact is exactly the image they need for the end of this day, in this world of astounding variety. "What a story," says Laurits, whooping, breathless, and then he says more quietly, "but she must have blacked out, surely the force of the wind must have knocked her out."

"I suppose so," says Catherine, and she pauses above a sliced tomato. "Tell me, Laurits, if you had your choice, would you go through a tornado like that conscious or unconscious?"

"Good God, Catherine," says Laurits, "I'm going to make you answer that one yourself."

III

One hot afternoon in September while Laurits and John were testing the new kiln, Catherine took herself for a walk along the back roads of the section. There had been no rain for weeks, and the hushed crops and weeds were coated with a film of dust from the baked roadbed. Catherine strode along in spite of the heat; her body was strong from the months of outdoor work, and she felt vital and continuous to herself beside the stretching fields. The landscape to some eyes would have seemed monotonous, she supposed, but she was coming to exult in its apparent plainness; here her eyes could spread out, rested, and her mind could empty itself, and she could be seeing nothing but straight road, fields, fences, and predominant sky until one detail—a changing of light, the thwacking up of a pheasant from a thicket, or a stream of water, invisible from a distance, cutting through the surface fertility—would simultaneously define for her both the plainness and variety of her surroundings, like the first stroke on a sheet of blank paper.

Today she was thinking how much this vast swelling land seemed to have retained its character of primordial ocean floor, and her own eyes were seeing it: the knowledge of a progression through millennia to this present moment of late-summer dry lushness and quiet was passing through her, making her a special child of the universal elements. She stepped off the road and sat down in the minimal shade of an Osage orange tree, looking up with curiosity at the globs of wrinkled greenish fruit. It was true: she felt almost like a child, and what was more, she was gradually understanding that her own lost child was being returned to her, not as she in her suffering had dreamt of the reunion, but simply as she herself was moving to the embrace.

She rested until she became thirsty, and then she got up and continued on the last two-mile stretch, lowering her eyes slightly under the sun, tasting dust on the dryness of her lips; and but for this chance direction of her gaze, she might have missed the dead frog: levelled by a car in the dust of the road, it was like the perfect shadow of a leap, yet really there, paper-thin and dried, complete with flattened eye sockets and delicately spread feet. She bent down to study the creature, her own shadow a foreshortened shape beside her on the dust; and toward this desiccated carcass that like a hieroglyph said purely, *frog,* and toward the even more cryptic configuration of herself she felt a quickened outpouring of that which long ago had come to be called love.

Merrill Joan Gerber

At the Fence

She is standing on her neighbors' doorstep, seeing herself as they will see her in a second: a cranky, middle-aged lady with a complaint. For an instant she is *them* seeing herself come up the walk in a polyester dress, her hair going gray, peering into their screen door, into their private life, prepared to introduce some petty irritation into their newlywed bliss.

She can see the young man lounging on the floor, his back against the couch cushions, watching the end of the Yankee-Dodger game. He has just come home from work and is drinking a beer. At first she thinks he might be wearing his underwear, but sees with relief as she puts her eyes to the screen that his shorts are of the jogging or swimsuit variety. His wife is in the kitchen, heating another frozen pizza. Anna believes—because of the nightly odor of oregano and sizzling mushrooms—that the young couple must eat pizza for every dinner during the week; on weekends it must be steak because then Anna can smell the fire-starter burning on their outdoor barbecue grill.

"Uh, yes?" the young man answers to her unwelcome knock, getting up reluctantly and glancing back at the TV screen. He shakes a long lock of black hair out of his eyes.

"Excuse me," Anna says, "I'm sorry to bother you, but I'm your neighbor, Mrs. Mazer, I live next door, and your dog was barking as he often does till after two o'clock in the morning. He has a very loud bark."

The young man looks behind him, and there comes the dog—a

sleek black Doberman trotting right to the door, his long snout coming up against the screen, his stubby tail wagging.

"Yeah, he does, doesn't he?" the young man says, and bends protectively to pet his dog.

To show her good will, Anna says sincerely, "He's really a beautiful animal." Just then the man's wife swings into view, wiping her hands on her blue jeans. She is perhaps a year or two younger than her husband, about nineteen, the age of Anna's oldest daughter, Karen, yet she comes to the door as if she owns not only this rented house, but also the world with Anna in it. She puts her hand on her husband's bare shoulder; only then is Anna aware of the thick black hair on his chest, the private hole of his navel looking at her eye. The girl has cornsilk blonde hair, long and thick, and she twists it, ropelike, over one shoulder as she stands there looking out. Her breasts are heavy and loose inside a blue T-shirt.

"Hi, I'm Liz," she says conversationally.

"The dog—" Anna continues. "I realize it's a new place for him here, but I would like you to be aware that he whines and howls all day when you're both at work, and last night—I guess you were out late—he was really frantic, running from one end of the yard to the other, barking hysterically. Even if you *are* home he tends to bark in the middle of the night, but it's worse when you're gone. I guess he stopped barking when you came home, around two."

"Yeah," he says, "that's when we came home, around two."

Anna wonders where they went, and what could be more enticing than this new little house, their bedroom at the back with a glass door to the garden, the kitchen so handy to warm up frozen foods in. The husband looks over his shoulder at the TV.

"I don't mean to disturb you, really," Anna says, "but it's agonizing to be trying to sleep and to have that bark never stopping. It makes me feel desperate, as if I have no control over my life."

Too melodramatic, I'm telling them too much, she thinks, moving away from the screen and down a step, to show she is going, won't take any more of their time.

"Yeah, well, we hope he quiets down." He scratches his thigh, and adds, "But he's not going to be sleeping in the house—we got a new rug."

"Look —" Anna says, suddenly thinking of how her heart pounded last night as she listened to that piercing, perpetual racket and of how she considered calling the police, then realized they could do nothing more than some official preliminary paperwork, "the thing is I work at home, I do calligraphy, and I often work outside on the patio, or in my bedroom, and I just can't concentrate with all that noise. Even when it's quiet, I know he's going to start in a minute again, or *could,* and I just can't function." To her surprise, she hears her voice crack and feels tears heat her eyes. She didn't know she could act this well; at least she thinks she's acting because she didn't know she felt this bad.

The young man is bored now. She can see him wondering how this crying woman got here just when the Dodgers were going up to bat. But she can't leave without saying just a few more things. "The point is, I can't *do* anything to control what's happening to me," she begs in spite of herself. "I can't stop your dog from barking and there's no room in my house where I can hide. I hear him *everywhere*—even in the closet! If only I could contact you during the day to tell you about it! It's been going on for a whole month now, since the day you moved in."

"Well, I guess he's lonely," the wife says suddenly. "What he needs is another dog to play with." She snickers. "But *it'd* probably bark, too."

"I don't understand why you have a pet, just to leave him alone all day. Why do you need a dog? You both work!"

"Hey!" the husband says with a flare of anger. "That's *why* he's here. I mean, if we were both here all day, why would we need a watchdog?"

"Well, I'm home all day," Anna says, backtracking with a weak smile, believing for an instant she can convince them to give their dog away and make her their watchdog. "I could watch out for you. I mean, I always look out my windows. If I saw anything funny going on, if I saw a truck in your driveway, I could call you. Is there someplace I could reach you during the day?"

Her voice is reedy with guile: she really wants to be able to call them up and scream, "Come home and shut him up! I can't listen to that noise another second!"

"If she saw a truck in the driveway," the wife says, "it'd probably be one of your buddies." She elbows her husband and laughs.

"Well, me," he says, keeping to the point. "I'm a housepainter, so I can't be reached, and she — well, she works in a store and you can't call her there." His voice is protective and mean now, he's had enough of this, and to show it he bends down and pats the dog again, lovingly. "Good boy, Fletch, yeah, we'll get you some of that good food soon."

Anna feels worse than she did in the middle of the night. It's gone wrong. The young man is really hostile now, and she's gotten nowhere, just a crank on his doorstep.

"You know, I like animals, I really love them," Anna says in a last effort to set it right, show them that she's a fair, nice person. "I mean, I'm all for pets. I have two cats myself — ."

"Yeah," he says. "*They're* probably what makes my dog bark. One of them was in my yard. I even fed it. I sure won't do *that* again." Now he's holding the dog by its red leather collar as if to keep it from springing at her throat. She suddenly remembers a half-dozen movies in which Dobermans were killers, one in which Rock Hudson is a mad scientist who discovers a way to age a human embryo to an old woman in a few short weeks. Anna thinks that it was just yesterday she was newly married, and now she's old. She doesn't believe the problems she's thinking about these days could really be her problems. She hasn't had enough of starting out, she's just getting used to being grownup, being married.

"We also have a little aviary — maybe you've seen my daughter's birds when your dog gets out the door and you come up between the houses to get him."

"He don't ever get out," the husband says threateningly, stepping back, his hand on the door now, ready to close it on her.

"But he does!" Anna says. "You were in my yard just yesterday morning."

"Not me," he says. "Sorry — we got to eat now," and he closes the door.

Anna's husband is doing a crossword puzzle at the kitchen table;

her oldest daughter has her book bag over her shoulder and the keys to Anna's car in her hand.

"I'm going over to Ben's," she says. "See you—."

Anna wants to ask, Aren't you going to have dinner with us? When will you be home? Do you have a sweater? but those are old records that spin soundlessly around her children's ears.

"What if *I* need to use my car?" she says instead, meanly, striking a bull's-eye.

"Do you?" Karen asks.

"No, I don't," Anna says, "but what if I did?"

"Then Ben would come and get me," Karen says reasonably.

"On his motorcycle," Anna says. "Well. . . go"—waving her away—"go see Ben."

Ben, her daughter's lover, is the wrong man for her daughter, but Karen says she will marry him very soon. Not *live* with him, which Anna often prays will happen, but *marry* him. Anna would much prefer the new arrangement for them so when Karen grows up and finds out how off-center he is, how insincere, superficial, humorless, stupid, the break won't be as complex as divorce. Anna also reasons that if Karen moved in with Ben, she would be out of her way, out of the house where now Anna has to witness her in her adolescent turbulence, its ugly, heavy, despairing side. She doesn't even want to look up from her desk these days when Karen comes in sullenly from classes at the junior college, doesn't want to say, How was school? as she said it, gladly, when Karen (bright and darling and lovable) was in second grade but going daily to do reading with the sixth graders. Karen has given notice that she is going to quit school to get a job so she can marry Ben. Ben has no plans, no interests right now, and even that isn't the trouble. It isn't his motorcycle, either—Anna is not that dense or backward. It's just that her heart hurts when she considers Karen's giving her life to that dull boy, a boy who makes rat-tat-tat sounds like a six-year-old playing soldier whenever he describes some fantasy film he's seen in which lasers shoot out of spacecrafts.

As she sets dinner plates on the table, her husband, Lou, absently raises the newspaper to let her get one under it. *His* mother was convinced Anna was the wrong girl for *him* more than twenty years ago, and she fought Anna like a banshee, with threats, scenes, blackmail, insults, curses. To no avail, of course—here they are, not having half the fun his mother was afraid they were going to have, and not anywhere as ruined as his mother predicted. But ruined enough, by normal attrition, repetition, the insidious deadening of responses. At least at the beginning there was that spark arcing over them, between them, encircling them, which clearly Karen has not got with Ben—there *is* no current as far as Anna can see, but Karen, in her dullness, doesn't even seem to know there's that to hope for.

The other children, old teenagers, come dragging into the kitchen for dinner; they used to set the table for her, used to check a wheelchart on the refrigerator for their weekly chores, used to vacuum, straighten up the bathroom, take out the garbage. Now they do nothing but wait to be waited on, and Anna hasn't the strength to fight back anymore. Arguing takes more energy than doing everything herself, though her energy level, in general, is very low, and losing sleep every night hasn't helped.

"That black dog," she says to Lou, "you heard him last night, didn't you?"

"Well, yeah, I suppose, maybe I did."

"Don't say that just for my sake," Anna says. "Did you hear that horrible barking or didn't you?"

"I think I was sleeping," Lou says.

God, she thinks, *heavy and impenetrable, like his daughter Karen. Hardly conscious sometimes.* Maybe if his mother had tried just a little harder, Anna would have been saved from him, from this life of servicing him and his children. Sometimes she says it aloud, that she doesn't feel she has her own life, and Lou or one of the children will say complacently, "Well, you have your calligraphy."

But she can't even do her calligraphy with the dog howling. Sometimes a distant fire engine or police siren will start the dog going, and he begins a thin wailing, less eerie than the coyotes' wailing she hears at night from the hills, but burdened enough, an outward-spiraling tornado of loneliness and misery. Then it will pause briefly before turning into an explosion of staccato barks, getting shriller and more panicky, till finally the animal is running from one end of the yard to the other, rattling the fence, clawing at the spaces between the boards, yipping and yapping in a frenzy that can go on, easily, for several hours without pause.

"They should require every person who owns a dog to have the dog's larynx removed," Anna says, dropping silverware onto the table. "No one has a right to do this, to destroy a person's peace, just because he likes the idea of having a dog. A man and his dog! —what a dumb, romantic notion."

At the same moment she is thinking that she would like Karen to marry a young man like the one next door. A man who has a dog —a man, who, with his woman and his beer and his ballgame, seems like the sort of man a woman should have, a man who protects his rights, who doesn't back down, who stands firm. She thinks of his hairy chest, and to her surprise something clutches low down in her abdomen, in the place where the estrogen is running low.

She wishes all her children would move out tomorrow and end it right there. She wishes Lou were really her father and she could live in the house with him but still go out in the world for adventure and romance, and then he'd be there to hold her warmly when she came in from her excursions in the shimmering night world.

Of course, it could never happen. Sometimes she feels she will never go anywhere again, and if she does, it won't matter where, she'll be bored and tired at any spot in the universe. As far as her success as a mother goes, if she has raised such a perfect child, her first-born, Karen, who knew the names of all the dinosaurs at three, how come a girl like that dopey blonde next door can figure out how to set up such a neat arrangement for herself, a handsome man, a bed, an endless supply of pizzas, while Karen falls in with a young man of no redeeming charm or beauty or intelligence whatsoever? Do all parents feel this about their children? Is it her duty to intervene and *forbid*? or at least try to? At first she thought interfering was against her principles, but now she realizes she just hasn't the energy to do it. What difference can it make? In the end she will have to recognize that her children aren't perfect people, no matter how much of herself she handed over to them —they're just ordinary, mixed-up kids who have all the predictable problems.

Besides, how can she know if her instincts are correct? What if she insists that Karen never see Ben again. . . and then Karen never in her life meets another man who wants her? Then she'll live forever with Lou and Anna — she'll be a spinster of fifty and Lou and Anna will be seventy-five, and she'll be taking Anna's car out to the cotton-spool factory where her job will be to spin cotton onto plastic spools. Who will do Karen's laundry when Anna and Lou have died? No one; she'll never wear clean underpants again, and won't care, either.

It's getting away from her. Anna serves dinner. Later, when she goes to bed, she watches the cold computerized numbers of the digital clock and thinks how buttons are taking over the world, video games and phones and microwave ovens and food processors and word processors and machines on which you can play carnal movies in your bedroom. Warmth has gone out of everything. She shivers with a chill, and at that moment the dog starts to bark and her body flares with anger or sorrow or with a vindictive hormonal flush, and then she feels as if she is burning in hell.

Judge, she says to herself, getting her case in order, *do you think it's fair? Don't dogs belong in big country spaces where they can roam and explore? Isn't it a true crime to lock an animal in a yard and then leave it alone all day, and long into the night? And isn't my home my castle? Shouldn't I be able to take a nap, or read a book, or make love* (as long as we're envisioning the ideal life) *without either the threat of sudden barking or its actual occurrence? Is there no way justice can be done in my favor?*

She will not tell the judge her other fantasies: how the young couple shake the little house with the force of their passion (a young wife does not have soft swinging breasts for nothing), how, after the beer and the pizza and the ballgame, the young man takes his other satisfactions before he has to go out into the cold morning world to smooth fresh new paint over old walls.

And is it the appearance of this dog in her life which is really the greatest injustice that has been done to her? And what about the moral wrong done to the black dog with his long moist snout as he daily runs from one end of the yard to the other — hardly a watchdog, hardly a man's best friend, just a whimpering, crazed abandoned creature, without a mate, without a friend.

On the next weekend night, long after the coals in the barbecue grill on the other side of the fence have died out and the couple has roared away in their pickup truck, when the full moon is overhead, Anna gets her two biggest pot covers and takes them out into the backyard. She holds them poised like a cymbal player waiting for her cue in the pit of a great orchestra. In the house her remaining daughters are sprawled on unchanged bedsheets, sleeping in old sweatshirts and torn cords. Karen has not come home from Ben's yet — she often does not arrive till three or four o'clock in the morning. Lou is posed in bed like a marble statue on a sarcophagus. On Anna's desk are a hundred blank sheets of beige bond paper on which she is to hand-letter wedding invitations for a high school friend of Karen's, a girl who is marrying a twenty-seven-year-old astronomer, handsome and highly placed in a government job.

Anna waits, counting the beats, as breathless as if the stars are her vast audience and this is her debut. And when it comes, first the whine, then the howl, then the full-fledged bass and treble of the mad dog's great range, she runs in her nightgown, barefoot, across the damp grass of the yard, runs to the fence and crashes the pot covers together in a series of clashes, bangs and shrieks till the night sky shakes with the lightening and thunder of her fury.

Then. . . silence. She has terrified him. She feels her lip curl. Hah, good. She imagines the dog to be like a native in the jungle who witnesses a meteorite fall. He will be cowering now under the oleanders, his ordinary restless anguish changed to full terror. Well, this is only the beginning. She will teach him.

Back in the house, she sees that she has actually awakened her sleeping daughters. They are stumbling, bleary-eyed, down the hall. What happened, they wonder. A car crash? Only her husband still sleeps: no kiss, no catastrophe, no symphony can wake him.

Anna replaces the pot covers in the cabinet under the stove, but not before a sliver of silver metal, shredded from the edge of one of the covers by her wild banging, pierces her finger, drawing bright blood.

The next day she buys a pair of ear plugs, little cylinders of wax and foam, and at night jams them into her ears as if she is corking up her vital fluids. After she inserts them and lies down under the covers she hears only the pounding of her heart, each beat pushing the ear plugs, little by little, out of her, as when her husband, that last, long-ago time, fell asleep during lovemaking and in slow pulsing degrees slipped from her body.

She tries to sink down to sleep, but now anxieties of what she cannot hear reach her consciousness—the phone (her old mother, stricken, or Karen on the night streets in the old car, stranded, raped); the creaking of a door (a burglar); the whispering of passionate noises in her ear by her husband (he is not ninety; he is only facing in his way what she is facing in hers).

But then, as though through deep water, the dog's barking reaches her mind, blurred but stirring, a call to her energies: she is needed out there at the fence, she is wanted. This time she carries the tape recorder into the yard and carefully, like a technician fully versed in the uses of the buttons of destruction, presses "RECORD," gathering evidence for the judge in her case against the young couple, those lucky folks, so obliviously licking oregano from each other's lips, or peacefully, deeply sleeping.

The next day she writes the newlyweds a letter on a piece of the beige wedding-invitation stationery, taking a risk. Her daughter's friend probably will not count them, will never know Anna has only sold them ninety-nine sheets and taken pay for one hundred.

Dear Neighbors— [she writes in her best italic script] —
I am not well due to the barking of your dog. Please
put him in the house or take him with you wherever you go.
You have brought chaos into my life by moving to this quiet

*block, and I will have no recourse but to call the police
if you do not take proper measures.*

Anna Mazer

It has taken her almost thirty minutes to write this, using her finest, most graceful golden nib. She ought to send them a bill for her services. They probably have more money than she has — after all, they eat steak, which Anna never buys, and they haven't got three sullen children to buy clothes and educations for. *Someone* ought to pay her!

Making sure they have left for work (both cars gone), she strides out past her walk and along the street to their mailbox, where she leaves the letter. Then, thinking better of it, she takes it out and carries it by hand to their kitchen door, where they enter every night after the day's work. She slides it under the door. As she does so, the dog comes trotting into view from the backyard, and she is within a foot of him as he pushes his snout against the space between the boards in the side gate.

It occurs to her that she will poison the dog if his owners don't fix up the trouble in her life. The dog yips, and absently she pats him through the fence as she plans what she will do. Valium in a hot dog, perhaps. But it probably won't kill, just sedate. If necessary she will go into the city and find a real drug pusher on a street corner. (She could probably ask Ben; no doubt he would know the right people.) A calculated number of barbiturates would do it. She wishes she were more knowledgeable in this seamier side of life.

The dog is licking her hand, dancing with pleasure at her company, his rear end wiggling in rippling convulsions. No one has been that happy to see her in a long time. She kneels and begins to croon to him, "You hate them for the way they leave you alone, and *I* hate them for the way they leave you alone. We should join forces, you know. Why don't you kill them, like the dog tries to do in the Rock Hudson movie?" She laughs. This is all very silly. She feels suddenly happy, not having laughed in some time.

"So long, kid," she says to the dog. "Try to have a nice day. Try meditation. Don't get so tense about everything."

Back in her house, she sits down at her desk and begins work on the wedding invitations. If Karen were to marry Ben, would she have to be personally responsible for a big party? For wedding invitations, dinners, a band, liquor? Would she have to make hors d'oeuvres and pass them around on little trays to Ben's friends who are wearing Star Trek T-shirts?

His parents are divorced and living on different continents. She thinks of his short stubby fingers and his brash thighs, riding her daughter. Perhaps — who knows about such things? — even sluggish, dull daughters might feel something.

When the dog begins to cry, she goes out in the yard and gives him a hot dog through the fence — to get him used to the idea, she tells herself, but he comes so fast to the fence, looks at her with his liquid brown eyes so longingly, that she feels her heart leap with gladness. She goes back into the house and brings out the whole package of hot dogs, feeding them to him one by one, watching with satisfaction as he devours them with pleasure.

Yet late that night, when the barking begins just as she has fallen asleep, she flails out in frustration, groaning, and strikes her husband in the center of his soft stomach.

"What? What?" he says, sitting bolt upright, and then he hears the sound. "The dog again, eh?" he says. "Are they home?"

"They don't hear *anything*," Anna says.

"Well, now *I* hear it." He looks to his wife for approval; finally now, after so long, he hears it. He once again has something in common with her.

"What do you want me to do?" he asks. "Call them?"

"Why don't you?" Anna says. She feels suddenly excited, her husband is going to stand up for her, like the young man with the beer and the dog stands up for *his* wife, doesn't let anyone call her at work.

"Look up their number," he says, but she already is pushing buttons on the bedside phone; she has known their number by heart from the beginning. The digital clock reads 3:33. When her husband takes the phone from her as it begins to ring, she dashes into the kitchen and lifts the extension.

"Hullo?" finally comes the dull voice of the young man, heavy with sleep or sex. She can imagine him standing somewhere in that honeymoon cottage, naked, hairy, hot with the beating of his young blood.

"This is your neighbor," her husband says in a deep voice. "We're having trouble sleeping because of your dog. Could you do something about it?"

"God damn!" the young husband says. "Get the fuck off our backs, will you? We don't want fancy letters from your wife, either. You're just a couple of fucking old farts,"—and Anna hears him hang up the phone.

She comes back to the bedroom, her face flushed, her blood pounding in her head. Already her husband is calling the police, his anger causing his fingers to tremble as they search among the buttons. She listens while he tells the police the story, gives the address, hangs up. "They're coming over to talk to the guy," her husband says. "I won't be treated that way. I'll go to court! If necessary I'll go over there and kill it!"

Kill it. For her. She is overwhelmed. She turns the lamp off and gets into bed beside her husband. She embraces him, turning on her side toward his stretched-out body. They lay tensely, waiting for the lights of the police car, which finally come washing up over the ceiling.

They can hear the policeman knocking on the front door of the little house next door. There is a low interchange of polite voices. Her interests are being protected, she is going to be taken care of. They hear the door close, the police car backing out of the driveway, driving away.

"Well, maybe now we can get some sleep." Her husband pats her shoulder, moves her arm off his stomach, and seems instantly to be breathing softly, drifting into sound sleep. All the breath goes out of her. Now she is filled with fear. The young man is the type who probably has a gun in his house. A real man has a dog and a gun. He will blast her children in the yard. Or strangle her cats. Or slash the aviary wire and let out her daughter's precious birds—she can see the flutter of finches and doves as they ascend over the house and fly away forever. It will end as a headline in a tabloid newspaper. Her husband will kill the black Doberman with his bare hands and the young man will get out his gun and shoot her husband. Karen will marry Ben. Her other daughters will run off to a commune. The wind will blow away her wedding invitations, and the ink will come out of her pen nib in blots.

She imagines the young man right now stroking the polished barrel of his shotgun, and she feels herself arc out of bed and land on her toes like a ballet dancer. She hurries into the backyard. The stars are as sharp as at the beginning of creation. A tall palm at the far end of the yard is fanned out against the moon. There is a rustling in the brush on the other side of the fence as she approaches it.

She whispers, "Here boy, come here," and the beautiful black dog with his princely face comes to the fence and thrusts his warm nose through the crack till it is cupped in her fingers.

"Listen. . ." she says. "Just wait here and be very quiet." She walks on the sharp, damp blades of grass to the door at the back of the garage and returns with a hammer. By the light of the moon she pulls and pries at a board in the fence until she wrenches it from the bottom rail. Making a tiny kissing sound with her lips she holds it aside and the dog pours through like a waterfall, shimmering and coursing down the length of her leg. She kneels and puts both arms around him, long enough to feel his hot breath on her face.

"Come with me," she says, standing and leading him by his red collar up the patio steps, into the house, and across the soft carpeting of the living room. He follows her out the front door and into the wide street where they both stand in silence, panting in the cool air. His ears are up, his hind legs spread slightly apart. She bends quickly and gives him a sharp rap on his rump.

"Go!" she commands. "Go!"

He starts forward like a thoroughbred, like a whippet, a black arrow flying into the dewy night. She watches him gallop till his image begins to fade against the slurry blacktop. She doesn't breathe as she sees him pause, tense, and then leap in a single bound over the horizon. At that moment she realizes she has forgotten to climb upon his back.

Lester Goldberg

One More River

Just six months out of North Plainfield High School, in the winter of '32 when I hit the road.

Five dollars a week, my old man had promised me for working on the chicken farm. He and I shook hands on it. He never paid out a solitary dime and I saw how things were, just couldn't bring myself to ask him. My father came home from his cutter's job in the garment center in New York, and let's get a move on, he'd say, grab the tool box and we'll fix that fence post before supper.

He'd watch me for a minute, and when the saw bound in the four-by-four, he'd snatch it out of my hand, saying, Call yourself a carpenter, you're a shoemaker. In the morning, he'd hammer on my door before six, and I was happier when he went off to work and I could take care of the moldy chickens without his advice.

Those few nights my father couldn't find any extra jobs around the chickens, I'd hustle over to the social center supported by the forty Jewish families in the rural area west of Plainfield; they called themselves the Settlers, mostly cloak and suit union men, one cap-maker.

I belonged to the Jack London Cultural Club, fellows and girls from eighteen to twenty-four, three jobs among twenty of us. The club's literary contest, a tradition for four years, was almost scrapped that year because part of the group wanted to use the money to send a delegate to the Scottsboro trial.

The ten-dollar first prize went to the essay "The Scottsboro

Boys—A Lesson in Economic and Social Repression." But there was a big fight in the club because the treasury was bare. The left-guard activists had raided the treasury to send telegrams to the governor of Alabama from different parts of the state of New Jersey—Newark, Bayonne, Plainfield, Trenton, Atlantic City—all protesting the Scottsboro conviction. I had enough hassling with my old man, and I didn't take sides.

Just about that time, my father and the other chicken farmer–garment workers organized a cooperative to buy feed and eliminate the middleman. They bought a carload of cornmeal. The first shipment arrived in a railroad car in Bound Brook, forty tons to the car, one hundred pounds to the bag, eight hundred bags. The feed was low-priced: ninety cents a bag. Six volunteers helped unload the car and then sprawled on the bags, guarding the shipment. Ziggy from last year's football team and I wangled my father's truck and we got the delivery job. My father would get gas and five dollars for the use of the truck; Ziggy and me, two dollars apiece.

The chairman gave me seven dollars and the list of orders, then went off to work. We lugged and unloaded from eight in the morning until nine o'clock that night. I dropped Ziggy off down the road, then bone-tired I drove home and unloaded forty bags of feed into our shed. Dark in there, and I didn't stack them the way my father would want them stacked.

In the kitchen, I took off my boots, shoved them under the table, and stretched my toes. Where's Pop? I asked my mother.

With the chickens, she said, where else. Rest, I'll get you a meat-loaf sandwich.

My father came storming in, face like a red pepper. I counted thirty-nine bags. Where the hell is number forty?

I didn't panic. I'll restack them in the morning, Pop.

Thirty-nine bags. I counted them. That's ninety cents, almost a dollar wasted. Can you find ninety cents lying in the street?

He's standing right next to me now. I remembered the pushes and shoves: my father's a pusher; when I didn't move fast enough, he shoved me along. I started to get up. For chrissakes Pop, ninety cents, I'll look—

He grabbed my shoulder, and smacked me across the face with his open left palm.

I'm up and swung on him, the first time, I swear it's the first time, and I looped my shot down so instead of the side of his jaw I've poked him in the chest. He swarmed over me, strong son-of-a-bitch, gurgling—hit your father, hit your father—his right hand at my throat, clawing at me with his left. I grabbed his right wrist with my right hand and chopped him on the chin with my left elbow, and I saw another pair of hands encircling his neck, my mother's hands yanking his chin back. I heard my mother screaming, stop it, stop it, you'll kill him, and he let go of my neck, and my mother's in between us, first shoving him on the chest, and when she shoved at me I just turned around and ran upstairs to my bedroom.

I closed the door and propped a chair under the knob. I threw myself on the bed, still in dirty work clothes. I couldn't sleep. I started repeating in my head four o'clock, four o'clock, and it worked because I awakened before my father, stole downstairs, got my shoes from under the kitchen table, and got out of his house. He welched on me, never paid me the five dollars a week; I hit him—had to—to even things a bit. My mother wouldn't miss me. She had my two younger brothers.

I walked past the chicken coops in pitch darkness; could hear the chickens messing around, maybe laying a couple of eggs, puffing up and squeezing the eggs out.

Tramp along until daylight when the iced-over puddles at the sides of the road start to crack and lucky to grab a ride on U.S. 1 into Philly. The first thing I do is go to the post office and buy a stamped envelope and mail my father the five dollars for the truck hire. I'm sorry I hit him but he had it coming. I still feel his fingers on my right cheek. Granted, he couldn't pay five dollars a week, but five dollars a month? Or every three months? A man needs real work, not chores. That leaves me with two dollars, my only payday in the last eight months. I cuss myself for a week for giving up the five dollars.

Now I'm getting freer and freer, so around the corner I buy six loose cigarettes, light one and put the others in my shirt pocket. A skinny kid with a curled-up used butt hanging from his lips asks for a light. I give him a fresh cigarette, and he lights up and puts the used one away. He sucks that smoke in, and a look comes over him like he's being invited into heaven.

Name's Willie Klinger, he says, walking alongside me. I keep walking but don't know where I'm walking to. I'm from Klingerstown, Pa., know where that is?

I shake my head no, in a friendly way.

Sunbury then. Same no shake from me.

My daddy's an undertaker, Willie talks on. I've been to mortician's school, learned how to paint them up, stuff cotton inside their jaws, make 'em look better than new. Nothing to undertake now, he says deadpan.

I grin, seeing as he expected me to.

Now my daddy says nobody's coming in, but the people hungry as they are must be dying even faster than before. My daddy says if we had a flood, and the Susquehanna overflowed, all those bodies buried in the backyards would just rise up and float down the road.

He paused, out of breath, not for long though. I'm backsliding Lutheran, he says. What are you?

Just living.

But what are you?

I was born Jewish but I don't hold with it. I'm called Miller.

I can see you don't know much, Willie says, so you better come along with me, and he turns right and I follow. How about another butt, he says, stretching out his hand.

After we eat, I'm starved.

You're one damn fool for not holding with the Jews. They give the best handouts, and I'd go with you, you just tell them we're both Jewish.

The hell with that!

The steam engine runs the West Virginia hills, hugging the mountainside, dragging the boxcars and open gondolas and black tankers along, running over the rickety trestles, the engine straining up the long grades, then charging down the hillside, the boxcar I'm in tip-ping so the floor where I'm lying slants when you see the front of the swaying trestle. I stretch out, the wheels clacking and squealing under me, rest on one elbow and look through the partly open car door, smoke rising from the hillside cuts and then a glimpse of a cabin chimney. I see a mule pulling a Hoovercart, a sawed-off car rear with a dog lying on the leather seat, a boy swatting the mule with a branch, and I wouldn't mind being on the road and driving along instead of freezing to death inside this coffin-dark freight, while outside it's getting darker, a deep purple and ink-blotched darkness and we hit the flat along the river and as we flow with it at a steady pace I can see the silhouette of the train floating along upside down, and I'm floating and I stick my head out the door aways, hanging on to an iron car brace, and look for my head in the water and then I see it riding upside down, and the engine slows and the cars clank together and I hear one clank after another and the door jars closed and I catch it with my hand before it cuts my head off.

It gets real quiet and the thirteen or so bums in the car sit there not stirring and Willie gets up, I'll be right back, and he jumps down. I watch him go into the bushes and squat down. A couple of guys get up; water stop, one says; they jog around, swinging their arms to get warm, when suddenly the train jerks forward and stops, then starts again, and as it picks up speed, Willie bursts through the bushes. So I shove the car door back and hang out, ready to give him an arm up, but we're going faster. He sprints for the door, one arm swinging, the other holding up his pants, and then he stops. I just raise my hand and he raises his.

Now it's just me. On the car floor, Willie's blanket that he left behind, wrap it tight around me and close my eyes. The old man's feeding chickens now. I loosen my belt and tuck in the newspapers that Willie made me stuff around my back and sides. I move away from the cutting wind coming through the door and take a last look at the stars flying by. Close my eyes and open them. Someone's coughing his guts out in the other end of the car. I close my eyes again and hold them closed, drift off and then the rail shrieks along my spine, the train halts and my head smacks against the wall. A many-layered bum near the door shouts in a conductor's voice,

Richmond—Everybum Out—Last Stop.

Near the yard I find a dump of a coffee shop, and with my last coin I buy coffee and a stale roll for a nickel and get a dirty look when I ask for a phone book. I go out and walk around and the regular people are stirring, the ones who walk as if they got jobs to go to, easy to tell them from the bums who've just crept out of storefronts and move in no direction at all. I ask a guy in a veteran's cap, setting up his box of apples, for the way to the synagogue.

A stocky man in a long black coat is sweeping in front of the place. I wait while he finishes and then he goes to the high black iron gate and starts to open it.

I stand next to him and finally he has to look up at me. Can I work for a meal? I say.

I do the work, he says. That's all the work.

I'm Jewish sticks in my throat so I just stare at him.

The man says, go home!

I can't.

The rabbi is still asleep, he says. I wait. He pulls out a little notebook, looks in it, turns to a blank page, and holding the book against the synagogue sign on the fence, he talks as he writes. He digs in with his stubby pencil, go around the corner to Resnick's Restaurant, tell him, you shall love the stranger, and after you tell him, and after you eat, go to this address, and he gives me the note, then shoves me hard on the shoulder—another pusher, a Richmond pusher—Go!

What's gonna be, Miller? Miller, what's gonna be.

Miller, you're a bum!

Resnick, dirty white apron around his healthy belly, is frying eggs, six yellow bullseyes in butter and do they smell good and when I could get his attention, I deliver the message.

He wipes his forehead and looks at me hard. Rabbi Gershon again, eh, with his same cockamamie scriptures, go sit down there, you like eggs, yes, I see you like eggs, so sit on that stool, you smell better than Gershon's usual clientele.

That night I sleep free of charge in the attic of an old hotel, and just before I close my eyes, I remember my father never took charity and only one loan in his entire life, from the Jewish Agricultural Society, and this loan, his chickens and his sweat in the shop have almost paid back.

one more river to Jordan

Go on and going south now, and I hear, stay away from Flomington, Alabama, the railroad bulls will push you off a moving train, and I go through Greenville, an experienced bum now, where it's Schneider and Friedman, and they tell me Montgomery's a tough place but you can't avoid it, it's a rail center, but I get through and begin to forget the names, Lipschitz and Dolgow and in one place a guy called Merriweather but he was a Jew too. It's hot enough for anybody in Pensacola, Florida, and every place they tell me to go home, until I start saying that I'm an orphan so they'll leave me alone.

I eat raw shrimp from a can in back of a crazy Frenchman's truck in Gulfport, that's how hungry I am, and then in New Orleans I almost get caught for good. They stuff me with food and put me up with Chernetzsky, a housepainter, and he pays me wages and I sleep in his house. I've got the orphan story down pat, tell them I live with a cruel uncle on a farm, nothing to eat and the uncle won't let me go to school. After the second week I'm painting houses, all outside work, and Chernetzsky finds a niece for me and tells me I'm like a son to him and praises my work, but nags, nags, nags, at least call home.

A couple of days later, I cut out early in the morning. Ten dollars in my pocket and I'm heading for the Chicago World's Fair.

In the town of St. Louis, Missouri (really nowheresville), and I'm no country hick anymore. I've walked New York from the Battery to Spuyten Duyvil, and even Newark has Ruppert's Beer and the Newark Bears. I'm enjoying it all: Sally soup kitchen, Hallelujah, I'm a bum, Hallelujah, I'm a traveler, get moving from a cop and a shove with his nightstick when my feet dirtied the sidewalk in a good section of town, and twenty-five cents for taking out the slops in a greasy restaurant. I give a whole dime to go in to see *The Sign of the Cross*. Oh, the innocence of that milk-skinned Elissa Landi. The chariots go charging around the arena, and Frederick March gives the villain his comeuppance, not like real life—the Scottsboro Boys under death sentence again. At the end of the movie, March with a noble look on his face joins Elissa Landi and they both wait in the Roman arena to be served up to the lions.

Fox Movietone News. Jimmy Foxx cracks a home run. Then a cowboy-and-Indian cartoon flashes on. Three scouts are fleeing from a horde of howling Indians. One scout is dressed like Daniel Boone, coonskin cap and long rifle, but the other two are hunchbacked and have long noses, and their hats look like *shtreimels,* the black round hat you see on New York's Lower East Side. A stream of cussword symbols is pouring out of Boone's mouth and from the other two, I can hardly believe it—right to left, too, like my old primer—Jewish hieroglyphics appear on the screen. Boone is desperate, no more ammunition. He tells the two hook-nosed fellows: prepare to die bravely. They're holed up among a pile of rocks on a hillside. An Indian chief is climbing a cliff to attack them from the rear. One assistant says to the other: Herschel, give him a *zetz* in the *tsainer.* I can't make out Jewish anymore but can translate this into: Harry, give him a sock in the teeth. I laugh out loud. I roar. I howl. No one's joining in. Isn't it funny? Hilarious? My laugh's hollow now, can't stop; someone yells shut up and I know that in the entire theater not one person is laughing. Harry hits the Indian as directed and the other hunchback grabs the two pack mules, punches small holes in the huge packs, and sends the mules off at a gallop. The trade goods fall out and all the Indians chase after it, stopping to pick up pieces as the stuff falls. Boone, Harry, and the assistant hop on Boone's horse and the three escape. When the lights go on, I just sit there, can't make myself get up; fellows and girls walk out holding hands, and fathers herd smaller kids up the aisles. Guess they forgot hard times for a couple of hours.

one more river

I'm heading north: what's gonna be, Miller? Miller, what's gonna be! Don't seem to see the scenery anymore, don't know anyone, there's hot places and cold places and trees and railroad yards and more cops pushing and the Jewish Centers, the Young Men's Hebrew, and they're all saying, go home, go home and it all looks the same.

I'm sitting in a car with a bunch of hobos, like the last bunch, just more Negroes down here, and the 'bos seem younger, almost kids some of them, fifteen or sixteen, when it hits me—I'll go to Decatur —thousands of miles ago sat it out in Jersey while my friends screamed—screw literature—send a witness—I read in the paper that the Scottsboro trial had been moved to Decatur after the first conviction was reversed, and Sam Leibowitz of New York was on his way to meet the other attorneys and organize a defense. The trial was on now in late March.

When I hit Decatur, I'm pretty stubbly-faced to attend a trial with a bunch of strangers. A nice-looking town, reminds me of my home-town, Plainfield, with its broad tree-lined streets, branches arching over and meeting overhead so the country follows you right into town. Lots of good large homes with big porches on the front and fine lawns. The town's boiling up for so early in the morning, wagons filled with overalled farmers going by and carloads of men all going in the same direction. Shotguns and deer rifles are lying in the back seats of a couple of cars. I drift along and take off my jacket and then my sweater, roll up the sleeves of my blue-striped shirt, the shirt's cleaner than the sweater, and hope I'll pass muster. Reach the Decatur courthouse, a white brick building with those big Confed-erate white columns out front and a large oak tree at the side en-trance with four National Guardsmen standing in front of the tree. They're carrying rifles, and an old farmer walking by points to the tree and calls out, there's the hangin' tree.

I get on the line for whites and as we approach the door, two town marshals begin frisking everyone. Why'd you bring that handgun, I hear one big marshal say to a guy wearing a black suit jacket over blue overalls. Just bein' prepared, the man answers. The marshal gives him the thumb and he cusses his way down the courthouse steps.

Finally I'm inside, one of the last to make it. I sit down third seat from the door. The fans are lazily spinning overhead and all the south windows in back of me are covered by dark shades, but it's hot as blazes and smells like a barnyard. There's a small Negro section off to my right. The Negro men are very quiet and stare straight ahead. Almost everyone's in shirtsleeves; some farmers in overalls, teeth brown-stained from chewing tobacco, a few better-dressed people in shirts and bow ties, carrying straw hats.

The nine Scottsboro Boys are sitting up front and they're not handsome. Patterson, the tallest, looks like a good guy to avoid if he hopped into your boxcar; but I'd swear there are two little fellows no older than my brother; they couldn't be more than thirteen or fourteen. Those kids, rape someone? There's Leibowitz. He's listening as carefully to Patterson as if that ugly mug is his son. I want to wave to him. He looks cool for a big guy, beginning to put on weight. Good old Leibowitz: the heavyweight champion of defense lawyers. Wonder if he'd take my case: defend a man who's accused of stealing a ninety-cent bag of chicken feed. In back of me I hear, be a miracle if he leaves town alive. Then in front, one young farmer is telling another about a baseball game, the first of the season: that goddamn referee was a Hartselle man, weren't one of ourn, he Leibowitzed us right out of the game. Fellow next to me says, where you from, son? I look at him, don't like the twist to his mouth. Answer, Georgia, I'm from Georguh.

He gets up then, a stringbean of a fellow; he's wearing a seersucker jacket, and as he walks away his jacket opens, and I swear I see a handgun in a holster at his side. This lawman walks down the center of the aisle and standing next to the judge is a hefty gent with an even bigger gun tied down, and the skinny fellow, without turning his head, is talking and his chin is wagging in my direction, and the fat fellow is nodding his head.

I'm up, slide fast over the two fellows between me and the aisle, almost step into the gold spittoon on my way out, and I scoot down those steps. Force myself to slow down: the place is ringed with Guardsmen in leggings commanded by a Guard officer in polished brown boots. I look back but don't see anyone following and I walk faster, heading toward the railroad station.

I hide in a culvert near the station until dark. It turns colder when the sun goes down so I decide to pop into the men's room and warm up, then grab the first freight going north. I stay in the bathroom about a half-hour, and figure better not press my luck so I swing the

door open and step out. Slide right back in. They're out there, three
of them, and I wonder if they've seen me. I chin myself up to the
screen-covered window at the side of the john and spy the skinny
marshal and two others with him, swinging clubs. They're moving
very slowly but they're ambling toward the john. Certain they'll peer
in. Worse if they catch me inside, with the station deserted; more
'bos must be waiting somewhere for the night freight but not around
here. I walk out the door trying to appear unconcerned. Drifting,
they're drifting toward me, closing the circle, the thin man in the
middle and the other two swinging wide to either side. I turn right,
walking toward one club, and still the skinny guy is closing in,
doesn't say anything but he's opened his jacket and his thumb
latches onto his belt. I'm up to the man with the club, just a second
fella, he says, and I bolt for it, dash to the left and cut back, and run
like hell down the entire length of the platform, certain a bullet will
slam into my back. No one yells and I can't look back. I head for a
small shack at the end of the platform; if I can duck around it, the
shack's between me and the guns. I slip on the gravel, hear two shots
in quick succession, puff of dust off to my side, and I roll aways and
spring to my feet, dodge behind the shack, keep running, cut into
the woods, come to a narrow stream, leap across it, keep running,
smack my head on a branch, crash through a thicket, can't go much
farther, and I stop for a second to listen for the hounds, can't hear
any hounds, easy now, Miller, easy Miller—can't hear anything except my own heavy panting, the moon's out, a half-moon, but I'm
seeing double up there, two half-moons. I hear the night-train
whistle. Missed it.

Spend the night shivering in a thicket like a hunted rabbit, and in
the morning I work my way deeper into the woods; later drink from
a cold brook and eat two hard biscuits, left over from yesterday's
breakfast. Afraid to forage for food, I skulk in the woods the rest of
the day. Toward evening, guiding myself by the sound of the train
whistles, I begin to work my way out of the woods. I'm afraid to go
into the station so I wait just outside, figuring I'll get on the middle
of a long, slow one, hop on as it's pulling out but hasn't picked up
speed. I'm hungry enough to eat my belt. I poke deep into my

pockets and pick out a few biscuit crumbs and suck them off my fingers.

I let SOUTHERN SERVES THE SOUTH roll by, every last faded red, cracker-barrel boxcar, and wait for anything else. Now one's headed in the right direction—NORTH—and I let leventeen or so cars go by and then burst out of the woods and head for an open door and scramble aboard. Four-five hobos stretched out in the back. The train pokes along through a small dark woods, then an overgrown field with a bony white horse foraging in the moonlight; up a slight grade now, and as the train slows down—first one, then another, then a third black guy appears draped over the car door ledge.

Next car, next car, I hear someone holler from the shadows. The three Negroes perch half in the car, elbows and hands on the car floor and bodies hanging out. An overalled guy, detaching himself from the darkness, moves toward the Negroes with a shuffling, dancing step. He's a tall blond-haired kid, and he's prancing in front of the three Negroes. He's wearing torn black high sneakers; moving forward, then back, motioning toward the three with his palms as if he's scattering chicken feed. Suddenly, one hand shoots out and stiff-arms the Negro nearest him on the shoulder and the boy slides back and drops off. The other two still hang there. The blond kid dances toward them, in a fighter's crouch, shooting lefts and rights into the air.

What's gonna be, Miller?

Miller—what's gonna be!

The train is picking up speed. The utility poles flash by. Murder, to push them off now.

End of the line, Miller. On your feet, Miller!

I stand up at last. I sway, can't focus on him. A lean boy in the usual overalls. Little taller than me, not as heavy.

Lay off, I tell him. We don't do that. He turns. I face him, the open door to my left; afraid to stand between him and the guys hanging onto the lip of the door. I fix on his left overall buckle, broken, a safety pin's holding it together. The train's clipping along. My hands hang loose. I don't bring them up, don't want to force his hand, give him his pride. I lock his eyes, the color of washed-out jeans. To do any finger-stomping now, he's got to turn his back on me—I'd grab his overalls and take him down from behind. He turns away and slouches to the back of the car. The two Negro boys get on and go to the other end. I sit down in the middle. No one says one word. I'm light-headed again and starving.

one more river to cross

Over one hundred years ago, before there was a Depression, my father took me to New York to the old neighborhood to show me where he used to live on the East Side and to break me into the egg business. We'd had the farm only two years then, I'd just turned thirteen.

We finished carrying the eggs into the market and were leaning against the fender of Pop's truck. My father had just bought me a bag of hot chestnuts, so hot I could hardly hold the bag in my hand. I kept juggling the bag from one hand to the other. A sturdy old woman, carrying a rope-tied, large black valise, walked up to my father. She dropped the valise at his feet, and pulling her shoulders back, she stood erect. Take me to Long Island, she said, in Yiddish.

He stared her down. What do I look like, a taxi driver?

The woman said, I need you to take me.

Get in, my father said to her. To me he said, she's crazy. Doesn't she see my Jersey license? Son, help her with the valise. He shoved me so I'd move faster but it wasn't a hard shove.

The car floor is cold and hard. I sit cross-legged, rocking forward and back to the rhythm of the wheels. I turn my face toward home.

Robert Henson

Billie Loses Her Job

When I came out of prison in 1936, a man named Jax was waiting at the gate to sign me up for a personal appearance tour with his carnival: "Jax Shows—Pre-eminent in the Field."

I said I didn't have nothing to tell. "Besides," I said, "he's been dead two years."

"Oh Billie," he said, "if I could just show you the newspaper clippings, the magazine articles, even the movies! Ever hear of this new guy, Humphrey Bogart?—it's him right down to the grin! What's the biggest draw at the FBI in Washington, D.C.?—his .38, the straw hat he was wearing, his sunglasses. John Dillinger's a legend, Billie, an American hero!"

I said it was news to me.

"The lodge where him and the FBI shot it out—Little Bohemia, remember?—that guy's got a gold mine, tourists beating a path up there just to look at the bullet holes!"

"I wasn't there," I said. "That's what I mean."

I was going to Neopit, Wisconsin, to visit my mother, then on to Chicago to find work. Inside I'd learned how to *do* something for the first time in my life, even if it was only cutting shirtwaist patterns. My supervisor told the parole board I was the best worker she ever had. But . . . outside it was still hard times—especially for women, Indians, and ex-cons. How'd you like to be all three? When Mr. Jax looked me up again several months later, I'd left Chicago. I was back in Neopit.

He didn't have the look white men usually had when they knocked on a door on the reservation. He said, "I knew I was in the right place as soon as I saw that tepee." He meant the fake tepee refreshment stand for tourists that was in the middle of town. Indians were just show business to him.

"Actually I'm only half Menominee," I told him. "Of course, it's the half that shows."

"You got a nice smile, Billie," he said. "You got beautiful eyes. I still want you to join the midway. People'd take to you if you didn't do nothing but smile and say, Hello, I'm Billie Frechette. Crowds are one thing I *know* about."

They'd been playing lots in Illinois for a month and were fixing to loop down through Missouri, Kansas, and Oklahoma. "If you joined us now you'd have a whole month before we start hitting the fairs and the big crowds. However," he said, "in case you're still hesitating, I've got this great big ace up my sleeve. Guess who you'll be on the platform with? John Dillinger *Senior!* Just signed!"

I couldn't think of what to say. We were sitting at the kitchen table, wind blowing straight through the house from front to back. My mother never closed a window from June to November. Mr. Jax looked at the wall behind me where there was an old calendar picture of Lindbergh in his aviator's cap.

"An American hero, Billie, just like Lindy!"

"I've met Mr. Dillinger," I said.

"All the better! Did you know he started going out two weeks after Johnny was killed! Vaudeville, midways, he's even given talks at Little Bohemia. Don't that tell you something? But *this*—his dad and his only true love on the same bill! We'll pack 'em in! Don't get me wrong," he said. "This here'll be an office attraction—that means my own personal management. It won't be no freak show, I promise you."

I wasn't thinking about that.

Sure enough, before we ever got to the fair dates, he called me in for a talk. "Billie, Billie, Billie," he says, shaking his head, "you could go down in history as the *one woman* in John Dillinger's life. But you know what's gonna happen? The Woman in Red's gonna take your place. Not the woman that stuck by him, but the one that sold him out! How could you let that happen?

"I'm gonna have to let you go, Billie," he says.

The way he used to shake his head, and say my name over always reminded me of Louis Piquett, Johnny's mouthpiece. "Billie, Billie, Billie," he'd say, "Johnny wants to *marry* you! Doesn't that mean anything to you?"

Well, he wanted to marry me as soon as he met me. I was working hat check in a nightclub in Chicago. The first time he come in he leaned across the counter and said, "Know something?—you got beautiful eyes." The next two nights we had drinks on my break. He said he was from Indianapolis and had to go back on business but he'd send for me if I'd come.

"What kind of business?"

He opened his billfold and took out some clippings from Indiana newspapers, all about a daring new bank robber who'd walked in with a straw hat tipped over one eye, announced a stickup and then—instead of pushing open the teller's door—jumped up on the ledge and vaulted right over the cage.

"Why'd you do that?" I asked.

He said he didn't know why, he didn't even think about it—"All at once I was just flying through the air. Will you come if I send for you? I know we've just met but, baby, I've fallen for you in a great big way. Say razzberries, but to me that means just one thing. I want to be with you forever. . . ."

He always did talk like a popular song. It wasn't what he *said* that made me go to Indianapolis a few months later. In fact, I told him right off that I was married and couldn't get a divorce because my husband had been sent up for fifteen years and I didn't know where. He gave Louis Piquett a standing order: "Find the louse."

Louis had contacts in every pen in the forty-eight states, but finding Sparks wasn't that easy. He told me in private it was hard to believe I didn't know where my own husband had been sent.

I said, "Well, he wasn't tried in Chicago, it was in St. Louis. So I couldn't be there."

"And he never *once* got in touch with you after he was sentenced?"

"I guess he was ashamed."

When I first met the man I married, I asked why everyone called him Sparks instead of George. He said it was because he was an electrician.

I was crazy about baseball in those days. On Saturdays I used to hitch a ride into Shawano with my girlfriend. Usually we'd just stand around, but if there was a baseball game that's where I'd be. He turned up one summer playing first base for the Shawano team. He was Menominee but he'd gone away to Haskell Indian School in Kansas, then did odd jobs around the country.

He took me to Chicago after we were married. There was supposed to be a lot of work for electricians because of the World's Fair coming up: "A Century of Progress." That sounded good to me. Next thing I knew he caught fifteen for armed robbery.

A friend of his took me on at the nightclub. He was the one that changed my name to Billie, said it went better with Frechette. He used to tell people I was French and Indian—"French where you want her to be French, and Indian where you want her to be Indian." I was used to the jokes. Before long I had me a Persian lamb coat and a long bob, and I'd learned how to cover smallpox scars with makeup.

Louis finally tracked Sparks down in Leavenworth and gave him Johnny's message. "What're you telling me for?" Sparks says. "We ain't married. I didn't even know she was using my name."

"Billie, Billie, Billie . . . you've lied to me so much," Louis says, "trying to keep me from finding this so-called husband of yours. Why did you give me all those names—George Welton, Welton Sparks, George Sparks? Why didn't you just tell me to look for George Welton Frechette, nicknamed Sparks? Why did you let me think Frechette was your maiden name?"

"All I'm asking you to do is check on his story before you say anything to Johnny."

"All right, tell me again where you were married."

"Chicago."

"Not Shawano?"

"We stood up in front of a preacher in Shawano, then when we got to Chicago, we went to city hall to make sure it was legal."

"So you were married in Wisconsin *and* Illinois."

"And one or the other's bound to have a record of it," I said, "if you just keep looking."

He always liked me, Louis did, but Johnny was the one he'd do anything for. He served time for the same rap as me—harboring a fugitive. I seen him just once after we both got out. He still looked like a kewpie doll with his big round eyes and round face. "I never told him, Billie," he said. "At least I spared him that." I couldn't figure out what he meant.

"He died not knowing that you could have married him *any time.* . . ." Tears actually rolled down his cheeks when he said it.

Mr. Dillinger always introduced me as Johnny's wife—at least until he got sore and stopped introducing me at all. "I first met the little lady *you're* waiting to meet," he'd say after his own talk, "back in April 1934. My son brought her to the farm. He had many women friends, so they tell me, but only two he ever brought to get his Dad's blessing.

"I warned him against the first one. I said, 'That girl will not stick by you,' which proved correct as he later admitted to me. But when he come leading this little lady by the hand—never mind state troopers watching the road, and G-men watching the house—I said, 'She's the one for you, Johnny,' and he said, 'Dad, I'm glad to hear that because I want you to meet the sweetest little wife in the world—Billie Frechette!'"

That was my cue to step out on the platform.

He knew from experience what people liked to hear, but I never doubted he believed every word he said, especially if it was something Johnny told him. He was supposed to have been strict in earlier days. Wouldn't lift a finger to save Johnny from his first long stretch —wouldn't pay for a lawyer—wouldn't even go to the trial. Prison didn't change Johnny, except to make him a pro. The month he got out he robbed ten banks in a row. It was Mr. Dillinger that caved in. He used to tell audiences, "My boy lived longer in forty minutes than I did in forty years"—something Johnny said once to a bunch of reporters.

I never knew my own father—he was gone before I had the chance. If I'd met him later, I wouldn't have cared two hoots in hell what he thought about me. Johnny was just the opposite. I couldn't get over the way he beamed when Mr. Dillinger took me around at a family reunion introducing me as "Johnny's wife" and "my new daughter-in-law." I was dying for a cigarette. "No—he don't believe in women smoking!" Johnny whispered, nearly paralyzing my elbow with his thumb and finger. His sister Audrey had to sneak me out behind the barn. I was twenty-four years old!

There were relatives and friends from all around Mooresville at that reunion. Naturally no one expected Johnny to show up—it hadn't been six weeks since he busted out of Crown Point jail with his "wooden gun," and the FBI had just promoted him to Public Enemy No. 1. But when he got word from Audrey that there was going to be a reunion, nothing could keep him away. "Fix yourself up," he says. "I'm taking you to meet my dad."

We drove down from Chicago a day early, got there just before dark. State police had the turnoff to the farm staked out, but he said he had a secret way to get to the house that he'd used since he was a kid. Nobody knew about it except him.

No wonder. We left the car on a back road, crawled through a barbed wire fence, and started off through this maze of gullies and ravines, some so deep I could see tree roots over my head. He was carrying his Tommy, so I had to carry the overnight bag. I was wearing a skirt flared at the bottom but tight around the hips, a blouse with a lace collar, bolero jacket, and high-heeled shoes with ankle straps. Fix myself up!

"The least you could've done was warn me to bring another pair of shoes," I said.

"Go barefoot."

The gullies were sandy but with a lot of little flat rocks. I remember thinking how tender my feet had got. Time was I could walk on cockleburrs and not feel a thing.

Mr. Dillinger nearly had a heart attack when he answered the back door, but right then, I'm sure, is when he took a liking to me. Not when Johnny got around to introducing me, but when he seen me following him barefoot.

State troopers and FBI cruised back and forth all the next day but didn't have no reason to come onto private property. There was just local people coming and going. Audrey and the others set up a big chicken dinner out back where Johnny could keep out of sight while everyone else let themselves be seen walking around and acting natural.

Afterward Johnny told everyone to gather around, he had a big surprise. He reached in his pocket and pulled out a wooden gun blacked with shoe polish. "Here it is, folks—the gun that locked up eight deputies and twelve trusties at Crown Point! Audrey," he says, "I'm turning this over to you. Don't you part with it for any price. Keep it and pass it on to your kids!"

For some reason Audrey flickered me a glance. I was hoping I didn't look more surprised than anybody else.

They all got out their Kodaks and begged him to pose with the gun. He said he'd do even better. He went in the house and got his Tommy. Mr. Dillinger stopped him on the porch. I don't know what he said but Johnny answered in a voice *everyone* could hear, "This Tommy's as harmless as that wooden gun. Sure I keep it loaded, but I never shoot except to throw a scare into someone that's trying to shoot *me*. That's one thing you don't have to worry about, Dad. I've never killed a man and I never will."

That night I asked him where he got the wooden gun. He gave me a hard look. "Why?"

"Well, you never showed it to *me.*"
"I made it in jail, just like I said."
"I don't think Audrey bought the story."
"Did she say anything to you?"
"No."
"Well, don't judge everyone by yourself."

Newspapers and public officals raised a terrible stink about that reunion. All those good people knowing the whereabouts of John Dillinger on that day, and not a one calling the law! He was still collecting newspaper clippings about himself. Only one thing bothered him—the way they kept referring to me as an "unidentified female companion."

"Now Dad will think I lied to him."

Mooresville people got their backs up at being called pro-crime. They sent a petition to the governor asking him to give Johnny a full pardon if he turned himself in. They said banks were as guilty as he was of taking people's money, only banks never got punished. They also said he wasn't violent, which was proved by the fact that he'd never killed a man. They wanted him to be given a chance to start over.

He was shook up by the petition. He said he'd written to some of the very same people at the time of his parole hearing, asking for letters of recommendation. "Not a fucking one answered! Now they see they were wrong—they want to make it up to me. They're good people."

I said, "I guess you're going to turn yourself in, huh?"

For a second I thought he was going to punch me—he couldn't stand not to be taken seriously. But all he done was say with kind of a sneer, "Why don't you wake up, Billie—broaden your horizons." A remark I haven't figured out to this day.

Once down in Florida he beat me up so bad Pete Pierpont had to drag him off me. That was Christmas Day 1933. Two black eyes, kicked my leg so hard I could barely walk, busted my lip. Red Hamilton, Boobie Clark, Chuck Makley, and Pete were downstairs, them and their girlfriends, having breakfast. It's funny Pete should be the only one to help me—his girl started the trouble, Mary Kinder.

She was a tiny little thing but red-haired and mean. Johnny had gone down to the table and found his place wasn't set. In front of all the men, Mary said her and the other girls were tired of doing my work, said I never done my share, said she bet I was still putting on my makeup that very minute. Which happened to be true because of the smallpox scars.

I knew about how much good it'd do me to say that or anything else when he come slamming into the room yelling at me to get my ass downstairs and fix his breakfast! I said, "Well, what are you having?"

"Whatever the others are having!"

"Well, I hope it's bread and gravy, because if there are drippings I can make gravy, but that's all I know how to cook and I've told you that before."

"Then start learning!"—and he sends my makeup crashing to the floor.

I grabbed my long nail file. "I'm not starting *anything* just to please those bitches downstairs, and especially that one bitch!"

He swung on me, caught me in the mouth. Twisted my arm to make me drop the nail file. I went down on my knees to get it and he kicked me on the leg two or three times, hard. When I tried to stand up, I fell sideways on the bed. I went limp. I covered up my face with my arms and said, "Go ahead, show what a big man you are, prove you got power! The worst mistake of my life was to believe it myself!"

Then he begun accusing me of fooling around with someone else. That's what he always brought it down to. He never knew what I meant by power. "Tell me who it is or I'll kill you!"

So I said, "Charles Lindbergh."

He jumped on me like a mad dog, and I believe he would have killed me if Pete hadn't run in and stopped him. He was Johnny's best friend from prison, the only one he would ever listen to. Pete managed to get him out of the room into the hall. I didn't even care what they were saying, I was busy sopping blood from my lip with a wadded-up corner of the sheet.

Pretty soon Johnny come back alone. Didn't say a word. Grabbed me by the arm and made me sit up. Took my suitcase out of the closet and threw it on the bed, threw down a roll of bills. "Go back where you came from," he said, and walked out.

About an hour later I was limping down the stairs. Halfway down I heard Mary sing out, "Come on, everybody, let's open our presents!"

They were standing around the tree when I went by in the hall— taking their cue from Johnny and pretending not to notice me. Just as I got to the front door, Pete broke away. He said, "Wait on the porch. I'll call a taxi."

I said in a loud voice, "Don't bother, I got a car," and I jingled the keys to Johnny's new Ford. He'd left them lying on the bureau.

Pete stood there like he was frozen. After a couple of seconds Johnny said, "Let her have it."

So I went back where I came from—Neopit, not Chicago.

I could be gone a year and my mother wouldn't act no more surprised than if she'd seen me the day before. She'd always say she was expecting me because of a dream she'd had. I used to tease her. I'd say, "Oh, you're getting just like Grandmaw!" She thought she'd turned her back on the old ways, but she believed in dreams to the point where she didn't even say she *dreamed* this or that last night, but this or that *happened* last night. She looked down on the people over at Zoar, where they still lived in bark huts and belonged to the Medicine Lodge. She turned Catholic, she married a white man, she wanted overstuffed furniture, linoleum, and running water in the house, like the people over at Keshena. Still, there wasn't nothing she liked better than getting together with her cronies to swap tales about love powders and witches. On State 47, Neopit's right in between Zoar and Keshena.

When I drove into the yard she said, "I knew it was you. I seen your face in the water last night, so I knew you'd be crossing Wolf River today." I said, "Oh, you dreamed that because you want running water so bad." She pretended to think for a minute, then said dead-pan, "I believe you're right, Evelyn, and I seen your face because you're going to pay for it."

She was teasing me back. Other girls left the reservation and worked and come back with money to buy nice things. I usually showed up with nothing but the clothes on my back. This time, though, I had the Ford and the roll of bills.

I hadn't even counted it. She sat down and counted it first thing. Almost a grand.

"Well, it's all yours," I said. "Buy yourself a radio, get some furniture, have the front door fixed."

She acted uneasy. "I'll put it away and use it a little at a time." She wasn't worried about where it come from, only about being witched if someone got jealous.

A few days later snow begun to fall. "What are you going to do with that car?" she said.

"Leave it where it is, I guess."

Made no difference to me if it was buried in the snow. It got me where I was going, I didn't have no more use for it.

She went and borrowed a tarpaulin from a neighbor. *"You're* the one that's like Grandmaw," she said.

Mr. Dillinger used to tell people that Johnny was just an average American boy except for not having a mother after the age of three. He said Johnny liked to read Wild West stories, especially about Jesse James. He admired Jesse for fighting railroads and the money boys back East. Jesse was the one, he said, that inspired Johnny to respect women.

While he was giving his talk, he used to hold up baby clothes and a toy car he said was Johnny's favorite plaything and copies of Wild West magazine and family photographs in frames and souvenirs he said Johnny had sent him from different places, like a pillow with "A Century of Progress" painted on it. Then, at the end, with the crowd as quiet and respectful as church, he would unfold the suit he said Johnny was wearing the day he was shot. When he held it up you could hear people catch their breath because of all the bullet holes.

"That old man's a natural," Mr. Jax said. "Pay attention to what he does."

Because when I went out it was just like air leaking out of a balloon. Pretty soon I'd hear people muttering, "That ain't Billie Frechette." Crowds would get smaller after a few days, and by the end of the run there'd be hecklers. Mr. Dillinger could make people blubber, but it was me they were waiting to hear from.

Not long ago a woman reporter told me something about Johnny as a kid. The summer he turned thirteen he organized a gang bang for some of his pals. He didn't know any more about sex than they did—it was probably his first time. But he found the girl, gave a demonstration as best he could, then stood lookout while the others took their turn.

She asked if he'd ever mentioned this to me. I said no, but it didn't surprise me. I was wishing I'd known about it when me and Mr. Dillinger had our blowup. Just an average American boy!

Mr. Dillinger was plenty upset as it was. I said, "If you knew as much as you think you do, you'd know he lied to you about being married."

"You're the liar," he says.

"I was already married. And even if I *had* married him he would definitely have been second or third choice."

"Liar!"

I said, "You call me a liar again and I'm going to forget you're an old man and do something we'll both be sorry for!"

Mr. Jax had to step in between us.

Later he said, "Sometimes the Indian in you really comes out." I'd heard that before too. It could mean anything.

People didn't want to listen to another set talk after Mr. Dillinger got finished. They had to ask questions or bust. What was his favorite sport? What was his favorite song? Questions were tame back then. Usually they knew the answers better than I did. The first time someone wanted to know his favorite song, I said, "Home on the Range," and half a dozen people called out, "What about 'Happy Days Are

Here Again'?" "Well," I said, "can't a fella have more than one favorite?" I couldn't remember anything special about the way he dressed. I don't think I *ever* knew what he liked to eat. Things like that didn't make no impression on me.

Mr. Dillinger would get mad enough to have a stroke. "My son's eyes was blue—not brownish-green or greenish-grey or any other color except *blue!* He dressed in style, he had a ruby ring and a five-hundred-dollar gold watch! Bread and gravy's what *you* like to eat," he said. "You're the one that likes 'Home on the Range' and baseball games!"

"Is that true?" Mr. Jax said. "Is that what you've been doing? Christ, Billie," he says, "it's only been two years. How could you forget? Those were the days!"

Louis visited me right after I was sentenced. Johnny had just made headlines again, shooting his way out of Little Bohemia Lodge. Six people dead or wounded, something like that. President Roosevelt went on radio to tell people not to glorify criminals. Everyone knew who he meant. Louis said J. Edgar Hoover put him up to it because Johnny kept making the FBI look like fools.

But Johnny was depressed, Louis said. "He's had enough, Billie, he wants out. This time he means it. First he has to have plastic surgery. While that's going on, I'll file your appeal. He wants you out in time to go with him to Mexico."

"Don't do it," I said.

He wasn't listening. "Even if we lose, he'll be waiting for you when you do get out. He said to tell you that. He said to tell you he'll do whatever has to be done. You're the only woman he ever loved, Billie."

He looked more like a kewpie doll than ever. I said, "Well, tell him to take care of himself."

"Take care of himself! Is that the only message you have to send?"

"It's a good message for him."

Which it was. Two months later he was lying dead in the alley by the Biograph Theater.

One afternoon someone asked me how I felt about the Woman in Red—"him taking up with her and all that while you was in jail. . . ."

People had Anna Sage and Polly Hamilton mixed up then, or rolled into one. I wasn't clear about them myself. He walked out of the Biograph with two women, but one dropped out of sight so fast hardly anyone noticed her. Actually she was his new girlfriend—a call girl Anna had been using for bait. But it was Anna, wearing that red dress and fighting to collect the reward, that stuck in everyone's mind.

I said, "Well, I never expected him not to have another girl just because I was in jail, so I don't have no feelings about her one way or another. I never did have," I said.

Mr. Jax was waiting for me in the tent, shaking his head. We were getting near the Oklahoma line by then, "heading into real Dillinger country," Mr. Jax said. "We've got to get your act in shape."

I said, "Tell me what you want me to say and I'll say it."

"Next time someone asks about the Woman in Red, don't say you weren't *never* jealous, say in this case you didn't have no *reason* to be. Say you know from reliable sources that the Woman in Red was just a friend, someone that encouraged him to think of her as an older sister he could talk to and trust. She let him hide out in her place, then betrayed him—for money! Say you'd forgive him even if there was more to it than that: 'All of us have faced temptation and fallen. I will not cast the first stone. But I truly believe I have nothing to forgive him for. He was betrayed by a woman, yes! but not by the woman he loved!' "

"Well," I said deadpan, "if you want me to remember all that you'd better write it down. I'd never think of it by myself."

He lost his temper. "You claim you can't remember the color of his eyes, you claim you never got jealous! What the hell *do* you remember? What kind of feelings *did* you have?"

I don't know why everyone expected me to be jealous, like a witch. It was always the other way around. We hadn't been together two months before he took it in his head that I was making eyes at Eddie Shouse, a driver they sometimes used. Good-looking fellow, always had a girl on each arm and another one waiting in the car. I liked him but never paid no attention to his flirting. That's just the way he was.

But one day Johnny come storming in and pulled his .38 on me. "Get your hat and coat, you're going for a ride."

This was in Chicago. We were sharing an apartment with Pete and Mary. They heard him yelling at me, and come out into the hall in time to see him prodding me along with that .38. Pete says, "Use your common sense, Johnny. Shouse'll make a pass at anything in skirts. That ain't Billie's fault."

"She's leading him on. He wouldn't have the guts."

"What if she is?" Mary says. "She has a right to go for any guy she pleases. If she likes him, who are you to stop her?"

Which might sound like she was on my side, but really she was trying to stir him up more. It wasn't the first time.

He made me drive to a deserted stretch on the lakefront and park. "You got anything to say?"

"No."

"You don't seem to realize you're gonna *die,* sister!"

I didn't answer, just stared out the window on my side and thought about the wind blowing through the house, bare floors, bare walls, like sitting in the cockpit of a plane.

He said, "Remember what I told you when we met—that if you'd be on the level I'd give everybody the go-by for you?"

I said, "Well, I've been on the level. I can't help it if you don't believe me."

"I told you if you couldn't feel the same towards me as I felt towards you, then not to come when I sent for you—remember?"

"Yes."

"Why'd you come?" I couldn't think of any answer that wouldn't make things worse.

He said, "It's not enough for me if you just respect me, Billie. If you can't love me, I'd be better off not ever seeing you again."

I went on looking out the window. I wasn't going to beg.

"What's Ed Shouse got? What do you dames see in him? What makes you get all wet between the legs just because a guy's good-looking and has a fancy line?"

I turned and stared at him, disgusted.

He started rambling—all the women that'd let him down . . . his wife divorcing him while he was in the pen . . . a girl breaking off their engagement because she didn't want to settle down . . . another one skipping town with a square . . . he thought I was different, he was planning to take me to meet his Dad, etc., etc.

I thought, "Maybe he'll get it out of his system"—and sure enough, he trailed off after a while and lowered the gun and just set there. Then he all of a sudden grinned. "One thing I will say, kiddo, you don't lose your head easy."

I said, "Well, you ought to know that from just last week." I meant being with him in the Terraplane when he ditched four police cars—the wildest chase Chicago had ever seen. "I didn't lose my head because I know you're a good driver. You take chances, but I never yet seen you wreck a car."

"Put that in your purse till we get home," he says, handing me the .38.

He parked in front of the building and put his arm around my shoulder as we went up the walk. He rung the bell instead of using his key so Pete would have to look through the peephole. Pete really whooped: "They're back safe!"

"What happened?" Mary said. Johnny put on his best shit-kicking grin. "I couldn't do it. . . ."

I went on down the hall and into the bedroom. Mary followed me. I don't know what she had in mind, but before she could open her mouth I pulled the .38 out of my purse and pointed it right in her face. "Say one more word against me, bitch—*ever*—and there'll be some dead snatch around here!"

She backed out of the room, white as dough. She knew I wasn't kidding—and knew I wasn't just talking about Eddie Shouse neither.

She was at it again, though, in Florida. And twenty years later still at it. One July a Chicago newspaper run an "anniversary story" on Johnny's death, and reporters rustled her up for an interview. Not that it was ever hard to do. They asked if she knew what'd become of me. "Oh no," she said, "she dropped out of sight. Billie was a very unusual person," she said. "She didn't have a single good feature except her eyes. She didn't know how to dress or use makeup or do her hair. The rest of us couldn't understand what Johnny seen in her—except he was always for the underdog. . . ."

I asked him to stop teaming up with Pete. When the gang rented more than one hideout, him and Pete always went in together. I said, "I can't get along with her in the same *house,* much less the same *bedroom.*"

"What are you talking about?" he said. "You and her don't do nothing."

"Well, neither do you and Pete, so what's the point?"

"The point is, he's my pal—and he likes company."

The questions the reporter asked made me realize how much times had changed. She looked like she hadn't been out of college more than a couple of years. Pretty too. But right away she wanted the dirt. "Was there any group sex in the gang?" I said I didn't think what we done could be called that—just sometimes we'd be in the same bedroom. "Was that Dillinger's idea?" I said it was the men's. "Did you detect any homosexual overtones?" No. "Did he force you to continue after you objected?" No.

And didn't force me to go to Tucson neither when he come after me all the way from Florida. *"That's* what people want to hear," Mr. Jax said. "Not how you wouldn't cook his goddamn breakfast!"

He drove into the yard and honked the horn. I looked out the door. "I'm here to repossess my car," he says.

"Well, it's right there in front of you, and the keys are in it."

"Who's gonna drive this one back to Chicago, that's what I want to know."

It was the first time he'd ever seen Neopit, and vice versa. My mother didn't have no idea who he was, even after I introduced him, but she said, "I knew somebody was coming. Last night Evelyn took the tarp off the car. I asked her what she was doing, I said it might snow. 'I know,' she said, 'but I feel restless.'"

He looked funny because the tarp hadn't been taken off the car, it was still there—but "restless" was just what he wanted to hear. He followed me into the kitchen. The first thing he saw was that picture of Lindbergh. "Nice-looking fella," he grins. Then started in on me to go with him to Arizona. The others were already on the way there from Florida. "I told 'em I had to go by way of Wisconsin. . . ."

"What's in Arizona?"

"A new life, Billie. I've got fifty thousand in cash. I've made my mark. Out there we'll be just a hop, skip, and jump from the border. After that . . . well, what do you say?"

It wasn't the money, it wasn't Mexico. I can't explain what flashed through my mind, but clear as daylight I saw that what was going to happen had already happened, and now I had to go through with it or it would always be waiting for me.

He'd dropped Red Hamilton off in Chicago. He went back to pick him up. They were supposed to meet me in three days in Aurora.

Instead he come by himself. We started driving day and night without stopping. I forget just where we picked up a paper with the headline, *Dillinger Wanted for Murder*. It turned out him and Red had robbed a bank in East Chicago but had been surprised by the police. In the shooting, Red was hurt; so was a cop. Now the cop had died. So it had finally come around. "That makes three of you," I said.

"Yeah, but they ain't got a case against *me.*"

No use reminding him that the only reason they had a case against Pete and Chuck was because they killed a sheriff springing *him* from Lima jail. He was too busy gloating over witnesses that were coming to his defense in East Chicago. "Listen to this: 'A woman who was cashing a check started to hand her money over to Dillinger but he refused it, saying politely that he was robbing a bank, not the people.' . . ."

All the papers played up how he turned back when Red was hit and helped him to the car. ("Hell yes," he says, "he was carrying the money!") "Four policemen had a clear shot at him during those moments when he refused to desert his accomplice, but as usual he was miraculously untouched in the hail of bullets. . . ."

Things like that sent him sky-high: "Miraculously untouched! That's me!"

What they couldn't do in Chicago, Indianapolis, or Minneapolis-St. Paul, they done in Tucson. Someone recognized Boobie Clark from a picture in the post office. The cops spent a day trailing us around, picking us off one or two at a time. No big gun battles, just a wipeout of the whole gang except Red Hamilton.

Three states wanted Johnny; Indiana finally got him. They took him to Crown Point because a new wing had just been added to the jail there, guaranteed escape-proof. To make sure, they put extra guards on duty around the clock.

The girls were packed off to Indianapolis—all except me. I suddenly found myself on the street, and Louis was handing me some money and a railroad ticket to St. Paul. "Rent an apartment and keep in touch. Johnny's orders." That's all he'd tell me.

The girls served thirty days. The fellows never made the street again. They were tried in Lima for killing that sheriff. Pete and Chuck got the chair. Boobie got life.

Johnny was charged with murder too. I went to St. Paul and sent the address. It wasn't over yet. I knew I'd see him again.

A month later he was knocking on the door.

There wasn't nothing miraculous about the escape. He had a real gun.

"Billie, Billie," Mr. Jax says, "how could anyone smuggle a real gun into the jail where *John Dillinger* was being held! It's against common sense."

"Well, how could anyone smuggle enough guns into Pendleton that Pete, Chuck, Boobie, and six others could bust out? But Johnny fixed it—the biggest break the state pen ever had. He fixed that, and Louis fixed this. Money," I said. *"That's* what's common sense."

He took two hostages and drove off in the sheriff's own car. He'd grabbed a machine gun by that time, but when he turned the two

men loose at the edge of town, he reached in his pocket and flashed a
.45 in front of their eyes. "Want to see what got me downstairs,
boys? Wood and shoe polish!"

They made the mistake of telling this to the newspapers. They
said they thought he was pulling their leg—it looked like a real .45 to
them. The tier guard that'd had it poked in his stomach said the
same thing. Nobody else got a good look at it. As soon as he got to
the ground floor and a machine gun, he put it in his pocket. Pretty
soon, though, everybody was talking about that wooden gun. It was
his story they believed.

In St. Paul, I asked him to show it to me. He said he'd left it with
Louis in Chicago—didn't want to lose it—someday it'd be valuable.
"I suppose you think it's a lot of hooey," he said.

"Well, seeing's believing."

I was joking and thought he was too, but all of a sudden he got
sore. "You'll see it," he says. "Don't judge everyone by yourself."

At the reunion Audrey slipped over to me. "I hope you don't mind
him giving this to me."

"Oh no."

She had a funny little smile. "Did you know I'm thirteen years
older than Johnny?"

"No. Why?"

"Oh, no reason. I'm the only mother he ever had," she said.

I told Mr. Jax I couldn't prove it, but in my opinion that wooden
gun was a cover story for Louis. Louis knew people thought Johnny
could do anything. If he said he rounded up eight deputies with a
wooden gun, you could forget about anyone suspecting a fix.

Mr. Jax got as sore as Johnny. "That gun's part of American
history! But if it *was* a cover story—which I don't believe—then it's
to his credit that he didn't tell you."

No use saying that wasn't the reason.

I said, "Know who else he didn't tell? Pete and Chuck. They tried
the same thing on Death Row, using soap intead of wood. Chuck
was shot to pieces, and Pete burned right on schedule."

He said, "Billie, if you want people to like and respect you, you better get over trying to debunk John Dillinger. That's not what you're getting paid for," he said.

Funny, but the night before that reporter was due I was sitting at the kitchen table and all at once I could remember letter-perfect everything Mr. Jax and Mr. Dillinger ever wanted me to say. I thought, "Well, better late than never." I needed an operation for a little growth on my neck—I was hoping she'd help me out, me giving her an exclusive interview and all. I was ready to start with how it was love at first sight when Johnny walked in the nightclub, and go on from there.

She was polite but she set me straight in the first ten minutes. "Billie," she said, "I'm not here to get the same old Robin Hood line. The angle I'm working on is the truth behind the macho legend."

He had a gun in St. Paul I hadn't seen before. It wasn't wood, though—it was a pistol-sized machine gun that he could hide under his coat. He'd had it made special. He tried it out on jobs in Iowa and South Dakota while they were still looking for him in Chicago, and he used it when they finally caught up with us early one morning in St. Paul. He fired through the door, driving them back, then tore the hall to pieces while I flew down the back stairs wearing nothing but my slip and Persian lamb. I backed the car out of the garage, but he wouldn't get in—he kept shooting up the rear end of the building. "For God's sake, get in!" I screamed. He didn't care who he killed.

He was bleeding in one leg, so I had to drive. How we got to Minneapolis I'll never know. All I can remember is what a relief it was to see daylight again. In St. Paul we had to keep the shades drawn, couldn't go out till after dark, had to sneak down the back stairs. I never did get used to hiding out.

He was stretched out on the back seat. I heard him mumble, "You're okay, kid."

"Thanks."

"Yeah—you too," he says after a second.
I looked around. He'd been talking to that gun.

This reporter had her own ideas about guns. She brought up
Clyde Barrow, George Kelly, Baby Face Nelson. The only one I
knew was Baby Face. Kelly's wife, though, was on my tier in Milan.
She had it in for me until she saw I wouldn't pull rank on her. I
never talked about Johnny at all; she talked about George all the
time—mostly trying to convince us that she'd been the real brains of
the Kelly gang, and if he'd listened to her, they'd be out "drinking
good beer," as she used to say, instead of doing life. She liked to
read his letters from Alcatraz out loud and make fun of the mushy
parts. She said she didn't know how he ever got the name "Machine
Gun" Kelly—people might *think* he could write his name on the wall
with bullets, but he couldn't even *hit* a wall. Her name was Kathryn.

I was picked up not long after Nelson joined the new gang, so I
didn't know him very well—though as well as I wanted to. A mean
killer. It was worth your life to call him Baby Face. As far as I could
tell, his wife was crazy about him.

Johnny took him in after Crown Point, along with some others of
the same kind. The only one left from the old gang was Red. On the
Iowa and South Dakota jobs he shot out windows, kicked hostages,
cursed at women, and went out of his way to kill. "I don't like it no
better than you do," Johnny says to Red, "but that's the way they
want it." By "they" he meant the cops, the FBI, the banks. The
same line he peddled at the reunion.

Red wasn't fooled. "Johnny won't have to worry about his rep,"
he said to me on the sly, "as long as he's got Baby Face."

It was Baby Face the public got down on. Once when they were
using two cars, someone threw tacks under his tires but not
Johnny's. He died in a ditch. The body wasn't even claimed.

Johnny was laid out in state in the morgue. Lines a quarter of a mile long. Someone selling pieces of cloth they said had been dipped in the blood in the alley. Mr. Dillinger went to get the body. Lines outside the funeral parlor in Mooresville. Big mob at the cemetery. Couldn't hardly get the coffin out of the hearse. Tombstone chipped to bits as quick as it was put up. Mr. Dillinger said he had to have the casket dug up and set in concrete, then concrete slabs poured in the dirt over it. "People wouldn't believe he was dead, they wanted to see with their own eyes."

You couldn't feel sorry for him—he was too pleased and proud. "Audrey chased two fellers back to their car one day and seen California license plates!"

From Minneapolis we went to Chicago, then to the reunion, then to Indianapolis, then back to Chicago. I could almost feel the wind at my back. We shouldn't have gone near Chicago—the heat was on worse than anyplace. But he was in an ugly mood, he wanted to see Louis in person. "I'll give him one more chance. And then—" He cocked his finger at his temple. He was hell-bent on making good that lie about us being married.

Louis tried to get out of meeting him; he was sure he'd be followed. But Johnny wouldn't take no for an answer and wouldn't explain what he wanted on the phone. Finally Louis agreed to meet him in a bar on North State Street about ten p.m.

I knew he'd spill the beans if I didn't get to him first, so when Johnny was parking the car I said, "Let me go in ahead of you to see if the coast is clear."

He looked at me kind of funny—I didn't usually volunteer—and besides that, the Feds now wanted me for harboring. Then he said, "Okay, but if he ain't there, *scram!* Don't hang around."

The place was crowded—I couldn't see him—but I hung around for a few minutes in case he was in the men's or something. I heard a car horn blasting away—I don't know why it didn't register sooner. I beat it for the door—I could hear a motor being gunned—tires squealing. I run right into the big paws of the FBI.

"What's the matter?" I said to Mr. Jax. "Does it sound like I'm blaming him for making his getaway? Tell me what you want me to say. It wasn't his fault; I done it to myself."

He wouldn't answer, just looked at me.

"Well, not on *purpose,* " I said, "if that's what you're thinking."

We hit a spell of cyclone weather down near the corner of Missouri, Arkansas, and Oklahoma. Twisters like rattlesnakes all through that section. We'd be coming to a town and see a rooftop hanging in a tree, or a telephone pole sticking through the side of a barn like a toothpick. Everybody's nerves were on edge.

One afternoon—I remember how sultry and still it was—a woman asked me how many scars Johnny had on his body. I'd never been asked that before, maybe it seemed too personal; but whether it was that or the weather or what, I went blank. I said, "Well, he had a scar from climbing a barbed wire fence as a boy. . . ."

There was some shuffling around, people cutting their eyes at each other. "She means from the times he was shot," a man said.

"Well, he was pretty lucky, you know. He got creased a lot of times but he didn't really have what you'd call scars—no, not that I remember."

"She ain't Billie Frechette. . . ."

Mr. Dillinger had been laying off me for a while—now he landed with both feet. "My son was hunted and hounded and cut down in cold blood, and you tell people he didn't have no scars! I was the one identified the body, I *seen*—" He broke clear down.

"Well, I didn't say *no* scars, just none I could remember."

"If you can't remember, who can?" Mr. Jax said.

All of a sudden I screamed, "Anybody'd think I spent my whole life with John Dillinger instead of one piss-ant year!"

Mr. Dillinger turned and walked out. "I won't be on the same platform with her no more."

Mr. Jax didn't run after him. He knew who was leaving and who was staying. "Billie, Billie, Billie . . . you're just not making 'em believe that you were the love of his life."

"Or vice versa."

He wasn't interested in that, never had been. "I'm gonna have to let you go, Billie."

He was right about one thing—the Woman in Red took my place. When I left the carnival, I pledged not to talk about John Dillinger again. Every now and then someone would track me down, but I stuck to my rule for thirty years.

I didn't mention money until this reporter was in the house. "I've had to scramble these past few years. Take a look around," I said, wishing I hadn't had my hair touched up—her eyes went right to it.

She was interested in what I told her about Kathryn Kelly. "Mightn't she have been saying he wasn't so hot in bed—'couldn't hit a wall' with his gun?"

"She was disappointed in him, but *brains* was what he didn't have."

She asked if Johnny had anything to "compensate for." "Was he underendowed, for instance?"

"That'd have to be in his opinion, wouldn't it?"

"Not necessarily. *Was* it his opinion?"

I said I didn't know.

"What about Harry Pierpont?"

"Pete? How would I know? Ask Mary Kinder."

"She's been saying for a number of years that they weren't lovers, more like brother and sister."

"Well, that's news to me."

"Did you ever sense that Johnny was showing off for Pete—to help him along?" I thought: If any of this is true, no wonder Mary Kinder hated me!

I wasn't surprised when she begun to lose patience with me. I could read her mind a mile off—I was one of those women that men make doormats out of. Half Indian besides—probably didn't care much about sex, just laid there. My opinion of her was she had a one-track mind.

"Listen," I said, "I'd like to help you, I could use some money, but as far as I'm concerned you're barking up the wrong tree."

She asked what I thought her angle should be. I couldn't explain. I kept wanting to say, "Well, he was deceitful in the way the old people say evil spirits are. He didn't really have a shape of his own, he could only *take* shapes." I thought, "The older I get, the more I go blanket, just like Maw. . . ."

When I was in the hospital with my neck, I found a book by Lindbergh's wife on the bookcart—diaries and letters telling how they met and such. I felt sad seeing pictures of him looking the way he looked on my wall. He had a smile that lifted right off the page, the clearest eyes. I remember when I first tacked his picture up. I was seventeen. My mother said, "Who's that?" Without even thinking I said, "Someone that's got Power."
"What do you know about Power?"
She never had told me about it, of course, but I must have picked it up somewhere. "I don't know if it's the same," I said, "but if a white man can have it, he's got it. I can tell by the eyes."
His wife saw it too. Oh, she fell hard when she met him. She told herself she wasn't going to be taken in, but something burned like a bright fire in his eyes. He made her feel like he could do anything. The minute he proposed she said yes. She didn't expect it, didn't want the kind of life he was offering, but what could she do? There he was, she said—she had to go.

My mother studied that picture several days before she said anything. Then all of a sudden she started talking about the old ways. "When I was a girl, I went out in the woods and fasted so that I would see the future. Back then young girls who seen the sun or wind believed they'd find happiness, they'd get a good husband. But in my dream the wind was pressing like a hand against my back, pushing me faster and faster along a road until I was almost skimming. I turned my head and seen a tall dark shape, but I couldn't make out any feature except his eyes—cold and blue as ice, but at the same time they burned. I told my mother and she said I'd seen the Wandering Man, a spirit who never rests but goes round and round the earth with a burden on his back. He takes many different shapes, but when you see him, it means misfortune unless you perform special ceremonies."

"Did you perform them?"

"I started to, but I quit because I was in school; I was afraid to ask the Sisters for time off."

"About payment—" this woman said.

"Forget it," I said, to save her the trouble. "I never could make anything out of John Dillinger."

David Long

Home Fires

Longer than anyone knows, fir and tamarack had clung to the sharp slopes of the canyon, ravaged by lightning fires and bark beetles and gravity, their tenacity witnessed only by the moody northwestern clouds, by birds of prey whose serrated wings bore them on the tricky thermals, by families of deer carefully following trails beside the fast gray water. In this century Jeep roads intruded until the entire eighty miles could be traversed by a strong rig, though it was never thought of as a way to get from one place to another. Then in the 1960s dynamite and giant earth-movers left a two-lane blacktop highway that matched the river's twists, ascending in places hundreds of feet above it through unguarded switchbacks.

It was an early morning in the dregs of a September that had frosted early. Scattered stands of aspen and weeping birch fluttered in the shadows. Down in the heart of the river, kokanee salmon were making their first run, a few now to be followed by great numbers, swimming upstream toward the waters of their spawning—surely it was a kind of miracle that they should ever find their way back, no longer feeding, their bodies already soft and pulpy in preparation for death.

Traffic on the highway was sparse, relieved of the sluggish flow of motor homes and top-heavy camper outfits from other states. A few feet past mile marker 44, where the road climbs into a smooth northeasterly bank, a fresh pair of double tire tracks continued straight that morning, through the chunks of reddish clay, into the dry brush and the feathery upper branches of the firs.

The truck lay upside down, back end crushed like a soda can, cab folded into so dense a bolus of steel it would take Search & Rescue better than two hours working with welding torches and hydraulic jaws to discover it contained no body. Up slope, scattered among the outcrops of shale and limestone, in the trees and resting here and there on the flaps of freshly gashed topsoil, white packages of frozen fish were strewn, still rock-hard, though the exposed sides would feel mushy to the fingers of the first county deputy to huff down the slope, midafternoon. The truck had nearly made it to the river, stopped only by a slug of granite twice its size, where now the man named Pack squatted, head between his knees, glancing up every few seconds at the wreckage.

He could not understand why it did not include him. He should not have survived such a mistake, should not first have made it. He tried to picture the night just elapsed, the route that had led him to the lip of the road. He had no precise memory of it. Surely he had fallen asleep. Drivers fear the graveyard hours, though that fear is so close to the heart of what they do that it remains unsaid. They ride behind the wheel, pumping Dentyne or cigarettes or Maalox, half-thrilled by the power of the diesel and the reach of the head-lamps, half-terrified by their limitations. They flick cassettes into the tape player and set the volume so high the treble jars them out of that dreamy hypnotic mood that comes just before the moment their heads drop. They sing, they banter with one another on the CB, they juggle weights and distances and velocity in their heads. Anything to keep them sharp until it is light again. In the end, though, the fear itself provides the energy.

But Pack was never like that. Driving those hours he found a kind of peace, a solitude that was its own reward. The darkness outside seemed to illuminate his loneliness, seemed to tell him it was only the natural way of the world. He aimed the passenger mirror inward at his own face so he could watch his eyes in the halo of dash lights. He never used the radio except sometimes to tune in an all-night talk show from the coast and listen to the paranoia and longing that gave the voices their peculiar timbre. He kept to himself at the truck-stops, letting his cup be filled and refilled as he watched the other drivers kill their nights off under the acid lights. He would be privately pleased when the phone would ring and the waitress would wipe her hands and grab for it. It would never be for him.

He could not remember choosing to be a driver. He had fallen into the pattern of it a job at a time, found it suited his disposition. He had been to college but picked up nothing lasting there except the taste for reading, another solitary pastime. Sometimes on long nights he thought about his wife, but it was in the same drowsy distant way he thought about what he had read. He did not doubt that he loved her, but he could not remember choosing her. She had been with him as long as he could recall—the adolescence she'd marked the end of only a blur now, dotted by occasional points of shame and excitement. When he came home to her, his desire quickened and he'd hold her and listen to her deep sure voice and be happy, but driving again, at night, he knew that the two were not one, after all, but two.

Pack sat on the crown of the boulder, surrounded by the quiet and bird songs, trying to make sense of what had happened. He saw himself popping out the driver's door as the nose of the truck first hit, his body flipping backward through the branch tips, pitching like a dead weight into the snarl of laurel where he'd come to.

He ran his fingers up and down his legs, over his ribs and back, finally touching around his skull, searching for the fatal exception to his good luck. Though he was dizzy and his forearms were devilled with long scratches, he could find nothing dreadful.

He climbed off his perch and bent over a sheltered pool. His face was thin and droopy-eyed, fringed with a beard the color of clay dirt. His eyes were the blue of an undeclared predawn sky. He smiled into the calm water, and it was then he saw that his front teeth were gone, ripped out by the roots. He touched the gums delicately, felt the clots forming over the holes, withdrew his hand, and saw the fingertips evenly stained, as if his body were nothing but a bucket of blood.

At that moment the sun first crossed the ridgeline and Pack squinted up the steep slope, bathed now in keen September sunlight. The dizziness gave way to a rush of clarity, as if he'd only now begun to wake up, not just from the accident and from the night, but from ten years of living in the dark. He looked at the crumpled truck, the torn earth. Clearly he was supposed to be a dead man.

He knows his loneliness better than he knows me, Elisabeth Pack, called Willie, wrote her sister who had moved east. *Maybe I am a jealous woman after all.*

She put her pen down, stared impatiently out the side window where the two pear trees had dropped their yield into long sweeps of grass. The leaves were brittle and gold. The road dead-ended here. If there had been children, it would have been a safe place for them to play, away from the hazards of through traffic. But there were none. In the distance, the parched foothills hung in a blue morning haze, curving out of sight toward the mouth of the valley where the river flowed wide and tame, accompanied by the tracks of the Burlington Northern and the placid interstate.

But I doubt it, Willie wrote.

She was a handsome woman, six feet even—slightly taller than Pack—with clear hazel eyes and soft lines around the mouth. At thirty she wasted no time mourning the woman she was or might have been. In uniform her presence was striking. Intensive-care patients were guarded by her skills, comforted by her manner, perhaps mistaking her reserve for serenity or for a larger, more merciful view of things, one in which the sick always healed and the grieving were granted peace. It was good consuming work; with Pack gone so often she was happy for it.

His homecomings have become unbearable, she wrote, frowned at the words and stopped. It was not exactly what she meant to say. She preferred her letters to remain simple and full of news; even in the ones to her sister she was seldom confidential. She was embarrassed by the heaviness of her words. The fact was, though, his returns *had* become more difficult to cope with. She had long-ago accepted that Pack—for all her love of him, for all her willingness not to judge him—was a man who came and went. In the ten years of their marriage he had gone off on the fire lines their first summers, after that had shuttled rental cars back to the Midwest, traveled with a bar band called *Loose Caboose,* and in recent years driven truck on the long interstate routes.

He was always edgy just before he left, and she would have to turn away from him to avoid a fight. He always returned with a high-spirited exhaustion, coming to her bed for a spell of love-making, hard and wonderful for Willie, though lasting too long now, leaving her body sore and her spirit cut by resentment. She saw his passion soon spoiled by restlessness, as if she were not an object of love but of release. It had not always been like that, but she had to admit, privately, it was now. Still she forgave him that. What worried her more was that even between jobs he seemed to come and go, as though tracing an elliptical orbit around her and the part of his life that remained fixed. Sometimes she believed he might swing too far, snap loose, and keep sailing out into space.

"How do you put *up* with it?" her friends sometimes asked over coffee.

"I don't see that it's really a problem," Willie said, willing to defend Pack from loose talk. She could handle the Pack whose nature it was to come and go, who hadn't settled into a life's work the way she'd imagined he might, who seemed an odd character put up against their husbands. But she knew they also meant: *How can you trust him to be faithful?* Faith was private, Willie thought. It irritated her the casual way her friends rated their husbands' performance, almost eager to see them fail and at the same time scared to death of losing them, especially to someone else. She was not afraid of losing Pack to another woman.

Once she told him: *I don't mind sleeping alone.* "No?" Pack said, smiling at the darkness, rubbing her wide damp stomach. She had meant that it kept her from taking him for granted, that the emptiness of her bed, at night and again in the morning, stayed with her as a reminder even when he held her and warmed her. And she meant it as a kind of triumph, too, because it had not been easy for her at first; she had needed to learn to be alone.

Unbearable, she had written.

She craned her neck and squinted through the white sunlight at the clock on the kitchen wall, saw that it was already afternoon. She finished the letter quickly, dismissing her remarks as a morning's bad humor, sealed it, and laid it by her purse.

Though it was still early, she grabbed her uniform from the hook back of the bathroom door and slipped into it. She sat on the edge of the bed and double-knotted her white-polished Clinics, rising then for a quiet inspection in the big mirror. She liked to see herself in the white uniform, her wheat-colored hair drawn smoothly over the ears and gathered in a silver clip at the neck. She liked not worrying about the quirks of fashion, but more than that, the whiteness itself pleased her.

She closed up the house and walked out to the Volvo and idled it lightly in the driveway, a kind of nervousness overtaking her, the feeling that she'd left something undone. The afternoon light seemed suddenly frail, as if this were the exact moment the season turned. Her thoughts about Pack troubled her. She wished he were here, she wished he could walk down the hospital corridors beside her, feeling what she felt: the terrible precariousness of the lives and their links to one another. She wished he understood that.

Veins of worry began to dart through the halo of bright amazement surrounding Pack as he studied the ruined truck. The tires pointed absurdly in the air, splayed and flattened; the painted lettering emerged without meaning from the jammed aluminum. Unignited gasoline mixed with freon from the fractured cooling unit and gave the air a gray stink. It was past time for precaution, but Pack was overwhelmed with being too close. All the sounds he had missed in his flight now swarmed into his ears. His stomach balled up like a fist.

He backed along the silt-caked stones, hands tucked into the tops of his jeans, staring at the wreckage as it diminished and began to blend with the other debris along the river. He walked upstream until the current bent sharply around a deposit of harder rock and he could no longer see the truck, kept walking a long time, the click of the small hard stones ringing in the narrow canyon. The roadway was high above him, out of sight; he wanted no part of it.

When he stopped, the sun was nearly overhead, its light broken into rich shadows by the low-hanging limbs of the cedars. As he knelt he felt the shakes coming on strong. He got up again quickly and caught the glint of orange rip-stop nylon, across the river and a short ways up a feeder creek. Above it rose a thin braid of smoke, the first sign of life Pack had seen. He waded into the shallows, the water rising over his boottops, then out where it was deeper, bending his knees against the current. Approaching, Pack saw two women crouched by the fire, for the moment unaware of him. The one facing him was slight—*wasted,* his wife would have said—even in a down vest. She pulled her blue stocking cap down over strands of pale hair as she leaned to flip a pair of fish skewered above the coals. The campsite looked small and orderly. The other woman, who had been sitting back smoking, head down, suddenly caught sight of Pack and grabbed up a shotgun he'd not seen resting beside her.

"Hey!" Pack said, freezing.

The woman aimed the gun at Pack's midsection and appeared willing to squeeze off a shot.

"There's been an accident," Pack said, hands lifted in a victim's posture.

"There could easily be another," the woman said. "You alone?"

"No trouble," Pack said. "OK?"

The woman in the vest got to her feet and squinted at Pack's face, turned, and shook her head at the gun. Her companion slowly lowered it until it pointed at the pine needles around Pack's feet.

"Tell us what happened," she said.

Pack moved in gingerly, squatted, and told them what he could remember. "I was headed home," he began. It sounded like somebody else's story, though the throbbing in his mouth reminded him it was neither made-up nor borrowed.

The women seemed to listen with special attention. Finally the one with the gun cracked a smile, but it was thin-lipped and made Pack more nervous. "It should be that easy," she said.

Pack looked at her, not understanding, not knowing what to do next.

"Here," the other said. "You want some food?"

Pack shook his head. He was beginning to feel truly bad. "You think it would be all right if I maybe laid down?" he said.

The women checked with each other. The one in the stocking cap nodded toward the tent. As Pack stood she caught his arm and said, "Let me . . . ," dipping a corner of her towel in a pan of hot water, then dabbing at the blood dried around his mouth.

"Don't you get weird on us," the woman with the gun said. "You understand?"

Pack nodded. He crawled heavily into the tent, slid across the warm nylon and collapsed, watching the leaf shadows twitch above him.

While Pack slept the truck was spotted by a young man who had stopped above the ravine to photograph the eagles circling above the salmon run. He trained the long lens of his Nikon down the embankment, scanned the river bank for signs of life, and wondered what the little squares of white were. After a while he walked back to his van, dialed the CB to channel 9, and began calling for help. He was joined eventually by two county deputies, the highway patrol, Search & Rescue, and the coroner. The photographer followed the police down to the wreck and stayed until the light failed, snapping pictures of the truck and the broken slope and the faces of the workers, listening to their speculations, pleased to be so close to it all. The plates of the truck were checked through the Department of Motor Vehicles and identified. In Pack's darkened house the phone rang every hour, beginning at dinner time, continuing late into the evening.

Pack woke abruptly and saw that it was fully dark. It seemed as if a great flood of time had swept him away. He thought for a moment that he had dreamed but realized what he had seen and heard was the power of the fall itself, magnified and reiterated in the stillness of his mind. He ached everywhere; his lips and gums were swollen hard around the missing teeth. Peering from the tent flap, he saw the woman who had cleaned him sitting alone by the fire. Pack joined her. She smiled in an easy, sisterly way. It was as if they had gone in and studied him as he slept, reading into the man he was and deciding he was not a danger to them.

"Rita believes these are desperate times," she said. "She believes it's important to be armed and ready. Are you any better?"

"I don't know."

"That was a miracle," she said.

"I don't know," Pack said again.

She laughed, her cheeks glowing round in the firelight. "Any fool could see that."

"Kyle . . . ," Rita said, breaking the circle of light, armed now with a load of firewood, her voice reedy and careful. She knelt and dumped the wood, looked back at the two of them.

"Kyle," she said, "what have you told him?"

Kyle stared into the flames. "I just told him it was a miracle."

"Yes, that's true," Rita said. "But what will he do with it?"

"I don't think he knows yet," Kyle said gently.

Rita dusted the wood flakes from the front of her sweatshirt, then stooped and poured coffee into a tin cup and handed it to Pack, its steam puffing into the cold air. Pack nodded and took it, and it felt good between his hands.

"They'll be looking for you, of course," Rita said in a minute. "They'll figure your body fell into the river and was carried downstream. You could have gone several miles by now. It's not uncommon. For a while you'll be called missing, then presumed dead."

She stopped a moment to let that sink in. Kyle moved closer to Pack.

"I was missing once," Kyle said, quiet excitement in her voice. "My husband looked all over for me. No telling what he would have done if he'd found me. He'd done plenty already."

"Beaten her," Rita said.

"At first I was hiding upstairs at the hotel with a wig and a new name. I didn't know what I was going to do exactly. I couldn't sleep. Sometimes I could see his truck going down the main street and one night I saw it parked outside the Stockman's Bar, and he came out with someone else. I wasn't surprised. The next morning I took the bus to Pocatello."

"Yes," Rita said. "He was a bad man. A real prick."

Pack heard the tinkling of a brass windchime hung in the tree, drank his coffee in small careful sips.

"Still," Rita went on, "Kyle was smarter in the heart than I was. I waited until I was barely alive, barely able to help myself. But all that's changed now, as you can see."

"Can you eat yet?" Kyle asked Pack. "I saved a fish for you."

She tugged a bundle of tinfoil from the edge of the coals.

"You'll need strength," Rita said. "Whatever you decide."

Pack took the fish into his lap and cracked it open and lifted out the long limp spine and tossed it into the fire. The meat crumbled in his mouth.

"But you're not a bad man, are you?" Rita said.

"What do you think?" Pack asked her.

"I think you're a lucky man," Kyle said. "But luck's only the start of it."

"Let me be blunt about this," Rita said. "They will be looking for you, but they don't have to find you."

As she spoke she stood behind Kyle, her fingers lightly stroking the shoulders of the down vest. The smoke twisted up before them, through the fringe of trees to a wedge of sky overcome with autumn constellations.

"Brother," Rita laughed, "have a new life."

Right then Pack stopped chewing and looked hard at the two women. *"New life . . . ,"* he said.

"Clean slate," Rita said. "Maybe you have the nerve, maybe not."

"I don't know," Pack said. "I can't tell you exactly how I feel."

"That's right," Kyle said. "That's how it is at first. You feel sick."

"You get this unmoored feeling," Rita said. "But then you start to see destinations and you go ahead." Her soft white face shone with patience. "Don't tell me you wouldn't like another chance."

Pack was silent.

Rita stood over him a moment, then said, "Now, we're going to bed. You can stay with the fire as long as you need, but it's going to be very cold here soon. Believe me."

Passing by, Kyle whispered to Pack, "Don't think it was an accident," and disappeared toward the tent.

"Thanks," Pack said.

He stayed watching the fire until the last cedar log burned through, showering the air with fine embers, stayed remembering the fires of his life, the blue-gray smoke of branding fires and the stink of burnt hide, the scattered fires of his childhood. He stayed listening to the steady clamoring of the creek, imagining the water's descent, how it wept from remote snowfields, came together, and followed high country drainages to the wide rivers that passed under the city's bridges disappearing west toward the sea. He thought of all the lighted places where he had stopped, the extravagance of his curiosities, and the careless ways he had broken faith with his wife. When he bent later to crawl into the tent, he heard the powerful contentment of the women sleeping. They had left one bag empty for him and were together in the other, holding each other like twins. Pack backed out and stood alone in the cold, measuring the foolish turns his life had taken.

The phone back in its cradle, Willie Pack let her uniform drop to the linoleum of the downstairs bathroom, wrapped herself in a terry-cloth bathrobe, took the Valium bottle from her purse and carried it to the kitchen, lit the gas under the tea kettle, stared at the clear blue flame until the water steamed, turned it off, and sat finally at the breakfast table, surrounded by the bright enamel, the saffron scalloped curtains, lacing her long fingers together in front of her, sure that this moment of control was a fast-fringing lifeline.

Save your tears, she could hear her mother saying. As a child she'd imagined great fetid reservoirs of unshed tears. *Save them why?* How lame and remote her mother's efforts were. Yet Willie knew, perched in the solitude of her own kitchen, that she had grown so much like that woman, believing life was best treated with caution and reserve, believing that loved ones could suddenly trade places with darkness.

Missing, the sheriff had stressed, his voice like fresh gauze.

All her life she'd wanted the exact names of things. Beneath his words she heard this: We haven't found a body yet—in country this wild we may never.

"What does *missing* mean?" Willie said.

"Anything's possible," the sheriff said. "I'm sorry."

"Thank you," Willie Pack said.

So in that time before the confusion and the shouting and crying took possession of her, she held her own hand and rested in an aura of clarity not unlike the one that had settled around Pack hours earlier, as he contemplated the boundaries of his good fortune. This is what tears were saved for.

She had long-ago accustomed herself to his absence, but though it looked the same as always it was not. She felt a flush of shame, to think she had ever enjoyed having him gone. Solitude meant nothing if it was infinite. She thought about death, the way it was taught to her in school, the predictable steps the minds of the living and the dying took in confronting it. Month by month she practiced its sacraments, sometimes finding in her discipline an antidote, mostly not. The farm wife died whispering: *Tell them. . . .* The twenty-year-old logger witnessed the bright splashing of his blood with a pure and wakeful knowledge. She heard the halting voices of old husbands turn suddenly eloquent in the white hallways, reciting an Old Testament catalogue of suffering and accommodation.

She thought then of Pack's missing body. She remembered the feel of her fingers sliding down over the arch of his ribs, she pictured his beautiful hip-swinging gait through the downstairs rooms, the angle of his fingers resting across this table from hers. The image of that body torn and broken rose in her like a searing wind, bringing a wave of sadness—for Pack's body having to die so far away and alone.

She drew a long, controlled breath. For the first time since the telephone call she forced herself to see Pack's face, straight on. It was then, in a burst, she understood what she'd hidden from herself: that she had not seen Pack as he actually was in a long time. What she saw now was not the face she had guarded in her imagination, the one she had married as a teenaged girl, the one she had always reckoned her own happiness by. What she saw now was a face with eyes crimped and glazed, a mouth constantly biting at something, a thumbnail or an emery board or the inside of his lip. It told her Pack had been missing long before this night.

She lurched to the sink and threw up and kept heaving though there was little in her stomach except the dark residue of cafeteria coffee. She ran the water and watched it swirl over the grate, gradually washing away her nausea. In a few minutes she straightened and snugged her bathrobe.

She spilled the blue pills on the table, spacing them evenly with her finger, imagining the sleep they would bring, each one clarifying it like sudden drops in the thermometer, until the muscles no longer flexed and the heart beat indifferently. The rooms were still dark around her: the front room where Pack's book was spread flat on the carpet beside his coffee mug, a book on snow leopards and survival; their bedroom where his workshirt had been carelessly thrown; the bathroom where Pack taped messages to the mirror—no longer the boyish love notes he'd once left, more like the one there now: . . . *and this our life, when was it truly ours, and when are we truly whatever we are?* from something he had read.

Another chance, she thought, sitting again. She studied the pills lying before her, the tears beginning to burn her eyes. She scraped her hand across the tabletop, scattering the pills across the kitchen, spilling back the chair as she stood and ran out into the darkness of the house, turning on lights, screaming *Goddamn it* at the tears, screaming *No* at the treads of the stairs. *Goddamn it. Goddamn it,* throwing open doors, flipping switches, every one she could lay a hand on, until the whole house was burning and raging with life.

It was dawn again. Dawn of the husbands, Pack thought. He had been quiet all the way back, not letting on to the trucker who'd stopped for him who he was: the man presumed dead. It was still a private affair. The driver played a Willie Nelson tape, mostly ballads, and hummed along in fair harmony, blinking constantly at the road beyond his windshield. Pack hugged his arms inside the sweatshirt the driver had lent him. This was always a nervous and transitional hour, one kind of thought giving way to the next. Pack remembered how much of his life had disappeared working like the driver beside him, only with less sense of destination than this man surely had. He remembered the few times he had left a woman at that hour, the sadness of strange doorways and words that disappear like balloons into an endless sky, the whine of his engine as it carried him away. He thought of Kyle and Rita waking together in their tent, joined by affection and the belief that the only good road leads away from home.

Pack thanked the man and got down from the truck at the edge of town. He walked slapping his arms. The full white moon floated above the unawakened houses, above the familiar rise and fall of the mountains. In the next block somebody's husband had gone out and started a pickup in the semidark. Steam flared from the exhaust. Soon the heater would throw two rings of warm air at the frosted windshield. Pack broke into a run, loping through the empty intersections, cold air slamming into his lungs.

He stopped in the mouth of the short street that deadended at his house. Men on the road talk about coming home religiously, though they are not religious men or even, Pack thought, men who are at peace being there. What they want is to be welcomed each time, their return treated like the consummation of something noble, which is too much to ask. Unnecessary risks, Pack thought, too great and foolish to be rewarded with love. He had somehow thought he was immune.

Panting hard through the gap in his teeth but warm for the first time in many hours, Pack looked up to see the lights blazing from his house, even from the twin attic dormers and the areaway at the basement window. He could never know the fullness of his wife's grief, how it came with as many shades of diminishing light as a summer twilight, just as she would never know why his lonely disposition took him always away from her, or precisely what had happened to change him. Sometimes it is a comfort to believe that one day is like another, that things happen over and over and are the same. But accidents happen, and sometimes a man or a woman is lucky enough to see that all of it, from the first light kiss onward, could have gone another way. Pack ran to the front door of his house, alive, thinking *dawn of homecoming, dawn of immaculate good fortune.*

Helen Norris

The Christmas Wife

His name was Tanner, a reasonable man in his early sixties, desiring peace, a measure of joy, and reassurance. All that was submerged. The tip of the iceberg was a seasoned smile that discouraged excesses and a way of looking, "That's fine but not today." His marriage had fitted him like a glove, but now his wife Florence was dead for three years. And so it came to pass that Christmas was a problem.

Not a large problem, but one that niggled when the weather turned and got a little worse with blackbirds swarming in the elm trees, on the move. And here he was looking out at the falling leaves, chewing his November turkey in a restaurant down the block, and going nowhere. Except to his son's in California (Christmas with palm trees!), to his daughter-in-law with the fugitive eyes and his grandsons bent on concussions, riding their wagons down the stairs at dawn, whaling the daylights out of their toys. During the long, safe years of his marriage his hand had been firmly, as they say, on the helm. He had been in control. It alarmed him that now he was not in control, even of his holidays, especially of Christmas. A courtly man with a sense of tradition, he liked his Christmases cast in the mold, which is to say he liked them the way they had always been.

Now, the best thing about Thanksgiving was its not being Christmas. It held Christmas at bay. But then the days shortened and the wind swept them into the gutter along with the leaves. And it rained December . . .

He had seen the advertisement several times that fall, a modest thing near the real-estate ads in the Sunday paper, the boxed-in words: "Social Arrangements," and underneath in a smaller type: "Of All Kinds." He had thought it amusing. At the bottom a phone number and then an address.

Actually the address was a little elusive. He passed it twice without seeing the sign. It would have been better perhaps to have phoned, but he wanted to maintain a prudent flexibility. Inside, the lighting was dim and decidedly pink. It proceeded, he saw, from a large hanging lamp that swung from the ceiling, an opulent relic with a porcelain globe painted over with roses. The wind of his entrance had set it in motion and he stood in the rosy bloom of its shadows. He was conscious of pictures in massive frames — one directly before him, a half-draped woman with one raised foot stepping out of something, perhaps a pool — a carpet eroded slightly with wear, a faint sweetish smell of baking food. To his left a man was bent over a desk. Incredibly he seemed to be mending his shoe. Filing cabinets flanked him on either side. For a silent moment they studied each other. What Tanner observed was a dark, smallish face of uncertain age, possibly foreign, with a dusting of beard, a receding hairline, and rimless glasses with one frosted lens. He managed some irony: "Are you the social arranger?"

"I am at your service." The man swept the shoe neatly into his lap, and then he repeated, "I am at your service."

"Yes," Tanner said. "Your ad is tantalizing but a little unclear. The scope of your service . . . "

The man interrupted. "It is very clear. We make social arrangements of all kinds."

"Splendid! Then perhaps I can rely on you."

"We are discreet."

"Oh, I assure you, no call for discretion." Then he laid it before them both, making it seem a spontaneous thing, almost as if the occasion inspired it. The arranger clearly was not deceived. With his unfrosted lens he seemed to perceive how long it had lain on the floor of the mind, how a little each day it had taken its shape and resisted being swept with the leaves to the gutter.

"I am by nature a sociable man." The arranger inclined his head with enthusiasm. "I live alone. My wife is dead. Christmas has become . . . What I require is a Christmas companion. A lady of my age or a little younger. Not handsome or charming. But simply . . . agreeable. Reasonable health. A good digestion, since I shall look forward to cooking for the occasion."

The other was making notes on the back of an envelope. "My secretary," he said, "is out with the flu. An inconvenience." Then he looked up and past Tanner's head. "Overnight, I presume?"

Tanner said lightly, "I've consulted the calendar. Christmas arrives this year on a Saturday. Actually I should prefer the lady for the weekend. But I wish it to be most clearly understood: the bedrooms are separate."

The arranger put down his pencil and adjusted the frosted, then the unfrosted lens. He propelled his chair backward ever so slightly into the burning heart of his files.

"There is a difficulty?" Tanner asked, concealing his unease. "Christmas, I'm sure, is a difficult time. But there must be a few in your files who live alone and would welcome a pleasant holiday with no strings attached." He stared with some irony at the array of cabinets.

"My secretary at the moment . . . Your request is reasonable. We shall consult our files. There is the matter of the fee."

Tanner was ready. "I am prepared to pay a fee of five hundred dollars for a suitable person. And, I may add, a bonus of one hundred to be paid in advance to the lady herself in case she wishes to make some holiday preparation." He had made an impression. He saw it at once. And then, without really intending it, he explained, "I arrive at these figures by checking the cost of a trip to my son's and concluding that this would serve almost as well and be on the whole a great deal more convenient." He turned to go. "In the meantime I shall check on your agency."

"Of course. It is welcomed. Your name and number? A few facts for the files."

"I shall drop by again."

"But your telephone number?"

"I shall be in touch." He left at once. He was again in control of his life, his seasons. The knowledge exhilarated him. He took a deep breath of the chilly air. Halfway down the block he stopped before a store window and studied the objects on display with care. Some plumbing equipment, secondhand it seemed. He was not after all in the best part of town. The bowl of a lavatory brimmed with live holly. In the mirror above it his own face was smiling.

As he moved away he played with the idea of stopping it there, of letting the plan of it be the whole. He sniffed at the edges. The scent of it, crisp, indefinable, a little exotic, was in the wind as he turned the corner.

Before a profitable sale of his business had left him retired and now, as he told himself, dangerously free, he had been an architect. A few years ago he had built for a friend a small vacation house back in the mountains, a comfortable distance away from the city. It was quite the nicest thing of its kind he had done. "Do me something you'd like for yourself." With such an order how could he resist giving all of its contours his gravest attention? He recalled it now with a growing pleasure, how it made its alliance with rock and sky. It was in the year after Florence died, and perhaps it was some of his lost communion that he poured without knowing it into the house.

When he returned to the tiny apartment, haunted with furniture, where he had lived since the death of his wife, he looked at it with a critical eye and found it hostile to holiday cheer. He rang up his friend, who was now in Chicago. What about the house? Using it for the holiday? Well, would you mind . . . ? Well, of course he wouldn't mind.

When the key arrived in the mail he put it into his pocket and went for a walk. He watched the gray squirrels loitering in the park and the leaves crusting the benches and the sun going down through a network of fog. He reminded himself that what he wanted was the mountain air like a ripening plum and the smell of burning wood in the morning. He wanted the cooking. He wanted the house he had made and loved and the presence of a woman, simply her presence, to give it the seal of a Christmas past. There was no woman of his acquaintance whom he could ask to cancel her plans and give him a Christmas out of her life. In return for what? With a woman he knew, there would be the question, the expectation, the where-are-we-going? to spoil the fine bouquet of the season. In the morning he drove to the arranger.

Actually he had meant to check on the agency, but then it had come to seem that part of the adventure, perhaps the whole of the adventure, was not to do so. So that now the unlikely aspect of the office, with its lamp and the rocking circles of light and its unpleasant piney odor of cleanser, and of the arranger, today without tie and faintly disheveled, did not disturb but even elated him. He was startled and then amused to observe that one of the pictures on the wall had been changed. The one he had particularly noted before of the woman emerging half-draped from a pool had now been replaced by a pasture with cows.

"It occurs to me," said Tanner, "that I don't know your name."

"I have a card somewhere." The arranger rummaged, overturning a vase full of pencils. He was looking flushed, even feverish, but perhaps it was only the rosy light. "My secretary is out . . . " He abandoned the search. "But your name . . . we don't have it. Do we have your name? We require references for the protection of all."

"You have found someone for me?"

The arranger fixed him with the unfrosted eye and gave his desk chair a provocative swivel and coughed for a while. "I believe," he said, "we have just the party." After a pause he propelled himself backward into his files. He caressed the drawers lightly with delicate fingers and opened one with an air of cunning. And swiftly removing a card, he called out: "I think, I do think, this is what you require. I shall read you details, and then of course you can judge for yourself."

Tanner said firmly, "I don't at all wish to know the details. I rely on your judgment." It seemed to him suddenly to spoil the occasion to have the woman read out like a bill of fare.

The arranger was visibly disappointed, as if he had suffered a rejection of sorts. But presently he shrugged and closed the drawer carefully. Still holding the card, he propelled himself forward and into his desk.

Tanner said, "I have here a list of my own: pertinent facts, a reference or two."

The arranger took it and scanned it slowly. Then very quickly the matter was concluded. Tanner was handed a map of the city marked with an X where he was to wait for the lady in question to step from the 2:20 bus on the afternoon of the day before Christmas.

"But I should be happy . . . "

"She wishes it so," said the arranger reverently. And as Tanner was leaving, he called out gravely, "She is one who has recently entered my files. A rare acquisition."

Tanner bowed. "I shall treat her accordingly."

It had occurred to him of course — how could it not have? — that the whole thing could well be a jolly rip-off. While he waited with his car packed with holiday treats, no woman at all would emerge from that bus or the next or the next. The phone would ring on in an empty office. I'm sorry, the number is no longer in use. But because he so richly deserved this Christmas he could not believe it would really be so. And if it were . . . then he would drive slowly and quietly home and slowly and quietly get Christmas drunk. Part of the reward of growing older was precisely this trick one seemed to acquire of holding two possible futures in mind, of preferring one while allowing the other.

He found, on the whole, in the days that followed that it was best to assume that the lady would appear and to give his attention to preparation: a miniature tree, a wreath for the mantel, the mincemeat pies on which he prided himself, the small turkey stuffed with his own invention, the imported Chablis. He had always done most of the holiday meal when Florence was alive. He spent a great deal of time on the gifts, one nice one for her and several smaller things (he wished now that he had permitted himself a few details such as height and weight), a gift for himself in case she failed him in that department.

And of course the day came and the hour struck. With the trunk of his car neatly loaded, he was waiting by the curb. When he saw the bus coming he got out of the car. And there she was, the last to descend, as if she had lingered to look him over. Clutching a small bag, she stood alone looking down at the pavement and then up at him, the winter sun in her narrowed eyes. And she was so unmistakably what she was, a bit of merchandise sent out on approval, that he knew her at once with a catch in his throat and a small despair.

"I'm John Tanner," he offered and gave her his arm, and then as he assisted her into the car, "I've been looking forward to this for days." She wanly smiled.

After that as he drove and kept up a patter of talk to put them both at ease, he remembered how she looked, without looking at her: sand-colored hair (he guessed it was dyed), colorless eyes, a small thin face. He thought she could be in her middle fifties. She rarely spoke, and when she did her voice had a breathless hesitation — very soft, so low that he scarcely heard her.

So he said to her: "Don't be uneasy. I'm really a very comfortable person. This is new to me too. But I said to myself, why not, why not."

She coughed a little.

Then they were climbing into the mountains and the air became damp with fallen leaves and notably colder. When they reached the road that led to the house already the dark was lapping at the trees in the valley below. And around the curve was the house before him exactly as he had made it to be — clean-lined, beached on the rock with pines leaning into it, breasting the wave of sweet gums and oaks that foamed at its base.

He thought how much he had always liked it. "I built it," he said to her. "Not with my hands. Perhaps you were told I'm an architect by trade." He wondered suddenly what she had been told and if it had made her decide to come, or if after all the money was the whole of it.

"I'll go first," he said. "The steps are narrow." With a shyness he had not expected to feel, he climbed through a thicket of wild young shrubs that had marched through the summer to take the stairs. Her plaintive cough like the cry of a bird pursued him into the dusk that gathered about the door. It summoned the longing out of his soul. At that moment he wished that this Christmas were past, over and done with along with the rest. His hands were trembling when he turned the key.

Inside it was dark, with a faint little warmth from the windows that lately had drunk up the sun. He switched on the light and paused to see the great curving room spring to greet and enfold him, exactly as he had created it to do, all the sweeping half-circle of wood and stone, brown, rose, and gray. It calmed and restored him as it always had. He noted the lovely stone curve of the mantel and below it the faggots laid ready to light. Beneath his match they sprang into bloom. And when he turned round the fireshine was kindling the great tile stove, the hub of the wheel, the heart of the house, with its own special curve like a hive of bees. How he loved that stove! He had found it in an old hunting lodge near Vienna where he went for a week after Florence had died. He had bought it and had it dismantled with care and shipped to this place, then reassembled, while he ordered and implored, agonized and exulted, till again every tile was exactly in place — only one of them cracked and that still mourned and unspoken like a guilty secret.

He turned to share it all with the woman behind him, but she was warming her hands in the blaze of the fire. So now he would fill the hive with good oak and a little pine for the seethe and flair. Till the translucent bricks that encircled its base would be gemmed and ringed into amber and garnet. The hunting scenes on the creamy tiles would shimmer and glow and appear to change from moment to moment — the deer and the boar, the flowers, the trees, all richly orange and yellow and brown, as if honey had seeped through the hive to stain them. And the circle of the house would draw close and warm. Guests had always exclaimed: But where, but how? The children accepted without a word. They ran to embrace it and warm their faces. When something is right the children will know it.

He drew the curtains against the night. Then he showed her her room done neatly in white, and assured her the chill would be gone in an hour. While the daylight held he loaded the stove with wood from the generous pile banked against the rock outside. He unloaded food from the trunk of his car and all the rest. He busied himself and refused to think beyond the task at hand. He could hear her coughing in a stifled way.

While he was checking the fire in the stove he recalled with a start and a sense of shame that he had not asked or been told her name. Again she was warming her hands by the hearth. He stood behind her with an armful of wood. "What shall I call you? You must tell me your name." He made it sound as gracious and easy as possible.

She turned to him then. "My name is Cherry."

He found it a fatuous, unlikely name for the woman before him. He wondered if it had been invented for him. He would not trust himself to repeat it. He said instead, "Please call me John."

Her eyes were colorless, he observed again, and reflected the fire, the room, himself. He could find in them nothing of the woman behind them. They seemed in a strange way not to see him. The flesh beneath them looked faintly bruised. The cheekbones were firm and slightly rouged. There were small, parenthetical lines at the corners of a thin and somber mouth, which he noted with relief was free of rouge. He said to her kindly, "You seem to be coughing. Perhaps we have something here that would help."

She withdrew from him then. Her eyes shut him out. "Oh, no, I'm fine. It's just . . . well, I had the flu but I'm over it now. But when night comes on . . . I cough just a little."

He reassured her. "The flu is everywhere. I've really remarkable resistance to it."

"I'm really quite well."

"Of course," he said and winced to recall that clearly he had specified reasonable health. He could explain now her stifled voice in the car. "I've made a little light chowder for supper. Something very light. It will warm you up and be just the thing. I've always made it for Christmas Eve."

"That would be nice. I can help you with it."

But he would not have it. He placed her in a chair before the fire with a throw from the sofa around her shoulders and told her to rest her voice and be still. Then to get her into the spirit of things he found the wreath made of ribbon and holly and balanced it on the mantel before her. And he added a length of pine to the stove. He opened the vents to make it hum for her like a hiveful of bees in the manner its maker had meant it to do—a trick of construction he had never fathomed. The tiles had taken on a splendid sheen. He wanted to tell her to turn and watch.

While he was warming their supper in the kitchen, she came and stood in the archway, her eyes pale as glass, her hands, transparent with blue veins, clutching the sill like roots. He had put on his dark-rimmed glasses for the work. She looked at him with a kind of alarm as if he became even more the stranger, almost as if she surprised an intruder. But he led her back to the chair by the fire. He scolded her heartily, "I want you well by Christmas." The words and the gestures sprang naturally out of the last years with Florence.

He served them both from trays by the fire, making it all seem easy and festive. She ate very little. He poured her a glass of Tokay, and while she sipped it, her face now pink from the fire, he got out the tree and began to trim it with the tiny carved figures he and Florence had found in a shop in Munich before their son was born. He told her about them. She put down her glass and began to help. One of the small figures slipped from her fingers. When he bent to retrieve it he saw that her eyes were swimming in tears. "Don't worry," he said. "They're quite indestructible."

She fought for control. "It's my glasses," she said. "I don't see without them."

"Of course. Where are they? I'll get them for you." He rose at once.

She drew in her breath. "I forgot to bring them."

Or had she thought he would find them unpleasing? He was really impatient. Should he have specified in the beginning that he wanted a woman who could manage to see?

Finally he asked, "Shall I put on some music? Or would you just rather call it a day?" He did not like to say "go to bed," an innocent phrase that had been corrupted.

"It's what you want."

"It's what you want too."

But she shook her head. She was paid to pleasure him, to enjoy what he offered. He was suddenly struck with how easily the shape of a thing could change and take on the color of prostitution. A practiced woman would take care to conceal it, but in her innocence she underlined it. He rose and removed the throw he had placed on her shoulders. His voice was grave. "If I'm to have my way . . . I want you to have a good night's sleep."

The evening was gone. He could not retrieve it, nor would he have done so. His heart was heavy. He lowered the lights. Her face was uncertain but she moved away past the stove that sang softly like a bird in the dusk, throwing its shadows on floor and wall. She looked at it briefly and passed without comment. Perhaps she could scarcely see it at all. Her gesture summed up for him the failure of the day.

He tried to sleep. The wind had risen. The pines above his bedroom were stroking the roof. In the room beyond he could hear her coughing. Wasn't she after all what he had ordered — a nothing who would not intrude or assert or assess or be?

He tossed in despair. Christmas is dangerous, it's too hot to handle, it's a handful of roots breeding — what did the poem say? — memory and desire. Get another day. Fourth of July, Labor Day. Don't pit yourself against Christmas. You lose. You can't contain it. It runs backward into a shop in Munich. It echoes . . . It's calling your own name down a well.

He slept a little. And in his dream the social arranger took off his glasses and lo, behind them his eyes were laughing. The eye once hidden by the frosted lens was crinkled with laughter. Why are you laughing? Tanner approached him and saw, peering, that the eye was a stone and cracked into pieces.

He awoke, dispossessed. The dark ran liquid through his veins. The wind whipped him into some distant gutter.

When daylight came he lay grimly rehearsing his script for the day. If order prevails all things are possible and even tolerable. The key of course is to be in control. His shoulder was stiff from hauling the wood. He had raised his window to sleep in the cold, and now he heard the sound of a distant axe breaking, breaking the early day.

He had the turkey in the oven, the pilaff thawing, and the salad prepared before she appeared for her morning coffee. The patches of dark were still under her eyes, but her face was rested. She seemed to have taken great care with her dress. Her sand-colored hair was combed back from her face, and now he decided the color was hers. He could see the gray. She was wearing a wine-colored jumper with a gray-green, high-necked blouse beneath. They might be a nod at the Christmas colors. There was something childlike about her dress and her slender figure, and touching about her desire to please.

He drank a third cup of coffee with her, and some of the grayness drained out of his soul. She pronounced the smell of his cooking agreeable. In the glance of her eyes around the room there was something of readiness, almost he might say of anticipation. And suddenly the day began to be possible.

"Were you warm enough in the night?" he asked.

"Oh, yes. Oh, yes."

"You're not coughing today."

"Oh, no. I'm well."

After he had coaxed the stove into shimmer and the comfortable song it could sing in the morning after a night of lying fallow, he drew the curtains away from the windows, a tender curve of them like a sickle moon, the way he had planned them in the beginning. The mist was milk in the pines and the hollows.

Before she arose he had laid his gifts for her around the tree. She looked at them with a troubled face. "I didn't know."

"How could you know? It would spoil the surprise."

But she left him quickly and returned with an unwrapped heavy tin. "I was saving it for dinner." She handed it to him, then took it away and put it with the other things beside the tree. His heart misgave him. It was fruitcake of course. He had never liked it. But what else came in round tins painted with holly and weighed enough to crush the bones of your foot?

He put on some music. He made her sit in state on the sofa. Then he found his glasses on the sink in the kitchen and put them on her. "I want you to see. Can you see?" he asked.

She looked around her and down at her hands. "Oh, yes, I can."

"Are you sure you can?"

"Oh, yes. Oh, yes."

"Well, at least you will see things the way I do." He had to laugh. She looked like a small, obedient child who was given permission to try her father's glasses. They diminished her face and gave her an owlish air of wisdom. Then he handed her the packages one by one — first, the teakwood tray, then a fragile porcelain cup and saucer with a Christmas scene. For Christmases to come. And to remind her, he said, of this very day. Then a small, lacquered music box that played a carol. While it finished its song he opened the tie he had bought for himself and exclaimed at the colors. He declared that a friend had secretly left it on the seat of his car. She held her things on the tray in her lap and watched him with pale and troubled eyes, their trouble magnified by his glasses. "Do you like them?" he asked.

"Oh, yes. They're lovely."

Then he watched while she opened the tall ribboned box with the figurine, a bit of Lladro that came from Spain. She drew out the blue-and-gray girl with the pure, grave face and the goose in her arms. She held it silently. Then she touched the smooth, child's head with her hand. "Do you like it?" he asked.

"Oh, yes. I do."

"I knew you would like it." She looked at him, puzzled. "Oh, yes, I knew it . . . It reminds me," he said, "a little of you."

What he meant, he realized, was that Florence would like it . . . and that it also reminded him a little of her. But there was one box more, the largest of all. "But you've given too much." She was reluctant to open it, almost distracted. He could tell she was thinking of the whole of her cost, the somber transaction with the seedy purveyor.

"What is too much? This Christmas has never happened before." And he added gaily, "Whatever you don't like will have been too much. We can toss it into the stove and burn it."

She smiled at that and opened the box. She lifted the dark green, floor-length woolen robe, severe, elegant, very formal. "Try it on," he commanded. She did so obediently. He crossed the room to appraise it from a distance and pronounced it too long. He saw with dismay he had bought it for Florence, her height, her coloring. But it seemed to do now surprisingly well. It coaxed her colorless eyes into green. "I like it on you. You must leave it on till the room is warm."

But she took it off at once. "It's much too fine." She folded it carefully and put it back in its box.

The dinner went well, and she seemed to enjoy it. He insisted she wear his glasses while eating. It was prudent, he said, to consume nothing on faith. At his urging she took a second helping of pie. He allowed himself a generous slice of her cake and declared it superior. He toasted her fruitcake, herself, and the day. Her face was flushed to a pink with the wine. Her hair fell softly against her cheek. She brushed it away with the back of her hand, which was worn and expressive, with a tracery of veins. He had seen such a hand on a painting in Prague.

He allowed her to rest for a while after eating. Then he told her about the lake below the house, hidden from view because of the trees. "Would you like to walk down?"

"Oh, yes," she said.

At his bidding she put on a sweater he had packed for himself and then her coat. She drew a flimsy scarf over her head. He looked with doubt at her fragile shoes. But she said they were all she had brought along. "No matter," he said. "I'll keep you from falling."

Outside it was sunless and clear and cold. The mist had vanished. The path was hardly a path at all. He had to steady her over the rocks. She was light and insubstantial against him. In the trees around them festive with moss the squirrels were stammering, cracking their nuts and spitting the shells. Under their feet the acorns of water oaks crackled like flames. And then the lake was down below like a rent in the fabric of moss and leaves. Strange birds were skimming it looking for fish, with haunting cries that poured through the trees and summoned them to the water's edge.

He guided her down. Once she slipped but he caught her and held her safe. She was shivering a little. "Are you cold?"

"Oh, no."

He held her arm tightly to reassure her. The lake was polished and gray as steel. Across it a line of young bamboo was green, as if it were spring on the other side.

"It's very deep. And somewhere in the middle is a splendid boat that sank beneath me without any warning."

He watched her eyes look up and smile. "Were you fishing?" she asked.

"Yes, that I was. And the fish I had caught went down with the boat. When I came up for air they were swimming around me laughing like crazy."

He had made her laugh, in the way he could always make Florence laugh when he sounded foolish. Her laughter warmed him in some deep place that had long been sunless. Not the laughter itself, but the way he could pluck it out of her throat, summon it out of whatever she was.

He ventured, regretting the small deception: "You remind me of someone I used to know whose name was Beth. Do you think you would mind if I called you that?"

"Oh, no."

He was more than relieved to be rid of the name which he could not bring himself to repeat. He was holding her firmly. The edge of her scarf fell against his face as if she had touched him. It released him into the cold, still air. The birds were circling, ringing them with their plangent calls, weaving them into the water and trees. She coughed a little and the shudder of her body against his own was mirrored down in the polished lake. Her image in water joined to his was clearer to him than the woman he held.

As if it had lain in wait for him there, he remembered a time before the boat had vanished. It was in the summer they were building the house, the only one then for miles around. The workmen had all gone home for the day. He rowed himself to the middle of the lake and waited. He never knew why it was he had waited. And suddenly along the line of the shore a woman was walking who seemed to be Florence: the shape of her body, the way she moved, as she was in the years before her illness. Her head was bent. She was looking for something at the water's edge. He could see her reflection just below moving with her like a walking companion. Abruptly she knelt and, leaning over the slight embankment, she plunged one arm deep into the water. In the waning light he could see the gleam of her bare white arm as it disappeared. For a terrible moment he was sure she would fall and join the woman in the water below. The whole of the lake was moving in ripples, around him, past him to where she knelt. He could not call. He simply willed her, willed her to rise. And she rose and looked at him across the water. And then she turned and walked into the trees. He had never known who the woman was . . . or if she was.

The woman beside him coughed. "Do you swim?" he asked.

"Oh, no," she said.

He waited a little. "Would you like to go back?"

"Whatever you say."

They climbed the hill slowly, clinging together, pausing at intervals to catch their breath and release it in mingling clouds to the air.

A rising wind sprayed their faces with leaves. He felt they were plunging deep into winter. The rock supporting the house above them loomed pearl gray in the evening light. Below them the lake had been sucked into shadow.

In the night he awoke with a cold, clear sense that Florence had called him. He lay still listening. But of course not Florence. Then he heard the sharp cough, but it did not come from the room next to his. It came from another part of his world, and it seemed on the move like the call of a bird, caged in the circle he had made of a house. It shattered his dark. Finally he put on a robe and found her in the living room with her hands and her body pressed to the stove. She stood in darkness. But she had pulled the drapery back from the window, and in the moonlight he could see her clearly, motionless as if she were carved in marble.

He switched on a lamp. She turned to him quickly a face that was stricken with grief and shame. "I'm sorry, I'm sorry."

"Were you cold?" he asked.

"A little cold. But the cough is worse when I'm lying down. I was afraid of waking you."

He saw that she had thrown over her own dressing gown the robe he had given. "You're not to worry. I'm here to help." He noted her trembling and built up the fire.

"I'm sorry," she repeated. "I've spoiled it all."

"You haven't spoiled a thing." He fetched her a chair.

He found a jar of honey in the kitchen and a lemon he had packed; and he fed her spoonfuls of the mixture as if she were a child . . . as if he were giving Florence her medicine when she woke in the night.

"Thank you," she said. "I'm so sorry."

"You mustn't talk."

She sat by the stove, her body subdued, in an attitude of profound despair. He pulled the robe close about her shoulders and waited silently beside her chair. He felt he was on the edge of something, a depth, a life he did not want to explore. A lonely woman who had waited for years for a door to open and now was in terror of seeing it close? He drew away. Nothing is simple, he said to himself. Nothing is ever, ever simple. Though what he meant by it he could not say. He saw his own life as an endless struggle to make the complex simple.

Commanding her silence, he turned out the lamp. He drew up a chair for himself and sat near her, and waited as he had waited in the night with Florence after the stroke had forbidden her speech. The moonlight was cold on her trembling form. The circle of light at the base of the stove drew him down and ringed him with glimmering warmth. He sat half dozing in a strange sort of peace, because it was good to be with a woman on a Christmas night. And because he had bound her voice and its power to give him more.

After a time, when her trembling had stopped, he gave her another spoonful of syrup and sent her to bed with the rest of it.

In the night through the wall he could hear her weeping. He lay with some reservoir within him filling with tears. The walk through the wood had brought a memory of Florence, the sharpest one. She had been moving ahead through the trees of another wood. He had heard the rustle of her shoes in the leaves, and then nothing. He thought she had stopped to peel moss from the bark of a fallen trunk for her garden at home. And so he had come on her fallen body. Then the long limbo of her stroke and death, when slowly, slowly she had withdrawn. As he thought of it now, and had scarcely let himself think it before, there had been a period before that day when she had withdrawn herself ever so lightly. In fact for some years: "Whatever you think . . . whatever you like . . . if it's what you want." His will was hers, his desires her own. It was almost as if her helpless years were a further step in a long dependence. He had liked the deference of her will to his. He liked to arrange the life for them both. Perhaps it was true—he saw now it was—he had struck her down in her vital self and summoned compliance out of her soul. And in compliance was bred withdrawal. Yet surely, surely it was what he wanted. Making a house or making a marriage, always he had to be in control. Her death had ended his long dominion. He must admit he had reigned with spirit . . . and a certain flair.

Genial husband, genial host. And now in the dark he knew himself as the social arranger. That seedy figure in the heart of his files he had conjured out of his own deep need. The woman weeping behind the wall—weeping for a reason he could not explain—was made to his order. He remembered with shame how he had denied her a past or a name. As if he would grant her permission to be . . . what he wished, when he wished.

Sometime before dawn he made peace with himself, as a man must do.

He awoke with a start. The windows were opalescent with ice. The needles of the pines were threads of crystal. Their boughs lay heavy along the roof. He rose to shake up the fire in the stove with a thunderous clamor, for the final time. He built the flame on the hearth again. And when she emerged, her eyes faintly rimmed, the lines gone deep at the corners of her mouth, he stood before her in new humility. Today he allowed her to help him with breakfast, a good one to last them for the drive into town. Then while the kitchen was alive and steaming with the cleaning up, he asked: "If you hadn't come . . . " He began again. "If you had spent Christmas in the usual way, where would it be?"

She was washing dishes and did not answer. He heard her silence, again with relief. He said with good humor, "But the rule is you have to take half the leftovers back to wherever it is you would be if you weren't here now." He was restored as the genial host.

After a little he went into the living room and stood at the crescent line of the windows. He could see the frozen forest below, shimmering with amber light in the sun. Beside him the warmth of flame on the hearth. It seemed to him that this was enough forever—the ice-filled trees, the flame-filled room in the midst of ice, all this ice with a heart of fire. He was conscious that she had entered the room. For a moment he asked for the trees along the mountain road to break beneath their burden of ice and cut them off for another day.

He turned to see her. She was pressing her hands to the tiles of the stove—worn hands the color of the ancient tiles. "I'll show you a secret," he said to ease her. "There's a tile that was cracked, and no one knows where it is but me. And I've never told."

She seemed not to hear. It was almost time to put her back in the box, like the blue-and-gray girl with the goose in her arms. And so he told her, "I shall always remember this time . . . these days."

She sucked in her breath and turned away. He stopped and waited. She began to cry. "What is it?" he asked.

But she turned again and walked to the fire. "You're so good," she said in a stifled voice. "You're so kind."

He was moved. "But that shouldn't . . . "

"Oh, yes. Oh, yes."

He said something he had not intended to say then, perhaps never to say: "But it doesn't really have to end with this . . . But I can't go on picking you up at a bus stop."

She faced him, weeping, shaking her head.

"You've not enjoyed it?"

"Oh, yes. Oh, yes. It's the loveliest time I've ever had."

"Then why . . . ? I assumed . . . Why would you be in his files . . . why would you be willing to come at all unless . . . " Then a kind of light seemed to dawn in his mind, as if he had known it all along. "You work for him," he said. "You're the secretary who was out with the flu."

She did not deny it. She wept on into her handkerchief, coughing as if he had called up her illness. "Are you?" he asked. She nodded her head. She could not speak. "But it's all right . . . it's all right. Why should I care? I really don't care if you work for the charlatan. He made this weekend possible, didn't he?"

She gave him a final, stricken look. "I'm his wife too."

"His wife!"

She wept.

He was stunned. "But why?"

Through her tears she told him. "There was no one else. And we needed the money. You don't know. The bills."

"But his files . . . the files."

"They're full of other things, not names: cleaning aids . . . other things. We have nothing at all. I bought these clothes with the money you gave." Her voice sank to a hopeless whisper. "He said I should do it. It would be all right. He said you were safe."

"Safe!"

"He said you were . . . "

"Safe?"

She did not answer.

"No one is safe! How could he send you out like this? How could he know I was safe, walking in out of the street like that?" His anger released him from hurt and chagrin. He paced the length of the curving room. He said to himself: I've been taken . . . had.

He turned to her from the end of the room. The stove beyond him was deep in whispers. The ice outside slipped and fell from the trees. "Can you approve of this . . . man? Can you love this man?"

"He's my husband," she wept.

He was forced to see with what grace she suffered them both.

And so he did indeed put her back in the box. He drove her to the bus stop and waited in the car, talking lightly of the winter ahead and the spring when perhaps he would take a trip to the West. When the bus arrived he helped her on with her packages. The music box gave a stifled cry. He saw her safely seated at the rear. Then he watched while her bus moved off and away, picking up speed with a grinding of gears, moving faster and farther away past the winter and into spring and on through a shower of summer leaves, and never reaching her destination.

Nancy Huddleston Packer

Early Morning, Lonely Ride

Frances Benedict's husband, Emery, was a lawyer. Successful. Frances herself might yet become anything, having tried nothing. She was only thirty-three. She had three children and live-in help at home. Sleeping. She was nothing among strangers at a rich man's party. She said to Emery, "Notice how new money smells like a cross between wet copper and Cashmere Bouquet?"

"Please don't," said Emery.

"Cash, cashmere, coppers, copper, and a can of room freshener I think they call it wafting in from the downstairs drains. Rich people always trying to undo the natural odors of the universe. New rich. What about dying? Buried with a can of aerosol spray and a couple of lavender sachets?" She thought she was going just great, about to zoom off holding Emery by the collar.

"Grow up," said Emery, making his choice against her. "Please just grow up!"

"Right here?" she asked sweetly. "On his gorgeous handwoven rug? Think of the aroma for God's sake, Emery."

Gazing beyond her with the look of a guest who expects momentarily to catch the party's beat, Emery professed to ignore her, having other fish to fry or why had they come in the first place. To cope with her, she believed, required his full attention. Hell with it. She sat on a pumpkin velvet window seat and vowed to view the dark bay all evening. Maybe the rich didn't like smells but they sure bought the sights. If anyone noticed. Occasionally she nodded amiably

about her. Grins hung from her teeth like old moss. People seeing
her saw only Revlon and Maidenform. She was just one of the girls,
boys: chic, shrewd, and stupid. Look out. Their hostess, whose bar-
biturated face flamed up from a purple dress that weighed in at close
to five hundred dollars, claimed Emery, rescued a man from his
wife. From time to time, the host, porpoise of body but ferret of eye,
came to sit beside Frances and to press thighs with her. Frances
shortly ran out of amusing things to say and was a wallflower. With
contemptuous lack of embarrassment she warded off other wallflow-
ers seeking solace. She was not a woman's woman. With a cold blue
mirthless eye she forewarned idle men she might have ridden
straight through the evening. She was not a man's woman.

It was Emery's crowd, not hers. It was a tired coupling of business
and pleasure. She did not count. She was, if anything at all, only a
helpmeet the color of the background. Forgetting her, Emery enjoyed himself. At that thought, many grievances surfaced. The children slept like tops; like tops they were spinning on their own.
Strings dangled from her hands, cut loose by time and condition.
Nothing short of the rapt attention of everyone would satisfy her
and, sadly, she knew it. She grew restive. This was the world she
lived in, a world she never made, the best of all possible worlds, but
hers, alas, was not the hand that rocked it.

"O brave new world," she said aloud.

"Darling?" asked Emery, standing at the empty fireplace with
their host's brother-in-law, for all the world as if conducting the
world's affairs.

"That has such people in it," she finished.

Emery laughed gaily, apprehensively, and moved away. The
brother-in-law, who smelled of oil and litigation and pine needles,
cast her an appraising and impersonal look. The sort of man, she decided, who grandly bestowed upon a grateful wife a white Lincoln
Continental. (What's wrong with that? Emery might ask. If you
don't know . . . Did *she* give *him* a Cadillac?) Frances preferred
Emery, gentle, rational, accepting. Mutual. Slyly she coughed for his
attention and signaled for them to go home. He hesitated but then
set his face to stay. All right all right go fly a kite.

A waiter moved among them like a matador, a towel over his arm, a tray of drinks poised for the kill. He was Filipino, colors of golden hills and black patent leather. The host called him Robert. Soon, Frances called him Bob. An hour passed and she called him Bobby. He said, Yes Mrs. Benedict, and she thrilled at the sound from strange luscious lips. Later, having crossed the hearth to the other window seat, she caught his eye. One enchanted evening. His white teeth gleamed for her. She played with the thought of lust. She saw them naked and exhausted upon hot sand but found that she had nothing further to say to him. To fill the void, she curried, combed, painted, filed, smoothed, roughed in order that she would want to talk to him. Why? Reality, as usual, impinged and she saw him sliding down the corridors of forever, happily passing drinks to friends of the rich. Let him climb some other snow-capped mountain. Poor Frances, she thought.

Two in the morning came none too soon and Emery, she thought, was none too sober. He did not so much approach as accost her. He took her elbow. She heard his trumpets blaring and the martial beat of his drums. He had not forgotten her, but he preferred himself. She was not defenseless but she was demanding. She reclaimed her elbow. At the front door he swooped down on a half-finished and deserted drink and after proffering it to her downed it with a flourish. His gesture was at once a reprimand, a warning, and a defiance. He apparently felt deeply guilty at having deserted her, but nonetheless he proclaimed that he was his own man by right, be quiet.

By reason and a long-standing agreement, she should have driven home. By happenstance she did not, for their host marched them down the stairs to the car. Before such a client as that, dear Emery lacked the courage to let her drive. She might have insisted, made a small scene, but she did not, out of pity and fortitude and a desire to justify all her grievances.

Gesturing grandly, drunkenly, Emery slid behind the wheel of the car and unerringly slipped the key in the ignition. Smiling grimly, Frances announced to herself that she was going to die on the Bloody Bayshore because their host wished, under cover of darkness, to pat her bottom one more time. She contemplated giving the old fool a punch in his belly and her resentment reached a climax. Is this the age we live in? No one counted her, protected her, nor was she free and equal. She wished ill on everyone.

As Emery bucked away from the curb, she looked back and saw their host sprawled face down in the entrance to his house. Now that, she said, will do for a starter.

"There's a stop sign," she said.

"I'm not blind," said Emery.

"Oh?" said Frances. She withdrew into her most maddening silence.

"Great party," said Emery, making amends. He glanced at her quickly as if to judge her mood. What right had he to smile who had no right not to smile? What gift was this? He drove, did he not?

"Absolutely tiptop, one in a million," she said. "Shall I drive?" She extended her hand as if literally to take the wheel.

He heard, saw, ignored. "They're first-rate people, really first-rate. Know what I mean?" It was his way of making friends, but he had no grievance.

"Well now let me see," she said. "You mean salt of the earth, don't you? May I drive now?"

Emery appeared to ruminate. "It's going to be a very fruitful relationship."

"He said you were the greatest lawyer since . . . John Jay. I'd like to drive, Emery."

He laughed. "That guy never heard of John Jay. I'm doing all right, ain't I? Driving?" His voice was so reasonable, not thick, just very careful and reasonable. He bore no grudge. He was, in fact, managing the car well enough. He had smoothed out the clutch and he traveled at moderate speed. All the same, she wanted to drive.

"In the early years of their marriage," she intoned as if reading from a document, "they agreed together, both parties complying without dissenting voice, that so-called role-playing was less important than life-living, that error would be on the side of over-safety, that should one or the other imbibe too deeply, that one automatically relinquished his or her rights to the wheel of the car, the body of the baby, the tray of Orrefors, or the handle of the hot pan. It was a bargain struck in good faith and high reason. It has no doubt saved them many a goblet."

"Agreed," he said, turning up the ramp to the Bayshore. "So?"

She had been acutely alert to him for years and she saw the components of his resistance, the pride, the threat, the daring, the fear. Nevertheless, it infuriated her.

"Tomorrow morning you'll give me that cute little crooked little smile of yours and you'll say Boy was I crocked last night, I didn't know whether I could drive home or not. If we live until tomorrow."

"Goddammit," said Emery, speeding up, "you know I'm not drunk but you just keep pounding away as if your life depended on it, just so you can win the round, just so you can show me."

"Merging traffic," she said.

"I see the merging traffic." His face became, for him, brutal and flushed. Suddenly he braked and swerved to avoid a sideswiping Thunderbird. His face quieted. "Got your seat belt fastened?" he asked in rueful apology.

She quoted a headline. "Lawyer and Wife Killed on Bayshore."

He thought he had her, he looked delicious. "*Prominent* Lawyer and *Beautiful* Wife Only Injured." When he heard himself, his smile soured. "Not injured either, dammit. Why do you act this way? What do you want?"

"I'd be mad as hell if I got killed coming home from a party as nasty as that one," she said.

At first he laughed at the absurdity of what she had said. And then he surrendered to her anger and its demands for combat. He drew back his lips and said, "You just can't stand it, can you? How many years and you just can't stand it when people are more interested in me than they are in you. You just got to cut me down some way."

Her skin felt like plaster of Paris and her teeth ached, but her voice was gay. "It's a man's world, you know. Poor Emery. Poor dear old Emery, with his hag of a nag of a bag of a wife. I mean, what the hell, if you want to drive while intoxicated, what difference does it make that I'll get killed too?"

Sour and silent, he drove the car. Stubbornly they built up the battlements of silence. The Bayshore swept down the countryside to the flat country and the bay and darkness. The hills to the right held pockets of light. A jet swooped upward from the runway at the airport. The moon vanished. Occasionally cars sped toward them on the other side of the parkway. Rarely, a car passed them heading south. Their own car began to lug. Emery gripped the wheel. He shifted down a gear. The car began to thud and bump. He switched off the ignition. Understanding struck them both but Frances rushed to speak it.

"It's a flat."

"I know it's a flat," he said, turning off to the shoulder of the road. "I am not a fool."

He applied the brakes and the car stopped. His face was sober and ashamed. She relented at the sight and wished to touch his face, give comfort, offer love and forgiveness. She devised a smile but not soon enough.

"You are so superior," he said. "You never had a flat in your whole life. You'd have seen the nail, whatever it was."

Rebuffed, she said warningly, "Perhaps."

"From you, that's a concession."

She knew that all he wished was one kind word, to be asked to share in the comedy or rue that lay beneath their quarrels. He was a bookish man, not a fighter. He hated to quarrel, as he inevitably, too late, proclaimed. She saw clearly, not for the first time, how she drove him to it, with her vanities and irritations, her untapped powers and her vast need for consolation. She saw, too, that he had not this time consoled her but had instead himself concocted a grievance. She refused then in all conscience to help him. Was it ever different?

"You may recall," she said, "that I asked to drive. Perhaps, just perhaps but nevertheless perhaps, we might have avoided this flat."

"Oh for Christ's sake stop it."

"But you had to show everyone how big and tough . . ."

"Can you stop it? Can you please stop it?"

"If I wanted to," she said.

"Can you forego just this one time the intense pleasure you get from hammering on me?"

"He said, hammering on her."

Her stomach cramped and her jaws ached, but she smiled to prepare herself for further battle. He was what he was, but so was she.
She did not know what laws governed them. But loving each other
(for all they knew or cared), they rubbed mild abrasions into deep
rawness. Moments of contempt and anger had always come and
gone, had often wracked and strained them to breaking, and always
been inconclusively put away and forgotten. She was no fool, she of
course wished for peace. But she said, "Can you change a tire?"

"That's helpful, that's real helpful," he said. "Leave it to you to
make a man feel manly and confident."

He got out of the car, took off his coat and folded it neatly, placed
it on the seat, rolled up his sleeves, loosened his necktie, and idly
walked up and down beside the flat tire. Finally he got his keychain
and opened the trunk. Staring ahead at oncoming lights, Frances
listened to his work. She thought that she wished him success, but
she was not sure. He removed the jack from the trunk and placed it
under the back axle. Frances felt the car rise. She thought of going
to stand with him but gave it up. They would only antagonize each
other. She would create his mistakes. Once he had accomplished his
task, he would be so happy that they would be friends again. He
would be irresistible. If he succeeded.

She heard him bump the spare out of the trunk. He popped the
hubcap off the flat tire. She heard his startled cry of pain. She
opened the door and peered back at him. He held the heel of his
thumb to his mouth. Blood darkened his arm and shirt front.

"Damn thing slipped," he said.

She took the handkerchief from his hip pocket and wrapped it
around the wound. A car coming in their direction slowed. She
raised her hand in greeting but lowered it in fear. Who were they and
why? Emery turned, still holding his hand to his mouth. He looked
at Frances, gleaming and relieved, as the car stopped behind them.
Frances thought that she might herself have changed the tire. She
feared strangers at such an hour.

Three young men got out of the car. They wore sports coats and white shirts and loosened neckties. They smelled of men's cologne and stale whiskey. They stopped before Emery and bowed low. Their manners were comic, impersonal, and threatening.

"Sir," said the shortest of the three, a boy of twenty or so with a crew cut and glasses. The largest one came to stand before Frances. "Madame," he said with a low bow.

The third boy said, "You talk entirely too much, bear," and all three commenced to laugh. Frances backed away. The big one did look like a bear, with his short arms and heavy torso and triangular head. A bear.

"I'm awfully glad to see you boys," said Emery. "I seem to have hurt myself." He presented his wounded hand for their inspection. The shortest one grasped it and shook it vigorously. Emery cried in pain.

"Leave off, Larry," said the third boy, apparently the leader. He was sharp-featured, yet soft and sensual. The other two, the bear and the one called Larry, watched and waited for his reactions. The three were, it seemed to Frances, a closed group, performers and audience at once. She and Emery were only props for them. Or toys. "Okay, doc," said the leader.

The bear approached Emery and extended his hand. He said, "I make no pretense at being adept at the healing arts but may I look at your wound?"

Emery held out his hand and the boy took it. He held the wound close to his eyes, pulled the handkerchief away and carefully pressed open the still bleeding gash in the heel of Emery's hand. Emery jerked away.

"What the hell, are you crazy?" he said.

"I wanted to see what was inside," the bear said.

"He's a sadist," said the leader.

"I was a teen-age sadist," said the bear. All three boys whooped with laughter.

"You boys run along," said Emery. "Find your fun someplace else."

Frances wondered where the highway patrol was. The vaunted highway patrol. Cars were fewer and fewer now.

The smallest of the boys, Larry, pushed his glasses up higher on his nose and after a glance at the leader walked to peer under the car. He put his hand on the bumper and gently, slowly began to rock the car.

"Stop that!" said Emery. With his hand at his mouth, he started toward Larry. The bear touched Emery's arm.

"He isn't hurting you, is he, mister?" The bear shot a glance at the leader. "Ever heard the story of the Good Samaritans? I mean, anybody else stop to help you? He's just trying to help, mister, in his own little way. Don't kill the instinct for brotherhood, mister, not in our Larry."

Emery paused. "He's going to rock the car off the jack."

"Larry ain't mean, mister," said the bear. "Ain't a mean bone in that kid's body."

"By accident, maybe," said Emery. He didn't look at anyone, nor did he move. Frances knew that he was uncertain and nervous, that he was unsure of how to handle the boys. He wouldn't want to act on impulse or do anything dangerous. And he did want the boys' help. He hesitated, staring at the roadway and sucking the wound on his hand.

"Larry ain't accidental, either, mister," said the bear. "Ain't an accidental bone in that kid's body. Is there, Larry?"

Larry turned toward Emery. He was not smiling, but his expression was trancelike. He began to shake his head, slowly, rhythmically, as if dancing. On that signal the other two boys also began to shake their heads, to wear trancelike expressions, and to move toward Emery. They moved in quite close, shaking their heads, but silent. Emery looked at the highway, up and down the highway. Frances said to herself that the boys were obviously kidding, that they would fold if Emery just showed a little authority, confidence. They were just kids. Clean kids, at that. Out on a lark. Showing off for each other. Not dangerous, not if someone laughed at them and said Fix the flat or go away. Emery said nothing. He did not feel comfortable or strong, perhaps it was his aching thumb, or the quarrel. Seconds ticked off. A car whipped past them.

"You want this tire fixed or not?" asked the bear.

"I seem to have hurt this hand rather badly," said Emery. He appealed to them with a smile.

"We ain't asking for a health report," said Larry. "You're taking too much time talking. You want the tire fixed or not?"

Frances said, "Yes," and Emery said, "Yes, if you would be so kind." His voice sounded choked and she knew he was angry to ask directly for help, from them. He had taken too much from them. She shrugged off the accusing look he gave her. If she hadn't said Yes, would he have said No? She didn't think so.

"We'd be delighted to be so kind," said Larry.

The bear walked to Emery and laughed when Emery backed off. "I won't hurt you, mister, not a mean bone in by body either. I don't want your wife to hear this." Emery looked suspicious but allowed himself to be involved. The bear cupped his hand around Emery's ear as if to whisper and he brought his mouth close. In a loud shouting voice he said, "You scared shitless, ain't you, mister?"

Emery jerked loose and Frances thought he was going to hit the boy. He stopped himself but his face clenched. "Now look here," he said, "you boys are having fun, but I don't find it at all funny. What are you up to, what do you want?" He looked from one to the other, demanding an answer, a rational explanation.

"Easy easy easy," said the leader in a soft sibilant voice. He held his hands up and shook them, as if to forestall Emery. He seemed deeply embarrassed. Emery went on.

"I say, if you are going to help, then help. If you are going to change the tire, then change it. But if you are going to rob, then rob. If you are going to hurt, then hurt. If you are going to . . ."

The bear interrupted. "Rape?" he asked.

"Shut up," said the leader. He gestured for Emery to go on, that he for one found Emery's words interesting and he was intent on listening.

"I'm sick of it," said Emery. "I've had as much of your clowning as I am going to. Either . . ."

"Inside," said the leader, gesturing toward the car door.

Emery did not answer. He stared as if he did not believe his ears. Larry took a step toward him. Spacing his words as if for a particu-

larly stupid and stubborn person, he said, "Get in side. We will
fix the flat. Get it?" He turned to the other two boys and then
looked back at Emery. Very quickly he said, "The lady stays outside."

"Oh no," said Emery. He went to Frances and put his arm protectively about her shoulders. "Oh no," he repeated with finality. Larry
went to the back of the car and began to rock it on the jack, back
and forth, back and forth, with increasing tempo. He smiled sweetly,
as if deeply engaged in the music of the rocking car. The bear began
to move his hips and snap his fingers.

Emery pulled Frances farther away and then he turned back in
fury to the boys. Frances put a restraining hand on his arm. His
hands were locked in fists at his sides. She tightened her grip. She
had thought the boys meant no great harm; but if Emery challenged
them, would they be able to resist? What chance had a paunchy
forty against three young bulls who were twenty and raging? Emery
tugged at his arm but she held fast. Let them have their fun.

"Don't be a fool," she said. She pressed her body against his and
forced him to move backward. They walked away from the car. She
held his elbow and applied a gentling rhythmic pressure. She said,
"They're just showing off. If you try to take them on, well . . ." She
slipped her hand into his and they walked off hand in hand. Emery
seemed blind and agonized.

"Christ!" he said. He stopped, forcing her to stop too.

She said, "They could easily rock the car off the jack. What could
you do? You can't win. They could rock the car off the jack."

"Let them," said Emery. "I don't have to take their insolence."

She put her arms around him and leaned her head against his
chest. He strained his head over her shoulder, asserting himself at the
boys. Silently the boys watched and waited for Emery's next move, to
play out their game against him and to defeat him. They despised
him and Emery knew it and Frances knew it. But she thought it was
useless for him to try to remedy their opinion of him.

"I'm in it, too," she said. "You can't just decide by yourself to
start a fight."

"Start a fight Christ!" said Emery. He put his hands on her shoul-

ders to shove her aside, but she locked her arms around his back.
"Get in the car," she said. "Please. For my sake. You aren't a
child, proving something. What would be gained?"

"I don't know, something, I don't know." His breath was staccato, like obstructed sobs. Abruptly the strain left him and he grew
slack, surrendered. She knew he was ready, needing now only a bit
more persuasion. She wondered briefly, had it all been a charade, his
willingness to fight? She did not dwell on the thought nor did she
commit herself to it, but it was there. Automatically she marshaled
the opposing force: his tension, his anger, his self-respect, and, of
course, her own unfortunate instinct to comprehend the seamiest
motive of everyone.

She said, "For my sake. Think what might happen to me. Those
stupid toughs. Bully-boys. Bulls. Animals. Do it for my sake. Get in
the car."

She urged him toward the door, her arms still locked behind him,
as if they were dancing. He stared over her shoulder at the silent
boys, from time to time made as if to challenge them. At the door of
the car, she released her hold on him. Hesitancy gripped him and
then he folded into the back seat.

The bear and Larry began to change the tire. Frances leaned
against the front fender and drew her light jacket tighter. She felt
quite chilled, and as she looked at the sky it seemed to recede and
she seemed to shrink. She was on a vast empty darkened desert. She
was delicate and exposed in a senseless universe and she was mortal
and alone. All else was diversion, and useless.

She became aware of a presence near her and she was at once her
intact self again. The third boy, the leader, had come to stand beside
her, leaning, as she did, against the fender.

"You're a tough one, ain't you, a real tough one," he said. Polishing his teeth with his tongue, he nodded his head and looked at her
under lowered lids. "I like tough women. Not cheap: tough. Know
something? You ought to pick on somebody your own size, not a
little guy like that one." He motioned with his head toward the car.
"I bet not once, not once, you been with a guy as tough as you are."

How absurd, Frances cried to herself, how awful, she cried, and momentarily her body seemed to open wide and to close and she felt a chill on her neck and a tremble. As if by signal the boy pushed off from the car and came to stand face to face with her. He put his hands on his hips, thumbs hooked into his belt. He rocked back and forth, back and forth, from the balls of his feet to his heels, swinging closer and closer to Frances. He was grotesque, and lewd, a caricature, obscene, threatening, appealing. And she was herself and tough.

"You filthy little animal!" she said. "Don't dare touch me! You fix the tire and then leave us alone, all of you."

The boy laughed hollowly. "Tough," he said, "see what I mean?" He moved away and as he walked past the other boys he said, "Fix the tire like the lady said and then git." He shook a cigarette from a pack and went on to his own car. The other boys bent back to work. Frances felt the back end of the car go down and she heard the trunk slam. They were finished. With the leader at the wheel and without speaking or acknowledging Frances and Emery, the boys got in their car. Whatever they had wanted, they either had or would never have. Grinding, spitting stones, blowing smoke and the stench of burning rubber, the car sped away.

"They're gone," said Frances.

Emery's muffled voice came to her. "I hope you're satisfied. I hope one time in your life you're satisfied."

She did not answer. She knew what he meant, or thought she did, but she did not know what the truth was. After a moment she got behind the wheel and started the car. Slowly she gained the roadway and set out for home. Once home, she would consider Emery. She would help him. She would restore him with a final drink, with ice and coldness. She would persuade him, and herself, that really nothing important to either of them had been at stake. She would help him to discover the comedy of it all and to laugh. Slowly, between them, they would begin to build a little anecdote to relate to friends and to reduce the episode to dust. And in the darkness they would soothe each other's frail raw nakedness to a forgiving sleep. When they got home. But for now, as Emery wept silently in the back seat, she drove the car and she was exhilarated.

Pamela Painter

The Next Time I Meet Buddy Rich

We pulled into town just as the sun was coming up, dropped some stuff off at the rooms they gave us, and took the drums and other instruments over to the club. The debris of empty glasses, full ashtrays, disarranged chairs was still there from the night before, heavy with stale air. I unrolled my rug, set up my drums. Felt for the piece of gum Buddy Rich once gave me — now stuck at the bottom of the floor tom-tom. Vince hooked up the sound system and then we headed back to the hotel.

I carried in my practice set, calling to Gretel to open the door. Finally I used my key. Sounds of the shower running droned from the bathroom. Her clothes were scattered over a chair, suitcases sprawled open on the floor. Then the water went off and Gretel appeared in the doorway with a towel around her, a folded rim keeping it in place, flattening her breasts. Her hair was piled on her head and held by one barrette. Beads of moisture gleamed on her shoulders, her legs.

"No more hot water," she said, as she pulled the barrette from her hair, shaking it loose. "I'm getting tired of these places. This is too far away from the club considering we're going to be here two weeks."

"We can move. We have before."

"It's the whole scene," she said pointing to the suitcases. "Where's it going? I know what you want. But sometimes wanting isn't enough."

I lay down on the bed and closed my eyes. I saw her standing in the towel. I took the towel away and looked at her full breasts, her stomach, a different texture of hair.

"Sorry," she said. "You want to listen now or later?"

"Later." I put the towel back and opened my eyes. She was looking out the window. I felt sorry for her living this way, but the words to change it all, to take me back to Erie, just wouldn't come. "Let's have a nice dinner after the club run tonight. Chicago doesn't close down like Kansas." She shrugged her shoulders. She was right. If you weren't playing, it was hard to care what you did out here. One room after another. A hundred tables in a hundred towns. The bed slid as I got up. I licked some of the water off her right shoulder. She didn't move.

"OK, later," she said. And I understood that everything would have to wait. That was OK too. She had been traveling with me for the past year, ever since we decided we'd eventually get married. We never mentioned settling down, but I could tell she was tired of being on the road. The band probably wouldn't be together much longer anyway with Jack pulling toward hard rock. Then I'd take my uncle up on his offer of being a plumber for him again. *That* I didn't want to think about.

So I arranged my practice set, fitting it around my chair. Settling it into the sparse pile of the rug to make it steady. "Bring me back two ham on rye," I told Gretel when Jack and Vince knocked on the door.

Vince understood. Five years I've been breaking my ass to get the big break, trying to make it happen. One night in Columbus I was talking to a drummer who was almost there, would be in a few years — by thirty you have to be. That's what I asked him. "How do you get there?"

He wiped his hands under his arms and said, "You practice your ass off all your life and the better you get the worse you seem to yourself and you're ready to give up; and then one day when your hands aren't getting any faster you say the hell with it. When you next sit down at a set of drums after you haven't touched them for days, weeks, like a vow you'd made — suddenly you're doing all the things you've been trying to do for years — suddenly there is a 'before' and 'after' and it's the 'after' where you are now — and goddamn you don't know why, you just know that you're finally there. Then it's only a matter of time."

And now my time was running out. The band close to breaking up. Kids, pets, hard rock up against the slower stuff. I looked down at my hands. Clean, now. The prints clean, sensitive to the smooth surface of the sticks. I hated being a plumber although I was good at it. All that grease, fitting pipes, welding. I straightened my back. Time enough for planning that later. Time to practice now. I pulled back the plastic curtains to let in the last of the hotel's sun. Then I started to play. Slow at first, just letting my wrists do the work, looking out past the sunken single beds, past the cheap print of some flower, using a little pressure, feeling how my wrists were somehow connected with the tension in my feet. Just feeling it happen like I was watching myself in the mirror. Trying for the sounds of Buddy Rich.

The next time I meet Buddy Rich it'll be at a 76 station in some crazy place, like Boone, Iowa, not at a concert, and he'll be all burnt out waiting for a cup of coffee and I'll go up to him and say—what I'll say I haven't worked out yet but it'll happen and I'll say it then.

I met Buddy Rich for the first time at Rainbow Gardens in Erie, Pennsylvania. I was playing a spot called The Embers and it was our night off. We went really early, to get good seats up close so I could watch him play, watch his hands and feet and the way his body moves. He's a karate expert — once said that the martial arts apply to drumming; they key your mind up for getting into it, coordinate your hands and feet. I want to ask him about this when I meet him next.

The Rainbow Gardens is an oval-shaped arena, a stage at one end and a big wooden dance floor in the middle of a bunch of tables. Loads of people and glasses and cheap booze. It was during intermission, on my way back from the john, that I saw him. He was sitting off to the side, just happened to be there — probably after changing his shirt. Not drinking, just leaning back in his chair. Looking out as if to say, "OK, show me something intelligent."

I walked past thinking, "That can't be." Somehow you think of stars as either living on stage or in their dressing rooms. No real life, no tired hands. Then I walked past again and got enough nerve to say, "Buddy Rich?" and he didn't say "no," so I went on and said,

"I'm Tony — I'm a drummer and I play with Circuit of Sound." The words kind of rushed at him like a spilled drink and just as effective. "I think your band is really great," I said. He seemed to lean further back in his chair. He had on a long-sleeved grey shirt and grey pants. His fingers were tapping on the table, tapping like they were just doing it by themselves. I fumbled in my wallet for a card with the name of my band on it. "Would you autograph this for me," I said. I gave him a pen.

His first words were, "Who do you want it to?"

"Tony," I said, "and good luck on the drums."

He looked at me kind of funny and then wrote, "Best Wishes." I nodded, disappointed. Then I thanked him and went back to my seat, knowing I had blown my chance. Where are the questions when it matters? I wished I could grab him by the collar and say, "Hey, I'm different. I'm not like all the rest of the people who don't understand what Buddy Rich is unless you're in solo. Who don't understand that you, Buddy Rich, are here for the band — while all these people are here for Buddy Rich." But I didn't say it. I drank down eight ounces of Schlitz — chugging it to drown my embarrassment, and dying a second time because I finally realized that he thought I meant good luck to him on the drums. As if he needed it. Shit.

I let about ten minutes pass. Watching him just sitting there, wanting to know what was going through his mind, wanting to know what was keeping his hands moving or still. What's in his mind when he's playing. He had a back operation in July and a night later he was on the bandstand, behind the drums. Later, on a talk show he said they should have done the operation while he was playing, then they wouldn't have needed an anesthetic.

Finally, I couldn't stand it anymore. I chugged another Schlitz and stood up. I hadn't talked to my date since I sat down and all I could do now was tap her under the chin — grateful that she understood.

"I talked to you a few minutes ago and nothing came out right — including asking for your autograph," I said. He seemed to appreciate my honesty because his eyes stayed on me longer and again I told him how great he and his band were and he said, "sit down," so I pulled out a chair across the table from him. Then I started to pinpoint all the different songs that I really enjoyed off his albums — some of them almost unknown. I counted on that. Like "Goodbye Yesterday," like how it talks to me instead of playing.

"It shows how close the musicians work — you know the music is in front of them, but no arranger, no charts could do it for you — it's the energy of the group that pulls it together, that makes it talk." I told him this and more about "Preach and Teach," and he was nodding his head and not leaning back anymore. Now he leaned forward on his table, looking at me. "You know," I said, "with you, it's not just jamming. It's structure pushed to the end in sound." We sat in silence for a few minutes thinking about it.

"Yeah, you do understand," he said. Then he kind of grinned that wide smile of his. "Hard to talk about, isn't it. Easier to play."

"If you're you," I said. "I'm still trying."

"You know," he said, "interviewers are always asking me about the future of music. Hell I don't know about that. For me it's playing two hours here then going down the road to Muncie, Indiana. It's the next night for me. Nothing more." His hands were still now and I saw them for the first time.

"You don't have any calluses," I said.

"Hell no I don't." He grinned again, spreading his fingers on the table. "If the pressure's right the sticks don't rub." Smooth. Magic.

Just then I noticed some kids standing off to the left of us waiting with their pencils and papers — finally having figured out who he was and who I wasn't. So I stood up to give them their turn and he reached out and grabbed my wrist. "Don't go," he said, "I'm not done talking to you." So I sat down. My wrist was burning and I knew that the next time I played, the next time my right hand had to make itself heard, it wouldn't be the same. "Sit down," he said, "I got a few more minutes before I have to play to this airport hangar." He gestured around the arena, the high steel-beamed ceiling, the cold aluminum walls painted yellow, pink, blue. It would never be the same for me again.

He held out his hand for pencils and paper and a guy stepped forward, a couple more shuffling behind him. Wondering who I was, sitting there like a friend.

"I really like your 'Sing, Sing, Sing,' " he said to Rich. Rich looked up at me sideways and winked and told him, "I'm going to play 'SSS' and 'Wipeout' in a medley just for you." The dumb ass should have known it was Krupa's theme song. I suddenly had a feeling for what Buddy Rich had to deal with, wanting to be liked and understood and yet running into people who kill off any generosity you feel for the public out there. Like the ones who come to hear his band — they're all looking for the drum solo — you can see their eyes light up as if the stage lights suddenly got switched around. They don't understand the dynamics and togetherness. They know the finished product in a half-assed way, but not how it comes about. Even the critics in the early days would say he plays too loud, or throws rim shots in where they don't belong. *Now* they know what they're hearing.

We talked for a few more minutes — then he said he had to go. Gave me a stick of gum — Dentyne. He stood up and leaned over the table and did a quiet roll with his hands to my shoulder. "I think you'll make it," he said. "I'll be hearing you some day." And he was gone. I guess I heard the rest of the concert. But now being there meant something else to me. And when I hit home that night the stick of gum went into my drum. Was there now. A small pink lump. I look at it just before I begin to play.

Gretel still wasn't back so I practiced a while longer. Then I moved to the bed and lay back, still hearing the sounds, my own sounds this time, and I lay there for one hour. Not sleeping but waiting for show time to come round. When she arrived with the sandwiches I ate them. When Vince called to check the program I talked. But I was hearing other things, I was making my own program for tonight.

Finally, I must have slept for a few hours because pretty soon Vince was pounding on the door yelling, "how we going to make it without our practice?" I knew what he meant. He plays a cool sax — sliding notes around like melted butter then pulling them together with a tension that tells in his back, in the way his arms move toward his sides when he gets up for his solo run. We might have made it, Vince and I; maybe he'll keep something together. "Meet you in the lobby," I yelled.

We took three changes of costume and all went in one van over to the club. We were starting out tonight in tuxes, then switching to sequined jump suits that remind me of kids' Dr. Denton pajamas, ending up in jeans. All a part of the act. Jack was driving and putting on his cuff links at the same time. He's a good guitarist and up-front man. Can talk to anyone—sifting his smile out over the audience behind his velvety voice. Carol, the vocalist, and he were a good pair. She was filing her nails. Gretel was out shopping.

The stage loomed in the back of the place away from the bar and the lighting was OK. Bad was bad. OK was good. There were a few early drunks sitting around before going home to the wife and kids and mashed potatoes—they'd be moving along as soon as the sound built—it always happened. I took a run on my drums—did some rolls—soft then faster and faster. I hit each drum firm, getting that crisp beat, starting with the snare and ending up with the floor tom-tom and then one closing beat on the bass to cut it off sharp. I set out two sets of new sticks because I've been breaking one or two a night. Then I rolled up my pant legs and sat there sipping coffee. Vince was off talking to the waitresses, trying to line something up for later—much later. It's hard—you have fifteen minutes here and there to make contact, change clothes, and sound like you're not coming on too strong. He's good-looking in a seedy sort of way and even then he's about 90 per cent unsuccessful. I just let it happen if it's going to. Sometimes classy groupies show up two, three nights in a row and you know they want to be asked out. Sometimes they think you'll be a temporary drug source, but they got us all wrong. If we find it we use it, but we don't travel with the stuff. Or play. If cops are even a little suspicious in some of those one-horse towns they'll rip your van apart in the middle of a cornfield—drum sets, suitcases, instruments, speakers, music. It happened once when Jack had some coke from another musician at a gig. But it wasn't on us. Who the hell wanted to be looking for bail in Boone, Iowa.

We were about ready to play, so I changed into my high-heeled shoes for a better angle. We started out with show songs, dance music—moving toward two shows a night. My solo is in the second. I usually start light, play something basic that people can tap their feet to. Then I build up by getting louder, and faster, bringing it back down to nothing then building to a finale with a very fast single-stroke roll. My sticks are moving so fast you can't see them. People relate to a set of drums before any other instrument—I guess because it's obvious what a drummer does—it's so physical.

We started playing and people began coming in. The usual crowd — single people needing movement and noise, countermen, clerks from the local record and sheet-music stores. Bored couples. And a drummer or two. I've met one or two in at least half the towns. Some I looked forward to seeing, some I hated running into again.

We didn't get any requests yet. That'd come later in the evening after a show, after Carol went into her act. A few songs. Talking at the tables, telling women about the men they're with, always on their side. Gretel wasn't here yet. I missed her. But it wasn't reason enough to make her want to stay.

While we were playing "Preach and Teach" something felt different. I moved into a double stroke roll. Not too loud, just testing. It was a feeling. And then I was going faster and my sticks were almost floating across the drums, washing the high hat, the cymbal and snare with rushes of sound. Solid sound. And suddenly I knew I had to stop right there. It was happening and I wasn't going to let it happen yet. Gretel still wasn't here. And I was afraid of what it meant for both of us. But I had to be sure so I changed into a quiet single stroke, hearing the sounds I've heard on my Buddy Rich albums, and my hands were going places they hadn't been before, moving to beats I'd dreamed of playing, sounds I'd played in my sleep, and tonight they were mine. They were in my muscles and fingers as if they'd always been there — even though I knew they hadn't, but this time I hoped they weren't ever going away.

I slowed way down as Jack went into his bass solo and then we took one more run at the chorus before ending. Then I sat there feeling the sticks in my hands, rolling them between my fingers like magic wands. I felt my back relax and curve into a tighter arc as I sat there marking that place and that time. The bar stretching off into the distance of lights and neon noise. Gretel now at our table center front. Gretel in her beaded Indian blouse. My brown coffee mug on the floor beside a bottle of Schlitz. Me at the drums, at twenty-six.

We took a break and I changed into my jump suit fast. Then I joined Gretel at the table. I wanted to tell her but first I wanted her to hear it — without words getting in the way. Anyway she avoided my eyes so I ordered a beer. The tables were filling up. Sounds, smells starting to multiply into that magic of late-night movement. A girl at the next table raised her glass to me. She had beautifully manicured nails — painted green. I nodded politely.

"I went to the bus station today. Checked out the fare to home," Gretel said, finally looking at me. Her eyes were tired. She used to look more alive slaving in the Head Start program where she was working when we met. "But I didn't get the ticket yet."

"Is that what you want?" I asked. My stomach felt like a drum tuned too tight. I knew what she wanted but now I wasn't sure I'd ever get the whole thing together. I covered her hand with mine.

"I don't know what I want anymore," she said. "This just isn't enough even if we wanted the same thing. You big and famous on the drums. Us." She looked around the noisy room and I followed her glance to the stage, to the light glinting on the steel rims of the drums.

"We *are* us," I said but she didn't hear.

"I mean what makes someone give up. I feel like giving up and you're still out there playing." There were tears in her eyes and she blinked fast to spread them away.

"You want to know where being on the road ends for us?" I asked. She pulled her hand away, but I caught her fingers, could feel the turquoise ring I'd given her. "You're afraid I won't know." I knew she was because I had the same fear — living on a dream till the real end of everything. It was almost enough to walk me out of that club, my arm around her, the sticks and drums left behind. Almost enough.

She nodded. "And I know I'd keep asking. Wanting two things at once. Like I don't want to go now but I think I'm going anyway. For a while. Maybe I'll be back in a week. Round trip." She wiped her eyes and laughed up at me. It was a laugh too weakly struck to carry, but, God, I loved her for that smile. Then she clinked her glass with mine.

"I might get home before you do," I said. I missed her already. Her waiting for me at tables. Sleeping, turning when I turned. Her trivia games on the road as we zigzag across Route 80 just to break the monotony, getting off to the county roads for a while.

"Don't say that, Tony. I don't want to expect you."

She was right. There was nothing for me to say that I could say.

Vince and Jack were back on stage, tuning up. The others were coming back fast. I gave her hand a squeeze. "I have to play. We'll talk later."

"I'll be back for the last show," she said. The light played on the beads of her blouse as she sighed. Softer than drums. Her lips smiled. I kissed her fast. I loved her, but I left to play.

Close to the next break I looked out through the haze, the smoke now thick with words, perfume sprayed on too heavily in the ladies' room. Through the conversations, words going as much past the other person as our music, past people not used to listening to anything beyond their own pulse. And with the drums I had two. I looked out through this, looked for the few who made it all come together, for the one person alone, here for listening. The one who was watching my hands go to where they're supposed to be, craning his neck to watch my feet make the beat.

These people were the ones I leaned toward, the ones I played to. They knew it, and I knew they knew it. And sometimes during a break I would go and sit at their tables. I listened to things Buddy Rich must have heard a million times. But I'm not tired of it yet, maybe because it wasn't true — that I'm the greatest. But I liked to hear it and I talked back, I looked at them straight. It was the same way I played. Sometimes they couldn't handle it — me coming to them, my hand on the back of a chair ready to join them if asked — maybe they didn't have the next three questions memorized — so I moved on. I loved them just the same, but I moved on, doing us both a favor. A time and a place and all that crap. I've been there.

That night I sat with Harry Ratch, an ex-drummer turned history teacher. He told me that once in St. Louis he sat in three nights for Flip Belotti when he had an emergency operation. Harry was the high school hero. History went down pretty easily for the next few months.

I ordered a beer, keeping my limit of two while playing. Harry Ratch was drinking beer too. He was past the physical fitness of a drummer — it was hard to be overweight in this business — but I could tell by the way his arms moved, his shoulders moved, that he once sat behind a set. Suddenly I saw myself ten years from now sitting in The Embers in Erie, Pennsylvania. Talking to some young kid. Telling him about the time I talked to Buddy Rich. Pulling my back straight to hide the tire around my waist. Hoping he'll offer to let me take a turn at his drums. Wishing I hadn't had three drinks already.

It hadn't happened yet. I focused back on Harry Ratch. He told me that Flip Belotti said the thing for beginners is to always practice. "If you're right-handed, do it with your left. There's always practicing to be done when you're not behind the drums." Harry was passing this advice along to me. I accepted it graciously. It made sense. I told him I hoped to see him again in the next two weeks. Maybe he could sit in on a couple of numbers. For a moment his eyes lost their sad history.

"I'll be here," he said sitting back. "I'll be here." It felt good to make someone's night.

I broke my sticks in one of the first numbers and started working with a new pair. Then we began to play the medley that led into my solo. Again I just moved into the drums. I held off till the last moment, catching the beat at the last possible second, almost afraid to know if it stayed, afraid to trust my knowing. But man it was there.

I could feel it again and I listened to my wrists making music I was born to hear. I was loose and tight at the same time. My wrists were loose and my forearms were keeping the pressure under control. I was arching over the set. I looked for Gretel and she was watching. And she knew. I was playing the answer. Her eyes were sad and happy at the same time; her hands flat on the table, still. And I was moving back and forth toward the sounds I needed to make, toward the sound Vince heard because he stood up, and — still playing — he turned and saluted me with his sax. I knew he was hearing what was happening to me as my legs were tight against my jeans and my feet were wearing shoes I didn't feel and I thought: this is what I always wanted to know from Buddy Rich. What do you feel? When I'm as fast as you are, will I feel what you feel, will I know?

These questions went through my head like lightning, their smell remained, and now it was what I knew that stopped me thinking. That pulled my sounds out of the forest of tables and noise like an ancient drum in some tribal ritual. It was my night. I heard the voices in the club lose their timbre, saw heads turn. There was no going back to Erie, only nights like these to keep me whole.

People were standing now. And Harry Ratch must have felt in his heart that he was helping me to what he never made. I was glad he was here to help me move, and then there were no more voices. One by one the band was dropping back and out, and only Vince and I were left – his fluid notes winding around the sticks I was moving but no longer felt. We were making circuits of sound. He turned facing me, leaning into his sax, giving his pledge with the notes he made before he too dropped out and I was left. I was dripping wet and winging it. The spotlight hung before me like a suspended meteor. I played as if waiting for it to hit.

Abraham Rothberg

The Red Dress

When Anna came out of the hospital, the sunshine was still fitful and undecided, but the wind had changed direction and was blowing the city smoke and the quiet-looking, detached clouds over the East River toward Queens. Waiting for Jessica—since Jessica had quit social work and become a housewife, she was never on time for an appointment—Anna smoked a cigarette and thought about the red dress. She had seen it in the window of one of the very expensive little shops on Fifty-seventh Street and from the moment she had seen it on the tailor's dummy, Anna knew that she wanted it and that it was impossible for her to have it. She had gone in nevertheless, noting the saleswoman's carefully calculated stare at her cheap tweed coat and her navy blue knitted cloche, enduring it because she wanted to know how much the dress cost. The saleswoman, a tightly corseted woman in discreet gray, with a high upswept mass of tinted black hair, had taken out a mate to the one in the window and Anna, hat and coat off, had held the dress, hanger and all, against her while she looked at herself in the full-length mirror. She saw the length of red silk fall beautifully away from her body and felt the softness of the material between her fingers as she held it to her waist. The saleswoman hadn't bothered to offer to let her try it on, and before Anna could ask, the woman carefully told her the price. "One hundred and thirty-five dollars," she said, smiling almost with relish. "Reduced from a hundred and fifty-eight fifty." Anna had put her coat and hat back on, murmuring a subdued thank you and, not taking her eyes from the dress, had then gone out onto

Fifty-seventh Street hating the coarse feel of her tweed coat and the sight of the well-dressed mink-clad women on the street.

That had been three weeks ago and she had gone by that store window on some pretext or other every single working day since. The dress had been there until yesterday, when in its place was a gold taffeta evening gown. Because it had replaced the red silk, Anna hated it fervently. She had mentioned the red silk to Jessica and Jessica suggested that they try the sample house where Carol Van Wyck, a mutual friend, got all of her clothing.

"Are you still mooning about that dress?" Jessica was standing in front of her, grinning her wide-mouthed friendly smile so that the crow's feet showed around her eyes.

Anna laughed and stubbed her cigarette out underfoot. As they fell into stride and walked crosstown, she said, "So help me, I feel like a case myself. I never was like this about any dress. It's almost like a fixation."

"You'll get over it," Jessie said. "I feel like that at least once a week, but Vince usually talks me out of it. Can't afford it, he says."

"How is Vince?" Anna said, asking after Jessica's husband.

"Still finding that there are hundreds of promising young lawyers in New York, and none of them making a decent living," Jessica laughed. "How about you? Handling a big case load?"

"About sixty active," Anna said, "but that's par for the course right now."

"No wonder you got a fix on that dress. You're overworked."

"Sure, but who isn't?"

"Anything special?"

"The usual, and the most painful, the kind you can't do anything about. Refugee whose lovemaking was done in D.P. camps without privacy so long that he can't make love any more. His wife wants a child, among other things. Old lady who can't swallow and doesn't know why. She thinks she's got cancer of the throat, but there's no trace of it. The psychiatrist says her children have been planning to send her to an old folks' home and she doesn't want to go. She wants to die, so she can't swallow food. Oh, you know what it's like, with stuff buried so deep they don't really know what's happening to them or what they're looking for." As she said it, Anna realized that her desire for the red dress was a search too, for something entombed inside her that she couldn't or perhaps wouldn't see.

"You been going out much lately?" Jessica asked after a while, just a shade too gently, Anna thought. Everyone was very careful now since she had turned twenty-five and was still single, even Jessica, as if she were now officially doomed to lovelessness.

"No, not much," Anna said.

Jessica nodded, clucking sympathetically, and they walked on in silence, a silence Anna was grateful for. Jessica always knew when to talk, always had, even when they'd been in social work school together. Jessica sensed when she had something on her mind, even if it was only a red dress. Or was it only a red dress?

Mae Rumage's place was on the fifth floor of a big, dark office building in the West Seventies. The elevator operator said, "Miz Rumage's place is the last one down on the left," and they walked through the dim corridors, feeling the strange quiet of an office building after hours. "Five thirty-six" had small rubbed-out black letters with the name, *Mae Rumage,* and beneath, in letters equally worn, the single word, *Samples.* Jessica knocked, first quietly and then loudly until the frosted glass pane in the door shook like chattering teeth, but no one answered.

"Guess she must have forgotten," Anna said, almost grateful that the place was closed. She shouldn't feel that way about a dress and if they found no one and went away, maybe the feeling would go away too.

"Carol called her for an appointment at two this afternoon. How can anyone forget that quickly?" Jessica asked, irritated.

"You looking for Mae?" The voice was behind them, hollow in the narrow corridor, and they whirled, startled.

Anna nodded almost automatically, seeing a hairy man in an undershirt, a razor in his hand, his face half-lathered, and looking completely alien in the impersonal, office-like corridor. In the yellow light, Anna saw that a leather belt around his waist ended in a holster that held a revolver. Anna stared at the gun, so inharmonious against the pale skin, the dark hair, and the washed-out undershirt, almost believing that Jessica's whispered "He's got a gun!" was her own voice echoing in her head. The man suddenly noticed that they were staring. "Don't worry, girls, I've got a license for it. I'm a private detective. See!" He pointed to the gilt lettering on the glass of his door. It read: *William Frey, Executive Surveys.* "That's my office. Come on in. I'll call Mae for you."

"No," Jessica said, "it's all right. We'll come back some other time." She took Anna's arm and began to pull her toward the elevator.

"She lives just down the block," Frey said, "won't be any bother. She probably just went home for a . . . bite. Probably forgot you were coming. She's a little forgetful, about some things."

Reluctantly they followed him into his office, and sat in the straight-backed chairs while he called. "Mae?" he shouted into the phone, "you gotta coupla customers here. Nice-looking girls too. Been waiting for you fer forty minutes. Maybe more. Said you had an appointment with 'em. Sure. Sure. But get over here fast." He hung up.

"You shouldn't have told her we were waiting so long," Jessica said. "She'll be angry. Besides, we only just got here."

"Won't bother Mae. But you better buy something. She'll cuss you up and down if you don't." He went into an adjoining bathroom, left the door open, and went on shaving. Anna could see the gun nestled at his waist as he raised his arms in shaving, looking like some darkly exotic corsage pinned there. She took out a cigarette, offered one to Jessica automatically, forgetting that Jessica didn't smoke, and then, with the cigarette in her mouth, discovered that she didn't have a match.

"Wanna match?" His face still lathered, Frey watched her rummaging through her purse.

She nodded. He walked into a room that led from the office and in a moment called from the other room. "Come on in here and I'll give you a light."

Anna looked at Jessica, and Jessica whispered, "Just yell and I'll come running." She grinned mischievously. "If you don't, I'll know you're enjoying yourself."

Anna walked into a room that had a large studio couch in the corner, turned down for sleeping, and next to it a large blond mahogany buffet. "You work late, Mr. Frey?" Anna asked.

"Who, me? Naw, nine to five for me." Frey picked some matches from the buffet, struck a light for her and lit her cigarette. "Drink?" he suggested in a hoarse whisper, leaning toward her, the match still burning between his fingers. "Scotch, rye. . . ."

" . . . no, thanks," Anna said, finding her voice, and discovering it had fallen to a hoarse, conspiratorial whisper like Frey's.

"How about the fights? I'm going tonight and we could make a time of it?" he said, looking at her hopefully. He waited another moment and then, shaking the match out, he dropped it, threw the book of matches back on the buffet, and went out ahead of her.

When he had finished shaving, Frey put on a white shirt he took from a desk drawer, and a dark tie, readjusted his holster, and turned away from them to tuck his shirttails into his trousers. When he turned back to them, adjusting his trousers, Jessica asked, "Tell me, Mr. Frey, why do you call yourself *Executive Surveys?*"

"Oh, that? Well, I only talk to the top executives, not the secretaries." He smiled, and suddenly he didn't look at all alien to Anna, but rather like a bright young man trying to get ahead, who had a wife, two kids, and a house in Westchester. With the white shirt and the tie on, she couldn't even remember the pale hairy flesh and the washed-out undershirt underneath.

"Do you trail husbands?" Jessica asked, grinning.

"Everybody always asks that first," Frey said. "I wonder why."

"Well, do you?" Jessica insisted. "Do you trail men when their women want something on them?"

"Why don't you ask about tailing women so their men can get something on them?"

He put his jacket on, tucked the holster away carefully so that even to Anna's eye, knowing it was there, it was invisible. "Mae'll be along in a couple of minutes," he said.

She was. A fat blonde in a loose green coat came in, grunted at Frey, and asked if they were the girls Carol had called about. They nodded and stood up. "C'mon," she said.

"S'long, Mae," Frey called after them. "S'long, girls."

"You know what you can do, Bill," the blonde called back. She led them down the corridor to her door, opened it, and let them precede her. When she followed them inside, she left the door flung open behind her. The room was an old high-ceilinged office with a huge unshaded and uncurtained window that ran from floor to ceiling like a glass gash in the wall. Racks of colored dresses lined the gray room and gave the only brightness it had. Left of the window a shipping table, a desk with a telephone on the wall above it, and a sewing machine sat in a carefully shaped U, as if whoever sat at the desk in the center had fortified herself against attack from both sides. Except for a few cane-bottom chairs and a full-length mirror against the wall, the room was bare. Everything seemed dull, covered with a film of gray and mousy brown, as if the place had only been recently cleared of cobwebs that somehow had been rubbed into the walls for coloring.

Mae Rumage dropped her coat on a chair and Anna saw a mountainously fat woman in a tight black dress, obviously without underwear beneath. Embarrassed for her, Anna turned her eyes away. When she looked back, the older woman's bleached blonde head was tilted to one side, one of her eyes lost in the fat folds of her face, looking them over consideratively. For an instant Anna thought she might be winking. Then the woman said to Jessica, "What's your name?"

"I'm Mrs. Carruthers, and this . . . ."

". . . no, honey, your first name. We're friendly here."

"Jessica."

"And you?"

"Anna."

"Anna what?"

"Anna Townsend."

"You ain't no Missus." She said it as if she were certain, as if, unerringly, she knew that Anna was unmarried. She didn't even wait for Anna's corroborating nod. She simply knew.

"Okay," Mae said. "You can call me Mae. Anna, you stand over there. Jessica, you sit down here and I'll show you some of my pretties."

The dresses Mae had were lovely and she showed them to Jessica first, keeping up a running chatter with Anna while she did so. Jessica had warned Anna that they were to tell how poor they were because Mae always charged what the traffic would bear, and so, when Mae asked what they did, Anna told her they were poor social workers. No sooner were the words out of her mouth than Mae Rumage snapped her fat ringless fingers and said, "My God, I almost forgot. Glad you reminded me. You chickens will excuse me. I've got to make a call. I got to get my sister out of the bughouse. She was a little off her trolley, but they're letting her out tonight." Mae walked to the phone and then turned and called, "Say, one of you got some change?" Jessica gave her a dime, and for the first time Anna saw that it was a pay phone, looking incongruous on the wall.

When she had finished telephoning, Mae came to the racks where they were examining dresses, and said, "Well, chickens, do you like my dresses?"

"They're lovely," Jessica said.

"How about you?" Mae asked.

"Well, Mrs. Rumage. . . ."

"Call me Mae," she said, her voice commanding, not requesting. "What are you looking for?"

Anna told her about the red dress, trying to make it sound like a casual interest. She had seen a dress she wanted in a Fifty-seventh Street shop. When Mae asked where, Anna gave her the name of the place, saying that she hadn't bought the dress because it was too expensive. Jessica had suggested that perhaps Mae could get it wholesale for her, but Anna wasn't sure that she could.

"Of course I can get it," Mae said, looking insulted. "I've got special pull. I used to be a big-time model. I can get sample dresses from the best houses because they all know me." She patted her hair. "I can get any dress I want."

Anna gave her the rest of the details of the red dress, wondering all the while how such a mound of fat could ever have been a model. Yet, she did have a pleasant face, with good features under the fat, and perhaps her figure had once been good too. Her dark eyebrows and gray eyes were striking, almost hypnotic, and as Anna told her about the dress, she had the feeling that Mae sensed how important it really was to her, knew it in spite of the fact that Anna had spoken of it as matter-of-factly as possible, fighting the urgency she felt out of her voice.

When she was finished, Mae turned to Jessica. "You gonna try these on?"

Jessica nodded, still looking at the dresses she had picked from the racks.

"Well, go ahead then."

"Isn't there a dressing room?" Jessica asked.

"Do you see one?" Mae asked. "This is all there is." Majestically, she waved her arms around the room.

Jessica lifted her dress over her head, laid it carefully on a chair, and began to try on the dresses. Mae brought her others, recommending each in the most glowing terms, and, each time Jessica undressed, looked at her slim, high-breasted body with envious longing. Mae helped Jessica in and out of the dresses, touching her whenever she could. To Anna there was something sick and ugly about it, and the little remarks that accompanied the stroking. "You've got a lovely figure, chicken." "That's a good bustline, Jessica." "This one shows off your pretty hips." Jessica finally bought two dresses, a blue boucle and a bright plaid jersey, and looked lovely in both.

"And you?" Mae turned to her.

"I came for the red dress," Anna said. "I really can't afford any more."

"Don't you like my things?" Mae said, almost threateningly.

"Yes, I think they're lovely," Anna said, honestly, "but. . . ."

" . . . but me no buts." She drew two dresses from the racks and said, "Come on, try these. We'll find a couple just right for someone with your figure."

Reluctantly Anna took the two dresses from her hand, feeling that Mae wanted more to see her undressed than to have her buy the dresses. She took her jacket off, her blouse, and stepped out of her skirt, watching Mae's eyes as she stood there in half-slip and brassiere.

"You've got something there," Mae said admiringly, looking at her bust. "I used to look like that," she continued, as if waiting for someone to contradict her. Someone did.

"I'll bet you did, Mae, but that was sure a hell of a while ago."

Anna saw the detective, Frey, in the hallway, looking her up and down. "She's dead right though, sister. You sure got what it takes." In the air his hands made the rounded motions of breasts and hips, and Anna, suddenly aware, covered herself with a dress.

"On your way, Willie boy, before your eyes pop out of your face," Mae said. "G'wan now, save your buttons."

"If you ever change your mind about that drink," the detective invited Anna, "just let me know. Or you either," he turned gallantly to Jessica. He tipped his brown fedora, mock-bowed to Mae, and then they heard his heels clack down the corridor toward the elevator.

"Don't you think you ought to keep that door closed," Jessica said.

"Too stuffy in here. Ventilation's no good. Besides, nobody but Bill Frey and maybe that elevator boy passes."

"Is that all?" Anna said, trying for the right sarcastic tone, but Mae seemed to miss it.

Anna tried on one dress after another, feeling Mae's slithering hands helping her, holding her. She felt a sudden quaking terror, as if she was walking along a steep cliff in a heavy mist and couldn't see her way. She might walk off the edge and into the surf she was sure she heard surging against the rocks somewhere below, but she didn't know which way the lip of the precipice was and so she couldn't know how to turn. The hands always seemed to brush her naked skin, casually, helping her in and out of dresses, caressing her arm, her back, her shoulder, once just flicking the edge of her breast, almost probing into the recesses of her heart, so that it set the sound of surf going in her mind and in her flesh. Finally, almost without looking, and knowing that she couldn't afford it, Anna chose a green crepe with piqué collar and cuffs so that she could get it over with. Then she got back into her own suit.

After they had paid, Mae asked for a deposit on the red dress, but Anna had no money left. She knew she shouldn't have bought the green crepe; she hadn't wanted it, but because it seemed that Mae would never let her go and stop touching her until she bought something, she had taken it. Anna promised to mail her a check that evening and they left with the smell of Mae's ginny breath hanging in the corridor, and the sound of her "Goodbye dearies" following them to the elevator.

In the street Jessica broke into burst of laughter. "Why . . . why . . . you look like you've seen a ghost."

"I feel like it," Anna replied, trying to smile. Automatically, she looked up at the darkened building, where only one window was lighted. "Look!" she exclaimed, pointing to the lighted window of Mae Rumage's shop where big letters that ran horizontally across the middle of the window spelled out *DRESSES*, and smaller letters in the lower corner said *Rooms.* As they were watching, the window went dark.

"I wonder what that means," Jessica said. And, after a minute, "It was weird, Anna, wasn't it?"

"That's the understatement of the year."

"Did you see the way that detective leered at us. I thought he'd start drooling any minute," Jessica said, lapsing into helpless laughter.

"You expect that from him, but her." Anna shook inside as the prickling of her scalp and skin and the sound of the surf in her head ran through her. "How she touched me!"

"Me too. I thought she was enjoying it a little more than the line of duty called for," Jessica said soberly. "You think she's. . . ."

". . . I don't know what she is," Anna said, uneasy about being asked to label Mae Rumage. "But whatever she is, I don't like it. She frightens me."

"What's there to be afraid of because a fat old ex-model gives you a couple of pats? You get worse any morning in the subway rush."

"This is different, Jessie. This woman's—I don't know how to say it without sounding ridiculous, or hysterical—but she's evil."

"Whoa! Anna! That's pretty strong."

Anna didn't answer. The woman had some strange power, something she couldn't explain. The oddly clear gray eyes under the absurd black eyebrows, so unlikely in the fat, pleasant-looking face; those eyes and the power that leaped from the sloppy fat body made her take that green crepe, although she didn't need it and couldn't possibly afford it. Yet she had bought it. Why?

At the corner they waited for the light to change and when they started across the street, Mae's voice came suddenly from behind them. "Watch out for the cars, dearies. Don't get run over." They turned and saw her coming down the street, surprisingly light and swift. She waved and said, "And tell all the other girls about my beautiful dresses. Don't forget."

Together, like a small chorus, Anna and Jessica said in unison, "We won't," and then Mae had turned the other corner and disappeared into a doorway.

At her apartment, Anna was too unnerved to prepare or eat dinner. Something was racing inside her like a car with its brakes on. Instead of eating, she poured herself a whisky to quiet her nerves and sat down in the living room to figure it out. Between sips of whisky she told herself that she was acting like a child, giving in to a whim about a dress and frightened of a harmless fat old lady. Let's break this down, and analyze this, she told herself. What's bothering me anyway? I don't really need that red dress any more than I needed the green crepe. What's more, I can't afford either of them. But I want it, the racing inside of her purred. But why? she asked herself, despairing of an answer. I want it and that's all, the racing said firmly, brooking neither question nor argument. Because she was unused to drinking, the whisky fogged her brain, and just before she fell into unquiet sleep, Anna wondered what was happening to her.

The next day Anna had the afternoon off, for she was on night duty on Friday, so she went shopping. She ransacked the small shops and the big department stores, but she couldn't find the red dress, and she hated herself while she searched. When she got back to her apartment, she was exhausted but she kept seeing the red dress flowing silkily against her body. When she awoke the next morning she felt as if she had not slept. She had had nightmares but what they were she couldn't recall, and she remembered she had forgotten to mail the deposit check to Mae Rumage. At lunch, Anna called and told Mae the check would be in the mail that afternoon.

"I'm sure glad you called, dearie, because I found that dress. Just like I said I would. I thought maybe you forgot."

"No, I didn't forget," Anna said, trying to be casual but hearing her own eagerness. "When can you have it for me?"

"If I get that check tomorrow, I'll have it in a day or two."

"Are you sure?"

"Soon as I get it, I'll call you. But first you mail that check," Mae said, businesslike.

Although she mailed the check that evening, it wasn't until Friday that Mae called. It was late in the afternoon, almost four, when the switchboard operator called Anna to say a Mrs. Rumage was on the phone. "Hello, Anna?" Mae's voice was metallic and distant.

"Mae? This is Anna. Have you got the dress?"

"Sure. I got your size too, so we won't need to alter it. You bring fifty bucks and it's all yours."

"But I sent you a check for twenty-five."

"The dress is seventy-five, and that's a good price. If you want it, come right away."

"I can't. I work late tonight, until eight."

"Bring cash."

"Where'll I get cash now? The banks are closed. Can't you take my check?"

"Cash, or no dress."

"Where will I get it?" Anna wailed, hating herself for not saying never mind the dress, and for the subterranean cry in her voice.

"Borrow it. Ask the girls. You want the dress, get the cash."

"All right, Mae," Anna said wearily, "I'll be there."

It took her until the time she left to get the fifty dollars. Anna was embarrassed, but she borrowed from the switchboard operator, from another of the social workers, from one of the residents she knew well and from an interne she didn't know at all, and even from Fannie, the washwoman.

When she finally got up to Mae's, it was very dark. Mae's window was lit, illuminating sharply the words *DRESSES* and *Rooms,* so that they seemed to have been carved into the light. The elevators were not running and Anna had to walk up the five flights, holding herself from rushing, because even if she couldn't wait for the red dress, something inside her knew that she must not let herself be carried away. She passed William Frey's *Executive Surveys* and smiled when she saw the light dim from the second room, with the bed and the liquor buffet. He didn't believe in working late he had told her, nine to five for him.

Mae's door was open and when Anna walked in there was only a little dark-haired woman sitting at the shipping table, carefully wrapping dresses. "Hello," Anna said, "is Mae in?" The woman did not look up. Her face was blank, the black eyes remote and expressionless, the mouth an unsmiling line. She said nothing, but she went on wrapping. Schiz, if I ever saw one, Anna thought, picturing the ones she had known. She remembered Mae's phone call the day she and Jessica had been there. This must be her sister, the one she was getting out of the "bughouse," Anna speculated. The woman didn't look like she should have been let out. She went on packing. She picked up a dress, folded it neatly into a cardboard box she took from the floor next to her, closed the box, and tied it with cord. As she finished tying each box, she snapped the cord between her fingers, her knuckles going white with the effort, but separating the cord from the spool before she dropped the finished box into a pile on her other side. Everything was in its place: a pile of dresses on the table, a pile of boxes on the floor, a roll of cord next to the dresses, all in easy reach. Watching made Anna nervous and she took out a pack of cigarettes and offered one, but the woman did not even acknowledge the existence of her outstretched hand.

"Well, if it isn't Anna." The booming voice behind her was close and Anna dropped the cigarette she had begun to light. It was Mae. "I didn't think you'd get here." Abruptly, as Anna was bending to pick up the cigarette, and almost leaping from place to place, Mae began to show her dresses, one after the other, style after style, color after color: blues and greens and yellows and reds, seeming to bring the clothes not only from the racks, but from the floors and walls and ceiling, and even out of her own big flabby body. Mae's black brows were unruffled but her gray eyes were shining with excitement and there was a film of sweat beaded on her upper lip as she displayed dress after dress. "The finest gowns in town. From the best places. You can see the labels." But Anna didn't see a single label. Every dress was placed against Mae's huge body so that each seemed slender against the gross black-dressed bulk behind. Each dress was the most beautiful, the one for her, Mae assured Anna, just what she needed to show off her best features. And with each Mae asked in an urgent, sensuous voice, "Aren't they beautiful? Have you ever seen such pretties? They're so lovely, my gowns, the loveliest," commanding appreciation, demanding response.

"Stop. Please stop," Anna cried, surprised at the loudness and intensity of her voice in the quiet room. "Don't show me any others. Please. I can't afford another dress. I can't afford any dress. I only want the red one and that's all."

There was a moment of silence and Mae said threateningly, "Don't you like my things?"

"Of course I do, but I can't possibly afford them."

Mae looked at her as if stunned, and then, curiously reasonable, said, "You don't have a chance to wear many clothes in your job, do you? What did you say you do?" Anna told her about social work. Mae kept plying her with questions, some she had asked before, some she kept repeating two or three times, sometimes at intervals, other times in succession. Where do you work? What do you do? Do you like to go out? Do you go many places? Where? Do you like pretty clothes? Do you have a nice apartment? Anna listened to herself giving Mae answers, picturing herself as a deprived unhappy girl who wanted another life, a life filled with going out and fashionable apartments and a red dress, and all the while she heard these answers, as if another distant, yet intimate, part of her spoke for all of her, Anna wanted to cry out, "I'm not like that at all. That's not what I want. I've got a good and full life." But somewhere the cry was stifled inside her. Mae stood there listening, nodding her head understandingly, but Anna saw the calm gray eyes measuring her, estimating her.

When Mae spoke, her voice was like oil on waves, soothing and deceptively calm. "I like you," she said, her eyes widening until the pupils looked large and blacker. "Maybe I'll give you some of my dirtied and mussed-up dresses for free."

"No. You mustn't do that," Anna said, feeling like a fool and a liar for having painted a picture of herself and her life that was so untrue. It was as if there were things she was feeling for and did not grasp, as if she was stumbling forward for solid ground that she would never again walk on, and she felt she was falling into the bizarre depths of those gray eyes and widening dark pupils, depths in herself from which she could never return.

"Now don't you worry, dearie. I like you and when I like someone, I like them. You want pretty things, don't you?" Mae asked for the fifth or sixth time, and, not waiting Anna's answer, plunged ahead. "Look, I tell you what. I've got a friend who has lots of nice clothes and wants to give them to someone nice . . . like you."

"How about my red dress?" Anna asked.

"Oh that," Mae said, casually turning to her desk. "I didn't expect you with the money. That rich friend of mine came up this afternoon and she liked it so much, I sold it to her."

"You sold it!" Anna gasped, her breath hard and panting.

"Don't worry, chicken. My friend'll give it back to you for nothing. Save you fifty bucks. She never wears a dress more than once or twice anyway. She'll give you the red dress and lots of other pretty things. She'll like you."

"You sold it," Anna repeated. "You sold *my* red dress."

"Now here, I'll write you a note and you can run right over and get it tonight. My friend won't mind. She lives down at the Hotel Germania. It's only a few blocks away. Her name's Mrs. Burtis." She sat down at the desk and began to write. She looked up at her sister for a moment and asked, "Say, Lydia, what's Mrs. Burtis's room number? And her first name?" Lydia didn't answer but went on with the automatic movements of packing dresses. She seemed not to have heard. Mae twisted her head to look at Anna. "Doesn't know a damn thing. She might as well be dead." Then she turned back and began to write again.

Lydia, Anna thought, what a beautiful name. A name to wear with that red dress. Lydia.

Mae got up and handed her a note on her business stationery, neat gray bond paper, the left side embossed with MAE RUMAGE'S EXCLUSIVE CREATIONS, the right side with a neat column of four words: *Dresses, Coats, Suits, Gowns.* On the paper Mae had written in a big green ink scrawl: "Give the things to this nice girl." Mae was still talking but Anna could hear her only as if her voice was coming through cotton stuffed in her ears, or over the telephone on a very long distance call where the voice grows softly blurred and the words indistinct. She was saying: "You walk down to the Germania and the doorman in front of the hotel will be there. Ask him for Mrs. Burtis. He'll say he doesn't remember her, that there are a lot of Mrs. Burtises, and you'll answer that there's only one Mrs. Burtis. Then he'll give you her room number. I forget the number but it's on the ninth floor."

While Mae went on talking, Anna stared at the note. Why this sounds like a password, she thought. And this Mrs. Burtis thing, with the doorman, and my red dress, and the free clothing, and the ninth floor, and my red dress . . . why, it's all insane. Abruptly, she cut short Mae's flow of talk. "No. I couldn't go to anyone's apartment for clothes."

Mae stopped and stared for a moment, and then, in a sudden springing movement, she tore the green inked note from Anna's hand. Mae almost ran to the far side of the room and when she turned, her face twisted and her body shaking as if with sobs, she shouted, "You don't have to! You don't have to!" In slow, deliberate movements, almost like her sister's, she tore the note and let the shreds float to the floor in front of her, a little white puddle. They stood there for minutes, silent, facing each other across the room, the only sounds coming from the rustling movements of Lydia's packing. And then came the snapping of the cord as Lydia broke it between her fingers, and the sound of it was an outcry in Anna's heart.

When next she remembered, Anna was at the opposite end of the hall, past the elevator, facing a glazed door that read *Equity Company*. She turned back to the elevator and rang the buzzer furiously, again and again. It wasn't until she heard noises from Frey's office and from Mae's that she remembered the elevators were not running. She walked down the stairs, barely keeping from flinging herself down headlong. In the darkened streets she wandered, unable to tell which direction she was moving in, walking until her aching mind and her aching feet reminded her that it was time to go home. A policeman was standing at the corner and Anna went up to him. "Which way is east?" she asked. "I want to take a bus crosstown to the East Side."

The policeman looked at her and pointed a gray-gloved hand. "That way. There's a bus stop right here, but go up to the next one." He smiled and went on kindly. "Funny things happen in this neighborhood sometimes and it won't do for a young girl like you to wait in the dark. You'll be better off walking the few blocks and waiting in the light."

Anna thanked him and walked blindly off in the direction he had pointed when she saw she was on the same street Mae's building was on. She passed it, frightened by its face, thin and long, crowded between buildings, its sides pressed together as if in a vice. When she looked up she saw Mae's light on and the letters *DRESSES* and *Rooms,* only this time, without a moment's reflection, she knew what they meant. She remembered that she had left the deposit on the red dress with Mae and was about to cross the street when she saw the dark brows and gray eyes, the shreds of paper floating to the floor and the beauty of the red dress, and she heard the strange loveliness of the name Lydia. In the distance ahead of her, squatting on the ground in a patch of light from the street overhead, she could see a bus sign, looking like an outlandish marker, a black and white arrow stuck in the concrete, and she made herself walk toward it, thinking all the time of the dress, the dress. And then, suddenly and impulsively, she was walking back down the street toward Mae's, and as she saw the face of the building staring down at her, rigid and disapproving, she knew she had returned for the red dress.

Janet Beeler Shaw

A New Life

Ronna told Kristin that it was time for them to give up caffeine, to cut down on grass, wine, french fries, to shape up, join a gym. In fact, to join The Limberyard, which was right down the highway from Kansas City Mutual Insurance, where they both worked in the mailroom. "Now's the time," Ronna said. "The big three-O is coming up for us both. We've got to save what we can before it's too late." Kristin thought maybe it was already too late. Ronna insisted. "We've got to take control here as a team." Kristin let Ronna talk her into buying a shiny black leotard and black tights just like Ronna's. "Wonderwomen," Ronna said, and signed them up for a trial run at the gym.

"I'm too skimpy for this gear." Kristin pulled a strand of her blonde hair across her lips and tasted balsam. Without looking in the mirror, she knew that her shoulder blades and the sharp bones in her hips stuck out. "There aren't any men here, are there?"

"What guy would come to a place called The Limberyard? Too bad, you could show off your classy rear." Ronna patted her own. "Mellow out now, and let's pump some iron."

Dressed in her new gym outfit and her old running Nikes, Kristin followed Ronna into the mirror-walled gym, where the thick, warm air smelled of sweat and a gardenia-scented chemical deodorizer. Over the loudspeaker a Ramones tape howled. A gray-haired woman in faded blue sweats and a red bandanna pumped a chrome machine known as a pec-deck. A tall woman hauled down the bar of the tricep-pushdown; her narrow nose and thin lips reminded Kristin of her mother's face, though Kristin could imagine the disdain her mother would have had for this place. The women on her mother's side had lived on farms and raised large families; they worked, they didn't work out. But, like Ronna, these women in the gym seemed full of energy and purpose. Maybe Kristin would catch it.

"Where do we start?" Kristin said.

"Don't you love it?" Ronna flung herself onto the sit-up bench. Her face was flushed, her forehead and arms gleamed as if she'd already been exercising.

Kristin crouched in front of the squat machine. She slipped her shoulders under the padded bar, as she'd seen the woman in the bandanna do, but when she tried to stand her legs trembled.

The gym instructor's husky command came from somewhere behind her. "Blow the weight up, honey. Breathe deep, then blow out."

Kristin blew, pushed, stood. It was a small victory, but she needed it. Anyway, this would be something to do. She wanted to keep busy, very busy.

After their workout, Kristin and Ronna showered, dried off, then sat in the sauna. Ronna squeezed water from her thick, dark hair onto the sauna floor. "I can't resist joining up, can you?"

"Something about it depresses me."

"Everything depresses you. You are basically a depressed sort of chick. That's what I'm trying to spring you out of."

"I don't like lying around in someone else's sweat," Kristin said.

Ronna tucked the top of her towel under her arm. "All you're talking here is damp orange vinyl. There's no place you can go somebody else hasn't already been, toots. We're all just passing around used goods."

Of course Ronna said that because her lover was married, but Kristin pushed her. "How about all *your* talk of a fresh start, then?"

"Everything is relative." She tossed back her hair and left Kristin alone in the pine-scented cave of the sauna.

By the time Kristin dressed and got upstairs to the desk, Ronna was already signing her contract, the instructor in her pink sweatshirt looking on. "Can't you hurry a little?" Ronna said to Kristin. "It's *Tuesday,* remember?"

Maybe it was because Ronna rushed her that Kristin signed her maiden name to her contract. She had to study the name a moment to realize that it was hers, the way she was sometimes startled to recognize that troubled, pensive face in a store window as her own. Kristin McKenna—she let it stand. Why not, if she was beginning a new life?

Driving them in her Fiesta to the parking lot of Shopmore, Ronna broke the speed limit twice. She had arranged for Kristin to meet Gene today. After work one afternoon, over beers at the Laurel Tap, Ronna had confessed to her affair with him. He worked nights on the police force; his wife, Sally, worked half-days as a legal aide. So the only sure time he and Ronna could get together was late afternoon. "We're crazy about each other," Ronna said. "But of course it's awful hard for us to have any kind of normal relationship. For example, he'd like to meet my friends. You're the only one I think would understand. You're older than the other girls, experiencewise." As much out of curiosity as to please Ronna, Kristin had agreed to the meeting.

Ronna parked by the bags of peat moss and the flats of tomato and onion sets. The sweet, rotting scent of fertilizer bloomed in the April sun as they waited. Then a blue Chevy wagon pulled up nearby, and a man jumped out and made his way to them between crates of potting soil. He was wiry, with thinning brown hair, glasses, an inch of beard. His shirt-sleeves were rolled up, and across his chest in a denim baby sling rode a plump-armed blonde baby, cheek pressed against the work shirt.

"He's got a child?" Kristin said.

"He was going to leave her for me, but damn if she didn't get pregnant! It killed me." Ronna's chin puckered and a rash flared on her throat as though she would cry, but she called, "Hi, sweetie!"

Then Gene was at Kristin's window. She saw a reflection of her face swim on the surface of his glasses. After a quick, assessing glance, he reached past her to grab Ronna's outstretched hand.

Ronna made a kissing sound. "Meet my pal Kristin. This is Gene Jacobson."

"I've heard about you," he said. "Ronna says you're the greatest. You really looked after her when she got this job."

Kristin touched the baby's soft arm tentatively. "Who's this?"

"Tim. Six months of relentless energy."

She looked for a moment at the carefully trimmed line of Gene's moustache, and then the baby turned his head and fixed her with his solemn gaze. His pudgy fist closed on a loose strand of her hair. When he pulled her head closer, she inhaled a sweet mix of soap, baby oil, and clean baby sweat. Blue veins threaded under the translucent skin at his temples. "Hello, Tim," she said softly.

The baby's delicately arched lips opened, but he made no sound. With her hand, she encircled the small fist entangled in her hair. His fingers felt like miniature shrimps.

"He's crazy about blondes," Gene said.

"His mother's blonde," Ronna said. "So I've heard."

"Want to hold him?" Gene asked.

As though they'd rehearsed the moves, Gene opened the door and Kristin held up her arms; he slipped off the sling and handed her the baby.

"Hop in," Ronna told Gene. "Let's go get us a soft drink." Then he was in the back seat, his hand on Ronna's shoulder, and they were driving north past the beltline.

The baby lay on his back in Kristin's lap. When she bent over he grabbed her hair in both his hands. "Tim." The ping of his name on the roof of her mouth pleased her. Guiltily — why would she think such a thing? — she imagined laying her lips on his. She would taste the freshness of his skin.

When she glanced up again Gene was leaning forward and joking with Ronna about a guy on the force who'd been ordered to knock off twenty pounds.

Ronna had told Kristin that Gene was her hero. She lived with her mom, so to be alone she and Gene drove off into the country and made love in the wheatfields or under the cottonwoods by the river. When he could get away, now and then, for a whole afternoon, he packed them a picnic of smoked turkey, deviled eggs, and beer, and they went to a motel on the beltline. Sometimes they took fancy underwear for her, kimonos for them both, cowboy boots. He's a wild man, Ronna said.

Gene pushed up his glasses and rubbed his eyes as though his head ached. The bridge of his nose was sunburned and peeling. "How'd you get in the mailroom game, Kristin?"

"I was teaching third grade at St. Thomas, but I got laid off. Lewis, my husband, taught math in the high school. Math's more secure these days."

"Have you got kids of your own?"

"She was widowed. I told you that." Ronna cut a corner close to swing into the carhop section of an A & W on the outskirts of town.

"I'm sorry. I just thought she might have kids. She seems to like Tim." Gene dropped his glasses back into place. Through the lenses his eyes were larger, their blue darker.

"It's okay," Kristin said.

"Not all of us *want* kids." Ronna yanked off the lavender plastic headband that matched her T-shirt and tossed it onto the dash. "Three root beers," she told the carhop.

"Take it easy." Gene stroked Ronna's throat. "Hey, your hair's damp."

Ronna let her head fall back, trapping his hand. "We joined a gym today. If we don't look after ourselves, no one else will." She'd told Kristin that she had been on her own since high school. Before moving back home she'd hitchhiked all over the West, working in Arizona as a short-order cook and in Utah as a ranch hand. She had gone to a junior college for a semester but had dropped out. "It was all baloney," she said of her college days. "I don't know how you lasted so long, Kristin. It's all hot air. With a diploma and half a buck you can get a cup of coffee." It looked as if she were right. Here was Kristin, sorting mail too, and although Ronna had her adventures to look back on, Kristin had only five years of scholastic drudgery and three years in a tiny grade school. And Lewis.

Kristin leaned down over Tim again. He gazed at her without blinking. Something about the baby made her think of Lewis—Lewis at the last, anyway, in the hospital. He'd curled into the fetal position, his knees to his chin. Meningitis, the doctor said. When the resident brought his sterile tray to give Lewis a spinal tap, the instruments had spilled onto the floor. The syringe rolled under the bed. Kristin ducked down and took it in her hand; had they chosen this enormous one because Lewis was so tall? She wanted to ask, but she was crying, and the doctor told her to wait outside. After Lewis died, she decided she was through with love. The pain of it spread out around her on all sides, like deep water difficult to move through.

Tim pummeled her stomach with his kicks, waved his arms. Ronna finished her root beer and handed the baby sling to Kristin. "Since you two get along so well, how'd you like to take him in that park for a while so Gene and I can take a ride and talk things over?"

Gene looked down into his empty glass mug. If they had set her up, Kristin didn't mind. The small park next to the A & W was filled with young mothers in jeans and kids playing on the swings and the jungle gym. It was better than going back to her little apartment alone.

"Does he have a bottle?" As she asked, she realized she'd made a choice, though she wasn't sure what she'd chosen.

Gene handed her a quilted plastic shoulder bag. "Seems like you know what to do."

"You're a living doll." Ronna patted Kristin's thigh.

Letting herself out of the car, she forgot to ask when they'd come back. She turned, but Ronna was already driving off, white dust spinning up behind her wheels. It was Gene who waved goodbye.

She was alone with the baby. The wind off the plains tossed the silvery cottonwood leaves. On the benches under the trees the mothers chatted and laughed. One nursed her baby under her shirt. When Kristin walked over they smiled, asked about her child. He nuzzled her shoulder, the damp circle where his mouth rested growing larger. Watching crows fill the pines along the field, she leaned back on the bench, the baby's weight a radiant warmth across her breasts.

The late afternoon shadows on the wheatfield beyond the pines reminded her of the farm. She'd lain on the porch roof and pretended the house was a ship sailing across the waves of wheat. Her mother raised four children there. If you had a child to care for, days took shape, simplified, held their own meaning.

The baby slept, and perhaps she did, too, though she heard the voices of women and children all around her. When he woke she gave him his bottle of orange juice, cradling him across her lap as the woman next to her held her child.

When Gene called to her she looked up, startled. He came from Ronna's red car across the park. She got up quickly, slung the bag over one shoulder, cuddled Tim on the other. "Are you okay?" he asked.

She nodded. Perhaps she had slept; she felt dizzy—though maybe that was from the exercise and the fresh air.

"I mean about this babysitting. Ronna can be pushy."

"I can take care of myself."

But, as though she needed protection, he took her elbow and they went to join Ronna, who rested behind the steering wheel with her head tipped back. She blinked up at Kristin with a dazed, satisfied frown. "How's your little boyfriend?"

On Tuesdays and Thursdays after work Ronna and Kristin met Gene at Shopmore. If the weather was good, Ronna and Gene went off in his wagon, and Kristin took Tim in the Fiesta to the park. If it was rainy, she took him into Shopmore, pushed him slowly up and down the aisles, stopped to sit in the cafeteria section. There she held him on her lap and taught him to hang onto her fingers, to pull up. He pushed his face against hers, his lips on her cheek. Soon he'd be talking. She'd teach him the names of things, her own name. She bought a book, *You and Your Baby*. On Mondays and Wednesdays after work she and Ronna went to the gym.

Ronna was doing crunchies on the inclined board, her gold chain with its teardrop charm swinging behind her as she raised herself, elbows to her knees. She'd braided her hair. She looked Indian, tanned already, although it was only May. "I wish I still smoked." She watched Kristin sideways.

Her knees cracking, Kristin did deep knee bends with a weighted bar. "But look what good shape you're getting in."

"I need something for my nerves."

"What's wrong with your nerves?" Kristin didn't speak to Ronna of her own. Lewis had been dead for over a year now, but still she often woke before light, her heart crashing. Something was wrong, something that couldn't be fixed, but she was unable for an awful moment to remember. Then, when she *knew,* no matter how she tried to arrange the pillows, she was unable to sleep again. More than anything else, she missed sleeping with him, curled against his long back, her arm over his side, her knees tucked behind his. It had been such a safe place. These days she gave up, fixed her breakfast, and thought of where she might take Tim; maybe there was somewhere she could show him puppies, kittens, ducks, some of the animals she grew up with on the farm.

Ronna lay back and chewed on the end of her braid. Upside down her face looked childlike, unformed. Kristin kept up her slow rhythm of lifting while Ronna talked.

"Sally's giving Gene grief about what does he do with Tim, where does he go, who does he see. Gene says it's hard to get away. Not that Sally's so crazy about having a baby. 'You were the one who wanted him,' she tells Gene. 'You take care of him. He's yours.' So he says. When she got pregnant, she said she wanted an abortion. But he said he couldn't live with that. So now she expects him to take Tim all his free time. It's wearing him down. Like, he's just burned out on these quickie meetings of ours. I tell him we should get married. He says he *is* married. He says he'd like to build another room on his house for me! It's all such a dead end. At first I thought I'd do anything for him, like I'd lie down and die if he asked me. But I'm coming apart. What do you think, Kristin?"

Kristin didn't answer. A fist of anxiety blocked her chest. How would she see Tim?

Ronna reached back and grabbed Kristin's ankle. "Hey, don't be so sad for me. Wonderwomen, remember?"

When Kristin caught her breath, she said, "That's a comic strip, Ronna. I don't hear us laughing."

Kristin crossed the gym to ride an exercycle. She pedaled fast, pumping heat fiercely into her chest. She could bike all the way across the plains and over the mountains, a single, long, ferocious effort all this exercising and clean living had prepared her for. She could swing Tim onto her back and run away.

How had it happened that she loved this baby? She wasn't the kind even to notice other women's kids. The subject of children had barely come up between her and Lewis. First they'd had to get through college, then they'd needed jobs. They spoke of a family as something they'd attempt when they had some savings, maybe even a place of their own. And, after all, they both worked with kids all day. But none of those she'd taught had ever seized her heart. Tim was the only one to do that. She loved a child who wasn't hers and she wanted *him*. Not another. Oh, god.

On the way to meet Gene at Shopmore the next day, Kristin offered Ronna the use of her apartment for their meetings. "It's homier, and it's close by. You'll have more privacy. I put out clean towels."

Ronna teared up. "You are a goddamned sister, you know that? What can I do for you?"

"Take some hamburger out of my freezer to defrost, if you think of it. That's plenty. Let's not talk about it."

Ronna grabbed her hand. "I'll get Gene to start your supper for you. He owes you, too, and anyway, he loves to cook. He should have been a mother. When we go to a motel he always wipes out the washbasin so the maid won't find it watermarked."

Kristin slid the house key into Ronna's shoulder bag. "You think he'll go for this?"

"Will he ever!"

When Kristin let herself in that evening she smelled onions, tomatoes, browned beef. Rice steamed in a separate pan. A damp towel was folded and laid on the bathroom hamper. The bed was made. Maybe it hadn't been unmade. Maybe they had spread the quilt on the floor, as she and Lewis had done on summer afternoons. She didn't want to think about it. She had enough beef and rice for two nights, and reheated it tasted even better. On Thursday she left chicken in the refrigerator and found a fricassee waiting for her.

Except for the delicious meals Gene made, and an occasional damp towel, she never saw signs that they'd used her place. Of course, Gene was a cop. Maybe he checked out the room, put everything back exactly where it had been, and picked up after Ronna, who habitually left hamburger wrappers and soda cans on the floor of her car until Kristin threw them into a dumpster. It was almost as though they hadn't been there at all.

Kristin, Gene, and the baby waited in Ronna's car while Ronna ran into Shopmore for shampoo and hand lotion. The day was hot, and Kristin sat sideways in the back seat, her legs stretched out, Tim dozing in her lap. Gene watched Ronna hurrying between cars and vans in her denim skirt and red T-shirt; then he turned and slung his arm along the back of the seat. "That old photograph over your rocking chair. I like it."

It occurred to Kristin that she and Gene had never been alone before. "That's my grandma and her sister. That's her sewing rocker, too. They lived on a farm next to ours up north of here. I think of their place when I'm in the park with Tim. I remember the way the wind blew day and night, and the shapes of the clouds, like fat animals in the sky." That she had said so much surprised her. She looked down at the sleeping child in her lap, the pearly sweat on his temples.

After a moment Gene said, "The cut-glass pitcher is nice, too."

"That was a wedding gift."

"I don't suppose you want to talk about your husband."

"I don't mind." He hadn't asked about her life before; she liked it.

"You probably miss him a lot."

"I miss the way I felt with him."

"Which was?"

He was watching her so closely that she looked out the window at the stream of cars pushing along the highway. "Quiet, I guess. We worried about things, of course, but as it turned out they were the wrong things." Then, with alarm, she heard herself ask — either to change the subject, or because she wanted to know — "How do you manage all this?"

"You mean Ronna?" When he smiled he looked less tired, younger. "Two lives."

"It's pretty much a mess. I want you to know that I *know* that."

When she didn't respond, he went on. "I've made some dumb choices, but I'm not dumb."

The drone of the traffic was a dull roar like the wind. A line of clouds moved seamlessly across the rolling hills beyond the shopping center.

"We shouldn't have gotten you into this," he said.

"What you do is your own business."

"I mean involved with us. You're not the kind."

She wished he would look away. She felt color rush to her forehead and cheeks. "I'm not involved, actually." Was she? Was she an accomplice, as they said in the movies? And maybe, in spite of what he said, she *was* the type. If you want to know someone, you watch what they do.

"You're a sweet lady," he said. Then he reached to open Ronna's door for her. As Ronna pushed her bag into the front seat, he went on, "Who did you say you were seeing now?"

"She picks up guys now and then." Ronna winked at Kristin in the rearview mirror. "They go for tall, blonde types. Short, dark chicks like me don't do so well."

"You're doing fine," Gene said to her.

When Kristin got home that evening, she found a pan of brownies cooling on the counter.

"He says I'm doing fine, but I'm *not* doing fine! I'm doing lousy!" Ronna had cried for a long time in the parking lot outside The Limberyard. Now she was inside, doing sit-ups and sniffing.

Stretching her hamstrings, Kristin lay beside her on the orange and green flecked carpet. "If you don't feel so good, we could leave."

"Do you think I care if I cry here? Who do you think I am, anyway, to care about what other broads think? You think *they* don't cry? This is a totally rotten life, and you know it as well as I do." Her face was swollen and splotchy, but she kept at the sit-ups, her braids swinging.

"Take it easy."

"I knew this was going to happen, that's what kills me! I predicted it!"

"Predicted what, exactly?"

"What I haven't told you. Gene says he doesn't see how things can go on between us. He says there's too much guilt for him in this sneaking around. Suddenly it's guilt! Where was his guilt when he was so horny last winter? What he means is that it's over."

Kristin pressed her forehead to her knee and closed her eyes. She let her breath out slowly. "Over? Just like that?"

"Two years of my life, two years and a half, I've given to that bastard!"

"But how can it be over?" Kristin was afraid to look at Ronna. She looked instead at her own pale, triangular face in the gym mirror. Take it easy, she told herself. But she was scared. Her neediness made her light-headed. Her ears buzzed, as though she'd drunk wine on an empty stomach.

"Well, maybe it's not completely over. He says he'll meet me today to talk it through." Ronna pushed up on one elbow, tears running down beside her nose. "I know this isn't our usual time, but please say you can babysit."

When they met Gene at Shopmore, Ronna had herself under control again. After her shower she'd smoothed on herbal lotion and pulled on new underwear, skin-colored and shiny. She dried her hair under the blower and threaded gold hoops in her ears. "Hi, honey," she called to Gene.

"Looks like rain." He bent to Ronna's window. "Let's get going."

Clouds massed in the west. Wind blew grit up from the parking lot, flinging it against the windshield. Gene had Tim's head covered with a blue blanket.

When Kristin held out her arms for the baby, Gene asked, "Where will you wait out the storm?"

"Here. If it passes over, I'll go to the park." She didn't look at him; she watched the rosy, smiling face of Tim, who reached for her, clung to her neck.

Gene fastened the car seat he always brought with him now. Marks the color of the clouds slanted below his eyes, as though he'd had trouble sleeping. Ronna jumped out, holding her skirt down, and ran to the station wagon, her gold hoops swinging.

Through a film of dust coating her windows, Kristin watched until Gene pulled away. Ronna was shaking her head, gesturing as though tearing cobwebs. Like the roof of an army tent, the khaki clouds sank lower. But Kristin headed for the park. She wanted the open space around her.

In early June the side ditches were already choked with Johnson grass and cockleburs, the pine tassels releasing their pollen into the wind like green smoke. Now and then a shaft of sun struck through the boiling clouds to pick out the tin roof of a silo. She drove beyond the farmsteads and into the prairie, which seemed to move eastward under the wind. It came to her that she was searching for her own house, though the place had long ago been torn down. All that would be left was a well cover and a windmill in the corner of some wheat or corn field. And wasn't it farther out, almost to Cross Plains? She hadn't been there since they'd moved to town, her senior year in high school, but in her mind she clearly saw the weathered gray house with its long porch, the collie sleeping under the ragged lilacs, the copse of black alder where she and her sisters played dolls. In the side yard her grandmother, in a flowered cotton dress, swung a chicken around her head to wring its neck. In the flat light of the kitchen her mother blanched and peeled canning tomatoes, squeezing seeds into a blue-speckled bowl. They did not talk while they worked, and they worked all day and into the long evenings. They were sturdy, joyless women. What needs they'd had of their own Kristin had never heard acknowledged. They were women without illusions who could not abide ambiguity. How had her own life become so confused and uncertain? She turned the Fiesta around in a lane and headed back to the park.

When she reached it, she pulled into the empty lot and kissed the top of Tim's head where his blonde, downy hair was damp, laid her cheek there. She felt as though her ribs had cracked, each breath pushing a shard of bone into her lungs. She recognized the pain: she was mourning, whether for the baby or for her own lost clarity and sureness she couldn't decide. "Let's get going," she said aloud, and lifted Tim from his seat.

The wind was a strong, steady hand on her back. It pushed her toward the pines, and when she'd crossed the ditch there it pushed her out until she was knee deep in the green wheat. All around the earth stretched out like a firm floor, but she thought now that the ancient explanations were truer: although the world looked wide enough, if you weren't careful you could fall off the edge. Monsters would eat you. You had to be very careful, and who knew what precautions would serve? Tim hung onto the collar of her plaid blouse, his large eyes narrowed against the wind. "Never play with matches," she said to him. "Don't run into the street. *Remember.*" But who can be another's protection from the interior dangers, which can't even be imagined until suddenly they are right there, close enough to touch?

Rain spattered across the wheat like buckshot. As she turned to run back, she saw that Gene's station wagon was in the parking lot, and that he waited for her in the passenger seat of the Fiesta. She threw Tim's blanket on him, bent over him as she ran. By the time she leaped into the car, her hair was plastered to her head, her face was wet, water streamed from her bare arms. When she unbundled Tim, he started to cry irritably—wet, cross, and teething. She offered him to Gene, but he shook his head, so she bounced the baby on her shoulder. "Poor little fellow," she crooned.

Gene leaned forward on the dashboard, resting his chin on his arms. Mascara was smeared like an oil stain on his collar. He slipped his glasses into his pocket and pressed his fingertips to his eyelids. "I broke it off with Ronna. She wanted me to take her home. She said you could bring her car by later."

Her chest collapsed from letting out a long breath. She had to comb her wet hair off her forehead with her fingers in order to see his face.

He scrubbed his eyes with the backs of his hands. "I used to think of myself as a good man."

"It's a hard time," she said cautiously. Tim was quieting, sucking his thumb.

"I've hurt people. I'm sorry for that. I told Ronna I was sorry."

"I don't imagine that helped much."

He looked at her as if she'd slapped him. Maybe she had. "No, it didn't help. But I'm going to straighten things out."

"Sometimes life just won't straighten out." She spoke against Tim's head.

"You sound shaky."

"It's just I'm so tired." Rain flooded over the roof of the car, battered the puddles that had already made a pewter lake of the gravel lot. Wheat lay dark and flat all the way to the horizon.

"I'd feel so much better if I could help you, Kristin. You deserve help."

"I get along—"

"We'll go to your place, the three of us, and I'll fix us some dinner."

"Your wife—"

"She's at an office party. I bought some rib-eye steaks for us, and you can fix a salad. You've got lettuce and sprouts."

So he'd worked it out. All of it. She imagined the three of them in her small kitchen, Tim in his seat, she and Gene at the round table, their plates heaped with steak, mashed potatoes, butter beans. Rain would drip from the eaves, squirrels scutter across the balcony, night come slowly on. A happy family scene.

Tim began to cry again, banging his head against her shoulder. He wanted his bottle, his supper, and to be put to bed. In her apartment, she and Gene would be alone while the child slept. "It's late for him," she said.

"A quiet supper is all." As though he had lost his balance, he leaned to her suddenly and brushed her cheek with his lips.

Her throat ached—to be held again. To have the baby near. Gene's thumb traced her chin, radiating a complicated pain.

"I'll follow you back. Drive careful," he whispered. "We all need a rest."

He opened his door, letting in a gust of wet wind that smelled of onion grass and mint. But she caught his arm. Quick, she told herself. Quick! Don't think about it. She handed Gene the baby, began pushing his things into the plastic bag. Her hands shook as she unhitched the car seat.

"Take him to his momma!"

"You need someone, Kristin."

But she was shoving Gene now. "You don't know. You can't possibly know. Get going!" She was in a panic not to weaken. Get him out of here, get the baby out of her sight.

He stood half out of the car, Tim thrashing in his arms. "Just at least let me fix you your dinner. We'll talk."

"I'm not going back now. I'm going to sit here and watch the rain. Go home." She turned her face and heard him shut the door. She closed her eyes, clenched her teeth. In a minute, over her thudding pulse, she heard his car engine sputter, then catch. Don't look. Don't think. In a minute more they'll be gone. A rush of water and wet gravel retreated behind the motor sound. When she opened her eyes, she saw his taillights reflecting long red ribbons on the highway.

Tim's blanket lay on the floor of the car. She picked it up, pressed it to her face, then clutched it in her lap, nesting her hands in the soft folds. The summer storm was already passing, the shimmering curtain of rain wavering eastward like the northern lights. Behind the rain the broken clouds were the ochre of windfall pears. She eased down in the seat, studied the sky. She wanted to feel relief, or even moral certitude. But she felt neither wiser nor a better person, only more alone. After what seemed a long time, though it may have been only minutes, she pushed the key into the ignition. As she lifted her head, she caught sight of a row of towering cumulus that the lower-passing rain clouds now revealed. The great hump-backed shapes like camels, the setting sun bronze on their hindquarters, drifted over the drenched plains.

Anthony E. Stockanes

Ladies Who Knit for a Living

Dover watches Lufkin gnaw at Thursday's second raspberry bismarck. Tuesdays and Thursdays Lufkin always has two raspberry bismarcks. Dover: fascinated by Lufkin's routine just as he sometimes marvels at his own invariable choice: I'll have (pause) plain toast and (smaller pause, lower lip sucked, nibbled, a tiny decisive hiss) black coffee please. And the waitress, celery-green smock with carrot-orange pockets, orange insets on the sleeves, orange piping on the lapels, stands with bony hip canted, pencil poised over a small green pad with orange lettering. Between "toast" and "coffee" she always pushes a frizzy comma of cement-colored hair away from her eyes with her wrist. Then she always says, "Juice?" Lufkin always shakes his head and Dover always pretends to consider before he says, "No, not today. Just black coffee."

When his coffee comes, there is always a waxed paper cone of milk on the saucer.

Dover wonders how these habits develop. What if one Tuesday or Thursday one of them did something else, not a big something else, just a minor change. Suppose Lufkin ordered two lemon bismarcks. Or even a single raspberry. Suppose *he* ordered *buttered* toast. Suppose he held her hand between toast and coffee. What would happen? Nothing would happen, that's what. Everything would simply stop, frozen. Habits, Dover thinks, are the gears of life. He believes that is a line worth saving.

Lufkin is again telling him to fire Miss Kronopius. His napkin is a mess because Lufkin always tries to eat the entire jelly center at once and always lunges to trap raspberry snails leaking from his mouth. "A dizzy, Dover. A birdbrain. A dimbulb. If nothing else, that laugh—chapeep chapeep chapeep, like some kind of I don't know what. You can't keep your mind on business with that going on. A business is no place for chapeep chapeep. One of these day's it'll snap your brain." Worn teeth peek through a ruby film.

After ten years of mid-morning snacks they remain as they were at first meeting, Dover and Lufkin. It isn't conceivable he would call Lufkin "Jerry" or even "Gerald"; Lufkin would never call him "Martin." A city friendship, sustained more by proximity than preference. He knows Lufkin's office, one floor below his, as well as he knows his own, but Lufkin's home in Skokie is a mystery, a queer and expensive structure constructed for him entirely of Lufkin's complaints. They have exchanged comments on their wives but Kathryn and Carol are distant, intangible. And yet, if asked, Dover knows he would probably say Lufkin is his best friend. But if Lufkin died Dover wouldn't know about it. Sometimes the knowledge bothers him but he doesn't know what to do about it. He can't say, "Lufkin, if you die at home be sure and let me know." And could he carry a card or wear a bracelet like one of those medical alert things with: I Am A Dover. Please Contact My Best Friend Lufkin (No First Name) Somewhere In Skokie?

He watches Lufkin cram the doughy rind in his mouth and grind it to a lump of paste. "She's O.K."

Lufkin's throat sucks the wad below his tie knot. "No, not O.K. Very much not O.K. You can't tell her nothing, right? Listen, how many times have I been in your place—your place of *business,* Dover—and you tell her she's screwed something up, what does she do? Chapeep chapeep—aughh!"

Lufkin is only partially right. Miss Kronopius takes correction in a flippant way, with a tinkly laugh as though she doesn't care. But she never repeats her mistakes; the laugh is habit, not attitude.

"She's O.K." He doesn't say, "Lufkin, you have to be tolerant of people's habits. Besides, if I fire her as a secretary, how do I keep her as a mistress. This is a problem in employee relations."

Mild for late June, the heat pleasant. They take the long way back instead of cutting diagonally across the street. Lufkin on the outside as usual, they turn left, stroll a block south on Wacker, come back to Clark, turn north to Wells.

"So how's the missus?"

"Fine," Dover says. He seem himself in a store window, doesn't think he looks his age. In the window a mannikin models sportswear, cream slacks and a breath-soft blue sweater. Dover is tempted to come back in the afternoon. Where can he wear slacks like that? To Miss Kronopius's on a Thursday evening? Brush against anything, the dirt is going to show. And expensive! Seventy-five dollars for a pair of pants, that's crazy.

Dover knows he will come back.

Dover (again) imagines how it would be to have an exact duplicate of every bit of money he's ever handled. An inspired fantasy. Of course the serial numbers would show they were phony, but only two with the same number would never be noticed. The security of his dream is a comfort. Imagine, a perfect copy of every bit of money. Not just his own but every bill, every coin he ever held; change made at Griswold's when he was working Saturday mornings, the bank deposits for T & L, his first real job. Incredible, the money a man touched in his life. An immense pile of fives, towers of singles so tall you couldn't see the top, various loans taken out in crisp hundreds, mountain ranges of quarters, a dull brown ocean of pennies with here and there a new one glinting like sunlight. Just the dimes—a fantastic amount of money passes through a man's life. Suitcases full of money, black steamer cases full, closets so crammed the door would have to be braced by a chair. Dover never imagines doing anything with his treasure. Just having it again, all at once, what he once had, would be perfect. No strain of figuring out complicated deals, no translating numbers on a statement. Just to have it all back again in hard cash, to be surrounded by what he once had . . . a splendid vision.

Lately he has become more cautious, but it's much too late to save for his old age. While he was thinking of it as far off, hidden by a jumble of days, his old age came up and squatted on him. And "old age" isn't what it should be anyway. It isn't much different from "middle age" (he can't look back and see that as a definite period; it had no end, nobody rang a bell and said, "That's it, Dover, time's up. You're not middle-aged anymore. Now you're in your old age.") Old age isn't a different time, a time for relaxing, for sitting around on a bench by Buckingham Fountain feeding pigeons. It isn't anything. The big surprise is the lack of much change at all, in his life, in himself. You got some wrinkles when you were young, years later you had more wrinkles. Who could say this is an old wrinkle, but this little rascal here popped up when I got old. A wrinkle is a wrinkle. The only way to measure the time spent would be to have, all at once, every bit of money . . .

Once, on a mild day like this, walking the same route, he tried to tell Lufkin about the money, but he didn't know how to start. Casually, he asked Lufkin what he would pick if he could have anything he wanted. After Lufkin told him some mundane thing, he would tell Lufkin about the money. Lufkin would be impressed.

Lufkin bounced along with his penguin strut, toes angled out. For almost a block he didn't say anything and Dover thought Lufkin hadn't heard him. That was all right. It was a childish question.

Suddenly Lufkin stopped. "Anything? You mean just one thing, no matter what? Like maybe being invisible, something like that?"

People eddied around them. Dover was uncomfortable; he had never considered being invisible. "Something like that."

Lufkin's hands, speckled, hairy, had the sharp-tendoned delicacy of age. "I'll tell you . . ." He hunched over, locked the index finger of his left hand over the little finger of the right, waggled his arms. "Firestone's South Course. The 16th. 625 yards. A ball-buster. Nicklaus, one of the big bombers, somebody like that, just bogeyed it." He studied the imaginary ball with an intensity that made Dover see it, glaring white on the sidewalk. People flowed around them, impatient, amused, irritated. Two young men in vibrant shirts stopped to watch. "Two long wood shots and right in front of the green you got to pitch over." Heads ducked automatically to avoid the club head swinging back, cringed as the ball leaped away from the sweet solid "tock," arced in a sublimely smooth line above the trees, rolled to the pin. The two young men, a microcosmic gallery,

Lufkin's Legion, applauded. "I birdie it," Lufkin said with the only smile Dover ever saw on his face.

Dover didn't even know Lufkin played golf. After ten years.

They walked back to their building in silence. Dover remembers the scene often, the brief poignant exposure of a curious man's curious dream. His own seems sensible and insignificant and normal and petty compared with Lufkin's. He never told Lufkin about the money.

A depressingly small stack of mail, advertising flyers and bills, and Miss Kronopius's impersonal daytime smile welcome him.

"How's Mr. Lufkin?" The question another habit.

"Fine." He riffles the thin sheaf of call-back slips. "Billy say what he wanted?"

"Santiago's copy stands. You put a hold on them."

The Brothers Santiago never pay without a nudge. "O.K.," Dover says with depthless reluctance. "I'll give them a call."

He closes his door behind him. God, he is tired and it's only a little past ten. He does not want to press Santiago. Where does the money go? The office gobbles up so much, is so unnecessary. A mail-order business like this, who needs a fancy-shmancy office? A small space at the warehouse, a desk next to Billy's, would do. But the warehouse is in such a grubby neighborhood, two rented floors in a decaying brick building that stares at the river through grilled paneless windows. A man would simply rot inside if he had to go there every day.

He sits behind the desk and stares at the two black-and-white enlargements on the opposite wall. Both have a misty, nostalgic quality. Black-and-white is inaccurate; they are shifting blends of infinitely varied grays, insubstantial as smoke. On the left, a study of the city's skyline taken from a boat. He can remember the morning it was taken, the water immensely deep under the rented boat, the sounds of the city muted—not so much traffic then—the quiet slap of little waves, the rippled echoes of a tanker moving out beyond Navy Pier and close to shore the sail-less masts of the moored pleasure boats moving like windshield wipers across the buildings. The creaking of something, a buoy maybe. The most peaceful morning he had ever known. And such a long time ago.

The other picture shows—suggests—a bird, a winged shape at least, settling on a column or a piling or a stump. He can never remember when that one was taken; he found it on a roll of faces he'd snapped at random. Maybe it wasn't a bird at all, simply the face of a stranger blurred, transfigured by some freakish accident of the shutter. *Camera Yearbook* printed both of them. Somewhere he still had a dozen copies of the magazine unless Kathryn had thrown them out. The pictures had even been selected for the museum show that year.

He scrubs his eyelids with his fingertips. Such a long time ago. He was never sure whether they were actually that good or whether the titles Kathryn gave them, "The Death of Water" and "The Cruel Dove," were so opaque they gave the photographs an enhancing mystery. No matter what the reason, nothing else had ever been as good. Or at least nobody thought so. In a way, they were more Kathryn's pictures than his. Maybe not even hers. That was when she was reading Gibran all the time. No titles she suggested after that were ever as good, either.

"Santiago, you make me sick."

He was going to free-lance, be a regular artist with a camera, travel all over with Kathryn, maybe collaborate with Lowell Thomas. Brady, Atget, Eisenstadt and Dover. Portraits he didn't want to bother with he'd send over to Karsh, and Karsh would be grateful for the references. People would shuffle over to Bachrach when he turned them down. The slick magazines would say, "Get Dover. If not, we'll have to use that new guy, Avedon. But, Jesus, he's no Dover."

After the museum show the old *Sun* wanted him, but he turned them down. Well, he was still alive and kicking and the *Sun* was long gone.

The chair creaks protestingly as he swings around to watch the tiny slice of lake visible from the window. When he first rented the office the building had been one of the ten tallest in the city. Even then it wasn't cheap. But a great location.

I don't know (a dubious Kathryn). That's an awful lot of money. What if things don't work out . . .

Look, I can still work at my own stuff (Dover, a colossus, a magnificent impregnable shell of bravery enclosing the squirming worm of uncertainty) and run the business during the day.

Everyone was taking pictures, cameras were like radios, everybody had one and once you had a camera there were always a dozen gadgets you thought you needed. Buy cheap in wholesale lots and mail them out at a 60% mark-up. Like coining money, that's what Bern said, gently insinuating the pen into Dover's fingers. Believe me, if I didn't have this stomach I'd never sell. In a couple of years people would think of "Dover" like they thought of "Eastman."

If—no, when—they shoved up one more building he'd lose the last slender piece of lake. He hadn't used a camera in twenty years. Maybe he should bring one in, capture the lake before Rubloff snatched it away forever. From here, a 50 mm lens. Use f/8 at 1/25 and maybe a #6 paper for contrast . . . Twenty years ago the sun would fill the room in the morning, lay wide trapezoids of creamy light on the carpet. Now he was in perpetual shadow.

Miss Kronopius buzzes him. Another habit, another useless expense. "I'm taking my break now." With only two of them in the office she could open the door and holler.

"Right. O.K."

"Did you call Santiago?"

"No, not yet." See, Lufkin? That's diplomacy. If I called someone her phone button would light up. "Miss Kronopius . . . "

"Yes, sir?" So formal. Somebody should be here to see how proper and dignified the office was run. Dignity—once you lost that, the whole thing was shot.

"I may go out this afternoon . . ."

"All right. Billy said Testrite is . . ."

"In case I don't get back before you leave, it's Thursday."

"Oh, I know that." You could tap the phone, who would find anything suspicious in that? Her laugh does sound like chapeep chapeep but Dover thinks it's pleasant.

His fingers know Santiago's number. Dover, you're sixty-eight years old! Why do they make you sweat like this? Where's the dignity? The voice that answers is different again. Santiago must have a harem. Which Mr. Santiago does he wish to speak with, please?

Paul. Oh, Mr. Paul Santiago is in Boston and isn't expected back until the first. Luis. Oh, the voice is inexpressibly sorry; Mr. Luis Santiago is in a meeting and *can*not be disturbed. May the voice take a message? Is Leon in? Oh, the voice is devastatingly sorry, Mr. LEE—own Santiago has just this very minute stepped out. May the voice take a message, Mr. Grover? He leaves his name, angry and relieved. He doesn't owe *Santiago* money, for chrissake, Santiago is into *him*, so why should he be the one sweating? If he gave Testrite the runaround . . . It's really a wonder the business has survived this long, Dover tells the photographs on the opposite wall.

Right now, this very minute, he should be living quietly someplace. If he had taken the job with the *Sun* and if they had kept him when they merged with the *Times*, he'd be three years retired. And doing what? For one thing, drawing a little pension—that would be a good thing, at least a little something steady coming in. Seventy-five dollars for a pair of pants, another forty for the sweater. Well, you couldn't get those on a skimpy little pension. So what do you have now? The business, barely scratching along, a little in savings—very little because of Miss Kronopius, a lot less than Kathryn thinks and someday *that's* going to blow up.

So let it blow up! Whose money was it anyway? Who sat in the apartment all day and who came out every day, rain or shine? Who was she to dump on him?

Years ago, when he thought things would always change and improve, when old age wasn't real, was a phrase, an impossibility, something that would eventually happen to somebody else, a different Dover, he was going to keep a record of Kathryn's faults. Every time she pecked at him—and after he turned down the *Sun* job she really started—about some piddley little thing, he couldn't remember the countless things she did and he lost arguments simply because he didn't have a good memory, because he was too tolerant, overlooked too much. God, her memory was total then. Every penny he spent, months later she remembered. Every word, every little word, that might—just might, if you twisted it—be a criticism, she tucked away and then, weeks later, brought them all out like shish-kabob on the sword of her tongue. She probably even made some of them up. She brought them out with such clarity, such venom, it was only later, walking around trying to cool off, that he was certain he hadn't said them in the first place. But after patiently explaining what you meant, you couldn't go back and say you hadn't said them.

He should have started the file when he first thought of it, not put it off. He shouldn't have let himself be trapped into the undignified arguments. No, the thousands of flaws should have been saved, a neat record on index cards with the date and time and exactly what she said and did. That would have been the way to do it. A special shallow closet right over there beside the window. Three, four, sometimes ten a day, a precise inventory: the way she licked her spoon and stuck it in the sugar, the toothpaste tube strangled in the middle, lipstick on the water glass in the bathroom, matches around—never in—the wastebasket, books with pages dog-eared because she couldn't be bothered with the bookmarks he supplied by the pound, the radio turned down but not off so he was gradually conscious of a buzz like a mosquito and had to go looking for it, the times she put away a magazine he'd been reading, the way she . . . each one on its own index card, a permanent damning record stored in the closet, expanding every day like a potential avalanche building, snowflake by snowflake, while she picked at him for no reason. Maybe two closets, side by side, with a special wide door.

THEN—! after years of not saying anything, of perfect dignity, when she made the ultimate piddley carping remark he would silently bring her up here, lead her to the closet, point to it. And when she opened it the avalanche would come down, burying her in the astounding history of her intolerance. "See what you did to me," he would say with a resigned smile while only her toes poked out under the permanent damning indexed weight of her nagging. To have all her faults dumped on her, all at once . . .

Staying together, another habit? Maybe it was because he never kept the record and so never collected enough evidence to show her—or himself—what she had done.

Occasionally he takes Lake Shore Drive, audaciously going to his mistress right past his own building. Talk about expense. But it was a great location. You mentioned your address, people were impressed. This evening he rolls the window down and stutters his way leisurely through the traffic lights on Lincoln. A mistress at his age, that's something. Should have done it years ago. Of course, years ago there was no Miss Kronopius to delicately suggest it, but, if he looked, there probably would have been somebody. Who knew how many somebodies?

Through the afternoon the heat has accumulated, feeding on itself, collecting truck exhausts, tamping itself into the canyons formed by buildings. How could people live like that, no air conditioning, hanging out of windows hoping for a little breeze? And the shops! Mile after mile of grubby businesses. He was crazy to stick with it in a city where block after block after block of tiny stores shoved against each other, store-front restaurants, twenty lawyers to a block, fourth-floor podiatrists . . . crazy, all these people trying to gouge the same buck. What insane vision would drive someone to open the A & A Grill ("Today's Special—Beef Stew Homemade Pie") on the same seamy block that already held the Ace Restaurant, Corky's Grill, El Toro Taco Shop, Bonheur's Fine Foods, the Elite Cafe, Cavanaugh's Red Hots, the Food Hut, Maxine's Grill? One lousy block where the Tip-Top Grill, Berkowitz's Restaurant, the Eagle Eatery, the P & G Cafe and the Ace-High Cafeteria had died, the legend of their daily specials dead-white graffitti on plate glass, the interiors dark.

And porno movies! Oh, god, that was something else. How did they stay in business? Mob-money. Had to be. Some kind of tax gimmick. Any time you went in, what was there? Ten guys, a dozen? You couldn't dent the overhead on a dozen customers. In the Loop the big movie houses were crying and they had a hundred times the business.

Block after block of it, a regular Potemkin village. It wasn't surprising that so many died; what amazed was the survival of so many, the new ones endlessly opening where so many had failed. So who are you to wonder, Dover? You could look in the yellow pages, that would scare you silly. Start with Photo Color Prints, go through Photo Finishing Retail, finish up with Photoprints, there were thirteen pages! Everything from International Camera Corp's big ad (a ball-buster, Lufkin would say, an ad that size) to Level Optical's skimpy single line. His own modest two-inch, column-wide ridiculously expensive notice lost in the confusion of page 1088. A crazy world. Why stick with it? Why not just sell out? To whom, Dover? Are you going to hold your stomach like Bern and grab somebody off the street? No problem. There's always somebody with a positive lust to get wedged into those thirteen anonymous pages.

So, sell.

And then what?

A horn behind him brays a warning and he lurches forward. In the rear view mirror he watches the cabbie's mouth form words.

And then what? For one thing, get out of the city. Who needs air like the inside of a vacuum cleaner bag, a thirty-minute hunt every time you want a parking place, fruit that looks good on the outside and tastes like paper, gum on your shoes all the time, tons of paper just drifting through the gutters . . .

The whole city is falling apart.

Used to be, you could drive through here or out on Irving Park or the south side, there were communities, real neighborhoods; Lithuanians, Poles on Division, even Swedes up around Belmont. Real little ethnic pockets. All that was gone now. Everywhere you looked it was blacks or Puerto Ricans or Mexicans—every other sign was in Spanish, for God's sake—or some kind of Indian running around in a turban. Half of Athens must be over here, there are so many Greeks. His cuff is grey, gritty. Perversely he leaves the window open, enjoying the city's decay.

Miss Kronopius lives on Wilson, the street here lined with trees that curve up in a cool arch, lay mottled, restless patterns on the pavement. The trees here have an air of permanence, not like those skimpy things strung out along Michigan, stuck in concrete like bare twigs. A few quiet brick apartment buildings between staid rows of narrow houses with porches; the houses hold themselves away from the sidewalk with steep wooden stairs. Residential, this is the way the city should be. But you go just a little back, around Broadway, and you might as well . . .

Miss Kronopius—Loretta now, after five o'clock, on Wilson rather than downtown—never automatically pushes the buzzer, makes him identify himself. He doesn't resent it. Not too much.

Better be safe than sorry with all the crazy things going on. Even here, under the cool, weathered trees, you're not that far from the craziness.

Just a few years ago I could take Kathryn for a drive up to Winnetka or maybe over to the Edgewater Beach and it was like being in the suburbs as soon as you got past North Avenue. Now the suburbs are out in Iowa someplace. You can't blame her for being careful.

Still, it would be better, more dignified, to simply press the buzzer and have the door open like he was welcome. Even better would be his own key, but he can see her thinking on that. Just for Thursdays, who needs a key? But since it's just on Thursdays he should be able to march right in without having to go through the rigmarole. Bending over to give his name to the speaker—did they expect only midgets to want to get in?

The whole business isn't what he anticipated. A little thing like getting in peels away his dignity: pushing the buzzer like a peddler, bending over, trying not to whisper "Martin" to her question—and too often she almost slips and says "Mr. Dover?" . . .

The stair light is out again and he has to feel his way. The stairwell smells musty.

You can tell this used to be a really good place. Little details, the pediment over the entrance, the grillwork around the speaker, those showed taste, somebody caring. Now it's just another place. And overpriced—one of these days Kathryn is going to find out about the beating the savings've taken this year.

He is breathing hard when he reaches the third floor. He leans against the wall, his shirt wet, listening to his harsh wheezing fill the space. He touches his chest. When you were sick, really sick, you got some attention, people excused things. People got annoyed if you were sickly, but they paid attention. Except for that once, he had never been sick in his life. But that once was wicked enough to count for something . . .

Kathryn didn't even get dressed, drove him madly through the twilight honking the horn like a crazy woman in her flannel robe.

He shakes his head, feeling his chest squeeze his lungs tightly, the rapid stutter of the pulse in his neck. That was something, all right. Racing through the streets with Kathryn holding the steering wheel like she was driving a fire truck and telling him to try to relax, it was going to be all right, he thought he was going to die. That was something.

The pain was such a surprise, so incredibly complete. A heart attack, you think it's going to be something in the left breast—in spite of the x-rays and everything he read about it later he still thinks of his heart as a plump, unattached valentine, literally heart-shaped, floating in the pericardium—but it isn't like that at all. It got you right in the stomach and spread like an explosion and you thought it was going to splinter your head.

"At your age you have to expect something like this, Mr. Dover," after they've put him in the room that cost an arm and a leg. What did a young shrimp like that know about what he should expect at his age? So many things he *had* expected never happened, who could say at fifty-five you can expect this, at sixty get ready for that? A heart attack—even a mild heart attack—was a serious thing, it *should* be a serious thing!—and it was always unexpected, no matter when it happened. Somebody keels over at thirty, everybody says, boy, that's terrible, such a young guy. Was it less terrible at fifty-five? Why should a few years change it from a tragedy to something you have to expect?

But he didn't mind dying, that wasn't it. In fact, he was actually disappointed when he didn't die, when they sent him home from the hospital with the brown plastic pill bottles, the mimeographed diet sheet, the pamphlet of instructions on exercises, the ache in his arms from all the shots and a bill big enough to run Evanston a month. Dying, that was something special, no matter when it happened. But coming home, *not* dying, *that* should be something special, too.

He'd only been disappointed.

What stunned was Kathryn's disappointment.

Not that she would have been happy to have him dead, that wasn't it. And she wasn't really *un*happy when he came home. It was just that—she'd adjusted to his dying. So quickly. It was a letdown for both of them and that she felt that way was something so immense he couldn't even accuse her of it.

Now, when he lifted something, she told him to be careful, but it was an automatic warning, without real concern, a mother saying, "don't put things in your mouth," but saying it out of habit, not really caring if the kid was sucking his thumb or cramming a Buick in his face. And it was funny because even though he was disappointed in not dying, he *was* careful, paused after climbing stairs, hesitated before picking up anything as light as a grocery bag, clenched his teeth in anticipation of the quick expanding total pain in the cavity under his breast bone.

What he dreaded most of all was that pain—that was really something—but there was also the pain of recovery, of coming out to find nobody but Kathryn knew he went in in the first place and she wasn't kicking up her heels when it turned out all right.

Occasionally there is a slight stinging sensation like an ice cube is being rubbed over the inside of his skin and he rubs his chest with slow, cautious fingers—feeling stupid doing it; you couldn't rub it away if it came and, if Kathryn notices, "Trouble?" (She is never more precise.)

"A touch of gas."

Sometimes there is no sensation at all and he isn't aware of his absently stroking fingers tracing the memory of the pain. Then her "Trouble?" is irritating. He automatically says it's gas. And she looks very slightly worried. (She doesn't drive now; sometimes he thinks her concern is the prospect of another tire-squealing horn-blaring race through the twilight to St. Luke's-Presbyterian. He takes secret painful delight in the knowledge that the hospital is no longer on Indiana and rigid in the blistering cocoon of his pain he would have to direct her, over to Congress.)

He never says, "Nothing," when she notices his unconscious stroking because it would end even her slight concern and that frightens him.

Miss Kronopius—Loretta—opens the door at his tap. It would be better if he came up to find her standing in the doorway, maybe with a drink in her hand, instead of waiting for his knock. It's better to be welcomed without having to bang the door. On the other hand, maybe it wouldn't be better. He needs a minute or two after the stairs to catch his breath. There's no dignity in showing up sweating and panting. He is warmed by this concern for his feelings.

But it would be nice if she was wearing something—well, something more mistressy instead of white knickers, white knee socks, wide red suspenders, white tennis shoes. To him they look like tennis shoes. Somewhere a rich fairy designer was laughing at these young women . . . not that Miss Kronopius was all *that* young; a young lady, but a *mature* young lady. She calls these ridiculous outfits her "home suits," something to relax in, completely different from the respectable, almost old-fashioned skirts and white blouses of the office. They're different all right. Knickers. Like some kind of old-time golfer. A swishy old-time golfer. He has a quick vision of Lufkin in her costume and smiles. She smiles a response.

He dumps himself in a chair shaped like a partially collapsed balloon, a crinkly black deflating ball, and continues to smile.

The knickers make a dry scratchy sound when she walks. "You look like you need a gin and tonic."

He is tired of his smile, wants to put it away some place, doesn't know what to do with it, has no replacement. "That sounds good."

God, this is an ugly room, the worst of the chaotic sixties preserved. Miss Kronopius takes *Apartment Life* and is drawn to the most hideous ideas in that catalog of hideous ideas. None of the furniture looks like furniture: barrels halved, covered with floral paper and glued to other barrels; two-by-fours, lacquered mauve and chartreuse, fastened together with chrome bolts; a throne-like object that was originally a wooden milk carton, two oak coat racks and yards of weathered awning. Red, green, yellow plastic boxes in a variety of sizes hold paperback books, artificial flowers. . . . Dover closes his eyes a moment. On one wall a huge poster advertises an ancient Ken Maynard movie. On the adjoining wall a square yard of sanded, black-spray-painted plywood flaunts four burnished hub-caps attached asymmetrically. The hub-caps are from Maxwell Street. Miss Kronopius—Loretta—calls it "found art" and it is her own creation; in *Apartment Life* the plywood was painted a duller black. Dover remembers when Maxwell Street was really a place to go for bargains, when the words hanging in the air were plaintive *meshuggaas* and *fahtumult,* a kind of wailing poetry, instead of strident repetitions of "mothahfuckah," when gypsies knocked on plate glass windows to lure young men in for palm readings and, inside, invited-tugged young men into humid back rooms for more intimate palmings.

A year ago he considered moving his collection of Auchincloss to Wilson Avenue, to establish himself in this sanctuary. At fantastic expense he had everything Auchincloss wrote bound in moss-green Morocco leather with gilt stampings because he thought the man was an unappreciated genius. He gave the idea up; where would Louis fit in this jumble of beads and plastic?

From the tiny kitchen the tinkle of ice cubes soothes him; the kiss of glass and ice is light, summery, the sound of cool blue-green.

She sits with legs crossed on a platform of lumber and wire. "Martin, do you think you want to go to bed tonight?"

What kind of question is that? The basic idea of a mistress is you come up the stairs and you're made to feel dignified and reasonable and wanted and after some civilized conversation you go to bed.

And how can he answer? If it didn't happen like it was supposed to—up the stairs, torrid welcome (torrid welcome, but returned with dignity), a conversation about important, cultured things, into bed—what could you say? Like some kind of dirty old man, yes, I want to go to bed? Where's the dignity in that? Or, no, the idea never crossed my mind? How stupid. Did I spend forty minutes fighting traffic to come up here and sit on something that looks like a diseased bladder? Or, no, Loretta, I'm beat out from dragging myself up three flights of stairs so steep they should be against the law and I just want to sit here and feel the glass cool in my hand and my only desire is that my heart should quit threatening to race away my time like a crazy taxi meter? I just want to sit here and not move, not smile . . . could he say that?

"Why?" he says cautiously, unable to find an answer.

"My period started this afternoon." She smiles brightly and drains half her glass, wrinkling her nose at him over the rim.

He is relieved. And disappointed. And sad. He doesn't want to go to bed at all, has dreaded it. It's been a nagging threat in the back of his mind. But, after all, when you're paying for a mistress, even a one-day-a-week mistress, there's an obligation, a disappointment when things don't work out as they should. And he is saddened, not only by her menstruation—mistresses did it just like wives; it just wasn't something you considered—but by her language. Kathryn would never come right out and say "period" like that. "It's that time of month," that was graphic enough when Kathryn still had the problem and there was a wealth of unspoken detail in the varied inflections she gave *that*. In some ways Loretta was not quite the lady Miss Kronopius was. Miss Kronopius went to the ladies' room during the day; but on Thursday evenings Loretta went to the toilet . . .

This is the fourth Thursday in a row nothing's happened. Well, that's not quite true. So they didn't go into the bedroom with the weird copper-finned contraption dangling from the ceiling, the octagon of stained glass suspended in front of the window. He can sit back, relax—as much as he can relax in the odd chair—and talk. That's not a bad thing. Maybe it's better than flopping around. Miss Kron—Loretta—is a good listener, sometimes a super listener. It's a good thing, having someone young listen to you, be interested in what you're saying. Like keeping a diary. Only better.

The witty epigrams: "Loretta," looking through the glass into the distance with a slight smile . . . more of a half-smile, really, wry, experienced, "Loretta, marriage is an education. It has its own three r's: romance, resentment, routine." Getting that just right, arranging it so it seemed to come out spontaneously, the sudden bloom of wisdom on the stalk of a sophisticated life, took some practice. In fact he'd driven past Wilson all the way up to Peterson working on it. But it was worth polishing because now it was locked away in her head.

Years from now Miss—Loretta—would be married. Or maybe she wouldn't be married; an old lady, maybe, who'd look back through the years to the precious, exquisitely brief Martin Dover time and tell her companion (someone; at times he imagined a grandchild, but that complicated things. More likely, a dewy-cheeked young girl who looked up to Miss Kronopius): "My child, years ago a very wise friend"—she'd smile at that, a secret wistful smile for the "friend"—"once told me something I've always remembered." A pleasant thought, the knowledge his precise sentences would be lovingly passed on, held gently and examined, gaining lustre with the retelling. When he imagines it he gives her perfectly coiffed white hair and dresses her in a version of her office uniform; knickers don't fit the picture.

He can tell her things and she pays attention. He makes her know what it is to be young when Chicago was a different city, when West 63rd was a world apart from the Loop, when the most delightfully foreign treat was a can of peaches stolen from the topmost shelf of the towering white cabinet on the back landing and eaten warm in the secret cave formed by sunflowers bobbing on scratchy green legs behind the garage.

She is very good at paying attention to the thoughts he discovers, the memories he finds stacked away in dim corners of his mind, their colors amazingly fresh when he brings them out.

"You know," he mused once, "It's really hard to figure out just who you are. Not you personally. I mean everybody 'you.' "

"Oh, you know who you are." When she yawns her face is very young. Dover vows to bring a camera to capture the sleepy innocence of that expression.

"No, really. For example, my father died when he was thirty-five— "

"That's too bad."

" —and I can remember him as being—oh, what kind of man? An old guy. That's something, eh? Imagine, an old guy at thirty-five. I was ten years old, to me thirty-five was as old as you could be. And big. So now I'm *almost* thirty years older than he was when he died, but I still think about him as being so much older than I am . . . it's a strange feeling."

"I imagine."

A mistress is a wonderful thing. You can tell her what's on your mind and she sits and listens, doesn't just sew and nod without really paying attention.

"Lufkin said a very interesting thing to me today." He never mentions Lufkin's attitude toward her; he can't discuss her with Lufkin, but tries to share Lufkin with her. "I've been thinking about it all afternoon. He said—I don't know what we were talking about, it doesn't matter—but he said his father once told him there are only two kinds of people in this world. One kind is ladies who knit for a living. Isn't that a great line? It's so—so quiet, so com-

plete, you get the whole idea—bang, just like that. Just sitting there
your whole life, just knitting away, miles and miles of yarn strung
out behind you, never finishing anything, just knitting away, spending day after day . . . ''

"I don't think people knit much anymore." Two triangles of tiny
creases touch the corners of her eyes when she frowns. "A lot of
people do crewel though. That's really in. I've got a friend who
works at the Merchandise Mart—she's really an actress— " her eye-
lashes flutter like little wire brushes when she's excited and she leans
forward with her shoulders pulled back. To Dover she is the figure
on a ship's prow. "She got called back once for an audition at Second City, but she was too tall. She does crewel all the time. She says
it helps her relax. She's got cushions all over, on all her chairs. All
the cushions have dogs' heads. Or lions. Her whole place looks like
it's full of animals."

Dover sighs. "That's not really what I mean. 'Ladies' aren't just
ladies, it's men, too. Everybody. And knitting is—you know— "

Loretta prowls her friend's creweled apartment. "It's really great
for her because she's crazy about animals but she can't keep pets.
She's allergic."

"That's too bad."

"What's the other one?"

Dover often finds the disconcerting flit from topic to topic de-
lightful. Often, but not always. "Other what?"

"You said Mr. Lufkin said his father said there were two kinds of
people. What's the other kind?"

Dover is nonplussed. "Isn't that strange? I don't remember. I
don't think he said. Maybe it's not important."

"Mr. Lufkin is very strange."

Dover surrenders glass. Sighs. Wishes this were a more traditional
arrangement. A mistress is a wonderful thing to have, but Thursdays only . . . still, those are her terms. And she will not quit her
job. These days a woman has to have her career, Loretta says with
animation. Dover doesn't insist. Maintaining her full time would be
economically devastating. The weekly envelope he never quite feels
comfortable leaving on the plexiglass-and-sewer-tile table are drain
enough as it is.

Driving home along the lake he thinks it is a very satisfactory arrangement, all things considered. But sometimes he studies his satisfied dissatisfaction. It would be better to have a mistress he could visit when the mood struck him, someone breathlessly waiting no matter when he arrived . . . but then, the mood doesn't come that often. Between Miss Kronopius's exuberantly healthy embrace and Kathryn's last phlegmatic grunting there is an enormous span.

The first time in Miss—Loretta's apartment was almost like being with the mustached gypsy on Maxwell Street. Except instead of being too quick he was too slow. Nothing happened. Not that it was anything to be ashamed of, those things happened, even to young men. But he'd felt so damned helpless, so—undignified. Lying there, watching her fingers work, all those turquoise rings chilling him, puckering his flesh into a soft stubborn curl, he didn't know what to do with his own hands, found himself patting her shoulder. He'd spent the whole day imagining how it would be, how her little gasps would sound (they would sound, he imagined, just like Kathryn's had sounded during the early years, soft explosions in her throat, an accelerating breathiness, almost laughter, almost weeping), even had to adjust his trousers around the unfamiliar tightness when he envisioned her without the oddly exciting plain white blouse. She touched his chest with cold ring-wrapped fingers. "That's all right, Mr. Dover . . . "

"Martin."

" . . . sometimes it happens that way. You're probably working too hard. Next time you'll probably come three times." Her skin picked out glowing light points from the glass suspended in front of the window. In the cool blue twilight she had been a soft statue, a Venus. It had been years, scores of years, since Kathryn could sit like that, her legs tucked under her.

When Dover remembers the first time he thinks of Kathryn and when he remembers his hand on Loretta's blue smoothness he shudders involuntarily.

Nothing is quite as it should be, is faintly blurred at the edges. Just a little out of focus. It would be nice to have a mistress waiting for him all the time; but he doesn't mind *not* being expected to pop up at odd times. No matter which way you look at it, it's O.K., and, as Lufkin would say, not O.K.

Dover devises a plan after that first failure. He leaves the office early on Thursdays and goes to a pornographic movie on Clark for preliminary stimulation. He is surprised at how expensive it is. He has to go all the way out to Lawrence to find a theater that charges less than two dollars and that's too much trouble. Eventually he settles on a Lincoln Avenue movie; it's convenient and it advertises 16 mm films. Dover equates this with amateurs—God knows, there are a lot of amateurs taking sexy pictures. You can tell that by some of the handwritten questions in the mail—and he thinks watching amateurs will be more exciting than watching professionals. For a while, a matter of weeks, his plan works fairly well. When he is in the apartment on Wilson he closes his eyes and remembers the movies. Loretta, knees tight against his ribs, rides him with a massaging action she says is very exciting. Dover is wordlessly grateful to her.

But the movies become boring.

The stories never change.

The men are usually the same and Dover cannot empathize.

The performances are professional and the camerawork is hopelessly amateurish.

He continues to visit the movie on Thursday, locked into yet another habit, but often he dozes after the performers take their clothes off. Awake, he finds himself concentrating on odd details: the men never wear shorts. Don't their trousers chafe? So many of the performers have bad teeth. Not rotten, just yellowish, uncared-for; the close-ups of mouths seem to be shot through beige gelatin filters. And there are so many blemishes, so many pimples, especially on buttocks. Dover returns to the street unrefreshed by his nap.

He took Miss—Loretta—to watch C. J. Lang (after a number of critical viewings he thought she looked, dressed, quite a lot like Loretta) to see what her reaction would be, to see if she would identify with—and perhaps imitate—Miss Lang. As far as he could tell she didn't have much of a reaction.

"What did you think about it?" He never suggested Loretta do anything like that and she never volunteered.

"It was O.K.," she said and there was such a lack of anything in her voice he didn't know how to interpret it. "What about you?"

"It was O.K.," he says carelessly. He took her to an Armenian restaurant and she was enthusiastic about that. Dover envied her appetite.

He parks in the basement garage, but instead of taking the elevator he wanders back outside, walks to the corner, walks across the street to the lake. A gentle wind moves the water with the heavy caressing sound of Miss Kronopius's thighs brushing when she wears the scarlet velvet trousers. Looking down he sees the jumbled footprints in the sand as though he is above a cratered desert. There is a strong smell of decaying alewives from the beach. For a long time he stands against the railing watching the boat lights moving far out beyond the breakwater.

He should sell out, that would be the smart thing. If he doesn't, there is no telling what will happen. Or specialize. Now that's an idea. Get a really hot salesman, take on just a few lines as an exclusive manufacturer's rep and concentrate on those. It's not too late to start something. All these years, he should have some kind of reputation . . . business is going to hell, little by little. A sudden drop, that's one thing. But the chipping away, that's worse. There are so many Santiagos now.

Tires hiss on the pavement behind him.

Things are in bad shape, there's no use denying that. He rubs his hands on the scaly railing, wonders why he feels no panic. There have been so many moments of crisis, bills not only unpaid but unpayable, he's been almost desperate enough to visit a couple of doctors for sleeping prescriptions. Somehow, while he planned on how many pills he'd need, things worked out, even when he was sure they never would. But things never *stayed* worked out.

He has not—yet—told Miss Kronopius this. The truth begs for the proper setting: it would be nice if she had an apartment with decent furniture. And a fireplace. Definitely a fireplace. It would be good to lean against a fireplace mantel with a glass in his hand. Brandy. Or an expensive port. Things you said had more—dignity—when you could lean against something, one hand in your pocket.

"It's something you learn with time, Loretta. You're much too young yet . . . " she would pull her lips together in a soft negatory cave. "No, I mean it. Only with time." He moves his glass in little circles, reflects. "You learn that all your life you're in tight spots and sometimes you think you'll lose your mind. It's very bad and then, for a while, it gets easier, but once it's been bad you never really relax because you know it's going to be bad again. Finally, one day you're in the same tight spot you were in originally and you think nothing's changed and nothing's ever going to change except you suddenly realize you're not desperate this time, you accept it as natural and you figure, what the hell, it'll work out again. And it does. Oh, sometimes you wake up thinking, 'Not *this* time, not this time!' and you want to jump out of bed and just run around the room, beating your head against the wall. But you don't. You just go back to sleep."

He must polish it, reduce it to a few sentences at once stunningly simple and faceted as a diamond so that she can store it away because it's important she get it right.

"Dover, I'm asking for a favor."

Dover's stomach contracts. The coffee shop turns dark and ominous. Lufkin is going to destroy their friendship, touch him for a loan that, even if promptly repaid, will alter their relationship in a terrible way. Lufkin, don't bring money between us! "Lufkin, business is so bad right now— " in the moment of panic he realizes he sounds like Lufkin, his voice too high, the words chopped off, the phrases Lufkinish. He takes a deep breath. "Lufkin, I got an inventory that just sits there like it's nailed to the floor. Billy, my warehouseman, tells me ten times a day— " the words a roar of despair, torn from the pain in his chest.

Lufkin watches him warily. "Dover, don't be such an ass."

"I thought you wanted . . . "

"I thought you wanted—aaghh." Disgustedly, Lufkin waves a shred of Friday cinnamon doughnut. "I said a favor, a personal thing. I need money, you think I got to go to strangers? Aaghh. Listen, what I want from you, I want you should change with me. You take Wednesdays, give me Thursdays."

Dover is conscious of a huge swelling emptiness, the hungry feeling he had coming home to Kathryn's lack of joy. "Are you telling . . . "

"Wednesdays are a bitch for me. The only nights I got free are Mondays and Thursdays. And Sid Hampshire, that bazoola, won't budge on Mondays."

Dover spreads his hands, embraces the celery green and carrot orange of the coffee shop. "Sid Hampshire? From Busnell Reality, that Sid Hampshire?"

"A bazoola, that one. Dover, is it going to kill you, changing one day?"

"Miss Kronopius?"

"So what do you say?"

"Miss Kronopius? Lufkin—Lufkin, you keep telling me to fire her! Chapeep chapeep chapeep!"

Delicately Lufkin pats sugar grains from his mouth. "Dover, what's that got to do with anything? That's business. In a business, she's terrible. You can't run a business with her around."

Dover wonders why he doesn't feel sillier, why this queer betrayal does not destroy him. He sees his Thursday afternoons, free of porno movies and the Everest of stairs, stretching out endlessly.

"Lufkin, let me think about it. Maybe I should get out of the gypsy business."

Lufkin blinks with saurian disgust, his "aaughh" a soft belch.

Kathryn is watching television. At least the television is on. She doesn't seem to be paying attention. Her fingers work the seam of the tent-like slip she is repairing. She is always sewing something. How much time does she spend stitching rips in her clothes? She is really a thrifty woman.

"You're home early."

Dover shrugs. All of his muscles have weights attached. "One of those days. What law says I have to work til midnight every Friday?" It is almost ten o'clock. He looks around the apartment. He spends very little time here. Except for Auchincloss, a cold green rectangle, there is very little of him in the room. Kathryn's long-dead sister squints at him from a photograph on the mantel.

"I've been thinking. Maybe I should sell the business." He sits down gingerly, aware of throbbing aches in his thighs and shins. "And do what?" She doesn't sound curious. "I don't know. Maybe we could get a small place somewhere. Maybe move to Arizona." "Arizona." Her teeth worry a piece of thread. "We don't know anybody in Arizona." Where are they, the people they'd known, called friends. Lufkin, there is limitless cruelty in your "strangers." "We don't know anybody here." Her teeth, the second set, look strong enough to bite through steel. "I know Lena, Sandy Pressman, Alice, Steffie, the Brookmeyers, Juanita Paulikas . . ." Who are these strange people? The names sound familiar, road signs glimpsed briefly on a drive long ago, a litany of out-of-the-way places. "Lena who?" A commercial pulls her eyes up. "Lena is Lena. Lena in 27B Lena." Dover recognizes the name as he recognizes but cannot identify certain smells. It is tantalizingly familiar. Dover lets a minute, then another stretch themselves out. His belly and brain conspire in ineffable yearning. "Kathryn . . ." She wags her head at the television. "That's so stupid. Who cleans a bathroom in a dress like that? Why do they let them put that junk on?" "Kathryn . . ." "Mmmmmm?" He brings it to her from a great distance, offers it as a rare and precious gift borne across unmapped places. "Kathryn, do you want to go to bed?" Her head moves so slowly he thinks he can hear her neck bones creak. "No, of course not." She blinks at him in mild surprise across a grey wash of years. "Do you?" He thinks about it, seriously thinks about it. "No, what I'd like is some peaches. Right out of the can."

"Well, be careful you don't spill."

"We've got canned peaches?" It is a discovery of shimmering beauty.

"In the cupboard over the sink. Next to the green beans. Be careful you don't spill."

The muscle weights loosen. He smiles contentedly, but he doesn't get up. He talks to her, slowly at first and then, leaning forward, he strings words together in brilliant beaded strands and flings them in her lap. Occasionally she shakes her head at the television and mutters something. He tells her about Santiago, a hundred Santiagos, about Lufkin—what he knows or suspects about Lufkin—about the senseless sublime efforts of people to open new food shops all over the city. Without planning to, but working toward it inevitably, he starts to tell her about Miss Kronopius. He notices she has gone to sleep, mouth open, teeth slightly parted. She looks so old, so completely defenseless. He squirms back in the chair and tells her about Miss Kronopius anyway.

Her dry snores vibrate in the silence when he lowers the television sound. He brings a can of peaches into the living room and eats them slowly, being very careful not to spill. He goes back for another can and watches television without seeing it until the station signs off.

Barry Targan

Surviving Adverse Seasons

> The Universe is either a chaos of involution
> and dispersion, or a unity of order and providence.
> If the first be truth, why should I desire to linger in the
> midst of chance, conglomeration, and confusion?
> —Marcus Aurelius Antoninus

Britannia est insula.

So it began, again, for Abel Harnack. Another beginning in a life, lengthening, of many beginnings. And now a few endings. One at least.

Britannia est magna insula.

"And now, so that you will learn to hear as well as see the language, so that you will *feel* the beauty of it in the mouth, will you please read aloud? Will you," she glanced down at her class list, "Mr. Harnack, begin for us."

He read clearly and accurately the two lines and then the two lines following them to the end of the paragraph. *Britannia est patria nostra, sed Britannia est terra pulchra.*

It had taken him a year to get here, this far. Monday evening. Page one. *Britannia est insula.* But even that morning he had not been certain that he would do it. He had not felt compelled into it as, in the past, he always had been—urgent, hungry, charging into endeavor, racing after accomplishment. Now he did not feel that way at all.

"Go on," his daughter had said to him at breakfast. "Do it." He did not live with Vivian, but after her husband, Charles, had driven off to his work and the two children had left for school, he would come often to eat a later breakfast with her. Unless she had something else to do that took her away. Then he would walk on past her house and into the city and into whatever vagaries his life just then, that day, would tilt him toward.

He might conclude upon a group of workmen breaking a street apart to fix a sewage pipe. He would drift down the street to them like a heavy log in a slow stream and go aground upon them, caught in their activity, the shattered air, the blasting of the pummeling jackhammer, the sputtering of the blue arcwelder, the revving up and down of the gasoline engine generator.

They would all subside at lunchtime and he would drift on, free. Perhaps to spiral through department stores, sometimes to visit factories and small machine shops he had once known well. Through the summer past he had watched young men play baseball in all the city's parks. And in the evening he would walk home, past his daughter's house (though at least once a week to supper there) to his own house and to his evening in which he would do whatever occurred to him, unless nothing did.

At twelve or a little before, he would drink a small glass of Scotch whiskey and then go to a thorough sleep, unprovoked by fears or passions or expectations. And at six he would awake.

"Go on," his daughter Vivian said to him at breakfast. "Do it. Go on and do it. It will do you good."

"Good? Good for what?" he asked her.

"Oh come on, Dad," she said, turning from the sink and their dishes. She said no more. That was as far as they ever got upon that point any longer.

"Very good, Mr. Harnack," Sylvia Warren said to him. "Thank you. Now Mrs.? . . . Miss Green, will you take it from there?" Miss Green took it from there, from Britannia through Europa to Sardinia, to Italia, some being insula, some not, some being magna, some parva.

At the end of the two hours, at the end of the first and second conjugations and the first declension and warnings about the ablative case, Abel Harnack decided not to return the coming Monday.

"*Vale,*" Sylvia Warren said to them as they all gathered up their books.

"*Vale,*" they answered back.

Outside, in the parking lot behind the high school, the group of them broke off to their own cars, except Abel Harnack, who would walk.

"Do you want a ride?" she called to him when she saw him, alone, crossing the asphalt parking lot to Wilson Street.

"Is that your car?" he asked, walking back to her, although it clearly was her car, the small door to it already opened, her briefcase already dropped into the catchall area behind the seat.

"Yes. My joy." The car was an earlier model MG, the classic squarish roadster with narrow, wire-spoked wheels and headlights separated from the fenders, with a windshield that folded down, a walnut steering wheel, leather upholstery, the car a gleamingly waxed deep green. It was not the car he would have imagined her to drive.

But she was thin, lithe enough for it, her motions strong and quick. Nimble, he thought. And although she was gray, she wore her hair modishly straight and long, out like a helmet, square across her forehead and to an inch over her shoulders. And she smiled like the young, easily and without complication and at everything. Perhaps her car suited her after all, even if she must be, Abel Harnack guessed, fifty-five or more.

"That's a fine-looking car." They both waited beside it. "OK," he said. "But I don't live far. Only down Wilson Street about a half a mile." He went to the other side of the car. "How do I get in?"

"Like this. You sit in first and then swing your legs in." She did it. He opened his door and followed her example. "Fine. You did that just fine."

"I learn things quickly."

"I noticed that in class." The car burst to life. She backed up and then drove across and out of the lot, turning left on Wilson Street at his direction. She drove gracefully, snapping the gearshift through its pattern, pushing the car a little quickly, but well controlled. She drove with pleasure, Abel Harnack thought.

In two minutes she stopped before his house, where he had pointed it out, the motor running. He swung himself out of the car.

"Thanks."

"It's nothing." She shifted and started off slowly. "See you next Monday." Between gears she waved her free hand. *"Vale,"* she shouted back over her exhaust.

"Vale," he said softly.

Latona est irata quod agricolae sunt in aqua.

"Now here, you see," she said, *"quod agricolae sunt in aqua* is the dependent clause. It depends upon *irata* for its full meaning."

He had come back.

After the first class, at breakfast Tuesday, he had told Vivian that he probably would not go to the Latin class again; but when she asked him why, he could not say, except to say that he was not so interested in Latin as he thought he might have been and that, after all, it was not something he had been strongly decided for in the first place. He had gone and he had seen and that was that.

Vivian, sitting across from him, shrugged. After a year of trying, of anxiety and duty, she would have to go along now with him as he was. He was sixty, voluntarily retired for a year now, ever since his wife, Estelle, had died, in one week, in a wretched spasm of sudden dying for which you cannot prepare, and from which you cannot recover.

Abel Harnack buried his wife and then stopped. That was the only word for it, as if to permit himself to do anything at all again would be to accept again the world—his life, the possibility of life —as it had been. And that he would not do. He had too much decency for that, and besides, he learned things quickly. And what he had learned—quickly, in a week—was that all the assumptions of his life had been unquestioned, had simply been assumed the way a child assumes the universe: *post hoc, ergo propter hoc.* But what he had learned was that nothing did or *did not* follow from anything at all. Not the seasons, not the tides, and least of all even the smallest aspirations of man.

So for a year now he had sat out, finally neither in anger nor in contemplation. He would not get caught by the old—by any—assumptions again.

"And for next week I want you to review all we've learned about first- and second-declension nouns and to study the declension of *bonus* in all its genders. And I want you to read and translate the first three stories in Appendix A, which begins on page 280. Write out your translations, and remember, think of the principles involved."

After class, in the parking lot, he told her he would not be coming back to class.

"But why? You do so well. I'm surprised. You seemed to be enjoying yourself."

"*Bonus, bona, bonum?*" he asked her. "*Midas in magna regia habitabat?* I already know the story of King Midas."

"But this is just the start, just the beginning. Surely you understand that Latin isn't declensions. It's Vergil and Horace and Ovid. It's Catullus.

> *Vivamus, mea Lesbia, atque amemus,*
> *rumoresque senum seneriorum*
> *omnes uninus aestimemus assis.*
> *Soles occidere et redire possunt:*
> *nobis cum semel occidit breuis lux,*
> *nox est perpetua una dormienda.*

Do you know what that says?

> Come, Lesbia, let us live and love,
> nor give a damn what sour old men say.
> The sun that sets may rise again
> but when our light has sunk into the earth,
> it is gone forever.

Oh, no, Mr. Harnack. Declensions and exercises are just the beginning. The end is poetry."

Beginnings again.

It was the first week of October but summery yet. The lights defining the parking lot flickered through the still heavy pulsing screen of attracted insects, like candles wavering in a slight breeze. The sound of Catullus lingered as if reverberating back from the night around them. Had she spoken, declaimed, so loudly? Were neighbors sitting now on darkened porches across Wilson Street listening to this woman cast Latin poetry at him, themselves listening to it hovering in the evening air? But of beginnings he had had enough.

"It's too far between King Midas and . . . and what you recited."

"Too far?"

"Too long. For me. I haven't time. I'm not so young a man."

"Perhaps it takes less time than you think. Have you ever studied a language before?"

"French. In high school. And for two years in college. I remember nothing of it."

"Perhaps you do. Perhaps you unconsciously remember much in your past that you think you've forgotten. It's all there, you know. The past."

He said nothing.

"Well, come on. Let me give you a ride home." She walked away from where they were standing and to her car. He did not follow.

"It's a nice night, thank you. I think I'll walk," he called over to her softly. He did not like this openness, Catullus blatant in the wide night, the talk of endings, of pasts and possibilities for all, for the air itself, to know.

"Oh come on, Mr. Harnack. I've lost students before. I don't take it personally. Don't you. Latin's not for everyone. Come on." She got into the car and waited. He came over quickly and got in. To be gone and done.

In front of his house she stopped and he got out.

"Thank you," he said.

"I hope you'll reconsider," Sylvia Warren said and waved and drove off.

He continued with Latin, although he did not reconsider. It was his determination now, after a year, not to reconsider anything. He returned on the following Monday, his lessons prepared, his exercises neatly typed. He returned as if the effort of halting the small momentum of going on, slight as it was, would require of him energies he did not wish ever to use again. Now, after a year, he had started something about which he could not care, something about which there could be no purpose, no meaning or accountability. Above all, he would—must—avoid the traps of purpose. Latin was what he had come up with, an act too remote from him to count at all; an act that could not, would never, matter to him in the years, perhaps the decades, left. He did not particularly enjoy the Latin, but he would do it and he would not think about doing it again.

During the class the rain that had gone on all day thickened, drove down like a summer storm improbably late even for the warm October they had been having.

"*Cadens imber mari similis est*: the rain falls like the sea," she had stopped the class to say, gesturing at the windows. The rain came now in sheets so dense that the wind slapped them against the building, shaking it. At the end of class she called for him to come to her desk.

"I'm glad you decided to come back. Your work is really superlative." And then, "You'll certainly need a ride home on a night like this."

"I brought my car. Thank you."

She nodded and smiled and gathered up her books and papers into her briefcase, and they walked out of the room together as the janitor came in to turn out the lights after them. From the doorway to the parking lot the rain made the darkness palpable.

"It's a bad night to drive in," Abel Harnack said.

"It can't rain this hard for long," she said. "It'll taper off." The class had gathered into a tight knot at the door wedged between the two darknesses.

"Well, here goes," Sylvia Warren said. She hunched herself over, her briefcase tight to her chest, and tucked her chin and sprinted to her car. They watched her, students now to her daring, but in ten feet they could not see her, the light from the lamps around the parking lot squeezed by the viscous rain back into the quavering globes. Then the others followed, four to one car, three to another, several to another, and Abel Harnack to his.

The cars started up and eased out slowly into Wilson Street. In the instant before he drove out, through a gap in the rain he saw her car, low and dead. He circled back into the lot and drove up next to her. Then he saw that she was out of the car with the right side of the hood up. She was bent into the engine with a flashlight. Her rain hat had slipped back. He got out and walked around to her side.

"Damn thing," she said to him. The rain eased off for a moment, and then a moment more. "It's water somewhere. I'm getting shorted out, but I can't tell where. Inside the distributor probably."

"Try and start it," he told her. "I'll take a look."

After a minute or two he waved her out. "I think it's here." He pointed to an element fixed into the line leading to the coil. "This is a radio static suppressor."

"Yes, I know. I put it in."

"They're a bad business, I think." He pulled the plug apart and removed the suppressor and reconnected the heavy wires. "Try it now."

The car started at once.

"Thank you," she shouted out to him. She raced the engine, securing it, herself. "I'm sorry you got so wet. You'll have to explain it to me next week. Please, hurry in out of the rain." She pulled the door closed and turned on her driving lights. He opened the door before she could drive off.

"Wait," he said. "That connection is still too open. You might get it wet again in this weather before you got home. Stop at my house and I'll fix it right for you." He held his coat tight about his throat, but he was already wet through.

"OK."

He drove slowly, keeping her watery headlights in his mirror. He turned into his driveway and pressed a button on his dash that opened the door to the large garage. She drove in after him into the space on the left and got out of the car and shook herself like a retriever.

"Well," she said, looking about. "This is certainly more than just a place to put a car."

Abel Harnack's garage was a workshop equipped to rebuild or mend whatever was. Or to create what was not. A large metal lathe with various milling heads, drill presses, band saws and bench saws, sanding drums, levering and bending devices, compression tools, testing equipment, oxy-acetylene and electric arc welders, racks and cabinets of wrenches, tap and die pieces, hammers, chisels, hydraulic jacks, lubrication guns and nozzles, a motorized hoist that ran on an overhead metal beam. In a corner, stacked up nearly to the roof, were dozens of small drawers like those in the oldest hardware stores where one of the objects in the drawer was tacked to the front: springs, nuts, bolts, shims, washers, wires, rods, and stock until the mind could not comprehend the variety of pieces demanded by the mechanisms of manufactured life. From an overhead rack belts and hoses and rubber and plastic fittings draped down like stalactites.

And everything in perfect array, spectacular as much for that lucidity, for the enormous accomplishment of arrangement, as for the objective demonstration that there existed so many things from which to make so many things.

"Mr. Harnack, whatever do you *do*?"

He had already lifted the hood and was at work sealing the connection, remaking it, in fact. In less than five minutes he was done.

"There," he said, pointing to it. "Better than new. You won't get stuck from that again. Your next trouble is going to come from here." He pointed to the gaskets beneath the double carburetors. He could have told her more about her car, everything perhaps. But he thought that he had gone too far already. He closed the hood and looked for her. She was still turning about in the marvel of the shop.

"I've never seen anything like it. Not even pictures or anything." She was wet and shivering but did not notice, still warmed by her discovery. Her hair was shining and flattened against her head, the ridges and notches of her bone structure clear and pronounced as the cold drew her skin tight to her skull.

"Would you like a cup of coffee?"

"Yes," she said, turning to him now. "Thank you. That would be wonderful." She walked with him across the workshop to the doorway to the house. Instead of a doorknob or handle there was a square metal plate, brushed steel. She watched him run his finger in a design over the surface of the plate. The door opened. They walked into the warmer house.

"What are you, Mr. Harnack?" she asked as she followed him into the kitchen. "What magic is this?" She laughed in delight as children do at wonder, thrilled and unnerved at sorcery all at once. He had not heard her laughter before.

"Nothing," he said. "Retired." He said nothing more until he placed the coffee before her. Until then she looked about quietly at what she could see of the house from the kitchen through its two doors and over its counter into the dining room and living room. The house was as neat and clean as ice, like water poured into a mold and frozen and then left.

"My wife died about a year ago. A year last August."

"I'm sorry," Sylvia Warren said. And then there was nothing more to say, nothing more she *could* say. She understood boundaries. She bent to her coffee.

But it was not such a boundary that Abel Harnack wanted to exist within. He wanted to erect no special defense because there are no such defenses, and he wanted nothing to defend, only to avoid, like the bitterness that had at first consumed him. In the staggering weeks after Estelle's death, after drowning and drowning, he had surged into the thin air of life again. In a second life, only this time to be lived carefully balanced upon the interstices between events and attitudes, cautiously in the shifting spaces between the molecules of human concern. So he would talk to her in order *not* to care.

"I was an inventor of sorts. And a salesman."

"An inventor?" She put down her coffee cup.

"Yes. More a tinkerer, you might say. I understood how things worked and I figured out ways to make them work better. You'd be surprised. Sometimes just the slightest thickness of the metal in a gear or the gauge of a wire in a motor can make a big difference."

"I've never met an inventor before. I'm genuinely impressed. Whenever I think of an inventor I think of Thomas Edison." She raised her cup to him.

Her eyes were very young, sharp and quick, the whites blue with vigor. He did not want to look at them.

"I'm hardly an Edison," he said. "More a Mr. Fix-it. That's how I began, as a kid. By the time I started college I had a good business going, a real one. I was making enough to pay my way and then some. And it's what I came back to. Fixing things. And then small manufacturing. And then I got a little larger. And then larger. The usual story, I guess. After awhile I had become a businessman instead of a mechanic, so I sold out so I could get back to things themselves. I took a job as a special kind of salesman. I'd go into highly technical production problems and help the engineers figure out what equipment and materials they needed and where they could get it. It was a great job for me. A little bit of everything going on, but deep too, if you see what I mean. And it left me with enough time for my own projects." He told her more about the work he had done for the industries and companies great and small, and of the shape that his advice had helped to give to our material lives. He hadn't spoken so much to someone for a long time, excepting Vivian.

Sylvia Warren got up and went to the stove to make herself

another cup of coffee. As she began to pour the hot water into the cup, she stopped. "I'm sorry," she said. "How presumptuous of me. You made me feel too comfortable."

"Oh please, help yourself. Go on, go on," he motioned to her to help herself.

But it was true. He had spoken more than he had thought to. He had intended a cup of coffee's worth of civility. Now she had bound him to a cup more. A slight tremor of refusal tickled through his legs, a memory from his more recent history of agony and rage when his body crashed about inside itself out of control, his organs ripping themselves apart as directed by the hormones and enzymes of grief and confusion. But that had ended. When everything else had ended except the simplest activities of the life process, his body had come back to itself. Only sometimes, such as now, an old forgotten neuron would synapse; but it would soon subside, for there was no energy of special hope for it to subsist upon, for it to generate a potential for action. Nothing got you, nothing *either way*. In the dark night of his soul he had learned that, and it had saved him.

"Go on," he said to her. He was not a victim any longer.

She poured her coffee and came back to her seat, drier, softer, her color returning.

"How do you invent something? How do you do it? How do you think of what to invent? It seems so . . . so *mystical.*"

"Not so mystical," he said. "All you do is think about something that somebody needs. Then you figure out how to make it."

"For instance?"

"Well, take a door lock, like the one you saw. People are always buying them, more now than ever. So there is your need. Then I figured out how to make one better than the others."

"Tell me. Tell me about the lock. How does it work?"

He took some paper from a drawer in the kitchen counter and drew diagrams to explain.

"You see, the metal plate is really quite flexible even if you can't see it is. And here, in back of the plate, are thousands of tubes. By putting fluid into some of the tubes you make a design. That's the key. When you trace the same design on the metal plate you put pressure on the harder tubes which then push down here," he indicated where on the diagram, "and from then on it works like a conventional lock with tumblers that shoot a bolt."

"That's marvelous," she said. "I'll bet you make a fortune with it."

"No," he said, "The psychology of it is wrong. People want a key they can hold in their hand, even for all the trouble it gives them. And there are other problems, like in a large family with little children who couldn't learn the design. Or suppose you wanted a friend or neighbor to come in while you were away, to water the plants or feed the fish? Instead of leaving the key under the doormat, you'd have to leave a drawing of the design." They laughed together.

"Oh my," Sylvia Warren said. "How disappointing. Did you think of all that when you invented the lock?"

"Oh yes," he said, "I've had a lot of experience with that sort of thing. But I wanted to do it. It interested me. And I did get a patent out of part of it, so I might make a little money from that."

Then he told her more about inventing. About the complicated process of a patent search and other legalities and about the cost, which surprised her ("Between one or two thousand, depending upon the complexity of the thing") and about all the ways an inventor could go about trying to make while failing to make money. Then he told her about some of his successes, the little artifacts of his skill and imagination and knowledge of the world that had added up to a small place in the spectrum of invention, and to an income that had made it possible for him to stop.

"What next?" she asked at last, her own enthusiasms for such power over things taking over for him. But she had gone too far now for a certainty and could tell (though *how,* she could not tell) that for Abel Harnack his past did not predict his future. No longer. "Sorry," she said, faithful at least to her intuitions.

"What next?" He would answer her. *"Pericula belli non sunt* and the future indicative. What else?" Again they both laughed. She rose.

"You've been just splendid," she said. "About everything. The car, the coffee, everything." She slipped quickly, agile and firm, into her still damp coat. "An inventor," she said, flipping her hair over her collar. "I've never met one."

"I've never met a Latin teacher," he said.

"No comparison," she said, her mouth making a pretty gesture. "No comparison at all."

He almost said something.

She stood before the locked kitchen door.

"Open Sesame," she said to it, and flung wide her arms and waited. "I guess I didn't say it right."

"No, you didn't. Here." He reached to the side of the door and turned a switch and stepped back about six feet. "Open Sesame, or whatever your name is." The door snapped open. Sylvia Warren gave a little shriek. "It's a sound lock. Convenient in a kitchen when your hands are full."

Sylvia Warren awoke to the day bright and scoured by the cold front that had moved through quickly in the night. Autumn was firmly here now, and even some of earliest winter, though there would be weeks left to tramp about in the woods and fields. She got out of bed and showered, made her small breakfast and, over her second cup of coffee, opened her ledger to write in it and to consult the architecture of her day, of her life.

Tuesday.

She would spend most of that morning correcting and commenting on the papers from her Latin class and then preparing for the following Monday. In the time left in the morning she would answer letters to friends, pay bills, make plans and lists. Tuesday. She would go to the Books-Sandwiched-In program at the local library, noon to one, and then on to the Triverton Nature Preserve, where she and Mildred Latham would beat through the late fields with their nets and jars for insects to bring to the Biology Club meeting that evening. At six o'clock she would eat supper with Mildred Latham, as on Tuesday she always had. But before Tuesday quite began officially, she wrote about the day and the night before.

She wrote quickly and exactly, more a record than an examination of events, something like a progress report, the way building contractors complete a day with an accumulation of data about bricks laid and tons of cement poured and steel girders locked into place, or as ship captains make log entries about winds and tides and weather encountered, as if reality were only where we have been and not where we might go, or want or intend to go. When she arrived at Abel Harnack in her day, she wrote:

> Abel Harnack, late 50's (?), widower, good health, extremely knowledgeable and intelligent, fixed my car in a driving rainstorm and then later at his house. An *inventor*. His workshop a cave of magic. He is restrained? Shy? Perhaps the death of his wife only a year ago?? What does he do with himself now that he is retired? How can a man who was an inventor retire? More to be explored here.

She shut her ledger, dressed, and settled down at her desk, the exploration of the *terra incognita* of Abel Harnack put aside for now. She worked at the Latin exercises briskly. Besides pointing out what was simply incorrect in a student's work, she explained why in the margins and between the lines with little sharp indicators, her comments as much encouragement and exhortation as corrective.

Sylvia Warren had taught Latin (and some French and a little Spanish) for twenty-three years at the regional high school, with spirit and affection enough to have made the subject palatable and, finally, even attractive to those dwindling few who worked on past the grinding first year of declensions and conjugations into Caesar's *Commentaries* in the second and, ultimately, in the third year, into the sublimity of Cicero and the Poets and the difficult, silvery Tacitus. It was an odd, an anachronistic thing to do, she would herself at times consider, this teaching of smooth old Latin in a world spiky and clattering about in the exciting newness of gleaming technology and movement in space and swift-breeding opportunity. She did not defend the Latin itself— for what defense could beauty have or need? But she was not about to accept uncritically the old banners under which the Association of Classical Language Teachers marched each year in thinning ranks at the annual convention: Latin is the Language of History, or The Study of Latin Is the Best Preparation for the Study of English.

No. She could not accept that, and never had. Latin wasn't a tool. Had it been, it might have survived. Latin was its own reward; but what it could promise in that way was no longer worth enough to the young. And she could understand that. Latin was, had become, irrelevant. And Sylvia Warren along with it. Her job, not her person.

She had taught long enough to retire if she chose, though she could have stayed on at the school teaching some French and taking up other chores such as an extra study hall or two. She was fifty-three then. Her pension would be smaller than if she had taught to the end of her possibilities, and she was years away from her social security income, but she had saved enough to balance things out nicely. She could afford to leave if she wanted.

But she did not want to, not exactly. She had come to the high school when she was twenty-nine and within a year she had clicked into place like a well-hung door closing evenly. Within a year she had found the friends and interests and functions that had not changed even to this moment, that had grown larger and deeper instead, rich as wine that ages well. If satisfaction was *in itself* one of life's true joys, then in her wide contentment she was there, and shared the sentiment with Horace in the *Epistles:* "Whatever prosperous hour Providence bestows upon you, receive it with a thankful hand: and defer not the enjoyment of the comforts of life." So there were no sudden pleasures expected or gained, no longed-for excursions to exotic places or into acts that would come to her once free of her daily work. In or out of the structures of the last twenty-three years, little would change.

But she did leave the job even so, as if that step, small as it was, altering her life as little as it would, would make up the difference that she had wondered at in the smallest degrees, in the quietest of ways from the beginning: that nothing more had come about in her life than what had.

It was a curiosity to her, this lost dimension, but not a sorrow, that all her life energy and intelligence, her capacity for experience, had carried her into one experience and then another and from the fluttery and imprecise edge of each into the penumbra where an experience bordered on becoming something else, something more than the experience, fulfilling as it was, did at last become. As with her painting.

Throughout her large apartment watercolors in double-matted, deep, silver-colored frames determined nearly every wall, every room: barns, seashore villages, fishermen from riverbanks, countrysides in all their seasons. The competency of each, of the whole, burst forth in a wave of illumination that promised to come, that did not come, and the pictures fell from the near pinnacle of vision down to the flat plains of skill. This was her own estimation, staunchly held through the winds of sweeping praise her friends blew upon her at her yearly show. She did not know how to paint the explosion that she felt in herself when she would work in the rapid light, racing the sun, the shadows surely coming. But she knew enough about what she could not do to accept no man's praise as though she had.

On one wall were her photographs, compositions as logical and controlled as if she had set a huge outdoor stage with perfect sets and actors. Light and dark knew what they were doing to the people moving through their lives before her lens. But then the pictures, dried and mounted, failed to alert the viewer to the implicit dangers and predicaments of the human transactions they fixed, and instead of perception they became glances. Sylvia Warren would look at them and know that. And think that, however firm were her trills in the Mozart piano sonatas, the music fluttered but never soared. How in tennis she could never trust her second serve, as certain as it was likely to be good. Nothing, nothing at all, ever went as far as it might have. As it should.

And she had not married. Or known a man at all. And that had puzzled her more than anything else in her life. But it was not simple longing that she sat with, rarely, through a night. It was the waking urgency to truly know about those processes of life that sometimes inexplicably fail. She had always been attractive to men, and was still. If she had not courted them, neither had she built skittish barricades. At first, younger, she sought reasons in herself, like talking too much or being too enthusiastic, little alienating characteristics that she had read and heard and been warned about as a girl. But there were no reasons like that, or any others. There were no reasons at all. Sometimes people to whom something is bound by every likelihood to happen are simply missed, like the one survivor in a massive air crash or the millionth customer who stops just before he enters the store to tie his shoe and falls from Grace.

So there was nothing to reason about. She had begun as she was and nothing came along to change it. Or end it. No one, she had corrected herself. Yes, she had thought, that's right. Maybe.

She was not afraid to think about herself directly, to examine and explore the crags and crevices of herself. She had lived alone with her good mind long enough to respect it, to not be frightened of it when it was insistent. It was in *not* thinking that there was danger. That was the trouble with old maids, old maid schoolteachers, she would point out to Mildred Latham. They were afraid to think and so they acted badly, especially with men, about whom they wished to think least, tripping themselves into the safety of the dreary old flighty stereotype or bristling with hearty self-sufficiency.

She had left her job in the school because she thought then that, allowing her energies to be completely loose, perhaps they would meld together, concentrate into a creative juggernaut that would storm the battlements and . . . But nothing like that had happened. Only the old pleasures that filled her nearly to the brim.

Tuesday morning was concluded. Before she left the apartment she packed a small knapsack with the rough clothes and field boots that she would change into in the afternoon.

"Do you know how long I've looked for this, for *Vendalia tarda*," Mildred Latham said, shaking one of the five cotton-stoppered test tubes at Sylvia Warren. "And now to find it, in *October* of all times. In a plenitude. Eggs as well." A short, heavy but soft woman, she bounced about in her kitchen like a semi-inflated beach ball, bounding off in unpredictable directions. "Just listen to this," she came back to the table. She read from a copy of *The Entomological Review* splayed across the kitchen table, supper gone awry.

> *Vendalia tarda*, although not considered a truly rare species within the Coleoptera, is yet uncommon even within its natural range, which, in the United States, is mainly southern. *V. tarda* is seldom found above the thirty-second parallel in the eastern states, the thirty-third parallel west of the Appalachians to the Rockies. It is not yet discovered in the western coastal region.
>
> The uncommonness of *V. tarda* in its own range and its only seldom and accidental appearance north of its range is accounted for by the insect's highly selective necessity for light and temperature, specific conditions which must occur not only once, but twice for the insect's passage from egg to larva to pupa to adult. This condition of quadruple diapause in *V. tarda* is nearly unique among insects. Apparently the quadruple diapause condition is continuous throughout the life cycle, and it is not unusual for four or five years to pass between the laying of the egg and the development of an adult insect able to lay another egg. And longer periods have been recorded. (Bornstein)

Mildred read more from the article and explained. "You see, the creature has to pass up through and then down through the same light/temperature ratio for each of the four stages—egg, larva, pupa, adult. It has got to be, say, thirty degrees on a twelve-hours-of-light day as the egg goes into winter, and then the same after winter as the egg moves into spring and hatches. And listen to this."

> It is unfortunate that this apparently disadvantageous life cycle limits the numerical size of the species, for *V. tarda* is

extremely destructive of not one but five prey insects, all pests. The range of *V. tarda*'s appetite seems clearly to be a consequence of its necessity to develop in such specific stages, thus making certain that food will be available to the insect at widely divergent times within the more normal and limited insect "year."

She read on. About the difficulty of raising the insects in the laboratory because of the complex double cycles involved in the four stages.

The length of time that would be required to work out the possible light-temperature permutations would exceed the endurance (and resources) of even the most dedicated entomologist. The very few recorded successes in the raising of *V. tarda* have been accounted for more by chance than by knowledge.

Mildred slapped her hand down on the journal page. "It's just wonderful," she said. "*Vendalia tarda.*"

"Slow to live," Sylvia Warren translated.

"Yes, 'slow to live.'" Mildred Latham stood up from the table. "I've killed and pinned six of them for tonight's meeting. A special event, you might say. And I'm taking about a dozen to Dr. Alberts at the university tomorrow. I'll drive down in the morning. Do you want to come?" She rushed on. "I'm keeping the others to see what I can do with them. And I'll check what's going on at Triverton until I can't find them any longer."

"What can you do with them?" Sylvia Warren asked. "What do you mean?"

"Breed them. Try to raise them. Take my shot at it. After all, I've never had these critters to work on. Let it be my turn to fail. Come on now, eat up. We don't want to be late for the meeting."

"Eat up what?" Within the scattered paraphernalia of their afternoon—killing jars, bottles and vials, magnifiers, aspirators, nets—here and there poked up lumps of cheese, curls of torn bread, a can of sardines, an onion started and forgotten, cups of tea gone cold.

"Yes," Mildred Latham said, "I see. I'll tell you what, old Warren. I'll buy you a hamburger later."

In the car on the way to the meeting she explained more about the problems of breeding *Vendalia tarda,* the elaborate devices she would have to imagine and build, the special habitats she must create and control, the exact regulators. "I haven't got a chance," she gaily granted. "Even if I knew just exactly what to do, I couldn't manage it for sure. I was always a field person, never good with complicated lab arrangements, and such. I've bred plenty of insects, but this is going to be something different, more exploring than doing. But what the hell." They drove on.

By the first traffic light, Sylvia Warren had decided that maybe Abel Harnack *could* manage it for sure.

Wednesday.

Wednesday was the luxury of a morning uncommitted, neither to nothing nor to something, the half-day of rest in her week, the pause for one o'clock, when she would go to the Y for an afternoon of yoga and swimming and the steam room and the dry sauna; free before Wednesday evening, when she would play piano in a trio of old friends. But at eight-thirty she called Abel Harnack and explained as best she could.

"So you see," she concluded, "what she needs is some way to make . . . to make time equal light and . . . and both to equal temperature. Sort of. But look, I'm doing a terrible job of explaining this diapause thing, and the experiment. Perhaps if you could meet Mildred Latham and have her explain the problem. I'm sure it would all be clearer than it is now."

But he said no.

Sylvia Warren recovered and apologized and said goodbye.

In the basement of Abel Harnack's house, in nearly half of it, rested a cat's cradle of various-sized wires, knitted and woven, spliced and soldered together into an intricacy too complicated for the eye to comprehend. Only at the moment it all might blur into a meaningless tangle, it did not; it held, instead, taut as sculpture, which it might have been. But it was a machine. An attempt that Abel Harnack had worked upon for years, in time he tucked in between his job and his family and his more practical devices. What he wanted to do with this machine was take an electrical charge and, by amplifying it and modulating it in exquisitely calculated increments, make the charge go on endlessly, inexhaustibly under its own power.

"It's what inventors come to sooner or later"; he tried to describe to Estelle what he was doing. "But you see," he had told her, "energy is what we are all about. From the sun to a can opener. It's what we are always working with." Estelle would nod and go on cooking. She did not understand the details of what her husband did. All she understood was him. Which had been enough for both. Still, he would tell her at length the history of the search for the grail of perpetual motion: who had tried what, and why it always failed. The mistake of the past was to use gears and levers that took as much energy to move as the energy that they would try to continue to produce. But he would not use material that way. He would use the electron's energy itself, to continue to produce itself.

A year ago he had come to where he could keep a small charge alive within his mechanism for twelve hours before his meters read out for him the slow and then quickening dissolution. On his way home from work that day he knew what he could do to gain two hours more. Even before supper he could make the modification that he had figured in and out of all through that afternoon. But when he opened his door, Estelle was gone. Vivian was there instead.

"Dad," she said. "I tried to reach you." And told him.

He had come home from work one day prepared to gain a centimeter against the universe. He found Estelle gone. She had dropped into the hospital and he had never seen her, as Estelle, again. There was nothing he could do to help her, or himself, not even the smallest thing: his voice beside her, the pressure of his hand. There was nothing he could do to help her. And if he could do nothing about that, then he would do nothing at all, ever again. He had raised his fists against the colossal outrage of the vulgarity of her dying that stripped her of the basest dignity and crushed her, smeared her like a swatted fly against a window-pane. He shrieked against the badly designed and uncorrectable device called life. And then held still, free now forever from the obscenity of creation.

In class Sylvia Warren said, "But enough of the difficulties of the imperfect indicative. Let's spend our remaining time with some poetry." For over an hour and a half she had gone over last week's exercises, through the new lessons, and then had prepared them for the work they would do in the week coming. "Now just sit back and listen to this. Don't worry about understanding it. You probably won't understand it except for a word or a phrase here or there. Just try to get the sound into your head. Each week we'll do a little more of this and you'll be surprised how much it will help you. And what pleasure it will come to be." She read to them from the *Aeneid* and then translated.

"And now, *molliter cubes.* Good night," she said to them.

"Good night. *Vale.*" the class said back. Then rose and, piece by piece, left.

"Mr. Harnack," she said to him as he passed her desk. He stopped and turned to her. "I'm sorry about the other morning. That was presumptuous of me. *Mea culpa.*" she smiled, open, clean. "I certainly must appear to be a presumptuous person to you, though I am not. I really respect . . . boundaries." It wasn't the word she wanted, but it was all that came to her. "Anyway, I'm sorry." She held out her hand to shake on it. He took her hand.

"No need for that," he said. "I wasn't offended." They let go of each other. He walked to the door. And then he turned. He did not need to tell her more, but he did not want to make a point of that either. "I just don't get involved in projects," he said.

"Could I ask you for some information, then?" she said.

"Sure," he said and walked back to the desk.

"Could you tell us where we could find someone to design the equipment my friend needs?"

"Tell me again what she is doing."

When she had finished telling him, he took a piece of paper from his notebook and made a series of sketches, precise as drafting, sharply defining the problem.

"What she wants to do is this." He explained the drawings to Sylvia Warren, pointing to diagrammatic objects where she had given him Mildred Latham's ideas. "And this is a list of what she'll need." He made some quick calculations and then wrote. With small numbers in circles, he coded each item in the list to its place in the drawings. On the bottom of the page he wrote the address of a New York City firm. "Tell your friend to say in her order that I asked she get a professional discount."

"This is marvelous of you," Sylvia Warren said. "You've made it so . . . so *tangible*. We really can't thank you enough. Mildred will be boundless in her thanks. Just wait till you meet . . ." But she stopped. "Sorry. Thank you. I mean thank you very much."

"You're welcome," he said. "I'm glad I could help. I used to do this for a living. Well, *molliter cubes.*"

What he had rejected when she had telephoned him was his own old assumption that he would do something because he could do it. But even more he had rejected her passionate investment in Mildred Latham's scheme, the implicit invitation for him to join, for he knew well the sound of endeavor and the enticement to contend for form, and of such investments he would have no part. If it was an odd job that she wanted done, that was OK; she was a decent sort, and he would help her out. Fix a car, learn Latin, rig up some thermocouples to a few clockwork gears and timers—there was no danger in that. He drove home, the nights cold enough now for him not to want to walk in them.

The following week she spoke to him after class about a problem in the wiring. She described what she and Mildred Latham had done during the week. Too anxious to wait, Mildred had driven down to New York and back the same day. They had built as closely as they could to his plan, and when at last they turned on the lamps, after about five minutes the meter reading went up continually to dangerously high levels. Everything else seemed to work. Only the light and heat lamps seemed out of control. They could not work out the problem.

"Are you sure you've got a resistor here?" He pointed to where.

"Yes. Definitely. We double checked. We figured that somewhere we must be making a circuit around that resistor. And yet there must be some resistance somewhere. That's why it takes five minutes before it starts to climb. The current is building. We thought we might be shorting through this little chassis here with the switches on it. But that's as far as we could go."

"I'm impressed," he said. "You know about electrical circuits."

"Not much. Only a little. Mildred's worked with lab equipment somewhat. And me, oh, I've tried practically everything."

"Well, I'm still impressed that you know as much as you do."

She waited.

"Will you help us out?"

"Yes," he said. "I'm obliged to now. If what you say is right, then the fault is in my design, and I can't leave you hanging on that kind of problem. There would be no way for you to fix it. When do you want me to look at it?"

"What's good for you?"

"I'm a free man. The sooner the better I'd guess, if you're doing an experiment with living things. Tomorrow morning? Eight-thirty? I know you're up by eight-thirty."

"Tuesday?"

"Is that not good?" He had heard her patterns speak sooner than she did herself, but she heard them too.

"Tuesday will be just fine," she said firmly. "Eight-thirty. Here's the address." She bent to the desk to write it. "We'll throw in breakfast. How's that?"

"I'll have eaten by then," he said. "But thank you."

He came exactly at eight-thirty and started to work at once. He set up his testing meter and traced through the entire circuit, probing delicately from connection to connection, sometimes stopping to write numbers down. The two women watched him silently. After twenty minutes he said, "Here's the problem." He touched the glass-encased recording thermometer. "The safety fuse in here is larger than I figured. It's pushing current back across here." He ran his finger along the wire to where. "I'll have it fixed in no time." He opened the square black case he had carried in and took from it a soldering gun, some additional tools, and a different resistor. In two minutes he was finished. "Try it now."

Mildred Latham turned the switch, the lamps came on, the meter needle rose and held. For five and then ten minutes he continued to test the circuitry.

"You're in business," he said, turning to look at them at last. The women gave a little cheer.

"May I offer you a cup of coffee, Mr. Harnack?" Mildred Latham said. "At the very least."

"Why yes, Miss Latham. I think I would like a cup of coffee now."

They sat in the parlor of Mildred Latham's house drinking their coffee. She placed a dish of fine, thin cookies near him, but he ate none.

"It's not unlike being a doctor," Sylvia Warren said. "You've even got the little black bag for it. An electronic stethoscope. A thermometer. Instruments. Medicine called resistors and capacitors and whatnot. It's a good analogy. Dr. Harnack, you just made a house call and the patient is doing fine."

Abel Harnack looked down into his coffee, examining it so that he would not have to look up at her. The women looked across at each other blankly.

"I think you'd be very interested in insects, Mr. Harnack," Mildred Latham said. Whatever they had suddenly accidentally gone into, for whatever reasons, Mildred Latham knew to try to take them somewhere else. "They're a lot like machines, like mechanisms," she pushed at him. "No personality. There's nothing you can love in an insect, only think about." Her voice rose a pitch. What had happened? "Their attractiveness is abstract, if you see what I mean, not like with mammals or even birds. It's too easy to slip into *liking* mammals and birds, too easy to start caring about what happens to them. Not so with insects." She looked quickly at Sylvia Warren, stricken. "Insects are fascinating not because of what they might do—they're too perfectly predictable for that—but because of how they work, like beautiful chess games, I suppose, or more like elegant watches."

Abel Harnack looked down deeper into his cup. They were all sliding down. Mildred Latham, bewildered, struggling to pull them out, knocked them further in.

"Yes," she went on, "I'd think they would appeal to someone with your analytical skills and interests. Do you know why some insects can move their wings so quickly?" She started to explain. "There's what amounts to a spring in . . ."

"I'm too busy," Abel Harnack said sharply, looking up, like waking up, interrupting her. Then, quietly, "My head is too full of Latin these days." He stood. "I'll check the circuits." He walked quickly away from them, through the house to the rear room where the experiment had been established. Five minutes later the women followed him. He was working.

"I'm making some changes," he said. "Nothing much. I'll be through soon." In fifteen minutes more he packed up and said goodbye and left.

Diapause is a means for surviving adverse seasons. It is a method in which the insect enters a state of dormancy, in which all growth changes cease and metabolism falls to a very low ebb, only just sufficient to keep the body alive, so that any reserves of food that are available may last for an extremely long time. This dormant state, or "diapause," may supervene at any stage in the life history of an insect: in the egg, in the young or in the full-grown larva, in the pupa, and even in the adult—where the arrest of growth means the cessation of reproduction. It is not uncommon for diapause to persist for more than one season, and for a pupa to lie over two or three years before it completes its development and emerges. But the record is probably held by *Sitodiplosis mosellana*, one of the wheat blossom gall midges (Cecidomyidae), which passes the winter as a full-grown larva in a cocoon in the soil. In this midge dormancy has persisted for as long as eighteen years, and yet in the end the larva has been able to pupate and emerge.

". . . and yet, in the end the larva has been able to pupate and emerge." He reread the line. He could hardly believe it.

Halfway home from Mildred Latham's he had turned and driven back the other way, to the library. She had spoken of the perfect predictability of insects, used those exact words. Was it just an expression, or did she mean exactly that? She was knowledgeable about these things, certainly; but could she have meant precisely what she said, the "perfect predictability" of insects? Now he wanted to find out. He had not felt this important need to know something for a long time. For Abel Harnack, *a long time* had come to mean *since before.*

In the library he began with the *Encyclopædia Britannica* for general information and then moved on to more complete texts. He browsed in them and then settled on *The Life of Insects.* He read the first two chapters and then turned to the index to find "diapause." That was what she was experimenting with. Incredible. He shut the book and rose from the table to take it and the two others to the checkout desk. And there they were again, the two women together as he had left them that morning.

"Why, Mr. Harnack," Sylvia Warren said. "How soon our paths cross." And then she wanted to take it back, to unsay the playfulness; he was not a playful man, and she forced him, and that was no good. Mildred Latham stood by and examined his books.

"Insects," he said to them, holding the books up. "You made me curious about some things about them."

"Wonderful," she said. "Let me help you learn about them whenever you need help." He nodded.

"We're here for the Books-Sandwiched-In program. Every Tuesday at noon," Sylvia Warren said. Absurdly, she wanted him to know that he wasn't being followed.

"Have a nice time," he said and nodded again and walked past them to the checkout desk. He did not care why they were in the library. He had taken a leap he could not have imagined three hours before. Now his mind was elsewhere, closing in. Closing down.

And the winter came on.

Through it Abel Harnack stayed diligently at work upon his Latin, moving comfortably from the ablative absolute through the passive periphrastic to the declension of comparatives to such esoteric elements as the conjugation of *eo* and the constructions of place and time. His vocabulary grew. The system of the language pleased him. And little by little, through what they studied, through what Sylvia Warren would read to them and explain, he came to a feeling for the Latin tone and style of mind, the stoic and heroic or vicious and yet always urbane Latin of the Golden Age and beyond. And, so far as he would ever go into such things, he came to a feeling, limited and tentative, for the vast and tumultuous whirligig of ambitions and acts that the Latin language had shaped and was shaped by. Cicero on the nature of friendship, Horace longing for the simple country life on his Sabine farm, what Pliny thought of the races, Vergil creating a history.

From the greatest to the smallest concerns of the nation or of all humanity, from the most angry denunciations to the most outrageous flattery and groveling, a profound decorum permeated it all, a sensibility to order that resonated in the culture even when there was no order, only the persisting, fading dream of it, the pretense of it, of order that contained the violence of the heart.

For Abel Harnack the ordering of insects was altogether different but more fascinating and better understood. The more he read about them, the more he came to be convinced that the life of insects had achieved the perpetuation of energy in the only way it could ever be achieved. He had been on the right track with his wire net of a machine down in the basement after all, the idea that energy could only be endlessly preserved at its most fundamental and therefore efficient level. But his machine, as simple as it was, was still material first and last; even if it took a million years, the copper and the tin and the silver would oxidize away, back to primary electrons.

Only the insects were perfect, going on in an unending transmogrification of material at whatever pace was possible, like passionless molecules in a chemical formula, the elements of the insects unalterably attached into larger structures as precisely fixed as ions in a bond, as atoms of oxygen in a carbon ring. And even the parts were not necessary to watch each other, so ants could work without abdomens and mantises conspire without heads. Blinded, limbless, the insects could go on. And insects could freeze into crystals and thaw and be insects again.

Abel Harnack saw that the insects, incapable of comprehension or choice, were uninvolved in their fate and thereby had no fate, only function. And he thrilled to see such perfection in the universe, to see that what was prevented for humankind was not prevented in itself, that the dream of endless motion was possible, was *already* possible, though the price was everything else. And most thrilling of all to him was the diapause, where the insect lost even its own necessity and became an extension, a bloom, of the sun itself.

He read deeply about the insects through the winter, but he did not talk much about them to Mildred Latham on the occasions when they met. He listened to her, and he asked questions. But he did not offer. There was an important crossing point that he did not want to have to meet with her, or with anyone. She had meant that the insects were machine-*like*. He meant that they were *machines*. They did not even always need sex to reproduce.

The winter went on. He continued in his new ways, but in his old ways as well. The same hours, the same patterns. Many days he would visit Vivian in the morning unless the weather was too fierce to battle. Once a week he would eat with her family. She was pleased that he was active again.

"You're looking good," Vivian said to him.

"My health is fine. I walk a lot most every day if I can. I get enough sleep. I'm fine."

"That Latin must agree with you," she said. Charles was in the TV room, watching the news. The children thudded about upstairs. Vivian sat with her father in the kitchen, the dinner dishes stacked, the counter and stove already clean and ready for tomorrow.

"It's OK," he said. "I'm learning it."

"And the teacher? What's her name?"

"Miss Warren. Sylvia Warren."

"Yes. What about her?"

"What do you mean?"

"How are you getting on with her?" Vivian looked at him.

"What are you thinking?" her father asked.

"You know what I'm thinking."

"Well, don't," he said. "We're hardly acquainted, hardly even friendly."

"I've seen her. She's not bad looking."

"Stop it, Vivian."

"It's nothing terrible, you know," she pushed on past him, her voice rising with old impatience and new hope. "You're not an old man." She waited for him, prepared to duel, to fight him *for* him. The past was buried; he had a lot of future to think about. But he said nothing. "She's not an old woman." He would not answer her. At last she stood up from the table and walked around the kitchen picking at it, nervous and irritable at his refusal.

"You think you know so much about life," he said to her. "But all you really know about is man and woman, husband and wife."

"Maybe," she agreed. "Maybe that *is* all I know about life. And maybe that's *all* there is."

"*Less,*" he said, suddenly, startlingly, and stood up quickly, stretched to his full height, as if his truth had pulled him up. "*Less,*" he shouted. Then he stooped and kissed her on the forehead. He went through the house and said goodbye to the children and to Charles and went home, above vicissitudes.

The winter deepened. The earth froze and then the sky froze; landscapes and people hunched up, tight and limited, compressed.

About every two weeks he would get a telephone call or a letter beckoning him back to work. Even after a year the offers and the requests continued. His skills had been special, even rare, and so he had continued to be remembered. Sometimes, now, he would give a day or two to the technical problems of old friends. But he knew what limits were, and stayed within them.

In January he signed up for the second semester of the Latin course. The original class of eleven had shrunk to eight by the end of the first semester, and now only five, including himself, had signed up to go on. Five was the minimum. With fewer than five students, the course could not be offered in the extension college curriculum. But he did not sign up as a favor to her. Latin had come to serve him in the way that he had wanted, and if there had been no greater reason to begin than that, then there was now no greater reason to stop.

He won a judgment against General Electric in a patent infringement suit that he had begun five years before. He put the sizable settlement into a common savings account and left it alone.

The storms turned February thick, the snow wet and heavy. Once, when a major transmission line went down, he battered his way to Mildred Latham's with a small, powerful generator and hooked it into her house system so that the light and the heat for *Vendalia tarda* would not go out.

He went on. His days—decorous, predictable—filled up. He had come so very far from a year ago to this sublime calm that he could dare to test himself against memory. Cautiously he would open the door to his empty house that day, to Estelle gone, and would wait for the wave that once had tumbled and suffocated him in the bitter surf of chaos to burst against the clever bulwark he had devised. He would feel the power of the wave on the other side strain and shudder and subside, die and recede. If in his life any longer there was such a thing as pleasure, *that* was pleasure.

At the very end of February after class, before leaving the building, he stopped at the "Boys" room. The sign was still the first one, blue lettering on white porcelain, that had been mounted on the door when the school was built forty years earlier. Vivian had gone to this school. His grandchildren went here now. Outside the wind blew across the parking lot, not quickly or strongly but with steady pressure, weakening slowly what it pushed against, rather than knocking it down. The snow had melted and frozen and melted and frozen into a moon terrain, ripped, pocked, sharp-ridged and uneroded. Nearly to his car, he dimly saw Sylvia Warren on her knees by hers. Her arms were extended forward, her hands flat against the rough ice, her forehead resting against her car door.

He labored through the wind to her.

"Miss Warren," he shouted. She looked up.

"I must have fallen. The footing is treacherous." She looked to him as if she were resting, her eyes quiet. He waited for her to get up, but she stayed.

"Let me help you." He bent to her and took her under her arms.

"Yes," she said. "Please. I'm having trouble." Then she was standing. She had cut her knees.

"Are you all right?"

"A little shaken." She opened the car door and he helped her in.

"Are you sure? Do you want me to drive you home? You could get your car tomorrow."

"No," she said. "It was just a fall."

"He's a very nice man," Mildred Latham said. "He's certainly intelligent. He's quiet, but he'd got keen insight. And he's gentle. That's always a good sign."

"A good sign of what?" Sylvia Warren asked her. They were in her apartment. Barely audible Bach floated about, the volume of the sound inappropriate for the size of the music. "For a proper husband? Do you mean, Mildred, that you're still thinking about getting married?"

"Me?" Mildred Latham actually shouted. "Me? *You.*" But Sylvia Warren was laughing; of course she understood that Mildred Latham had meant her then, and had meant her for nearly twenty-five years.

"You're still trying to get me married."

"It's not that, really. We've talked about that. It's just that I can still never understand why you never did. You're so attractive." She trailed off into the Bach.

"I'm not about to change my life, Mildred. Or have it changed. It works pretty well as it is. And don't you do anything to make Abel Harnack nervous. He doesn't want involvements. I told you about him. He's a specially nice person to be with. Just leave it at that."

"I wasn't going to *do* anything, Sylvia. I'm not a fool or a child."

But the subject was closed. Sylvia Warren got up to make them both some tea. Once she had tried, in an act of disciplined imagining, to picture her life differently; but what would it mean to be a wife? A wife to Abel Harnack? The idea was vacant, empty, the vision of it impossible to form, the thought itself wrong, a disvaluing of themselves as they were. They were, all three, becoming good friends. Even if—*if*—life could have offered more, it did not *require* more. And she would not relinquish herself into new passions, whether offered or not. She enjoyed Abel Harnack's interestingness; she enjoyed the civility of their union. It was enough. Another pleasure.

By the beginning of April the experiment with *Vendalia tarda* had failed. The eggs had not hatched; they had not been brought out of diapause.

"But the eggs are still alive, aren't they?" Abel Harnack said. "Maybe they are going to skip a year, or even two."

"Then what do you propose—that we just let the experiment go on?" Mildred Latham walked slowly about the caged eggs, still shining ticks of matter, inert but glowing, undetermined yet. "For another year. Or another and another. Then leave the whole contraption to the university after we're all gone?" She flung her hand over the apparatus, wiping it out, her disappointment blurring it like a damp rag.

"Yes," Abel Harnack said.

He had come to supper with them. Again. The suppers they had begun to share had gone well, the talk always about Latin and insects, photography and travel and the measurable nature of things—how an electron microscope worked, why plastic took its shape, the use that windmills could have, the distance to stars.

"Our own Royal Society," Sylvia Warren had called them, even just that evening, even with the failure of *V. tarda.* Now, supper complete, coffee finished, they stood in the back room of Mildred Latham's house.

"I haven't the heart for it," she said. "Or the patience. And spring is here. Nearly." She put her arm across Sylvia Warren's shoulders. "Me and Warren here have to get out in the field where we belong. I want to see what *is* hatching from the eggs, not keep on looking at what isn't."

"What will we do with them?" he asked.

"Put them back where I found them, if you like. Would you like that? Come along with us next Tuesday to Triverton and we'll show you."

He agreed.

The natural world of Triverton, the varying terrain of streams and bogs, upland meadows and woods blending from pines to hardwoods, was as unknown to Abel Harnack as an automobile engine might be to most others. One knew *about* meadows and bogs as one knew *about* engines, which was not the same as knowing a thing in itself, the way Abel Harnack could picture actual steel-hot valves opening and closing and the oily black rocker arms compressing and releasing; or the way Mildred Latham would envision the translucent apical cells at the root tip of the skunk cabbage dividing and expanding down into the grainy earth. But here, where the life of things was objectifying fact, where the network, not the element, was the reality, he had never been. Now, late, he had come to a new boundary.

Bloodroot, hepatica, fiddleheads, the lance-sharp buds of beech, the crusted egg-cases of the mantises, fungi fruiting under the powdery bark of rotten trees, tiny mosses greening up, a kestrel darting through the trees, a rare shrew, waterstriders already dimpling the quieter waters. But it was too late for him to know this world as they did, like an elixir, like a potion. He watched them as they ranged widely ahead of him, tracking wonder; the older woman heavy, the younger woman firm, lithe, and effective. From where he watched them, she looked like a young girl,

prancing and excited. Both of them did that day, the place transfiguring them.

"Mr. Harnack," Sylvia Warren called back to him. "Come and
see this." Mildred Latham was bent down into the grass. As he
approached she stood up with a small snake in her hand. She
grasped it behind the head and with her other hand held it by the
tail and extended it.

"*Thamnophis ordinatus,*" she announced. "The common garter
snake. Are you familiar with this?"

"No, I'm afraid not. This is out of my world."

"It's a beautiful thing, a snake. You see here, on the belly,
where the single scales stop and the double scales begin? That's
the start of the tail." She told him more about snakes, about
the musk gland under the anal scale, about the Jacobson's gland
with which some snakes tasted the air, that most snakes were born
from eggs, but that *Thamnophis ordinatus* was born live like man.
She dropped the snake gently, and it disappeared with a soft snap
into the grasses. For a moment they all three looked at one another. The sun intensified, the slight breeze rustling the still
winter-dry fields. Crows called distantly. The scent of the loosening
earth rose all around them like a fume. "I am deeply moved by
all of this," Mildred Latham said. Her eyes glistened. Sylvia
Warren took her arm and moved off with her.

The day darkened quickly as only April can, going from a bright
blue glory to a dirty squall gray. The first light mist of rain caught
them far from where they had parked the car, and far from each
other. The women waved him to them. When he got to them they
hurried him into the woods to an enormous green-black spruce.
They lifted the lower branches up from the ground, like lifting
the hem of a floor-length dress.

"Go in," Mildred Latham said to him. He got to his knees
and crawled in and they followed. Inside, the heavy smell of the
spruce was dazing at first, then liquidy, like breathing underwater.
Inside it was dark, but enough light came through the infinite
hatchwork of the needles. The rain increased, but they were dry.
Years of soft brown spruce needles cushioned them.

"It was time to eat anyway," Mildred Latham said. She took from her knapsack a thermos of coffee and a package of thick ham sandwiches on dark bread. "I'm glad for the rain. I love this, getting under this tree, eating here safe from the weather, safe from everything. But you need the rain to make it count, so to speak." She passed around the sandwiches and the cup full of coffee. They ate and spoke a little about their day so far: the extremely early wood duck they had seen, the witchhazel scrub tree that had not cast its seed before the winter, the wild ginger already well started. The year was coming quickly.

"Well, Mr. Harnack, what do you think?" Sylvia Warren asked him.

"It's all very pleasant, Miss Warren. And quite a new experience for me."

"It's always going on," Mildred Latham said. "Winter, spring, summer, fall." She finished the cup of coffee and poured another and handed it to him. And then she said, "I could stay here. On days like this. And other days. I feel like I could stay here forever. Just set up under this spruce and go on until I died here."

"Yes," Sylvia Warren said. "I've had that feeling. Here. But other places too. And sometimes when I'm painting. Or playing music. Or reading Vergil." She laughed. He was startled. Her laughter, always so soft and easy, echoed in his head now, sharply, like a volley of sound shot into him. It was as if he had been told a great and shocking intimate secret, as though what she had told him was safe with him, would not matter though told to a man to whom nothing would ever matter again.

He did not know what to say, or that he could say anything. He understood what the women meant, but there was nothing in his own life he could gauge it by—except his life with Estelle, and he would measure nothing more by that.

He raised the thermos cup of coffee to his mouth and then, as with an attack, he jerked and the coffee spilled. Time sagged. The spilled coffee fell as slowly as life itself, a languid cascading moment, leaving time enough to think of everything before the liquid hit his knee. Time to understand that he had built his life upon defense again after all, but that there were gigantic subterranean waves of memory too strong for any barrier. He had betrayed himself. In the sudden discovery that the fortifications have been breeched, that the enemy is streaming in through the jagged rent, the mind twangs between panic and act. The decision made in that moment is the decision, clearly understood or not, from which all the decisions ever after must come.

So too had he once shared in the profound, harrowing, and wordless condition of love, the boundless, shapeless, measureless condition which is not chaos though it cannot be formed. In which he too would have chosen to stay forever and had, unlike these women, thought he would stay.

Why had he come here with them? What had they had to lose, or not to lose? He should not have come here with them, into this place of contagion where there was no safety at all, only the dangerous belief that there was.

"Oh," Sylvia Warren said as the coffee hit his knee. It quickly soaked through to his skin, but the heat was out of it. His spasm had passed. He handed her the cup. She drank from it. They finished eating and the weather changed back, as Mildred Latham had predicted. Following the women, he crawled out of the spruce shelter into the cleared April-blue day, with all his old vulnerabilities once again intact.

"As you know," she said to the class, "I do not give a final exam. Your grade will be based upon the work you have done throughout the semester." She went quickly on. "This has been a very pleasant year for me and I hope as pleasant for you. We have gotten to know each other rather well through this school year, and we've gotten to know a lot of Latin. I'm really proud of you. You've done splendidly." She went on with the small valedictory. "I wish that you would continue. Do not stop now, here at the beginning of this great adventure. Perhaps over the summer or next year you will find a means to go further."

He sat forward. She was saying something more than the words.

"I conclude with this from Marcus Aurelius." She gave them the Latin as usual, and then translated: "Then depart at peace with all men, for he who bids thee go is at peace with thee."

"*Vale,*" she said, and left before more than that could be said.

He had at first promised wildly that he would sever himself from the women and from Triverton. He would see them no more, and he would not come back. But he did neither.

To refuse to meet with them upon the terms they had established was pointless. He was interested in their knowledge and in their friendship, their companionship. They were fine people. They had taught him much. He could not allow himself to flee from goodness. For if he started to run he would never stop, and the old terror would return and this time there could be nothing that would stop it. He would go on about his life as he had come to live it since Estelle's death, only now the anger that had been reborn under the great sheltering spruce he would accommodate. The truce he had arranged was his mistake. There could be no truce while the battle still raged and wounded. He would continue to see Sylvia Warren and Mildred Latham as the occasions arose.

And he did go back to Triverton. They had taught him that. He returned often. Sometimes with them, sometimes with the nature-study groups that were conducted there in the summer. And sometimes alone. As now.

He could see them down in the glade of the hill he was sitting on. Mildred Latham was beating through the weeds and grasses with the heavier net in a general sweeping for anything that would tumble her way. Sylvia Warren worked with the lighter net, flicking after butterflies or other insects she might spot in flight. They moved slowly through the large field. Even from where he sat he could tell that they were talking to each other, laughing and touching, giggling like animated schoolgirls, their transfiguring gaiety turning them childlike.

Her blouse was as yellow as the thick goldenrod and the heavy late daisies. Her gray hair had tightened through the summer in the sun, white and mirror-like. He watched their progress, the rhythmic beating of Mildred Latham's net, the short, jabbing, staccato swing of Sylvia's. Every ten feet they would stop and deposit their catch in the jars and vials they carried in their knapsacks. Sometimes Mildred Latham would stop longer and set up her camera with its close-up attachments and take pictures. And then they would move on. Sometimes Sylvia would run in a small circle about Mildred, raising and lowering her arms like a butterfly herself. Once, even, Mildred Latham ran after her to try and catch her in her net.

Sylvia came to a tree stump wide enough to stand on. She jumped up on it and, flinging wide her arms, her net still in one hand, declaimed to the multitudinous sea of wildflowers and weeds, to the far hill, to the wide sky. Abel Harnack looked up to where she must be looking and smiled to think how she must think she was so alone. He guessed it would be Horace that she would be telling the world. When he looked down she was gone. Mildred Latham was running, trying to run, to the tree stump. He stood up quickly and hurried down the side of the hill to them.

She was lying flat out when he got to her. Her forehead, her cheekbones, the bridge of her nose were bright scarlet, as if she had been struck by a wide brush across the top of her face. Mildred Latham was by her side, weeping softly.

"What is it?" he said. The women did not show it if they were surprised that he should appear, as if they did not separate this day from others that they had shared. "What is it, Miss Warren?"

"I don't know, Mr. Harnack," she said up to him. "I don't know. I don't know. I don't know."

But she did, and as he swooped down to her and lifted her up in his arms, light as a molted shell, so did he.

At the hospital the doctor said to them, "Are you her family?"

"No," Mildred Latham said. "There is no family. We're her friends. We're very close friends." She was trying to tell the doctor what that meant, but he understood, or perhaps he did not care to know; family or friends, it did not matter to what he would say, would have to tell them. They were sitting in a small office down the hall from the emergency room. They had waited for hours.

"I'm sorry you had to wait so long. We didn't want to tell you nothing, and we didn't want to tell you anything until we were reasonably sure. We don't have many of the tests back yet, but it looks like a form of *lupus. Lupus erythematosus.*"

"Oh," Mildred Latham said, and could say no more.

"What is it?" Abel Harnack asked. The doctor explained: it was a rheumatoid disease related to arthritis or rheumatic fever, but much more serious; it was a blood disease where the body formed antibodies to its own tissues; it was a wasting disease, attacking mostly the connective tissues, but the vital organs as well, so that in time it crippled. So that in time it killed.

"How much time?" Abel Harnack asked.

"It's not predictable," the doctor said. "The disease is characterized by sudden periods of remission and then equally sudden attacks. There are too many variables, too many complications that can develop. We've already started with injections of a corticosteroid hormone. For the inflammation and the pain there's aspirin."

"Aspirin?" Abel Harnack said. It seemed too trivial to be possible. The doctor nodded.

"In the morning she'll go downstate to the university medical center. We'll need to run more tests and to do more examinations. Dr. Felner will be there. He's a rheumatoid specialist. We just can't say, we just can't even guess at what the chances are yet." Then he added, "With *lupus* you never can." They all sat quietly for as long as a minute. "I'm sorry," the doctor said. "I wish there was an easier way to tell you this, but there isn't." He pressed a button on the desk and a nurse came into the small room. The doctor left. The nurse told them where they were going to take Sylvia Warren and when they could see her and what they should bring for her while she would be in the hospital and other things that Mildred Latham did not hear. But Abel Harnack did, and wrote them down.

He did not sleep well. He awoke at four in the morning and dressed and ate a small breakfast and then drove off down to the university three hours away. He drove through the gray morning lightening and thought of *lupus erythematosus. Lupus.* The wolf. How terrible a name for a disease! To call it what it was, the disease that devoured like a ravening animal. But why not? And who was not ill? He did not think back to Estelle or forward to Sylvia Warren or beyond that to himself. He was through with all of that, now. At peace at last.

At the university he went to the library, which would not open for two more hours. He walked about the quiet campus as the sun rose higher and hot as yesterday. He walked to the woods edging the campus, but he did not enter them—just as a year before, had he been here, at this place, he would not have entered them, although, two days ago, he would have gone in to see what he might see. Not now. Now he knew that there was nothing to see anymore. The quickening heat burned off the slight wisps of steamy dew until, at nine, the day was as clear as it would be.

He had decided to be beaten no longer. He had come here to the library to do what he had once always done, which was all he could do—mend, fix what was broken, make better, improve. Try.

He took his little Latin and swung it like an axe, chopping rough, splintered pieces out of a thousand years of words, hewing for her as best he could a gift that should say in language better than his own what he would have her know. But there was no better language.

In the great glass cube of the university library he found his material, mostly from PA 6164 to PA 6296 on the third floor, the quiet east wing. Knowing too little to manage it, he set about piecing together a statement. Through collections, anthologies, and book after book of the Loeb Classical Library series of Latin faced by a page of English translation, he scrambled like a man on a canted, rock-strewn plain, no two steps certain. He would claw through pages of the English and, finding a passage, he would transcribe the Latin across from it.

And indeed in my opinion, no man can be an orator complete in all points of merit, who has not attained a knowledge of all important subjects and arts.

Thus Cicero mocked him, but he wrote it down:

Ac, mea quidem sententia, nomo poterit esse omni laude cumulatus orator, nisi erit omnium rerum magnarum atque artium scientiam consecutus.

His notes piled up. Some appeared before him that he could not account for:

Nigro multa mari dicunt portanta nature, monstra repentinis terrentia saepe figuris, cum subito emersere furenti corpora ponto.

But what could he do with that?

Many fearsome things, they say, swim in the black sea—monsters that ofttimes terrify with forms unlooked for, when suddenly they have reared their bodies from the raging deeps.

Could her infinite Vergil offer him no better? Frequently his eye alone drew him onward, as if directed and compelled by a spirit in him:

Just when the farmer wished to reap his yellow
Fields, and thresh his grain,
I have often seen all the winds make war,
Flattening the stout crops from the very roots;
And in the black whirlwind
Carrying off the ears and the light straw.

He plucked at the golden fruit where he could, often reaching for it and missing it and lurching on.

I am minded to sing of bodies to new forms changing;
Begin, O you gods (for you these changes have made),
Breathe on my spirit and lead my continuous song.

But it was too late for evocations.

He struggled on, Tibullus, Ovid, Propertius, Lucan, and the names of those he had no knowledge of at all, poets who clung to Being by the fragment of a stanza. He willed himself on.

Lucretius:

> Like children trembling in the blinded dark
> and fearing every noise, we sit and dread
> the face of light, and all our fears are vain
> like things the child has fancied in the dark.

Horace:

> Thaw follows frost; hard on the heels of Spring
> Treads Summer sure to die, for hard on hers
> Comes Autumn, with his apples scattering;
> Then back to Winter tide, when nothing stirs.

Catullus, her beloved Catullus:

> If a wished-for thing and a thing past hoping for
> should come to a man, will he welcome it not the more?
> Therefore to me more welcome it is than gold
> That Lesbia brings back my desire of old
> My desire past hoping for, her own self, back.
> O mark the day with white in the almanac!
> What happier man is alive, or what can bring
> To a man, whoever he be, a more wished-for thing?

From his storm of notes he hammered together a document, banging on it, adding and arranging until the pen at last stumbled from his hand. He pushed back from the books and considered what he had made. He read it, the Latin, which he could not understand, breaking in his teeth. The morning had passed. He picked up his pen and, winning and losing with every stroke, wrote to her for himself in his own voice:

> which is to say we are all as susceptible to death, as are the insects. Death is as absolute for humans as for midges. When metabolism ceases, autolysis begins, in *Homo sapiens* or in *Vendalia tarda*. If there is comfort anywhere, it is in truth, whatever the truth, and in this, the act of these words.

Then he got up and took his paper and walked out, leaving everything there just as it was.

Mildred Latham was with her when he came into her room. She looked well enough, though still marked by the red insignia. It looked like a birthmark. She had been told. He handed her the paper. She read it and wept and then dried her eyes and smiled, looked up at him beside her bed and nodded once. And together they settled down to wait for the long night surely coming on.

Jean Thompson

Birds in Air

That part of the country is, within itself,
as unpoetical as any spot of the earth; but
seeing it . . . aroused feelings in me which
were certainly poetry.

Abraham Lincoln

An electric fan sits on the refrigerator: it hums, rotates, billows the edge of the tablecloth. Only when it blows directly on me does it cut the heat from the stove and the heat of the day. Eat some more, says Grandma.

On her flowered tablecloth are cold ham, pickles, potato salad, tomatoes, olives, biscuits, honey, white peaches, corn, cherry pie. It is full summer and we live off the fat of the land.

You have some of that country gravy, down south they call it Mississippi butter, says Grandma.

It is thick white stuff with brown crusty bits in it. No one likes it.

It tastes bad, says my younger brother.

Hush, says my mother.

After dinner we sit hot and overfed in the front room. The furniture is dark wood with hard carved edges. The lamps are massive, pink-shaded, with clustered roses or shepherdesses at the base. I look through the white net curtains at the dusty trees, the leaves hanging down like tongues.

Why don't you kids do something, says my father.

It is hard to connect my father with my grandmother's old photographs. A boy in a sailor suit and Buster Brown haircut; odd, dramatic lighting.

Why don't you go to the dime store, says my father.

Where they sell wallets with little Mexican boys stamped on the leather, Souvenir of Spencer County, Ind., sneezing powder, string ties, china ashtrays consisting of a lady on a toilet, Cool Your Hot Butt In My Old Tub.

We've been there before, says my older brother.

You could go to the Lincoln Village, my father says.

Lincoln didn't live in the reconstructed cabins, with the spinning wheels and plaques and corncob pipes and buckeyes for sale. It was north of here somewhere.

We've been there before too, says my younger brother.

Grandma's quilts are all made by hand, pieced out of cotton and linen, red stars and checks, small faded rows of daisies, candy stripes. Sewn together with good white thread, the edges bound and scalloped. In the back bedroom, shades drawn against the afternoon sun, I run my fingers over their taut surface and whisper the names to myself: Wreath of Grapes, Drunkard's Path, Mexican Rose, Birds in Air.

Grandma comes to the door in her long cotton slip. Too hot to sleep, she says. Too hot to do anything.

She sits next to me on the bed. Looking at these old quilts? I nod. Which one do you like best?

My hand hesitates, reaches out to the Birds in Air. A pattern of triangles, like a thousand small wings, which cross and recross until they seem to lift from the cloth.

You can have it, she says, nodding. Her glasses slip and show a red nick in the skin on each side of her nose.

I think of manners, of the way my mother responds to gifts. Oh *no, I couldn't*—

I mean to will it to you, she says. I won't forget. She pats my shoulder with her brittle hand and leaves the room.

Every year there is the visit to the cemetery. Grandma sits in the front seat in her good blue dress. We drive east along the weedy road from town, slowly, my father pointing.

Here's where Lincoln might have played as a boy, he says.

There's his swing set, says my older brother.

Gray sheds and ponds and shade. The limestone cliffs along the river, chalked over with the names of high schools. Dirt roads that disappear into the green distance. I try to imagine Lincoln here. I try to imagine what was different.

We reach the brick pillars of the cemetery gates. We help Grandma from the car and her light skirt floats in the breeze.

I have no grief. I do not remember my grandfather. The sun is hot on the red clover and dandelion puffs. We stand with her a moment, not speaking. Her name is already on the stone beside his, and the date of her birth. Then the numbers 19, waiting to be rounded into four digits. On my fingers I reckon the number of years she can live without spoiling the stone. I promise myself I will never do that, never fix the limits of my life.

After a while we leave her standing there and walk on the long grass between the graves, looking for odd stones, the finger pointing upward marked Gone to Rest, the scrolls and cherubs above the infant graves. The stones are crumbling and we have a contest to find the oldest one. My mother wins with 1820. In the far corner of the lot my brothers start a game of chase.

On the way back we drive through town, the big car strange on the quiet street, the smell of its vinyl seat in our nostrils. Past the feed store and the grocery. There are roofs built out from the stores over the sidewalks, held up by poles buckling into the street. They make a narrow shade on the baked white cement. Peeling boards and black windows, the painted advertisement for a bank sinking into a brick wall.

Really, whispers my older brother, how can people stand to live here?

I frown, tell him to hush. My father is speaking.

That's the jail, he says. I remember once in a while they used to have a drunk in there and we'd sneak up to the window and try to see him. And here's where Great-aunt Norma lived before she moved to Evansville. I used to work in her garden and she paid me ten cents an hour.

My older brother looks straight ahead, but I know he is talking to me: The story that he walked ten miles because he overcharged a customer five cents, is, of course, apocryphal. There are many places where Dad actually spent the night, or some historical incident occurred, but we must separate fact from legend. I mean, I'd hate to see it all get commercialized.

In the front seat my mother, father, grandmother do not move. Perhaps they have not heard. Again I try to imagine, back a hundred and fifty years when the streets were dirt, the paint fresh, Lincoln, on a hot day such as this, barefoot, riding a mule in from the back woods, thinking this a fine place, a big place, the county seat . . . Now the town is full of old people—men in overalls with chapped pink faces, old women living in a fragile world of cats and nicked china and water-stained rugs. The whole back page of the newspaper is for obituaries. Grandma reads them carefully.

The car pulls up in front of the house. I think for dinner we'll finish off the rest of the ham, says Grandma. And maybe some beans, fresh snap-beans.

Help your Grandma do the dishes, my father says to me.   I don't need any help, my grandmother says, go sit down and watch television.   No need for you to do them all yourself.

You just sit down and let me do them.   Finally I take a dish towel from the cupboard and start drying. My grandmother's hands are soft from the water, like old gum erasers, and shreds of vegetables stick under her fingernails. Her hands move in and out of the thin film of soap on the surface of the water, rinsing the bright sharp prongs of the forks. She has one bad eye, with a stripe of blood crossing the iris and the black pupil always large and vacant. The kitchen light is bug-yellow and glaring and it makes the eye water. I see a thick milky tear stream down her face and tremble on her chin.

Grandma looks up, wipes the tear away with a fierce brush of her sleeve. Now you go, she says, and pushes me away from the sink. Go watch television.

Instead I go to the back bedroom, away from the others. Here there is a picture viewer, a stereoscope, with a wire holder for the cards and a wooden hood that fits over your nose and smells of old hair. The cards are heavy and chipped around the edges: views of Niagara Falls, Roman ruins, the Grand Canyon. The story cards are better, girls in pinafores eloping with country swains, ladies in draperies singing Only a Bird in a Gilded Cage. The two flat identical pictures on the card make one with depth and shape. Old jokes, old songs; for a moment they are almost real.

We take Grandma to see her friends. Old ladies who live in crumbling houses, as if the ivy is pulling them softly back to earth and decay. They have names like Dolly, Anna, Pearl. Bunch of old women who wear copper bracelets to keep arthritis away, says my mother under her breath. She does not enjoy these visits.

When Dolly and Anna sit inside they too use electric fans. But when they sit on the front porch they wave paper-and-stick fans with pictures of the American Eagle and Miss Liberty. I think Dolly's son died in the Great War because there are so many pictures of him in uniform.

They are so old, in the middle of a sentence they drift and dream. Even Grandma knows we can't stay long to talk. They wear shapeless lavender print dresses that remind me of the patches in the quilts. Their houses are full of doilies and rugs made of braided bread wrappers. Anna has saved every greeting card anyone ever sent her in the top drawer of her walnut dresser. Mistletoe and violets, angels, risen Christs For the Coming Year and In Sympathy she spreads for our inspection, and smiles.

How pretty. Yes we will. You take care of yourselves. Good-bye Anna. Good-bye Dolly.

Back in the car my mother exhales, as if she has held her breath the whole time.

Now ain't that pitiful, says Grandma. Poor Dolly can't hardly hear. Don't walk so good either. And she's two years younger than me.

We stop for gas at Elnoe's. Elnoe, who is maybe a man or maybe a woman, I'm never sure, immense arms and chest, a sleeveless shirt and jeans, red cheeks, cropped gray hair. How you all, says Elnoe,

grinning, showing two gold teeth. Elnoe's white frame house is just
behind the gas pumps. The original second story now rests on the
ground, a memory of the river's rising. Back home Grandma has a
scrapbook of newspaper clippings about the Great Flood of nineteen
thirty-something.

There are picnics on the river. From the high bluff we throw
stones; they fall into the muddy edges and the great curve of shining
water is unchanged. A fast-moving barge passes, blows its horn,
and is gone.

My father squats beside my younger brother and his shoes skid
pebbles along the riverbank.

Do you know what that is across the river?

The boy squirms at my father's hand on his shoulder. Kentucky.

That's right. Look, says my father, and his arm reaches out to the
water and the haze and the fields on the other shore. Pioneers.
Indians.

Uh huh, says my brother, and he runs off to look for snakeskins
and dead fish.

The sun sets and the light on the river turns opal, glossy.
Grandma locks her thin arms around her knees and says to me Your
hair is so pretty, it's like mine when I was a girl. It was my father's
pride and joy, whenever company came he'd say Della show them
how you can sit on your hair. And he sent off for a bottle of lotion
that cost a dollar to make my hair shine.

She laughs, pats her short tight curls. I bet you can't imagine me
with long hair.

I laugh and do not answer. Darkness spreads from the trees and
the crickets surround us. We gather the silverware, waxed paper,
pop bottles, chunks of soaked driftwood my brothers carry up from
the beach. You know you could take that quilt with you when you
go, whispers Grandma. I won't tell nobody.

No, I say, confused, they'd find out . .

I suppose, says Grandma.

You know what I'd like to do while we're here, says my father, is
start a family tree.

My mother is brushing crumbs from the breakfast table. What for, she says. You think you'll find royalty?

More likely find we're all descended from John Wilkes Booth, says my older brother.

We visit Mrs. Crawford. Grandma says she knows a lot about things like that. Her parlor is dim, with old pictures hung too high on the walls. I sit in a scratchy armchair. The room smells of dust, attics, and it makes me sleepy. The tables are piled with parchment charts hand lettered in permanent black ink. Birth certificates. The bound volumes of the County Historical Society, round-cornered books with thin, crackling pages.

Of course I knew your folks, says Mrs. Crawford. Walter's cousin George married my sister-in-law . . . The silver frames of her spectacles glint in the darkened room. The parchment scrapes as she unrolls it. She turns on a lamp. Now, she says, do you know when your grandfather was born? My father shakes his head. Together they bend over the table and their fingers trace the lines, lists, old records.

I let my eyes close. In the warm darkness their voices are small and far away.

Maybe it would be easier, Mrs. Crawford is saying, to start from the other end. Here was a settler in Virginia. If you could follow his descendants . . .

My father takes notes on what Mrs. Crawford says, and puts them in his billfold. They will stay there until the creases of the paper grow worn and soiled. Then he will throw them away.

My grandmother still keeps a desk drawer full of toys for us. Coloring books, rubber balls, airplanes made of balsa wood, pennies in tiny glass jugs. Only my younger brother plays with them now. It is afternoon and I am watching TV, an old I Love Lucy show. The screen is gauzy and flickering in the strong light from outdoors.

Grandma comes to the door and stands with her hands on her hips. She asks me if I want some pop: I got Orange Crush, Cream Soda, Root Beer.   I say no thank you.   Some lemonade? She'd be glad to make it.   No, I'm not really thirsty.

I tell you what, says Grandma. I'm going to take you down to

Lotus's shop, buy you a dress. Maybe a pretty blouse, would you like that?

I see my mother's warning face. Sure, I say.

We walk downtown. The heat from the sidewalk wraps itself around my legs. Now you don't worry about how much things cost, says Grandma. You get anything you like.

The windows of Lotus's shop are streaked with old whitewash. A dozen shapeless, limp dresses hang on the racks. They remind me of a church rummage sale.

Lotus has a thin rouged face and lacquered hair. She pulls a stack of blouses from a shelf—can you take an eight, honey?—and watches as I look through them. They are strange prints, like kitchen wallpaper. Patterns of teakettles, vegetables, geraniums. My hands move slower as I reach the end of the pile. I think I have looked at everything in the store. I hold up the last blouse. Can I have this one? I ask my grandmother. Can I wear it home?

The branches of trees meet overhead. The dirt road is a tunnel, scarcely wide enough for the car. You would not drive in these hills at night.

They call this Owl Town because only the owls live here, says Grandma.

Really? asks my younger brother.

People live here too but you won't see them, says my father.

People who will never be on anyone's census or tax roll. Children who would not know what to say to us if we met them, for they have never seen anyone outside their own family.

The air-conditioning chills the back of my neck. We must keep the windows shut. I squint through the tinted glass and try to penetrate the solid green around us. We are going too fast. At the top of a hill I see a path, a fence. I look back and they are gone, the leaves covering them like water closes over a stone. We must start back. It is almost time for dinner.

The bits of thread and cloth come together into blocks, the blocks form patterns. It is hard to tell where the pattern begins and ends, for it crosses and recrosses. My grandmother dies and the telephone company buys her house. But this is not the end. She has left me the quilt. Her fingers moved along its border as mine do now, locking the stitches in place; it cannot be torn, not ever, it has been made too well.

Perhaps it ends when we are ready to leave. Everyone says goodbye to her at least twice, too loudly. My father starts the car. And she comes running after us with her apron over her face. The house is full of gas, she says, pulling at my father's arm. I smell it everywhere. He goes inside with her and the rest of us wait.

My father comes out alone and gets behind the wheel. It was nothing, he says, nothing at all. The car pulls away and although I can't see her at the window, I turn around and wave.

Gordon Weaver

The Two Sides of Things

"Don't continually say *hit me*." My Uncle Adolph spoke clearly without taking his black-and-silver cigarette holder from between his teeth. "It irritates the dealer," he said—he meant that it irritated him. "All you need do is scrape the edge of the table like this," he said, rasping the dining room table's felt pad with the edges of the deck of cards, as though he were sweeping crumbs toward his lap. "The dealer knows that way you want another card, and you don't have to irritate people by saying the same thing all the time. Now," he said, "try it." I scraped with the card in my hand. "Good," my uncle said. "Now let's get on with the game." He waited, one eyebrow raised, for me to call for yet another card.

With the five of clubs in my hand, it made eighteen. He had a jack showing. "I'm good," I said; I knew better than to say something like *I think I have all I want.* "I'm good," I repeated, wanting to be sure he noticed I remembered the correct words.

"I heard you the first time," he said, and, "Dealer pays twenty-one," said with confidence as he flipped over his blind card, a king. I swallowed my disappointment and pushed my cards over to him. He clenched his teeth, making the cigarette holder jut erectly up from his mouth, as he added to his score on the pinochle tablet he kept just to his right on the dining room table. It made him look a little like a thin President Roosevelt, in the famous photograph with his pince-nez and cigarette holder.

I remember my uncle marking the score with a ballpoint pen, a fairly new product then—it was 1948, and Uncle Adolph was convinced they would not last on the market. I was eleven, so never dreamed of second-guessing him. He was drubbing me unmercifully. He kept score in dollars, blackjack at a dollar a hand, casino at a dime a point; he said it was more interesting that way.

"You're forty bucks in the hole," he said to me. "In Vegas that's small change for the one-arm bandits. You couldn't get your hands on the dice with a roll no bigger than that." I nodded, seeing my Aunt Osa look up to smile very tolerantly at her husband's back. She sat at her escritoire, visible to me over my uncle's shoulder, on those evenings we played cards. Either she read, translating with moving lips, in an inaudible interior whisper, the Spanish of *Don Quixote de la Mancha*, or worked at her correspondence with the authors of cook books all over the world. The Spanish Club of Waukegan, Illinois, and the art of cooking: these were her world.

And that is the capsule, the essence of my memory of them: Uncle Adolph, inserting a fresh Sano into his filter-holder (it carried a cartridge, filled with crystals which blackened, signaling time for a change of filter), shuffling the cards while he eyed me through the smoke wreathing his head, like a Vegas sharper about to take a fat pigeon fresh from Cedar Rapids with the egg money burning a hole in his bib overalls; Aunt Osa, quietly prevailing in a spotless domestic comfort richened by elaborate menus and the time-resistant excellence of Cervantes.

My aunt's watchful control was, of course, smothering to me then, and my uncle's shameless crowing over cards was galling, but when I came to stay with them there in Waukegan, which was frequently during the year my father died of a liver disorder, I think I became a real person, in my sense of the word, for the first time in my life. That in itself makes them worth remembering, makes them worth cherishing in memory—I was only eleven, and it might have been less pleasant.

Because there was chaos and crisis at home, in Gary, Indiana, because of my father's alcoholism (aquavit is especially destructive of the liver), my mother sent me away often that last year . . . to give me a more *homey* atmosphere, as she would have put it. My other aunts, Anna and Claire, lived in Chicago, but they were less suitable, both being divorced. Aunt Claire had lived alone in Chicago since the twenties, when she cut something of a figure there after arriving from the family homestead, downstate in Hambro, Illinois, a farm town settled almost exclusively by Swedes.

I suppose the era was too exciting for my Aunt Claire's marriage to last. Her husband had something to do with bootlegging, and she would admit, if I persisted, that a fellow she went about with for a time ended up face down on the floor of a garage on a particular St. Valentine's Day.

Aunt Anna's husband, my Uncle Knute, had become wealthy during the second war, selling a part of a machine that made a part of a machine that made something useful in war. They were divorced when he took up with a woman he met in Minneapolis on a business trip. Aunt Anna's divorce was too recent, in 1948, for my mother to foist me on her. So I was sent to Aunt Osa's and Uncle Adolph's.

I was attracted to my uncle to begin with. For one thing, he detested my name—I was given Bengt, after my father and Grandfather Berntsson both—as much as I did. I cannot recall him ever using it to speak to me. For another, he was not comfortable talking to his wife or her sisters, or my father (who was almost always inebriated), so he talked to me when we got together as a family. This is a novelty with some charm, when you are only eleven.

On the occasions we gathered, in Gary or Chicago, for birthdays, Christmas, and Thanksgiving, I was lost below the level of adults who recollected childhood days in Hambro, ate huge meals of (to me) unappetizing Swedish food, and drank aquavit with beer chasers, my aunts staying drink for drink with my father. In short, I was lonely; my aunts were all childless.

"Who's your favorite baseball player?" Uncle Adolph asked me, peering over the edge of the sports page. My father, for example, would never have thought to ask.

"Jackie Robinson," I said without thinking, merely eager to give an answer when someone had somehow taken the trouble to care if I had one. Uncle Adolph cared indeed, frowning severely at my reply. I had answered too quickly, forgetting his background, as told to me by my mother and my aunts.

"What kind of an answer is that?" he said. "My God, is there any reason you can't have a white man for your favorite, boy?" He snapped the newspaper together and folded it against his chest. "What's the matter with Ewell Blackwell? Now there's a man to be your favorite. What's wrong with Ralph Branca if it has to be a Dodger?"

He could always intimidate me. I weakly mumbled that it did not have to be a Dodger—I thought a lot of Blackwell, and Branca, and Dixie Walker too. At least we could agree that there was no use in caring for the limping Cubs or White Sox, either one.

My Uncle Adolph was born and raised in Memphis, and this part of him had not been exorcised by his travels. He was touchy about it, denying prejudice if my mother challenged him on it. He would respond with the story of betting on Jack Johnson against Stan Ketchel, which was, he smugly asserted, hardly the wager of a prejudiced man.

And he had traveled. He joined the navy in 1908 (an impossibly prehistoric date to me!), and prior to that had logged some time on merchant ships. I loved the stories he told, of course.

What I love about them now is that he told them with the idea, I think, of suggesting something special, something hideous, for example, that could not be spoken plainly of in front of women. Aunt Osa used to contend jokingly that she had civilized him, for all the Old South and its culture, by accepting his proposal there in Hambro, Illinois, when he showed up at the end of his travels to operate the telegraph for the Illinois Central Railroad, in 1916. These impulses, his and hers, are at the center of my *person*, my being a person at about age eleven, in 1948.

There was, for instance, the story of his shipwreck off the Borneo coast.

"The damn ship rolled over on her side like a foundered horse. The suction must have taken the others down with her. I made the half-mile in from the reef, not knowing yet I was one of two survivors—" he said before I broke in. We were playing casino this time, and I was, as usual, losing heavily.

"Who was the other one?"

"Galley slavey," he said, "cook's helper—boy, don't interrupt me that way!" He had some sense that my mother's sending me to stay for a few weeks involved his responsibility to teach me some masculine social manners. I did not mind; it implied my importance, that I must be worth the effort it cost him, that I was considered a potential gentleman, requiring such manners.

"It's *very* impolite to break into a man's story, boy! What's more, what did you forget?" He waited, grim behind the smoke of his Sano cigarette, while I tried hard to concentrate.

"*Sir?*"

"That's right. *Sir.* Show others respect and they'll respect you," he said. "You can walk with kings, and they'll respect you." He said this with a change in the expression around his eyes that tempted me to look behind me and see whether or not some royal entourage had, in fact, joined us from the kitchen to validate my uncle's proposition. What it expressed was the poignancy of his disappointment at never having walked with them himself—because he felt, I think, that they, those anonymous kings, *would* have respected him. In shaping my deportment he was treating his own sense of failure in life.

I recall this statement whenever I read the blurb saying horse racing is the sport of kings. Uncle Adolph also played the horses. After the fashion, that is, that his wife permitted. He subscribed to *Racing Form* and a couple of Chicago tout sheets; he concentrated on the season at Washington Park, recorded his bets, and the results, all without risking a single dollar. It was like our card games, all a controlled exercise of his pure fancy.

I have seen him sit close to my father on their visits to Gary, pushing his recorded bets between my father and the aquavit jug, pointing with the trembling tip of his mechanical pencil, showing my father how he was making a killing, killing upon killing, on the ponies.

"Look here," Uncle Adolph said, "three hundred this week, three seventy-five, three twenty, and this . . . this was a bad week, just over a hundred. A hundred is a *bad* week for me. Now repeat to me I'm dreaming. Right here in black and white. . . ." Maybe he was trying to persuade my father to stake him for a real crack at the horses with his system, for Uncle Adolph, who pushed a pencil in the production control department for U.S. Steel in Waukegan, could not afford to bet much, and my Aunt Osa would not allow him to bet anything.

What he dreamed of was just exactly the kind of fast and fat win the horseplayer and gambler enjoy. And I believe he wanted me to know this. I believe it was important to my Uncle Adolph that I should perceive, and should respect, this flash of colorful, exciting dream-wish that lay buried beneath his steady, reliable, dull and aging exterior. The proper manners, he said, enabled you to walk with the kings of the earth . . . and I was meant to understand that he, at least, was up to it, at least in imaginative achievements, no matter how utterly absurd this all was against the realities of his life.

"As I was saying before you interrupted. I didn't know until morning that there was another survivor besides myself. We met on the beach in the first light of day after our ship went down on that reef." He paused, as if bracing himself to deal with another interruption, but I kept silence, and, over his shoulder, my aunt's lips moved soundlessly over her Spanish.

"We began to cut our way through the jungle, because we knew that it couldn't be too far to some civilization. The Dutch had naval installations in the area, but we'd heard that the locals sometimes took a man's head for a trophy without first asking his permission. We were ill-equipped. I had a revolver, a big single-action smoker—which I always carried on my person in those days—and my partner had a butcher knife, which he'd had sense enough to grab in the galley before he hopped over the ship's rail.

"We had been going about a day and a half. I heard him scream out behind me—I was breaking trail at the time—" Here he stopped quite unashamed, for dramatic effect, and also, possibly, tempting me, to see if I had taken the lesson about interrupting to heart. He liked to do that, test my self-control. At blackjack, when he knew I was praying for a low card, a deuce or tray at most, in order to come in under twenty-one with five cards, and so chip two dollars off my mounting losings, he would delay the flip of the fifth card off the top of the deck. Testing me. But I could do it if I tried.

"He screamed," he went on, "and I turned around with my pistol already on cock, but it was too late. Some breed of boa constrictor had dropped around his neck from the limb of a tree. He was dead before I could shoot. It happened that fast."

"Really? Sir?" I asked. He was too sensitive, and not so cruel, as to construe that I suspected the whole tale to be so much malarkey; he understood that I merely wanted its emotional reality confirmed, a last time, by the man before me, who was the very horse's mouth. It allowed him, too, the opportunity to plant the suggestion that is the crux, or his half of it, of the sense of *person*, of being, of oneself, of identity in time and place, that was his real gift to me.

"That's what I told the proper authorities, in any case," he said, leaning back in the dining room chair, the suggestion of the too-hideous in his eyes, the flash of his teeth clamped down on his cigarette filter-holder as he leered at me, his hand seeming to reach out, unwilled, to give the deck of cards a one-handed sharper's cut. Oh, he succeeded!

Sometimes, in the right mood, I still reserve the right to think it *was* pure malarkey, that my uncle made it up out of whole cloth, simply to impress and delight me. But again, at other times, in other moods, I need—*need*—to believe there was something too terrible to give utterance. Might they not have argued over cards, for instance? Certain it is that my Uncle Adolph admired those who did it and got away with it, even if only for a short time.

I have heard him speak of the Chicago gangster who dated my Aunt Claire, the one killed on St. Valentine's Day. Uncle Adolph spoke of him, of his fashionable clothes, his fast car, the lump in his coat where his pistol rested, in a tone that made it clear he would have approved an alliance with that outlaw. He and Aunt Osa had rented a flat in Cicero for a time back then, and Uncle Adolph recalled the violence of bootlegging days fondly.

He had me stand up, there in the parlor in Waukegan, had me put out my hand to shake with him; I was acting the role of Deeny O'Banion, while my uncle was the uncaught gunsel sent to make the hit—my uncle had several theories about just how the gun was concealed in the killer's hand until the instant he raised it to fire.

Uncle Adolph held that, morally, John Dillinger was more respectable than either the woman in red who fingered him, or the FBI agents who shot him down in front of the Biograph.

"Granted he was a thief and a murderer," my uncle said, "there was nothing wishy-washy about him. Good Indiana farmboy stock to begin with. Someday we'll have to drive over to Crown Point and see the grave where they say they buried what was left of him." I was eleven, and it was magnificent.

My Uncle Adolph disliked Jackie Robinson, because that was bred into him in Memphis. But he knew better than to bet on Stan Ketchel, and he admired Satchel Paige for holding onto his arm long past retirement age for ordinary men. Nigger or not, old Satchel was still getting away with it! He thought the Black Sox were simply dumb, because they got caught so quickly and easily, and Shoeless Joe Jackson the dumbest of the lot, because, unlike Eddie Cicotte and the others, he got no money out of it.

His all-time favorite baseball player was a man named Snodgrass, who had played third base, years before, for John McGraw's Giants. "He played third," my uncle said, "and he was something to wonder at. When a man was on third, waiting to tag up and go to beat the throw home on a long fly ball, this Snodgrass I'm telling you about would slip two fingers under the man's belt, pretending to play close to the bag. Snodgrass would hold him up, just for a split second, enough to keep him from making it to the plate ahead of the throw. They had a center fielder, I forget his name, with an arm like a rifle. He did it for more than a year. Nobody knew how long he got away with it but Snodgrass himself, I imagine. They finally caught him out." That was the way of the world, my uncle's voice implied; everyone always got caught out in the end, even Al Capone, and it was worse than unfair; it was tragic.

"Some wiseacre thought to remove the buckle from his belt before he went up to hit. He got to third, there was a fly ball, he tagged up and took off, and there was Snodgrass with the ump and both teams and a park full of fans watching him, standing over the bag with the runner's belt in his hand."

Uncle Adolph looked away while lighting a fresh Sano; we grieved, both of us, for Snodgrass, and for the fact that nobody ever gets away with it in the end, ever.

It has to do with secrets. I learned that men have secrets that cannot bear telling—witness the forever uncertain demise of the cook's helper in the wilds of Borneo. I learned men have secret desires—for riches, for fast and fat triumphs that depend upon evil or inside information. Men want to walk with whoever passes for royalty in our country. I learned things are not what they seem, that behind my uncle's very ordinary facade lay elements unguessed by any except initiates to those secrets, like myself. What, for example, I began to wonder, waited inside my own alcoholic father's stony and indifferent exterior for me to uncover? What might lie, in time, within me?

It has nothing to do with finding out secrets. It is only that they exist to baffle and fascinate us. This I learned, and became something other than I had been, as I looked up to watch my Aunt Osa, preoccupied at her escritoire. And I knew I had learned it, which is yet another secret of being alive.

One has to learn there are secrets, and then one has to learn to live with them. My uncle came to this, this learning, when he met my Aunt Osa. He may have learned it already, but he came to accept it when he married her.

In 1916 he was thirty years old, and outside his navy-taught skill as a telegrapher, and the stories gathered in his travels, he had nothing to show for his life. On the contrary, when he landed the job with the Illinois Central and came to Hambro, he had been used rather badly. He was underweight and sickly from the experience of his last job, working the key out of a tiny relay station near Utica, Mississippi. My aunt, it seemed to me, could always find some excuse to tell her side of it.

The casino and twenty-one were over for the night, but my uncle kept on talking, and had gotten around to the general subjects of food and eating. I think he was telling me about the *frijoles refritos* he had eaten in Mexico once, the time he made a special trip across the border to meet and shake hands with Francisco Madero, who was encamped just south of Brownsville then. Uncle Adolph could not speak of food without bitterness, for he had had, a couple of years earlier, the ulcer operation that removed fourteen inches of his intestines. He evaded his rigid diet whenever he dared.

He said something like, "You take a gob of those beans on a *tortilla*, boy, and you dash some of that red sauce they grind up from peppers on a stone all over it, and then, by God, you stick the whole shebang right in your mouth. . . ."

My aunt looked up from *Don Quixote*. I prefer to think she understood every bit of what his stories meant to me. I prefer to think she understood, and so determined that I should see the other side of it —her side; the second of those two sides people always say exist about any question of import. She was being deliberately fair to me, not cruel to him.

She got up and came behind his chair. She put her hand on his shoulder, her wedding band prominent against the black of his unbuttoned vest. Although she pretended to be talking to him at first, her eyes never let go of mine.

"Oh," Aunt Osa said, "and why don't you tell him how much you liked goat meat." Uncle Adolph carefully placed another Sano in his filter-holder and lit it, turning off his attention, as though saying: I have heard all this before. This is for the boy, not me. I already know; I have already accepted.

"Adolph had a job relaying dispatches at some dinky little back-water station in Mississippi, just before he came to Hambro. The railroad paid a farmer and his wife to room and board him because it was the only house within miles of the station. The first morning there he found out what that was going to be like."

Uncle Adolph went *ungh*, once, but it may have only been the smoke in his throat choking him.

"He stepped out of bed," my aunt went on," straight smack dab with his bare foot in some goat dung." I giggled. "Yes! Right in the bedroom, and you could smell it all through the house! Goats in the house!" I think I laughed again, louder. My uncle shifted in his chair, pinned there by the gently resting weight of his wife's hand. She held me with her eyes.

"And how that woman fed him! Fried dough, just fried in a deep fat, and coffee with chicory in it, and very rarely some ham, because they kept pigs too. He nearly starved to death. He couldn't bring himself to complain, nor could he eat it.

"Then one day while he was working, one of the man's fool goats was killed by a train. Your uncle ran up to the house to tell him, and the farmer got his knife and ran down to the tracks and bled the goat and dressed it out. Well they ate goat. It was the first decent meat he'd had in so long, and of course they had no refrigeration, so there was goat, fried in deep fat, meal after meal." My uncle swallowed audibly, and closed his eyes, pulled steadily on the bit of his cigarette filter-holder.

"When that ran out," Aunt Osa said, "it was back to fried dough again—because naturally the man wasn't going to care what he fed Adolph; he got paid for room and board regardless. Now tell Bengt what you did then . . . when you couldn't stand any more fried dough."

My uncle looked at me, opened his eyes, discovering an expression I had not seen before. He carefully knocked the ash from the tip of his Sano against the glass lip of the ashtray before he spoke. As if to say: No matter how ridiculous, no matter how humiliating, this *is* the truth. Like Alphonse Capone's income taxes and syphilis, there comes, finally, to all men, that *truth* that defies our desires, no matter what the grandeur, the enormity, or even the triviality. Yes, I understood: we dream secrets, all of us . . . and they fail us, and we fail them. And we must live with that.

"I bided," Uncle Adolph said, as if he were reciting a piece committed to memory, "my time. Until I could be sure there was no one in sight. The farmhouse was over a rise, so it wasn't particularly difficult or long in coming. I enticed a goat down to my station shack, and tethered him there. Sometimes, later, I'd have it all planned, on a schedule, so as to have only a five- or ten-minute wait, me there holding the bleating goat by its horns. When the train came I'd shove the goat under the wheels and run for the house to tell the farmer. He'd get his knife."

"And they'd eat goat again," Aunt Osa said. "Goat meat fried in deep fat." She quaked at the thought of it. "And that," she said, "is what ruined your uncle's stomach." I knew that he had had a very rough time with the ulcer operation; he never really recovered his health again, though he was not to die for many years to come. "If he'd stayed there longer before coming to work in Hambro he'd like to have died long ago as a result," she said. And she meant that, literally. And he believed it too. She had made her point; she went back to Cervantes, and my uncle squinted through cigarette smoke as he shuffled the cards for a last game of casino before my bedtime.

Later, that same night, when she had left the room, he leaned close to me to whisper, "God though, boy," he said, "that old farm woman could make a goat taste like something!"

He did not tell his stories of Borneo or Mexico to provoke her, and she did not bring up his bachelor absurdities to retaliate. They merely recognized, each, their respective strengths. He could not survive without the flavor of foolish dreams, and she knew no one dared try to live except with respect for reality. This is what each sought to teach me.

My father's mother, Grandmother Berntsson, died giving birth to my father. Aunt Osa was nearly twenty then, and she shared the housekeeping with an old spinster woman named Sorenson, who had more or less tagged along on the journey from Sweden to Hambro, Illinois, with the Berntsson family. By the time Uncle Adolph arrived in Hambro, my Aunt Anna had married Uncle Knute and moved away. My father was an irretrievably spoiled child of ten; my aunts attributed his adult alcoholism, and his early death, to the indulgences he was permitted as a motherless boy. And by then, almost thirty years old, my Aunt Osa's prospects could hardly have seemed very favorable to her, especially in light of Aunt Claire's already showing signs of becoming too beautiful for a small town to contain. Claire was twenty by then, and Chicago was beckoning; Prohibition was only a few years away.

My Aunt Osa faced becoming an old maid, with a future to be lived out in the same house where she was born, with the care of Grandfather Berntsson and the spinster Sorenson to assume as they aged into senility.

Then my uncle came, knocked at the porch door to ask if he might take his meals with the Berntsson family, who lived near the railroad station; the Illinois Central paid, now, a per diem to spend, for that purpose, anywhere he pleased.

So it all ended rather happily, in a way. My father died of cirrhosis of the liver, but I was spared seeing much of that, because I was so often visiting my aunt and uncle. And in time, they died too.

Aunt Osa outlived him. The last time I saw him, they came to visit me and my wife, in Levittown, Pennsylvania, where I lived a few years ago. Uncle Adolph was, I think, about seventy-five then.

My wife and my aunt were getting up a little lunch in the kitchen —it was separated from the living room by a four-sided fireplace in a

Levitt house—and my uncle and I were watching baseball on television in the living room. I got up and said I'd go out to the shopping center for some beer.

"He's not supposed to drink beer, Bengt," my aunt stepped in from the kitchen to say.

"One little can won't hurt," I said. "We can't watch the game without beer." My uncle listened closely, finger pressing the earpiece of his hearing aid deeper into his ear. When it was clear she would not protest further, he got up and picked up his hat.

"I'll come along for the ride," he said. He had had his first stroke just about a year before. I knew it was the last trip east he would ever make; east or anywhere, it was the end of his travels, though I had no special premonition he would die before the year was out. I had to keep a firm grip on his thin, fragile arm as he walked to my car, for he refused to use his cane.

They had the ball game on TV at the small quickie bar in the shopping center, and Uncle Adolph suggested we get a beer while we were there, so as not to miss the Yankees' turn at bat. While he deprecated contemporary sports heroes—Mantle nor Mays, neither one, was a Ruth or a Rogers Hornsby, much less a Nap Lajoie or a Louie F. Sockalexis—still, he liked to watch someone with a good chance of hitting one out of the park. He attributed all the home runs to the rabbit ball; Frank Baker would have murdered the lively ball, my uncle said.

"Put a head on this for us," he said to the bartender when he had finished his glass. He made a great show of peeling a bill off his roll, tossing it on the bar to pay for our beer. He stood out at the bar, one spindly, pathetically thin leg up, pointed shoe on the rail, in the stance of a much younger man, one accustomed to bending his elbow for a couple of hours each day. My uncle scrutinized the chalkboard recording the baseball pool the bar ran with a professional eye; he could have told them a few things about odds. I had the silly notion that he was going to ask the bartender for the dice cup, then challenge me to roll for a shot of straight whiskey. But that was my imagination, not his.

Dressed in a suit with matching vest, the chain of his railroad watch looped across the slight bulge of his paunch, the authentic straw skimmer from his mature manhood of the twenties cocked on his head, he was like some piece of antique furniture in the chromed, paneled, tiled quickie bar. Or like a cutout, a figure removed from the photograph of a big-city saloon of forty years before, pasted in our midst, the whole a superficial ironist's collage. I could taste with my beer, smell with the smoke of the cigar he bought, peeled, pierced, and lit after sniffing, a sense of the dimension of time stronger than any I have known since.

He admitted the second glass of beer made him a little dizzy, so we went home with a six-pack.

After another beer, after lunch, after the game was over, he seemed to withdraw into himself. I suggested we play a little cards, blackjack or casino. Through college, the army, my married life, I had played no cards, but I wanted, for some reason, to get him talking to me. He won the deal on the cut.

"No," he said, breaking his silence as he dealt the hands, "you've done nicely for yourself, boy. Yes," he said, "you've got a job that you can be respected for doing well, you've got a lovely wife—your aunt and I think a great deal of the girl you married. You've got every right to look the world in the eye . . . to be respected." I do not know how he happened to hit on exactly what I wanted; I could not have said, then, that I knew that was what I wanted so badly to hear. It is the kind of thing that comes to all of us, I hope.

There are the moments when we suddenly feel we have failed ourselves, have betrayed or frittered away what was once best in us, when even our ambitions seem to have evaporated into a filmy mess, when only sour memories come to us when we call on the past for help. They are nothing, these moments, for a man to dwell upon, but they will come.

This moment passed for me, in my uncle's kind words, and then we played some blackjack. I decided to risk another card, the fifth, with fourteen. I scratched my hand on the table top, but he did not lay out my fifth card. "Hit me again," I said, looking up from my cards.

"Shhh," my aunt said softly, coming from the kitchen and taking the deck out of his hands. "He's dozed off from all that beer you gave him. He usually takes a nap in the afternoon at home."

I sat back in my chair and watched him, sleeping. From time to time there was a flutter under his eyelids, a twitch at one corner of his mouth, the way there is when a sleeping man is dreaming.

ILLINOIS SHORT FICTION